Barbara Hulanicki w̶a̶s̶ ̶b̶o̶r̶n̶ ̶i̶n̶ ̶W̶a̶r̶s̶a̶w̶ ̶a̶n̶d̶ ̶s̶p̶e̶n̶t̶ ̶t̶h̶e̶ ̶w̶a̶r̶ years in Palestine, where her father was the Polish Consul General. After his assassination in 1948, her family moved to England where she was educated at a private school and the Brighton College of Art. In 1964 she founded the legendary Biba shops, for which she was the sole designer, until the final Biba closed in 1975. She moved with her family to Brazil, where she lived for five years. She has travelled extensively all her life, and is at present based in the United States, where she specializes in the design of hotels, restaurants, clubs and furniture, and the creation and design of image and costumes for rock groups, theatre and video. She works mainly in New York and Miami, where she has been involved in many of the new projects in the Art Deco district.

This is Barbara Hulanicki's first novel. Her autobiography, *From A to Biba*, was published in 1983.

BARBARA HULANICKI

DISGRACE

Pan Books

in association with Sidgwick & Jackson

First published 1990 by Sidgwick & Jackson Ltd
This edition published 1991 by Pan Books Ltd,
Cavaye Place, London SW10 9PG
in association with Sidgwick & Jackson

1 3 5 7 9 8 6 4 2

© Barbara Hulanicki 1990

ISBN 0 330 31765 2

Printed in England by Clays Ltd, St Ives plc

FOR: FITZ, WITOLD, SUSAN

1

Milla was fourteen when she lost her virginity, and even that was with a French boy. It happened at exactly six-thirty in the evening, on October 21st, 1961. Milla was very careful about details and she checked her watch twice, to make sure that there was no mistake.

It had been raining in Kensington Gardens and the steps of the Albert Memorial were damp and slippery. Jean-Claude was upset by the mud that was all over the front of his trousers and scared of what his mother would say, blaming Milla for making him do it.

Afterwards, she took a bus back to Knightsbridge and walked down Beauchamp Place to the flat in Pont Street where she lived. She looked at her reflection in a shop window to make sure that there was no mud on her grey-blue overcoat, the uniform of the French lycée where both she and Jean-Claude were pupils.

Her Aunt's apartment occupied the entire first floor of an old red-brick house with high, spiked wrought-iron railings separating it from a broad pavement. The heavy oak door was opened by a uniformed janitor as she approached.

She took a deep breath as she walked up the curving, stained-wood staircase and braced herself, trying to adjust to the world that waited for her beyond the front door of the apartment. She stood for a moment on the dark landing, straining to hear any sound that might give her a clue as to what was going on inside.

There were overcoats hanging in the stone-flagged hall, both of them black, with velvet collars to match. Hanging above them was the bowler hat with purple lining that belonged to Lord Harley and the slightly rakish Homburg of his friend, Friedrich, Prince Ottenholtz. Aunt Eva's inner circle was in session. She could hear their voices coming from the sitting room, or the salon, as Aunt Eva insisted on calling it. Another example of her obdurate foreignness which made Milla cringe in embarrassment.

The thought of her and her guttural, East European voice and claustrophobic self-righteous formality made Milla writhe in frustration at the unfair fates that had placed this nightmare woman in charge of her destiny. For Milla was English through and through, and determined to stay so. Since the death of her parents she had spent her life battling to preserve her identity, hating her Aunt and the shame and despair that she brought upon her.

She tried to sneak past the open door into the long corridor which lead to the bedroom that she had to share with Georgia, her younger sister. Aunt Eva's grating voice called her back.

"Milla. Come here at once."

Milla hesitated, wanting to run to her room and slam the door against these unspeakable monsters who had taken over her life. Two years ago that was what she might have done, but now she knew better than to offer the slightest resistance to her Aunt's wishes. The days of grinding harangue with which Eva would punish even the most minute sign of reluctance, real or imagined, were simply not worth the brief thrill of rebellion.

"Yes, Aunt Eva," she called, forcing herself to sound carefree and happy at the request, and wondering what fresh torments her Aunt and her cronies had been concocting for her benefit across the dry martinis and whisky and sodas of the cocktail hour.

She stood in the doorway of the large, ornately furnished drawing room. Her feet were together and her shoulders as square as her Aunt insisted. Her school coat was still buttoned up to the neck. Her Aunt beckoned impatiently for her to come and stand in front of her and her two companions.

Eva was sitting on an oyster-coloured velvet sofa which dominated the area around the fireplace. The two men were seated in the matching, high-winged armchairs placed on either side of the sofa. Lord Harley – Bo Bo to his intimates – was on Eva's right. He was tall and running to fat, his stomach straining against the buttons of his waistcoat. Although beginning to thin, his hair was still fairly thick, the greying curls slicked down flat across his large head. His cheeks were plump and mottled with veins, giving him a jolly, Father

Christmas sort of look that was belied by his eyes. They were hard and calculating and devoid of warmth.

Bo Bo was a man about town. He had been born in an age when commerce and all that it involved were considered far beneath the dignity of a man of birth and station. The social changes of postwar Britain had caught him unawares, and for a while Bo Bo had faced extinction along with the rest of his kind. His suits had become threadbare and his meals infrequent. He would have gone under had it not been for a chance meeting with the newly arrived and very rich emigrée, Eva Lubinski. That had been over ten years ago and the fortunes of Lord Harley and his sister Lady Pamela had been in the ascendancy ever since.

On Eva's left sat the Prince, Freddie to his friends, and scoundrel and philanderer to his many enemies. He was a slight man with suspiciously jet-black hair, greased straight back from his high forehead. His face was thin, almost gaunt, and this evening his customary good-humoured expression was replaced by a look of forced severity.

The men were already dressed for the evening. Both were wearing dinner jackets with long, shawl collars reaching right down to a single button, placed low down, so that the top of their crimson cummerbunds showed as a slash of colour below their starched shirt fronts.

Aunt Eva was still wearing a tea gown. Milla had never seen this one before. It was made of deep blue panne velvet, with an elaborately draped front. She could see Aunt Eva's small feet encased in mules of matching satin, peeping out below the long, full skirt.

Her Aunt motioned her to stand in front of them, her back to the marble mantelpiece with its clutter of ornaments and the single silver-framed photograph of Eva and her long-dead husband, Jack Powers, the banker whose riches had supported Eva throughout the grim years after the war, and were now sustaining the lives of Milla and the twelve-year-old Georgia.

Milla's hatred of the plump and compliant Georgia was almost equal to her loathing for her Aunt. She was Eva's instrument of torment, spoiled and indulged and armed with a constant stream of spiteful little digs, always at Milla's expense, which she relayed each evening with solemn self-righteousness. Milla would squirm in her impotency, sometimes sitting, late at night, watching her sister's golden head asleep on the pillow, and imagining a terrible revenge. Then she would stand above her with her own pillow in her hands, lowering it so that it was suspended only a few inches above Georgia's face, her entire body trembling with tension as she felt

3

the power of life and death course through her. Afterwards, she was sick and spent, yet filled with great relief and elation at the knowledge that if her Aunt pushed her just that little bit too far, she would have the means to get her own back, once and for all. The thought sustained her through the endless hours of her humiliation.

She stood in front of them now, her back to the mantelpiece, wondering what was coming next. It was unlikely that the miserable Jean-Claude had confessed to his mother, although with these wet little French boys you could never tell. Perhaps she could say that she had been raped, but, she thought, thinking of Jean-Claude and his namby-pamby ways, they would probably not believe her. She braced herself for what was to come, taking care to hide her defiance as she fixed her eyes on the floor and clasped her hands in front of her, in what she hoped was a demure pose.

It was Lord Harley who spoke first. He usually did. Aunt Eva used him as a battering ram to open up the gates while she waited to pounce in the aftermath of the shock.

His voice was deep and mellifluous. He cleared his throat solemnly before he started. She could almost smell the fumes of alcohol and stale cigar.

"Your Aunt has asked me to talk to you. She has received a very grave allegation from the lycée. The headmaster telephoned after school. It appears that an extremely valuable gold watch is missing from the desk of one of the teachers, and certain of your fellow pupils have indicated that the culprit is none other than yourself."

Damn that stupid watch and damn the snivelling, creepy little telltales who had told on her. She had forgotten all about the watch in the anticipation of her tryst with Jean-Claude. Now she could feel its weight against her thigh as it lay, hidden and accusing, in the deep pocket of her coat. She wondered why on earth she had ever bothered to steal it.

Her annoyance was tinged with relief. It was much better to be accused as a thief than a harlot. She had a sudden, ridiculous desire to raise her skirt and watch their faces as she displayed her blood-stained underwear.

She said nothing, debating whether or not to deny everything and storm out of the room, but not knowing what she could do after that. There was nowhere in the entire neat and precisely ordered apartment that the watch could be safely hidden from the search that would be bound to follow. The alternative was to confess passively and then wait for the retribution that was bound to come pouring in from all sides.

She looked up at the faces in front of her. They were watching

4

her closely. Lord Harley, his task completed, was sitting back, cross-legged, with a look of pompous satisfaction. Her aunt was hunched forward. She was staring unblinkingly at Milla's face. Her eyes were glittering venomously; her lips were parted in anticipation. She was enjoying herself. She had finally caught Milla in a situation where her punishment could be both openly and justifiably severe.

To everyone's surprise, it was the Prince who spoke first. "This is really too distressing." His accent was almost perfect. He had a slight lisp, which he used to disguise his naturally guttural tone. He stood up and held out his hand to Milla.

"Come with me, Milla. It's quite wrong that your dear Aunt should be subjected to any more suffering. We will go and have a little talk together, just the two of us, and see if we can reach the truth of the matter."

He grabbed her by the hand and started to walk towards the door. She followed willingly beside him, catching a glimpse of the astonishment and fury on Eva's face as they went past her.

The Prince's hand was warm and clammy as he led her across the corridor and into the cold and darkened dining room on the other side, where he sat down in the formal, mahogany armchair at the head of the table. He kept her hand in his and sat silently for a moment, looking hard into her eyes before he started to speak.

"What are we going to do about you, my little Milla?"

There was a softness to his voice that she had not heard before. It made her uneasy and she tried to pull her hand away from him, but he squeezed it harder and pulled her closer to him.

"You're becoming too old for childish things like stealing. Very soon you will be grown up and all sorts of exciting things will happen to you that you can't imagine just now. And when that happens, I want to be your friend."

As he spoke, he released her hand and stood up. "Let's take off your coat," he said. He fumbled with the stiff button at her neck and then with the others, all the way down the front of her body. His hands moved slowly. She could feel them pressing against her until finally the coat was opened. He put his hands on the collar and pulled it back, away from her shoulders, clumsily, so that for a moment she was pressed up against him. She could smell his cologne and the starch on the front of his shirt.

Then the Prince gave a sort of stifled sigh and stepped back from her. He was holding the coat and he patted the pockets quickly, still standing in front of her. It was a big watch, gold and heavy and easy to find. He gave a grunt of triumph as he pulled it out and held it in his hand. They both looked at it in silence. Then the Prince put the watch carefully into his trouser pocket. He sat down on the chair and crossed his legs.

"Now we have a secret that only we can share. You realize what would happen if I told your aunt what I have found?"

Milla nodded and stayed silent. Somehow she didn't think that the Prince was going to tell anybody about his discovery. There was something about him that reminded her of Jean-Claude and how he had been that afternoon on the steps in the park: a trembling subservience in her presence that was new to her. She could tell that the Prince was going to be a powerful ally in the future.

Just to make sure she leant forward and threw her arms around his neck, hugging him tightly and pushing her cheek against him so she could feel his rough bristles on her skin. She turned her head and kissed him hard on the lips, letting her mouth linger on his for a brief moment, so he would remember what it was like. Then she pulled away from him and gave a little girl laugh, just to make him think that she was still a child and did not know what she was doing.

"What will you do?" she said.

The Prince's face was red. He recrossed his legs and for a moment he seemed to have some trouble speaking. Then he cleared his throat.

"I'll take care of the watch. You don't have to worry about that. I'll tell your aunt that we've had a long talk and that I'm sure that you're innocent. She'll not be happy but there'll be nothing she can do, not this time anyway. You must be more careful in future. It's stupid for a lovely young girl to risk her reputation on something so trivial. You must promise me that you'll never do anything so silly again."

Milla nodded her head. Taking the Prince by the hand, she asked if they could have other little talks like this in the future. The Prince said that they could whenever she felt the need, as he was going to be a very special friend to her from now on.

Then Milla said that perhaps they could have tea sometimes, after school was over for the day. She was worried that she had gone too far because the Prince gave her a funny look, but she stared back as innocently as she could and he smiled and said that perhaps they would.

Milla thought she might ask him to go for a walk with her in Kensington Gardens, but then she thought that she should wait a while for that. The Prince would hate it if his trousers became all muddy. So she thanked the Prince very much and gave him a little curtsey, as she had been taught. She left him sitting in the darkened room and went down the corridor to her bedroom.

6

She only had one worry left. Before she went to bed she must remove the mess from her underwear. She could hear Druska, her Aunt's maid, talking to Georgia as she prepared their supper in the kitchen.

Druska was a miserable old woman from some Slavic country whose name Milla was determined not to remember. She had been with her Aunt since she had lived in Poland when she was a little girl. Milla hated Druska. She was Eva's spy. Always going through her drawers and searching the pockets of her clothes so that there was nowhere that she had any privacy. Between Georgia and Druska, there was someone with her every second that she was at home. The only moments that she really had to herself were the twenty minutes or so that it took her to walk from Pont Street to her school in the Cromwell Road, and even then she was timed in and out of the house and questioned closely if she was more than a few minutes late.

The weekends were even worse. Saturday morning was devoted to her homework, which had to be finished before she was allowed to eat lunch. At around that time her Aunt would have finished in her boudoir and would be ready to emerge into the world. The afternoon would depend upon Eva's mood and that, in turn, relied upon the success of the previous evening and the amount of alcohol that Eva had consumed.

It was better for Milla when the evening had gone badly or when Eva was still suffering from the after-effects of the entertainment. These occasions happened more often than not and with increasing frequency as time went by and her Aunt's circle of friends grew static, with no newcomers to enliven the claustrophobic sameness of their lives. Even the efforts of the Prince and Lord Harley were no longer able to keep her amused.

On those days Eva would not leave her room until around two in the afternoon, too late to organize one of her usual Saturday-afternoon excursions to a museum or West End matinée, things that Milla longed to do by herself and which were completely ruined by the presence of her Aunt and the placidly co-operative Georgia who always accompanied them.

The outings invariably ended in tea at the Ritz, where her Aunt would meet with those of her friends who were still in favour after the events of the previous evening's amusement. These events would be dissected and remodelled to the satisfaction of those present and then dismembered and assembled again, over and over, until Milla felt she was going to pass out, overpowered by the boredom and the smell of the heavily scented old ladies perspiring in the mink

7

coats which they never took off, no matter what the temperature of the room.

The Saturday after the incident at the Albert Memorial, Milla could finally stand the claustrophobia no longer. After an hour of petty bitchery, as the chorus of malicious innuendo was hitting its stride, she turned her head away from the table and thrust her finger down her throat. She turned back with her face puce and cheeks bulging. The result was dramatic beyond her wildest expectations. She had only intended to be sick quietly into her napkin, thereby providing an excuse for her early departure, but as she twisted back to face the table, her throat constricted again and she vomited with great force, moving her head at the same time, so that no one was spared.

For a moment the conversation continued as before, slowly petering out into a horrified silence which was soon replaced by cries of disgust and consternation, a rush of waiters and brushing of fur coats, and muttered calculations as to the cost of the damage.

The party broke up quickly after that. Her aunt said nothing during the taxi ride home, but Milla could feel her glancing in her direction. Whatever the punishment she was planning, Milla thought it had been worth it.

2

Eva was still silent as they entered the flat, and she went straight to her room. Milla could hear the silver handbell that she kept by her bedside ringing furiously and Druska's shuffling footsteps as she hastened to answer its call.

Georgia had gone to watch television in the kitchen. Young as she was, her instinct told her to keep well away from Milla, in case she too was caught up in the terrible reprisal that was bound to follow.

Milla sat on her bed, her exhilaration slowly ebbing as over an hour went by. Twice she tiptoed into the corridor and strained to hear what was being said behind the closed door of her Aunt's room, but there was nothing except the sound of the television in the kitchen.

At last there was a ring at the front door. She could hear the voices of Lord Harley and the Prince as they handed their hats and coats to Druska, and then the sound of her Aunt as she went up the corridor to join them.

She cautiously opened the door and moved a few feet towards the entrance to the drawing room. Lord Harley and the Prince had voices that were both loud and penetrating and she had no difficulty in hearing what they were saying.

It was obvious that her Aunt had only just finished her account of the afternoon's drama. The two men were uttering sounds of shock and disgust.

"My poor Eva," said Lord Harley, "what a ghastly experience. After all you are doing for that wretched girl. The ingratitude is impossible to understand."

The Prince said, "Madame Eva, I can only sympathize with you in your distress." It came out "seempateeze wit", something which she would normally have found amusing, but now it only made her angry.

"I think that little Milla is in need of a man to talk some sense into her," the Prince continued. "A man like myself who has experience of the world and can counsel a girl of her age as though he was her father."

Lord Harley said that he had been going to say the same thing himself, but the Prince had said it first. He sounded relieved, as if that settled the matter, and then tried to change the subject, saying he had booked a table at Quaglino's for the three of them, and they should hurry as they were late.

Aunt Eva was not going to be satisfied so easily. Milla could hear her start the story once again as Druska helped them on with their coats. She was still talking as they went down the stairs, telling it more slowly this time, her own hurt and outrage gathering strength as the tale unfolded. Milla smiled grimly to herself. By the time the evening was over half of London would know of her disgrace.

She wondered when she and the Prince were going to have their little talk. Soon, she hoped. She would be fifteen in another few weeks. Properly used, the time between now and her birthday could be very much to her advantage.

She found a pencil and paper and started to compose a letter. It was quite a brief note, but it took her a long time.

The next morning Druska took the two girls to Mass at the Brompton Oratory as usual. It was the High Mass and sometimes her Aunt would go with them. They would have to stand about for hours afterwards, outside on the steps while Eva talked with her cronies. She would ignore the bows and greetings of a large number of foreign-looking gentlemen, usually rather seedy, whom Eva said were only after her money, although she seemed to enjoy the attention all the same.

Eva did not go with them that day, nor was she in evidence when they returned home. Just the Prince, who was waiting in the drawing room, still wearing his coat, although he was holding a drink.

He bowed to Milla, very formally. "Miss Milla," he said, "your Aunt has asked me to have discussion with you about your behaviour yesterday, which was such a terrible thing and has made her *très distraite.*"

Then the Prince said that they were going to have a lunch together. He called a taxi on the street, and he gave the driver an address in Notting Hill, which was on the north side of the park. Milla had never been there before nor, as far as she knew, had any of her friends. It was not the sort of place where a lady should be seen.

The Prince lived on the top floor of an old and decrepit house in a narrow street, close behind the Notting Hill Gate tube station. The front door was chipped and scarred and there was a piece of cardboard covering a hole in one of the frosted-glass panels. There was a time switch in the hall that turned on the light and Milla was shocked to see an Indian coming out of a door as they passed one of the landings. She had never seen an Indian close up before. He was dressed in robes of flowing white. He brushed past them in a very rude way, but the Prince said he was a prince too and did not know any better.

The Prince's room was small and rather smelly. There was a divan bed along one wall, a small round wooden table and two kitchen chairs in the centre, and a scruffy armchair against the wall opposite the bed. There was a washbasin and a cheap-looking wardrobe, and dirty net curtains hung against the smeared glass of the window. The frayed carpet was rotting around the washbasin and the place smelled of mildew and urine. She doubted that the window had been opened in years.

There was a paper bag on the table and a loaf of sliced white bread. The Prince started to take some thin slices of cut meat from the bag and put them on a plate. He seemed nervous and paused to take a bottle of red wine from the shelf above the washbasin, pouring the contents into a plastic cup.

Milla went over and sat on the bed. She was wearing a simple white cotton shirtwaister dress, with a gauze petticoat under the full skirt which made it balloon out from her narrow waist. Her legs were bare, ending in white cotton socks and matching flat-heeled pumps. She was still not quite large enough for a bra, so she was wearing a thin white cotton vest and white knickers. She sat very prim and correct on the bed, but allowed her skirt to ride up several inches above her thigh. She crossed her legs and placed her handbag on the bed beside her.

"Can I have some?" she asked, pointing to the bottle of wine. "All my school friends drink wine at home and I'd very much like to know how it tastes." She made her voice clear and innocent and slightly demanding. The Prince's hands were trembling as he poured the wine into another plastic glass and held it out towards her.

"Thank you very much." She bent her knee so that her foot was on the bed. She watched the Prince's eyes as he stared at the back of her thigh.

"Do you want to sit beside me?" she asked.

The Prince took off his jacket and hung it on a hook on the back of the door. The room was very quiet. There was a radio playing somewhere in the building. It was tuned to the BBC Home Service because she could hear Reginald Dixon playing his theatre organ. It wasn't very romantic, but then romance was not really the point.

The Prince came and sat beside her. His face was very red, but not as red as it was going to be in a minute. He put his hand on her knee and squeezed it slightly, and then moved it slowly up to the middle of her thigh.

"I think you and I are going to be great friends," he said. "It's about time that a man showed you certain things, the sort of things that your father would have shown you if he had been alive." His voice was croaky and he had to clear his throat as he was speaking. It gathered strength as he continued.

"These things are going to be our secret, just between the two of us. You would be in very serious trouble indeed if you were to tell tales to other people and your Aunt Eva would throw you out of the house and send you to a school for poor girls. You would spend the rest of your life washing dishes with no pretty clothes to wear." As he spoke, his hand moved up her leg until it encountered the elastic bottom of her underwear. Milla thought that was far enough.

"I would love it for you to show me things," she said, "but first there's something that I think you should read, because I think you may have made a little mistake." She opened her bag and pulled out the letter that she had drafted so carefully the night before. She had been right not to waste any time.

The Prince reluctantly took his hand away from her thigh. He unfolded the paper and started to read. He read very slowly and Milla was glad that she had used big block letters to make it easier for him.

Even so, it took a while for what she had written to sink in. She moved further towards the end of the bed so that she could watch his face. It was screwed up in disbelief. She had expected it to come as quite a shock but hoped that the Prince did not have a heart attack or a seizure or whatever happened to old men when they were under great stress.

The Prince suddenly jumped up. He said, "What is this? What is

12

this?" several times. His knees were wobbly and he clung on to the table.

She said, "It's quite simple really. All you have to do is to copy that out in your own handwriting and sign it properly, with the right date."

He looked at her in disbelief. "I will never sign something as wicked as this. It would ruin me and it's all lies anyway, complete lies. You have misunderstood what I was saying to you. I was trying to be your friend, but now we'll go straight to your Aunt and you will see who she will believe, you evil, evil girl."

He was working himself up into quite a state.

Milla stayed very calm. She had expected that he would be upset.

"I think I see a policeman outside and if you do not write that out at once, exactly as I have written it, I'm going to start screaming and I'll tell him that you have been molesting me. You do realize that I am still only fourteen, although I know I look older, and that means you will go to prison for years for what you have done."

The Prince stood shaking his head for a while and then a look of cunning came over his face.

"You are not as smart as you think, you little fiend. If you go to the police I will demand a medical examination right away and that will show that you are untouched and it will be you that goes to prison."

Milla looked him straight in the eyes and slowly shook her head. "I don't think that would be a very good idea," she said. "You see I have thought of that. My virginity is gone and it's up to me to say who did it to me." She pointed to the paper. "I'm not going to use that you know, only if you force me to."

The Prince uttered a groan and sank down on to one of the kitchen chairs. He was weeping. "You little monster," he kept repeating, but he wrote the confession all the same. She poured him a glass of wine to calm him down while he was doing it. She took one for herself as well and made herself a meat sandwich while she waited.

When he had finished she read the letter through carefully. It was quite short, but as long as it was in her possession the Prince would be in her power.

She felt light-headed as she folded up the letter and put it in her purse. She also felt sorry for the Prince. He looked so dejected, sitting at the table with his head in his hands. She went over to him and put her arms round his shoulder. "Don't be too upset," she said. "I'm not going to tell, not if you are nice to me." She rubbed

13

the back of his neck but he shook his head violently and jerked away from her.

He gave her a pound note for a taxi. She walked down Kensington Church Street and spent the rest of the afternoon wandering around the streets looking in shop windows and thinking about men and the power of her sex and how best she could use it. The Prince was much weaker than she had thought and she would have to be careful how she handled him, in case he did something silly.

When she arrived home, her Aunt was sitting alone in the salon. She must have been waiting for her. She seemed quite relieved that she was back. She asked how her afternoon had been and whether she had behaved herself with the Prince.

Milla said that it had been very nice, thank you, and that she thought the Prince was a very nice man and they were going to see more of each other from now on, because the Prince had many interesting things to show her, now that she was growing up.

Her Aunt looked at her sharply and Milla thought she might have said the wrong thing and made her suspicious, but the telephone rang at that moment and her Aunt had to answer it herself as Druska and Georgia had not yet returned. Milla slipped away and went to her room. She was worried about hiding the letter. She was sure that Aunt Eva searched her things when she was out and it would be a disaster if it was discovered. She decided to keep it in her purse, which was a risk but the best she could think of for the moment.

In the end she thought it might be safer to destroy it. It would make no difference; the Prince would never know.

3

Eva had always known that she was different. She had been different from the other children of the village, where she had lived until the death of her mother when she was four years old. So different, in fact, that she was kept apart from them because they were nasty, common children, whilst her mother was a lady and her father a great man with untold wealth who lived on the other side of the Vistula, which flowed, wide and forbidding, at the edge of the village. Eva knew that if she were to become like the other children, her father would be angry and would leave her behind when the time came for her mother to join him in the magic land across the river.

For as long as she could remember she had been taught that she carried the blood of one of the most noble families in the land, so it was no surprise to the little girl when, shortly after the funeral, the call finally came and a fine liveried servant arrived at the manor house where her grandparents lived to escort her to her new life.

What had been a surprise was the way she was treated on her arrival at the vast and sprawling castle that had been the seat of the Lubinski family for over three hundred years. Instead of a father to meet her at the massive oak door that was the entrance to the castle, she had been driven straight to the back door and given a small room in the servants' quarters, far from the family that she had been taught to believe was her own.

And there she stayed for eight miserable years. At first she asked questions. When was she going to see her father? Why didn't her father want to see her? And, finally, why didn't her father love her as he loved the other children, whom she would sometimes see riding on their ponies or taking a trip in a horse-drawn sleigh, laughing and excited, wrapped against the cold in great, shaggy pelts of bear or sleek wolf skin. And always the answer would be the same, whether it was from Hirschka, the housekeeper or one of the kitchen maids. "Hush yourself, you silly child, you don't know what you're saying." Until, finally, she ceased to ask.

She was different from the others, she knew that and the servants knew it as well. She had heard the housekeeper discussing her with the major-domo soon after she arrived. Although she had not understood the real meaning of their conversation, she realized from its tone and from the way the two retainers were whispering together, that there was something shameful in her position, something which set her apart from the rest of the household, gentry and servants alike.

And so she slipped into a half world between the two, accepted by neither, except for a young kitchen maid called Druska, who became her only friend. Although friendship was not quite the word to describe their relationship. From the beginning Eva dominated the young girl, who, in spite of being four years her elder, was content to accept her childish demands and help her act out her fantasies.

There was a game that they would play for hours together, where Eva acted the grand lady and Druska her willing and obedient servant, and slowly over the next few years the game became a part of their daily life. The simple Druska had a blind loyalty to the little girl that made her deaf to the jibes of her fellow menials. "One day you will see," she would reply to their taunts, as she washed Eva's underwear, as coarse and frayed as her own, or saved the best titbits from her evening meal so that Eva could enjoy them later on.

The only thing that set Eva apart from the other servants was the attention that Monsieur Ribot, the tutor for the younger children of the Lubinski family, paid to her education. Eva was naturally a bright child and quickly realized the advantage that the ability to read and write would give her over her fellows. She studied hard, delighted that someone from the Lubinski family had acknowledged her presence.

As she grew older, the housekeeper started to introduce her into the intricacies of running a big household. She became an expert on the economics and organization necessary to control such a complex mixture of people and skills. At the same time she was expected to contribute towards her keep by working in the sewing room, where, with two elderly retainers, she spent her days darning and stitching, steadily graduating from the mending of tears in ageing sheets to the intricate alterations to the fine gowns that were sent from Paris for the ladies of the family.

It was not until she was twelve years old that she was allowed to enter the part of the castle that was inhabited by the family. One day she received a summons from the Countess herself. The housekeeper escorted her through enormous, oak-panelled reception rooms and long, gaslit corridors until they arrived at the small suite of richly furnished rooms that was the private apartment of the Countess. She was a tall, imposing woman of about sixty years. Her hair was thick and white and swept back from her forehead above a strong face with heavy eyebrows and a determined jaw. She dismissed the housekeeper from her presence as soon as they arrived. Eva was aware of her scrutiny as she stood with her hands clasped in front of her and her eyes cast demurely downwards.

The Countess was sitting on a sofa, close by a window that overlooked the green parkland stretching away from the front of the castle. There was a herd of deer browsing on the bank of a lake. Her voice was harsh as she bade Eva to step forward to stand beside her.

"The Count and I have been hearing very good reports from Monsieur Ribot about your work and the way you have been conducting yourself since we took you into this household. We have decided that now you have reached the age of twelve it is time for you to further your education by becoming a companion to Pania Alexandra, who as you know is our youngest daughter and is lonely, now that her brothers and sisters are grown up. Your belongings are being moved to the room next to hers, which is just down this corridor. You will act as her personal maid and it will be a great opportunity for you to learn the ways of the aristocracy. Who knows, if you work hard one day you may have the opportunity to be the companion of a grand lady."

She was looking hard at Eva as she spoke and Eva choked back the bitter words that were forming in her throat. She knew that the slightest sign that she had any ideas above the station in life that the Countess had decided should be hers, and she would be back in the kitchen, or even worse, banished for ever from the castle and from any hope of eventual recognition as the daughter of the Count and a member of the Lubinski family.

Life with Alexandra was not particularly demanding. She was a pleasant girl, spoilt by her brothers and sisters and used to having her own way with the servants and nannies, all of whom had been in the service of the family since their own childhoods and had looked after Alexandra's brothers and sisters before her. Of the two boys, the elder, Stefan, lived in the castle with his own wife and children and was responsible for the running of the great estate that would one day be his own. After him came two sisters, both now married and living far away with families of their own, so their visits were rare. Finally, six years older than Alexandra, was the younger son, Andrzej, whose cavalry regiment was stationed near by, and who spent most of his free time at the castle, bringing with him an everchanging group of other young officers.

Eva had always been conscious of Andrzej. Even when she was a young child she had listened for his voice as he called out at play, and had recognized the hoofbeats of his horse as he rode, usually at a gallop, through the park. She had often imagined how it would be to have such a wonderful person as a brother and had gone to sleep dreaming of scenes in which she shared his adventures.

The next few years were happier than Eva could have possibly imagined. Although she was not accepted as one of the family, never eating at their table or sharing in their festivities, she was a part of their day-to-day lives, even allowed to go on little trips with Alexandra and once, when they were both fifteen, on a long journey to the family palace in Warsaw, where she was allowed to wear the dresses abandoned by Alexandra's older sisters and accompany her on visits to the opera and ballet and tours around art galleries and museums.

It was the first time that Eva had ever been to a city, in fact her first visit to anywhere apart from the villages that dotted the Lubinski estate. It was the people who astounded her the most. The riches and elegance of the aristocracy, the wealth of the merchants who fawned upon them wherever they went, and the miserable poverty of everybody else. She could see that to be anything less than an aristocrat was to lead a life of servility or poverty, in most cases both at the same time. Her anger at the Count and his refusal to accept her into his family increased as she saw what that refusal was going to mean to her for the rest of her life.

She was quiet and thoughtful on the long journey home. She was tired of having to share Alexandra's enthusiasm for all the things that were going to be hers by virtue of her birth. The servants, the palaces, the safe assumption that she would marry well into her own kind, and, above all, the careless acceptance of all the gifts that Eva, however much she yearned for them, was going to be denied.

Around this time Eva had started to change from child to young woman. It was a change the importance of which she herself had been unaware; apart from the bulging of her breasts and the first signs of puberty between her legs, she had assumed that her life would continue the same as before. It was the attitude of the men around her that took her by surprise. Most importantly that of Andrzej.

He had always spent time playing with his little sister whenever he had been at home, and Eva had been included in their games, more out of his good nature than for any other reason, but now the relationship was changing and Eva could sense that his visits to the wing of the castle where she and Alexandra lived were as much to see her as his sister. Often he would appear when he must have known that Eva would be on her own and he would sit for hours, telling her about life in the cavalry and bragging youthfully about his adventures and those of his friends.

He had taken to kissing her hand when they greeted each other. Formally, clicking his heels as an officer should, but there was something about the heat of his lips and the way he would look into her eyes that suggested there was much more behind their half-joking contact than the meeting of friends.

Eva's heart leapt whenever he was near. She tried the best she could to hide her feelings, desperately ashamed that she should have such feelings at all, for was not Andrzej her own half-brother? She wondered what the Count would think if he had any idea of what was starting to happen between them.

Fortunately, Andrzej's regiment was posted far away near the Russian border before the bounds of friendship were breached. Eva was left wondering what her reaction would have been if Andrzej had declared his love. Whatever she would have done would ultimately have caused him terrible hurt and she loved him too much for that ever to happen. In some ways she dreaded his return. She had avoided a farewell meeting with him, pleading that she had a sickness and, in a way, that was the truth, although the sickness was in her heart and not in her body.

For the entire time that she had been living in the castle, Count Lubinski himself was very rarely at home. It was rumoured in the servants' hall that he and Madame, the Countess, were not always on the best of terms and that the Count preferred the freedom of Warsaw and other great cities such as Paris and London, where he could lead his own life, unrestricted by his family. Whatever the reason, Eva had seldom had the opportunity to see him, let alone talk to him and discover what her father was really like. She could see why her mother had fallen in love with him. He was tall and dark, with a thin moustache and long, expressive hands, like those of an artist. To her mother, the daughter of a country landlord, he must have been the answer to all her dreams. Even though he had abandoned her as soon as she became pregnant, her mother had never said anything but good about her great Count and had died still certain that he would come back for them.

The Count always ignored her during his infrequent visits, busying himself with the affairs of the estate and seldom seeing his family at all. He slept separately from the Countess. His apartment was in the opposite wing of the castle. While he was at home the Countess kept to her own rooms and when she did make an appearance, she was tense and withdrawn.

The Count was at home, some three weeks after Andrzej had departed, when Eva received a summons to attend him in his study. It was in a suite of rooms that led directly from the great hall which was the centre of the castle and out of bounds for the children and all but the few close retainers who formed the Count's private circle. It was a large room, the walls lined with books and oil paintings, and there was a wood fire burning in the vast brick fireplace.

The Count was sitting behind a desk littered with papers and the Countess was standing at his side. From the looks on their faces Eva could see that what they had to say to her was going to be very serious indeed.

The Countess was holding a letter in her hand. It was she who spoke first. Her face was white and her voice shook. The Count's face was strained and he avoided Eva's eye as she entered, keeping his gaze fixed on the papers in front of him.

The Countess waved the letter towards Eva. "This is a letter from Andrzej, my son," she said. "It is addressed to you, as I discovered after I opened it." She glared at Eva, daring her to protest. Eva said nothing.

The Countess continued, "When I took you into my house it was as an act of generosity, and this you have betrayed. My son is a very young man with a great future before him, and I will not allow it to be ruined by some little foundling I have picked up from the hedgerow."

Eva was speechless. There was a buzzing in her ears and a whiteness in her eyes. For a moment she thought she would faint. Then she drew herself up and faced her accuser. All the resentment that had gathered over the years of humiliation gave her a strength that surprised her. She suddenly felt calm and in control, not only of herself, but of this unjust and arrogant woman as well.

"Madame," she said. "I have no idea of what I am being accused;

nor, I might venture to add, have you any right to accuse me. There has been nothing passing between your son and myself except the normal feelings of good friends and I can assure you that I am the last person who would ever wish him ill. What is more, I should be pleased if you would allow me to take possession of my letter." She held out her hand and kept it there, defying the Countess to deny her.

They stood in silence, eyes locked. It was the Countess who turned aside. The Count stood up. He was clearly embarrassed, but angry as well, used to having his own way. He took the letter from his wife's hand and handed it to Eva. "Read it," he said. "Read it now and then we will talk."

The Countess was trembling with fury. "How dare you side with this slut, whom you have forced upon me and my children, another of your little follies that I have to bear. She is your child and now she is your responsibility, but she will not spend one more night under my roof." She strode from the room and the door slammed shut behind her. Eva turned to face the Count.

Suddenly he looked like an old man, tired with the responsibilities of his life. He motioned her to a seat by the fire and sat down in an armchair facing her.

"You take after your mother and not only in your looks," he said. "There is a spirit inside you that will never be content while you are in this house. I can see that I was wrong to bring you here, but that is over now. Read the letter and you will understand why that must be so."

The words danced in front of Eva's eyes. She was too upset to make sense at all of what Andrzej had written; they were just phrases in which he had expressed his love. There were tears running down her cheeks when she handed it back to the Count. He took it from her and dropped it on to the fire. They both watched as it flared and was gone.

"He must never know that you are his half-sister," said the Count. "Things like that can destroy families, and the scandal would destroy you as well. You must leave this house, that is certain." He thought for a moment. "I own an apartment in Paris. I will send you there for a while and we will decide what you should do when I arrive there myself, a few months from now."

Two hours later, while it was still light, a horse-drawn sleigh drew up outside a side door, far from the sight of anyone in the castle, and Eva's few possessions were loaded aboard. She had asked Druska to accompany her on the journey and she had willingly agreed. It would be the first time in her life that she had slept outside

21

the castle. The Count was there to see them leave. Awkwardly, he kissed Eva on the forehead and for a moment he hugged her to him. "You are a good girl," he said, as he let her go.

She was weeping with happiness as the sleigh drove out into the icy tundra. She knew that she was loved by her father.

4

Georgia left school as soon as she was sixteen. She was neither glad nor sorry that her time at the convent was over, just vaguely relieved that she had managed to pass the last five years without any serious incident to upset the even, easy pace of her pampered existence.

Georgia was spoilt. She knew it and looked upon it as her right. Her blonde hair and blue eyes and the relaxed and friendly, if rather condescending, manner with which she treated the world around her made her instantly popular with everyone she met. The nuns who had been her teachers, her school friends and the everchanging members of her aunt's social circle, all treated her with a respect and affection that she had taken for granted ever since she was a child.

Aunt Eva had told her countless times that the world was divided in two: good girls, who did what they were told and achieved everything that their hearts could desire, and bad girls, who would get nowhere in their lives because they were ungrateful and wretched and deserved all the nasty things that would inevitably happen to them.

Eva would shake her head sadly above the tea cups, and say in her thick-tongued English, "You see what a bad girl is Milla, all the troubles she gives me which, God knows, I do not deserve. In a few years she will be walking the streets and you will be married to a rich man, and you will thank your Aunt who looks after you, because you are my little girl." Eva's rouged cheeks would shake with indignation at Milla's ingratitude. Georgia would reach for another *baba au rhum*, secure in the snug world that her Aunt had created, knowing that as long as she did what she was told good things were going to happen to her.

She felt a mild contempt for Milla and her stupidity in not accepting the life that had been offered to her. When Milla finally left the lycée and went to work in a clothes shop, she saw it as the final proof that her Aunt had been right all along.

Then Milla left the comforts of home to share a flat near the King's Road in Chelsea, with two other girls from where she worked.

"Shop girls," her Aunt sneered. "You will see, streetwalker is next. What have I done to deserve this shame on my family, who have been nobles for centuries, with a hundred servants to look after them?" Eva would roll her eyes and cross herself and Georgia would roll her eyes as well, in sympathy. She had never liked Milla, finding her anger and hatred a disturbance, always upsetting people with her tantrums and bad behaviour. She was glad that she had gone away.

Aunt Eva and Lady Pamela, who was Lord Harley's sister, spent many long hours discussing Georgia's arrival on the social scene. London was still the most prestigious place for a young girl to be launched into society. Its Season attracted would-be debutantes of wealth and family from all over the world. There was intense and sometimes bitter competition for the few hundred priceless places on the social round. Unless a young lady was born into the British aristocracy, there was no certain formula for success. There was no official committee that decided, no court of appeal if you failed. If your name did not appear on the invitation list for Queen Charlotte's Ball where, as the ultimate accolade of the Season, you would be presented to the Queen, you would be confined to hanging around at the many dozens of cocktail parties and private balls that made up the rest of the social calendar. In which case life became a nightmare of being nice to anyone who would bother to talk to you, in the hope that further invitations would follow.

It was to help avoid the trauma that such a situation would cause a young and impressionable girl, not to mention her parents, that Lady Pamela and a few others like her made the bulk of their not inconsiderable living. For a fee, which Lady Pamela was far too delicate to discuss in person – her brother did that – a young girl of wealth but no bloodline could be accepted into the ranks of society, where she would rub shoulders with the nobility and, who knows, if she were lucky and her fortune of a suitable size, she might even marry into the ranks of the well born.

In truth, the British aristocracy, such of it as remained, was desperate for such alliances. Its wealth decimated by postwar taxes, it needed the infusion of new money in order to survive. Parties were thronged with young lords and Honourable misters circling like jackals around the flock of fresh young lambs presented for their consideration each year. Great indeed was the competition for the wealthier offerings. The father's bank account would be as well known as the foibles of the daughter.

Eva was determined that Georgia would make her mark on this exalted company. She saw it as a way to establish herself, once and for all, as the acknowledged matriarch of the Lubinski family. At one time she had thought that Milla would be the vehicle to bring her to her rightful position in life, but her ingratitude was beyond forgiveness and so she had waited impatiently for Georgia's time to come. Now that it had finally arrived, she plotted every move and manipulation with the thoroughness of a military campaign and Lady Pamela was her willing accomplice. Both she and her brother were very aware of Eva's fortune. Rich friends were hard to come by, and both had earmarked Eva's riches as playing a major part in their own financial future.

Lazy and compliant, Georgia found the endless discussions of little interest. Conditioned almost from birth to be totally obedient to her Aunt's wishes, she knew that she must do whatever Eva wanted if she was to avoid the fate of her stupidly rebellious sister. But she saw no point in bothering herself with petty details or anxieties when she had such an expert as Lady Pamela to guide her and tell her what to do.

The two old women decided that Georgia should complete her education, such as it was, at La Circle, a finishing school where young ladies of wealth whose families wished them to rise to the upper echelons of society were taught the niceties of social behaviour: cooking – cordon bleu, of course – deportment, flower arrangement and French, all in the space of the few months that constituted the Season. In reality, admission to La Circle guaranteed a stream of invitations to the right type of parties. Unless the offspring were particularly gauche – or caught red-handed in some stupidity, usually sexual, that placed her beyond the social pale – her presentation to Her Majesty at Queen Charlotte's Ball was a foregone conclusion. All of which meant that a place at La Circle was much sought after and very expensive indeed, open only to the daughters of the excessively well-heeled.

Although the finishing school was less than a mile from the apartment where she had lived almost all her life, Georgia found the move strangely exciting. It was the first time that she had been away from the constant, hour-by-hour influence of her Aunt. She was both frightened and exhilarated.

On her first evening she sat on her bed in the room that she was to share with three other girls, and wondered what she was meant to do. There was no one to tell her and her roommates were yet to arrive. She had unpacked her clothes, as Druska had told her she must, and placed them neatly in the wardrobe beside her bed. After that there was nothing else for her to do. There was no television in the room and she found it boring to read. She was sitting, staring at the wall, wondering vaguely what was expected of her when the door was flung open by a tall girl with thick dark hair and a sun-browned face. There was a porter behind her, staggering under the weight of two large suitcases.

"Hello," said the girl. "I'm Chrissie." She held out her hand.

Georgia introduced herself and sat watching as the girl told the man where to leave the cases and then pressed a ten-shilling note into his hand. The porter was clearly both surprised and pleased at the size of his tip. He gave a half-bow and left the room.

Chrissie ignored the suitcases. She reached into the large handbag that she had been carrying, pulled out a bottle of vodka and taking two tooth glasses from the wash basin, poured them both a large drink. It was the first time that Georgia had ever tasted alcohol. It made her gag at first and she felt her face starting to burn. Chrissie finished off her own drink in two big gulps and poured herself some more.

"That's better," she said. "Drink up and have another. There's plenty more where this came from." But Georgia said that she was all right as she was.

Chrissie opened up one of her suitcases and started to rummage inside. Georgia had never seen so many beautiful clothes in her life. Silk blouses and satin evening dresses with big, bouffant skirts and petticoats to match; shoes spilling out everywhere, with high heels and pointed toes, all in the same colours as the clothes.

Chrissie pulled out a packet of French cigarettes and offered one to Georgia, who took it gratefully. Eva had forbidden smoking at home and Georgia felt daring and independent as she took her first puff. She struggled not to cough. She already felt inadequate enough beside her new companion.

"Come on," said Chrissie, "Let's go and have a look round this crummy place." She stood up.

26

Georgia was horrified. "What about your lovely clothes?"

Chrissie shrugged. "There's plenty more of those too. They're made by one of daddy's companies and I can help myself whenever I want. Help yourself, if you see anything you like. It's all the same to me."

Georgia thanked her very much, but Chrissie had lost interest in the subject. "Come on. There's a phone downstairs and there's a boy I want to ring. Maybe I can get out of here tonight, go to the Milroy Club or perhaps the Condor. This place gives me the creeps."

Lady Bacon, the principal of La Circle, was standing in the large, oak-panelled hall. She was used to the attempts of her charges to savour the delights of their new freedom, and took care that none of her young foals were able to bolt the stable until the rules of the house had been both explained and accepted. Unexpected pregnancies and highly publicized arrests for drunk and disorderly conduct were very bad for business.

The newspapers looked upon the antics of each Season's flock of debutantes as manna from heaven, using them to fill their society columns with a daily ration of scandal and innuendo. They could be the making or breaking of the careers of the very young women in her charge, electing the Deb of the Year, writing about all the parties and continuous searching for the slightest breath of scandal – which they would promptly escalate into a full-blown storm.

She inquired sternly where Chrissie and Georgia thought they were going, and directed them firmly to the sitting room at the back of the house, where a number of their fellows had already been corralled.

Georgia was surprised, even slightly dismayed, as she looked around the room at the crème de la crème, as her schoolmates were supposed to be. They were a strange and rather unattractive group. Most of them appeared to be foreigners: plump, serious-looking girls, eyeing each other suspiciously in the musty, overfurnished room.

Georgia found a seat beside a fat, dark-skinned girl who was stolidly eating her way through a box of dates. There was a pile of stones in the ashtray beside her. They sat in silence as other girls joined them, until there were about twenty of them waiting uneasily in the stuffy room.

Finally the door opened and Lady Bacon entered, followed by two other women, both in their sixties and both dressed in tweed skirts, twin-sets and flat-heeled brogues. In contrast, Lady Bacon was wearing a black taffeta cocktail dress, with a double string of pearls around her neck and a diamond bracelet that sparkled as she moved.

Chrissie had plumped herself down between Georgia and the dark-haired girl, squashing the other girl against the arm of the sofa.

"They're fake," she said in a loud whisper, nudging Georgia as she said it.

Georgia pretended not to hear. She was terrified that Lady Bacon would think it was she who had spoken, and dreaded a bad report reaching her Aunt.

Lady Bacon had a very frail appearance which was deceptive, to say the least. Her head snapped round at the sound of the whisper and she fixed Chrissie with a glacial blue eye.

"Miss Levinson, that is precisely the sort of rude and thoughtless remark which your parents have sent you here to have corrected. You are here so that I may place the final polish on your manners and behaviour, enabling you to go out into society as the finished article, ready to take up a position of standing suitable to your birth and upbringing. Believe me, you are all very far from being that polished product at this moment, no matter what you may think of yourselves."

She went on in a similar vein for well over half an hour, until she could sense her audience becoming restive. Georgia sat drinking in her every word. She was as determined to please her new teacher as she had been the nuns at the convent. She was sorry when Lady Bacon indicated that the lecture was over, and they should all go next door for supper.

At least Lady Bacon had broken the ice as far as the girls were concerned, and a buzz of conversation started as soon as they sat down. Chrissie's voice could be heard high above the others, talking about nightclubs and boyfriends and holidays in Switzerland, what her daddy had said and done, the presents he had bought her, and how La Croisette wasn't what it used to be, with all those common people buying yachts and spoiling it for everyone.

Glad that she was at the other end of the table, so that she did not have to listen to her, Georgia was sitting beside the dark girl who had been eating the dates. She still seemed to be hungry, as she ate everything that was placed in front of her and then asked if Georgia had finished with her bread.

At last, with nothing left to eat, the girl volunteered that her name was Farah Kalil, and that she came from Beirut, where her father owned a bank. Georgia felt rather stupid when she had to admit that she had lived her entire life only half a mile away, but the girl

28

just shrugged and sat staring straight ahead. The conversation was over.

It was early to bed for them all that night. They went up to their rooms with Chrissie complaining about the early hour and saying she would ring her father in the morning to have him send her somewhere in Switzerland, where they allowed you to have some fun.

There were two other girls unpacking their clothes in the bedroom. They were twins, Alice and Gloria Swanson. Tall, blonde and very American, they were frightening in their similarity and jointness of purpose, but Georgia liked them immediately. They were pleased to be in London and looking forward to the adventure, as anxious to please as Georgia herself. She was relieved to have them as a buffer against the self-centred and rebellious Chrissie. She hoped they would become friends.

She saw Chrissie on the telephone the next morning and assumed she was ringing her father. She looked very grim when she sat down at the breakfast table a few minutes later, so the conversation could not have gone as well as she had expected. Georgia wondered what it would be like to have a father. It was a thought that she had always kept out of her head as much as she possibly could, determined to be content in her comfortable existence with her Aunt. Now, on her own for the first time in her life, she let her mind wander over what might have been. She was close to tears amidst the clatter of plates and the buzz of excited conversation.

5

It did not take long for Georgia to discover that the two hours of classes each day, which were meant to prepare her for life as a lady of the world, were of no importance at all in comparison to the demands of the social calendar. In a way, she was disappointed. Classrooms were something she understood. She knew that as long as she did what she was told, worked hard and pleased her teachers, then everything would be all right and Aunt Eva would be happy.

Suddenly that prop had been removed and she found the new set of rules confusing and alarming and tinged with a frightening immorality. Boys had never been much discussed at the convent. They existed, of course, as a necessary evil that would have to be faced at some time in the far-off future. The nuns told little stories to the older girls, moral tales, but so obscure that Georgia and her friends rarely managed to understand their point, however hard they tried. It had been quite a shock when, at the age of sixteen, she had finally found out how babies were made.

Her aunt had been of little help. Apart from her constant digs at Milla and the life that she was now leading, Eva had been reticent on the subject of sex; Georgia often wondered if she really knew what it was all about. Her advice had been strictly limited to impressing on Georgia the importance of realizing that boys were after only one thing and that they were to be left waiting for it until marriage or that would be the end of that. She never said exactly what would be so disastrously over. Georgia would nod solemnly and assure Eva that she would take great care and Eva would sigh and gloomily shake her head, as if she had her doubts.

Georgia, who had been only a few months old when they had been killed, did not often think of her parents, but it was after these unsatisfactory discussions that she would wish that she had a mother who could explain things to her. Not that it was likely to have made much difference, judging from the ignorance of her friends.

But boys – their wealth, breeding and good looks, in that order of importance – were all that any of the girls seemed to talk about at La Circle or at the three cocktail parties, two lunches and a dinner dance that she attended in her first week, courtesy of Lady Pamela and her socially high-powered connections.

Most of the other girls had to be content with a single event that week: a cocktail party given by Lady Bacon and her staff as a pipe opener to the Season. It was an opportunity for Lady Bacon to see her girls in action for the first time, and to assess their potential for both social advancement and disaster. The score or so pupils that were under her wing were joined by a few dozen other, less fortunate young ladies, whose parents lacked either the wisdom or the funds to place them in the rarefied confines of La Circle, but whose presence was nonetheless necessary to make up an array of talent to attract a like number of eligible males.

It was the third consecutive night that Georgia had been to a party. She was already beginning to recognize some of the boys from previous evenings, and even with her lack of experience she was starting to realize that it was almost impossible to tell from either look or conversation what any one of them was really like behind the formal evening wear. They all seemed to have the same wolfish features, their hair carefully combed above pointed, predatory noses and narrow chins. Their attitudes ranged from a sort of callow, supercilious inanity to downright boorish rudeness. Deb's delights, the press had named them, but Georgia found them both boring and depressing. The thought of spending the rest of her life with one of them made her feel like vomiting.

The other girls at La Circle appeared to be delighted with what they saw, giggling at everything that was said to them and blinking their eyes and wriggling their shoulders so that their dresses were in danger of popping away from their naked shoulders. Georgia was shocked at the spectacle that they were making of themselves. She hoped that none of the boys thought that she was in any way the same as her companions.

31

Even Lady Bacon and her minions seemed perfectly pleased at the general standard of behaviour. They stood in a group at one end of the room, smiling benignly on their charges, some of whom were starting to become tipsy and silly as the evening continued. Many of the young men had been drinking heavily as well, or as heavily as the glasses of fruit cup and White Lady cocktails would allow, but a few of them had brought hip flasks, which they were handing around.

Chrissie Levinson had a crowd of admirers about her throughout the evening. She was holding court in the corner of the room furthest away from Lady Bacon and her staff, but her voice could be heard, high above the others, as she shrieked with laughter at some banal witticism. Her breasts shook as she laughed, the top of them wobbling slightly above the low-cut front of her dress.

The other two parties that Georgia had attended had been nothing like as bad as this one. Even the young men had seemed nicer somehow, polite and well-behaved in comparison to the crude and immature collection that Lady Bacon had managed to procure.

Georgia was standing, detached and uncomfortable in the merry crowd, when suddenly she found Lady Bacon at her elbow.

"Mingle my dear, you must mingle or no one will ever pay you any attention at all, which is something we must avoid at all costs." She gave a disapproving look and, for a moment, Georgia thought that she was going to pinch her hard on her forearm, but then she wafted away through the crowd, leaving a seething Georgia behind her.

It was the first time in her life that she had felt resentment towards authority. It frightened her and she tried to put it out of her mind, but the thought kept creeping back, nagging away at her, making her feel guilty but excited at the same time at the evil rebelliousness that it represented. It was something she would have to think about later.

Lady Bacon knew just how far to allow this sort of thing to continue. At eight o'clock sharp, the maids, who had been circulating with trays of drinks, suddenly ceased their rounds. After twenty minutes or so, the party started to thin out as the men realized that there was to be no more hospitality forthcoming.

Several of the girls had been asked out to other affairs. They stood in a line in front of Lady Bacon while she gave her approval or otherwise. She glared fiercely at the young men, asking each one his name, who he knew, who his parents were and who they knew, until she was satisfied that he was, on the face of it at least, socially acceptable. Then she called the girls aside and gave them strict instructions on how to behave. They were to be home by one o'clock or they would not be allowed out again.

To Georgia's surprise, she was asked by two different boys if she was doing anything that night. She told them that she was already committed and they both went away, but it made her feel better. She was quite cheerful as she went to bed. Some of the other girls were very miserable indeed for no one had paid them any attention. Two of them were weeping and another had just walked out of the front door saying that she was going home. The rest looked gloomily at each other, shocked at this first rejection by the world of which they had been taught to expect so much, and numbed at the prospect of a life of eternal second best.

It was late before Chrissie returned. The twins had sat up waiting for her, eager to hear how she had got along. Georgia was too sleepy to stay awake with them and had dozed off. She woke to the sound of excited chatter from the twins, but Chrissie was not in the mood for talking and went straight to bed.

She looked terrible the next morning and Georgia saw little red marks all over her shoulders, but she didn't like to ask what they were.

There were invitations arriving in the post every day and there was always a tense crowd waiting for the mail to be handed out. This was done by Lady Bacon herself, at twelve o'clock prompt. It was a solemn moment, attended by everybody who could possibly be there. Each invitation was ceremoniously opened and read aloud by Lady Bacon, its significance analysed and explained. The thick white cards were the counters of social success, milestones on the road to suitable marriage or oblivion. The tension was unbearable, for even Lady Bacon's reputation could do no more than launch the girls on the cruel waves of society; after that it was up to them and their families to take advantage of the flying, and very expensive, start that they had been privileged enough to secure.

Lady Pamela's support and connections meant that Georgia received far more invitations than any of the other girls, with the exception of Chrissie Levinson. The two rapidly became the stars of Lady Bacon's social circus. Chrissie revelled in the attention, going to every party to which she was invited, sometimes three or four on the same night. Georgia was much more selective, ringing Lady Pamela every day to tell her where she had been asked, and taking her advice as to what to accept and what to decline.

There was no doubt that Lady Pamela knew her way around the intricacies of the London Season. Although Chrissie's invitations were numerous, there were certain, very special, gatherings to which she had not been asked. It was the custom at La Circle for all the invitations to be pinned on a vast, green baize notice board, just inside the front door where no one could miss it. There was a section for each pupil, her name conspicuously displayed above it. It acted as a roll of honour, an instant guide to success or failure, obvious for all the world to see.

One day, at the end of the third week, Georgia was coming back from a tea party, at which she had received two more invitations, when she saw Chrissie standing in front of the board, staring at the section beneath Georgia's name. She had a little notebook in her hand, something all the girls were encouraged to carry with them, and she was noting down some of the details of Georgia's formidable list of invitation cards.

Georgia felt embarrassed that she had seen her and made to turn away, but she was too late. Chrissie spun round and stood, frozen with guilt as she saw her.

"I suppose you think you're clever," she said. "A nambsy-pambsy little goody-goody like you, who keeps her legs crossed and looks so innocent. I don't know what you're up to, but I'm going to find out, and then you'll be sorry you ever heard of me."

Georgia watched her flounce away. She said nothing, not knowing how to reply. There was something wrong there, something she had been feeling more and more, ever since she had arrived. It was all too easy and mindless. Just because she was well connected – with a rich and loving Aunt, and Lady Pamela to guide her – she was the envy of all her fellow pupils; even, she could now see, one so attractive and sophisticated as Chrissie. If that was what life was all about then she was not sure that she wanted to be a part of it, not of this sort of life, anyway.

She found the thought very worrying. She went for a walk in the park to pull her thoughts together. She passed by the Victorian grandeur of the Albert Memorial, taking comfort from its solidity and the true love that it symbolized. There was no one that she had met in the last three hectic weeks whom she had felt even the vaguest desire to see again, let alone with whom she might want to spend the rest of her life.

She sat down on a bench, watching the men sail their model boats on the Round Pond. The sun was bright but it was too early in the year for it to be warm and she wrapped her sheepskin coat around her, turning up the collar against the sharp wind. She felt alone and as desolate as the bare trees that stretched as far as she could see. She wished she could talk to her father, but Milla took after her father and Milla was bad, which meant that her father had been bad as well. She digested this thought, reluctant to take it any further; but if her father had been bad, then perhaps she was bad as well. There was a strange comfort in that thought, and she walked back across the park with her mind whirling. She was starting to see that she was different from her Aunt and Lady Pamela and Lady Bacon. For all she cared, Chrissie could have all her invitations. She didn't want them.

There was a party that night to which both she and Chrissie had been invited. It was going to be one of the big parties of the season, given by Lady Arabella for her daughter, Lottie Manting. Georgia had met the Honourable Miss Manting at one of the first parties she had attended. She was a thin, foxy sort of a girl, with a beaky nose and an offhand sort of rudeness that Georgia had come to accept as the normal behaviour of the true aristocrat. She had been surprised to receive her invitation, but had assumed that it was because of Lady Pamela and her influence.

It was embarrassing that she had to share a taxi with Chrissie Levinson.

Chrissie virtually ignored her as they waited in the hall for the taxi to arrive. She was slightly flushed and as soon as they were in the cab, she produced a silver hip flask from her bag and took a long drink. She didn't offer any to Georgia. She looked flustered and distraught as they pulled up outside the entrance to the marquee that had been erected in the gardens of the ultra-fashionable Cado-gan Square with much publicity and, no doubt, great expense.

There was quite a mob milling around the wrought-iron railings that led to the garden. There was a policeman standing at the curb, directing the traffic, and several men with cameras, flashing them at everyone who entered, and several crestfallen young men who had obviously tried to gatecrash and had been ejected by the two large bouncers who were scanning the tickets.

Chrissie pushed through the crowd and was soon far ahead of Georgia, who had recognized one of the young men and felt the least she could do would be to commiserate with him. He was one of the few people that she had met so far who had seemed in any way human. He shrugged off his predicament philosophically enough, remarking wryly that you can't win 'em all. Giving Georgia a kiss, he said, "Thanks anyway" before he disappeared hurriedly into the night.

Georgia was sorry to see him go.

The marquee was huge and glittering with light. There were about five hundred guests, all determined to enjoy themselves and, if it was in anyway possible, to attract the attention of one of the several cameramen from the national press who were slouching casually around, cameras conspicuous, enjoying their power.

Chrissie was already the centre of attention in one corner of the tent. Georgia suddenly remembered that she had been claiming a close friendship, almost an understanding, with Sir Cosmo Manting, the brother of their hostess. She could see him at the other side of the room. She recognized him from the many pictures that had been appearing in the newspapers during the past few weeks. If they were to be believed, he was most definitely the catch of the Season, which was why she had paid little attention to Chrissie's boastings about her conquest. She had imagined it to be just another of Chrissie's fantasies, but now she was not so sure.

She was standing by a long trestle table, close by the entrance. Its white cloth was already stained and soaked from the brimming glasses of the inexperienced guests. Sir Cosmo Manting was approaching, escorting two rather dowdy young girls to the bar. As he neared she could see that he was the very epitome of all that she was learning to detest. He was tall and slim with long blond hair, swept back carelessly, and the offhand air of the true gentleman of breeding.

He seemed to be polite enough, offering his two companions a drink from the vast array of bottles on the table and making conversation as he did so, but Georgia knew the type only too well and was turning her attention elsewhere when she saw Chrissie heading across the room, directly towards him.

She waited to see what would happen. As she stood watching Chrissie's progress across the crowded floor, a voice said hello in her ear and she turned with surprise to see the young man who she had last seen walking away so dishevelled. She automatically straightened his tie as she asked, "How did you get in?"

It was a rude thing for her to say, she realized that almost as soon as she spoke, but the young man didn't seem to mind. He smiled, grateful for her attention, and said, "Over the back of the fence, actually. Then I slipped in through the caterer's entrance. It's easy if you know how."

He seemed very proud of himself and his achievement. Georgia warmed to him at once. At least he was different. She was distracted by the sound of Chrissie's voice. She was still some way away from Sir Cosmo and she was shouting loudly, braying more like, a strained and unnatural sound, at once both aggressive and submissive, and Georgia felt embarrassed for her, though why she didn't know.

Sir Cosmo looked up in surprise as he became conscious of Chrissie bearing down on him. An expression crossed his face that was not exactly what Georgia would have expected from Chrissie's account of their relationship. It was hard to tell what it meant, but whatever it was, it did not appear to be one of any great pleasure.

Georgia was too far away to hear what was being said through the noise of the party. She saw Sir Cosmo introduce the two young girls he had been escorting and Chrissie giving them a stony glare and a toss of her head. Then it seemed that the Baronet was making his excuses. He bowed to his companions and slipped away in the crowd. Chrissie stared furiously after him and then looked round, frantically, to see if the incident had been observed. Georgia quickly ducked her head and turned to her gate-crasher friend, who was still standing beside her.

He said his name was Charles and he didn't usually come to parties like this because he had to earn a living. This one was a dare, but now he was glad he had come. Meeting her was worth all the trouble.

The rest of the evening was splendid, although Charlie was not the sort of young man who would gain Lady Bacon's approval. He was studying to be a stockbroker and earned so little that his parents had to send him ten shillings every week to get by. But he was fun, all the same.

6

There was no sign of Chrissie at breakfast the next morning; in fact breakfast was not a very popular meal at La Circle. Attendance was taken as a sign that the carousing of the previous night had not gone quite as swimmingly as expected. Usually the only people there were Georgia and the Arab girl, Farah, whose appetite made up for the absence of several of the others. Georgia found it almost impossible to hold a conversation with her. The only time she showed any animation was on the arrival of the food, after which she entered a trance that lasted until she had eaten her way stolidly through several helpings of whatever was available. Then she would belch appreciatively and disappear to her room, where she would spend most of the day, appearing late for the classes in which she clearly had no interest.

Georgia would have been lonely if she had not been so used to being by herself. She had hoped that she would make friends with at least one of the other girls, but they were all much too interested in themselves and their own social standing to have time for anything or anyone else. Even the Swanson twins had proved to be a disappointment, engrossed only in their own little world to which everyone else was denied entry. It was as though they had a secret that they were determined not to share. Georgia could not understand it. The competitive pressures that grew stronger as the Season progressed had little or no effect upon her. Indeed, she hardly felt herself to be a part of it at all. Not in the same way as the others were.

In a few months, when it was all over, she fully expected that she would return to live with her Aunt and get a job in an art gallery or kindergarten — something suitable until she was married, and that would be that. What type of man she should marry never crossed her mind, nor did she think at all about how her life would be afterwards. She knew only that she would finally have done the right thing and won her Aunt's ultimate approval — the only ambition that she had ever known.

There was a telephone call for her and she went out to the booth in the gloomy hallway. It was Charles. He wanted to see her that evening and was disappointed to hear it was not possible as she was already going somewhere else. He asked when she would be free and she realized that every moment of her day and night was fully occupied for the next week, at least. She tried to explain this to him, feeling sorry as she did so and anxious not to hurt his feelings; but she could sense that he was upset, and she felt depressed as she put down the telephone and went in to the sitting room, where she started to leaf through the new copies of the *Tatler* and *Queen* that must have been delivered that morning.

They were full of blurry little photographs of the previous week's parties. Shiny-faced girls, simpering at flushed young men, all beaming and determinedly having a wonderful time, although some of them appeared to have enjoyed slightly too much, judging by their disarrayed clothing and vacant smiles. There would be trouble in some pampered homes that morning.

The idea amused her and she caught herself actually relishing the idea of disruption to some of those smug, self-centred lives. Then, she felt ashamed of herself. How could she? After all Aunt Eva had done for her, and knowing the importance that she attached to the world of society. She shook her head, angry that such thoughts should even enter her mind. She wondered what could have come over her, and doggedly ploughed on through the glossy pages.

There was a picture of Chrissie at a party to which they had both been only four days earlier. She was standing beside Sir Cosmo, pushing herself up against him, nuzzling him with her head while he appeared to have his attention fixed on another part of the room; anywhere, in fact, except on Chrissie. They had spelt her name wrongly as well. She wondered what Chrissie would make of that and found herself looking forward to finding out. She hoped that she was not becoming too much like her.

Then she turned to the daily papers. Tanfield's Diary in the *Daily Mail* had used last night's ball as the main story. There was a picture of Sir Cosmo and, by a trick of the photographer, Georgia appeared to be standing right beside him. It must have been taken early in the evening, when they were quite close to each other by the buffet table. There was a caption beneath it that implied they had gone to the ball together, and another dig at the end that not too subtly suggested, that they might be slightly more than friends.

Georgia found herself blushing as she read. She knew that any of the other girls involved in the Season would give all they had to have their picture in the Diary, and to be linked with such a catch as Sir Cosmo was a prize beyond the imagination of all but the most ambitious. And she had managed it without any effort or desire on her part to push herself forward in any way at all.

She wondered what her Aunt would think. She hoped that she would not get the wrong idea and believe that she really was having an affair. Judging from her Aunt's reaction to Milla and her escapades, the reaction to her other niece being publicly acclaimed as a wanton, or near enough, would be extremely violent. She shivered at the thought, suddenly alarmed.

She heard her name being called from the hall. There was another telephone call for her. She fully expected to be on the receiving end of Eva's wrath but she heard instead the silken tones of Lady Pamela.

"Georgia, my darling girl. I haven't heard from you for ages. How are you getting on? I've been receiving some very good reports about you. Your Aunt and I are both delighted. Are you enjoying yourself? Although it seems unnecessary to ask, judging from that delightful little piece in the paper this morning."

Georgia was confused. She said, "I promise you, Lady Pamela, there is absolutely no truth in that, none whatsoever. I wasn't even standing close to him, although I know it looked like it in the photograph."

Lady Pamela was silent for a minute. Then she said, "How very charming you are, my dear girl, but sometimes these little mistakes can be very helpful indeed. Particularly to a delightful creature such as yourself. We all need something to raise ourselves just that fraction above the hoi polloi and I think it would be a good idea if you didn't say that sort of thing to anyone else. Leave things as they are for a while and let's see what comes out of it. I want you to ring me any time there's something you feel I should know. After all, that's what I'm here for, to look after you and see that you make the most of your great opportunity."

"What about Aunt Eva?" asked Georgia.

"That's a good thought, my dear," replied Lady Pamela. "I think that you and I are going to get along very well. It would be a pity if your Aunt misunderstood the importance of the right sort of publicity. We mustn't have her upsetting herself, must we? I'll be talking to her in a minute. Does she read the *Daily Mail*?"

Georgia said that she didn't think so, but some of her friends might and they would let her know all about it soon enough.

Lady Pamela said, "There's a clever girl," and rang off.

Georgia felt much better for the praise. Thank heaven she was doing the right thing.

There was another big ball scheduled for that night, to celebrate the coming out of Miss Amelia Piggot Smith. Georgia had never met Miss Piggot Smith, nor Mr and Mrs Piggot Smith, who had the pleasure of inviting her to celebrate the event. It was a sign that she was firmly on the list of those desirable young ladies, without whose presence no such function would be complete. How she had been elevated to this rarefied level, she had no idea, but she assumed that Lady Pamela and her influence had been at work on her behalf. However it had happened, it was gratifying to be there.

She was sorry for those of her fellows at La Circle who had not been so honoured. For them the daily ritual of the distribution of invitations was an absolute nightmare. They waited with bated breath as the large white envelopes were handed round.

There was a sort of bush telegraph by which everyone knew which balls and parties were coming up and when the invitations could be expected, and as the days went by and the coveted invitations did not arrive, there would be red faces and girls running into corners so that no one could see their grief-stricken faces.

Emotions intensified as the Season wore on and the pecking order became established. Grief was replaced by desperation as the unlucky ones struggled against their fate. The tea and cocktail parties became duelling grounds where the outsiders vied for attention. The society columnists were bombarded with appealing little stories, made up by despairing mamas and frantic fathers; anyone who claimed influence anywhere at all that might be of help was courted and entertained.

Georgia had heard stories that were quite shocking, most of them centreing around unscrupulous young men who claimed to have a connection helpful in these matters and who used their spurious power to plot the undoing of the innocents who believed them. The tales were told and retold so many times that in the end they were believed by everybody, to such an extent that anyone whose name appeared in the press was an object of suspicion, greeted with nudging and whispers as she entered a room.

Georgia assumed that she would be subjected to the same treatment from now on. It didn't worry her at all. She realized the jealousy and frustration that was its cause. It was better to be thought a scarlet woman than to be on the outside, wracked with uncertainty and the fear of failure.

In the short term, it was Chrissie she had to worry about. She thought it would be a good idea if she absented herself for the rest of the day, until it was time to change for the evening. It was going to be a bad day for Chrissie; even if she did not read it for herself, there were plenty of people at La Circle who would be only too pleased to do it for her. Chrissie with her presumptuous ways had not made herself very popular amongst her fellows.

Lady Bacon must already have read the newspaper. When Georgia went to ask her permission to spend the day shopping, her ladyship beamed on her with proprietorial pleasure and patted her on the arm, telling her to take care and be careful – though of what she did not specify. Georgia could tell that she was becoming a credit to the school. It gave her a warm feeling.

She walked down Queen's Gate, past South Kensington, until she reached the King's Road in Chelsea. She felt rather daring, wandering down there by herself. The King's Road was the sort of place where things happened. Not necessarily good things, but things all the same.

It was a nice day for early May. The sky was clear and the sun was bright, shining in her eyes so that she found it hard to see until it was behind her, as she turned left at the bottom of Old Church Street and started towards Sloane Square.

She caught sight of herself in the window of one of the hundreds of narrow shop fronts that lined both sides of the street. She was surprised how well she looked. Despite her height, she had always been inclined to excess weight, something that her Aunt and schoolteachers had remarked upon, tactfully of course, as she had grown older. But in the few weeks that she had been at La Circle, the pounds had rolled away, and her reflection was tall and slender and, she dared to think, rather attractive. She tilted up her chin and strode onwards. She could feel her long blonde hair brushing the top of her shoulders as she walked. Her looks and the sight of her picture in the newspaper gave her a surge of confidence and belonging that was a new sensation. She was not used to such a feeling and it made her half-dizzy with excitement.

Although the King's Road was the fashionable place to be seen, she found the shops boring — rows and rows of antique dealers, interior decorators and smart little restaurants, which were closed until the evening. The rubbish from the night before was still stacked in front of them. There were only one or two shops that held her interest. A Jaeger shop, considered *de rigueur* for young ladies when assembling their wardrobe for country weekends, and a new shop, just opened by Kiki Byrne, a girl who had a certain reputation of her own and whose name was most definitely not on the guest list of any of the parties that Georgia was likely to attend. She spent a while looking in the window. The clothes were different and exciting and she would have loved to try some of them on, but she was too shy to enter by herself, so she walked by.

Ahead of her was a coffee bar which everyone knew was the centre of a certain loosely knit group of young people, most of whom, like Kiki Byrne, would not be considered suitable friends for a young lady of breeding. There was a cluster of tables outside on the pavement and several patrons drinking cappuccino and enjoying the sun. They were mostly young men and she very deliberately kept her eyes to the front as she passed them. Someone gave her a low whistle of appreciation, which made her blush with pleasure as she pretended not to hear. She was nearly clear when she sensed one of them stand up and approach her.

"Excuse me, but aren't you Miss Fayne?" The man's voice was strong and relaxed and slightly amused. It would have been rude to ignore him. She turned round to see Sir Cosmo standing a few feet behind her. There was a frown on his face, half amused and half angry. She felt like running away. He was holding a newspaper in his hand.

"I've just been reading about our friendship in this rag here." He waved it in front of her.

She could feel her cheeks growing crimson. "That's nothing to do with me, I had no idea that my picture was being taken, and I'm not too pleased about it myself, if you want to know."

She wished she hadn't said that, it sounded rather childish, but Sir Cosmo smiled and said, "I'm quite sure you didn't. Anyway, seeing as we're old friends, do you have time to take a coffee with me? I would be very happy if you said yes."

To be seen having coffee with Sir Cosmo was about the summit of achievement for any girl involved in the Season, even if it was at the Sa Tortuga.

Sir Cosmo drew out a chair at an empty table and she sat down. He sat opposite her and ordered two coffees. He asked her how she had enjoyed his sister's ball and she said, "Very much, thank you." And then fell silent. She was not sure what to say.

Sir Cosmo waited a moment and then he laughed. "That was very polite of you," he said, "but I don't believe that you're being entirely truthful. You don't seem to be the same, empty-headed sort of person who thinks these things are the beginning and end of life, unlike most of the girls I meet."

"Thank you very much, Sir Cosmo," said Georgia, "but please don't say anything like that to Lady Bacon, she would be very upset and probably send me home."

He raised his eyebrows. "La Circle. I can hardly believe that you are one of the inmates and, please, cut out the Sir Cosmo bit, it makes me feel an idiot."

The people with whom he had been before her arrival were standing up to leave. "We're going now, Cosmo." It was one of the girls. She was obviously reluctant to leave, but Cosmo just waved goodbye and said he would see them all later.

He turned to Georgia. "Do you have to leave as well, or can I be your escort to wherever you are heading?"

Georgia confessed that she was not heading anywhere really. Just trying to escape from La Circle for a few hours before she had to prepare for the evening's entertainment. She did not explain why she had felt this to be necessary. It would have been too embarrassing.

7

Cosmo said he had some business to attend to down on Portobello Road. It was a shock to Georgia, the idea that anyone so elegant and sought-after should be involved in any sort of trade. She had always imagined that men of his aristocratic breeding would never lower themselves to the mundane world of commerce.

The surprise must have shown on her face because Cosmo laughed and said, "How did you think I made a living? I don't want to disappoint you, but as you saw this morning, the newspapers are not always completely accurate when it comes to little details like the truth. There may be something left for me to inherit one day, but that's a long way off and probably won't come to much after death duty and all the other taxes, so I have to do the best I can for myself."

Georgia wondered what Lady Bacon would make of such a speech, or Aunt Eva, for that matter. Not very much, if she knew them; and nor should she either, if she were to heed all the advice that they had been giving her. She was conscious of Cosmo watching her closely. She hoped that he could not read her thoughts.

"I'm most awfully glad to hear that. I'm sick to death of all those young boys living off their parents' money and acting as if they're God's gift to the female sex. They give me the creeps." She shuddered theatrically at the thought.

Cosmo smiled at her. "I hoped there was more to you than all those ghastly young girls who spend their time pushing up to me for all the wrong reasons. It would be funny really, if it weren't so pathetic."

They went round the corner to his car. It was a mini – the cheapest model that you could buy, and it had clearly been around for quite a while. The paint was chipped and scarred and there was a rip in the front passenger seat. It was the most disreputable-looking car that she had ever seen. She hoped that her Aunt would not catch sight of her while she was a passenger. Then she realized that she was being silly. If Cosmo was the owner, then it had to be all right. Even then, she thought, she was still being a snob, just like Chrissie and the others at La Circle. But, somehow, meeting Cosmo had already started to change her thoughts about the world from which she came. It was very worrying, disloyal to Aunt Eva and all she had done for her, but it was exciting as well, in a way that she had never before experienced.

The Portobello Road, near Notting Hill Gate, was not the sort of place that a young lady should visit on her own and Georgia had never been there in her life. It was a long, narrow street running downhill from them as they parked their car, with some difficulty, in the maze of residential streets behind Notting Hill tube station. The houses were large and dilapidated, as was most of the area north of Hyde Park, which provided a vast and natural buffer between the riches of Kensington and Knightsbridge and the squalid streets through which they were now walking.

It was natural for Cosmo to offer her his arm and equally right that she should take it as they pushed their way through the milling crowd that thronged the roadway between the antique-laden barrows lining the front of both pavements and the arcades full of small stalls that occupied the buildings behind them.

"Watch your handbag," Cosmo advised as they pressed through the mob, and she clutched it to her with her free arm, holding tightly to him with the other.

There was a curve in the road as it started to flatten out at the foot of the hill, and a public house with a narrow front was jammed between the entrances of two arcades. The inside was packed, but Cosmo forced his way to the rear where there was a large, rough-looking man with a stubbly beard and restless eyes sitting at a small round table. There was a wooden bench running along the wall and Cosmo found her room to sit down between a fat old lady whose breath smelled of drink, and a black man in a dark blue donkey jacket who appeared to be asleep.

They were close to one end of the bar and Cosmo asked what she would like to drink. Feeling foolish she shook her head. "I really don't know. What do you suggest?" It was the first time that she had ever visited a public house but she was determined not to display her ignorance.

Cosmo looked at her closely. She was grateful that he made no comment. He shouted up to one of the perspiring women behind the bar and ordered two hot toddies. She could tell that he was well known there by the way the woman took his order, ignoring the pleas of customers trying to catch her eye.

The drink was delicious when it arrived, piping hot and tasting of nutmeg and cinnamon. She sipped it, cautiously at first and then with enjoyment as a warm glow swept over her.

Cosmo had introduced the tough-looking man as Dennis. As she relaxed she tried to hear what they were saying, but they were mumbling together and it was hard to make out the words above the noise of the crowd. The big man did not seem too pleased with whatever Cosmo was telling him. He shook his head violently several times and Georgia was worried that he might become really angry, but Cosmo did not seem at all concerned and in the end the man relaxed and asked her how she was if she had anything in the way of junk that she was thinking of selling. If so, he was the very person to do her a favour and take it off her hands, for a fair price, of course.

Cosmo laughed and said, "Lay off it, Dennis. Georgia's a friend, so leave her alone. Anyway she has no interest in all this business talk, so let me buy you both another drink and then we must go."

The man became very nice after that. He told Georgia that he was a totter, which meant that he went round with a horse and cart to see if there was anything that people didn't want. Then he would take it away for them, for half a crown if it was small and maybe as much as half a quid if it were something like a bedstead and hard to handle. Finishing his drink, he said he had to be going and he left. Cosmo said to be careful if she ever saw him in the street because he was not too choosy what he collected, just so long as he could sell it for a profit He sometimes collected things that people wanted to keep, making off before they could stop him. He was all right once he got to know you.

The second drink had made her quite dizzy and she was glad when Cosmo said that they had to be moving along. It was getting late anyway and time for her to return to La Circle. Cosmo dropped her off outside the front door, but there was no one there to watch. He said he was looking forward to seeing her at the party that evening, but he had become rather formal and correct and she was worried that she had done something to upset him.

So she was feeling depressed as she entered the gloomy hall of La Circle. The ground floor was deserted but there was a buzz of noise and activity coming from the two upper floors as the girls who were going to early evening cocktail parties began to prepare themselves. Those who, like Georgia, were going straight on to the more serious and prestigious formal occasions were resting, or trying to rest, amid the excitement around them. The miserable few who were going nowhere at all had already stolen away, shamefaced, to hide their tears in the darkness of a local cinema. Two such girls had already abandoned hope and left for home, without saying goodbye. It was rumoured that there were others who would soon be following them.

There was a piece of paper bearing Georgia's name pinned to the notice board inside the entrance. It was from Lady Bacon, asking her to visit her in her study the moment she returned.

Georgia wondered what she had done wrong. Perhaps someone had spotted her in Portobello Road and Lady Bacon disapproved. Apart from that and the smell of the hot toddy, which must be still on her breath, her conscience was clear. She walked down the corridor towards Lady Bacon's quarters, combing back her hair as she went.

Lady Bacon was taking a sherry as she waved Georgia to an armchair in front of the log fire. "I'm so glad you saw the message. I was anxious to talk to you before you went to your room. We've had a little upset here while you were out, and I think you should know about it before you see the others."

Georgia wondered what on earth had happened that could possibly concern her. She nodded her head, but kept silent, not sure what she should say.

"As you may know, Lady Pamela and I are very old friends indeed, and we are both very happy at your good fortune and the marvellous publicity you received this morning, but not everybody is as pleased as we are. In fact there's someone who's really quite upset." She waited for Georgia to respond.

Georgia had an idea of what might be coming next, but she shook her head and said that she was very sorry to hear that and what could she do to help?

Lady Bacon gave her a searching look, as if she doubted her sincerity and Georgia was worried that she had overdone the innocence, so she looked back blankly. Lady Bacon raised her eyebrows and sighed, taking a drink of her sherry, before she continued, "It's

Chrissie, my dear, Chrissie Levinson. Of course the poor girl has not received the same advantages in her upbringing as someone like yourself – the refinement and spiritual depth that only breeding and association with gentility can endow. I understand her father made his money in the frock business, and it is starting to show."

All of which made Georgia none the wiser, although she assumed that the newspaper article was somehow involved and her own misspent afternoon had so far gone unnoticed.

"What happened, Lady Bacon?" she asked. She took care to keep her tone of utter innocence within believable limits. She didn't want to be thought a simpleton; besides, she was starting to enjoy herself.

Lady Bacon was staring into the fire, talking more to herself than to Georgia. "It's all so very different now. The war changed everything. In those days dressmakers were dressmakers and their daughters were simply that. They did the ironing and picked up pins and curtsied when one entered the room. Nowadays everyone who can afford it wants to be a lady. Soon there won't be any dressmakers left, or milliners either, or anyone else, for that matter. They'll all be ladies and we'll have to make our own beds and go to the butcher ourselves. Thank the Lord, I'll not be here to see it."

She sat in silence, wondering at the disruption to her orderly world. After a few minutes, Georgia gave a little cough and Lady Bacon blinked and returned slowly to the present.

"Chrissie." Georgia prompted.

"Ah yes, Chrissie. Well, I hate to say this about anyone, especially someone who is under my protection, but Chrissie still has a long way to go before she is a lady. She became very upset when she was told about your little piece in the paper, quite hysterical, in fact. She came down here, shouting and screaming, demanding that you be sent away, and ringing her father to have his lawyer issue a writ against the newspaper and make them publish an apology and heavens knows what other madness. Then her father arrived – all the way from Hampstead in his Armstrong Siddeley – and he started to blame me for his daughter's wretched behaviour and I had to ask them both to leave at once. So I'm afraid you have made an enemy, my dear, and not one to be taken lightly. That sort of person can be very emotional and vindictive, if they so wish, and that's a cross you are going to have to bear for the rest of the Season, I am sorry to say."

Georgia said, "Oh dear. What a nuisance. I had no idea that she would be so upset."

Lady Bacon shook her head in sympathy and started to mumble something about making silk purses out of sows' ears. She helped

49

herself to another glass of sherry and Georgia took her leave. It was rather scary to have an enemy. It was the first time it had ever happened to her.

She arrived at the ball about an hour or so later than the invitation had requested. It was being held in one of the banqueting rooms of the Grosvenor House Hotel. Not a very imaginative venue, but what you might expect from the family of the Honourable Miss Amelia Piggott Smith, a large, horsey type of girl whom Georgia had seen, or rather heard, braying loudly at several other social occasions. She left her coat in the vestibule, for the first time wishing that she did not have to wear the long, pastel-coloured ballgown that was the obligatory uniform of the debutante. It made her feel one of a herd of determinedly vestal virgins whose self-centred coyness was starting to suffocate her.

By this time in the Season, many of the girls were starting to pair off with members of the opposite sex and Georgia was one of the few to arrive on her own. Not that she was without admirers, but she saw no point in attaching herself to a young man, even for one evening, if she had no feelings for him; she dreaded the thought of the ride home in the taxi and the sweaty heaving and fumbling to which she would be expected to submit.

Lady Pamela had told her that the professionals, such as she and Lady Bacon, had a code about these things to ensure that the behaviour patterns of the escorts were common knowledge to the self-appointed corps of chaperones. The initials entered beside the name of each young man on the list of potential invitees were both explicit and, in some cases, damning enough to cause them problems for the rest of their lives – a social report card that they would never live down.

There was SIT – Safe in Taxis – and GH – Groping Hands – and the most damning of all, MWD, which was so dreadful that Lady Pamela had abruptly changed the subject and refused to tell her what it meant.

Not that Georgia hadn't experienced certain feelings of her own in that direction, but experiment for its own sake was not for her. Sometimes she wished that it were.

The huge ballroom was already full of guests, a sea of white shoulders above pale dresses, with the men in tailcoats and white ties. It would have been exhilarating if she had not seen it so many times in the last two months. But still, the Season was nearly over; next week was Queen Charlotte's Ball, and the presentation to royalty which marked its official end. Georgia wondered what would happen to her after that. There was no eager and acceptable young man thirsting to marry her. She hoped that her Aunt wouldn't be disappointed in her. She felt guilty that perhaps she had not tried her best.

Ken Mackintosh and his band were the main attraction of the evening. They were playing loudly at one end of the room and the dance floor was crowded, couples pressing up against each other in a frantic, near ritual, end-of-Season passion. Like the last night on-board ship, she thought, disgusted at the writhing bodies. Wondering why she felt so bitter, she decided she should have a drink to put herself in the correct mood.

Several young men said hello to her as she made her way through the mob in front of the usual long table that was the bar. She smiled at all of them but continued on, as if she were meeting someone else. Why she did that, she didn't know, but somehow she had no desire to land herself with anyone, and felt doomed to another night of boredom and forced gaiety. She saw Charles some way down the table, separated from her by a hundred or so tightly packed backs. He was waving to her and she could see him trying to force his way in her direction. She smiled and waved back, but half-heartedly, not wishing to offend him, but hoping that he would leave her alone.

She took a glass of champagne. It was flat and unpleasant but she drank it down quickly and then, hoping that no one was watching, she picked up another, and stirred it with her finger so that a few bubbles broke the surface. She thought she had better get a hold on herself, this was not like her at all.

As she turned to face the room, there was a sudden, rather violent stir in the crowd in front of her and she saw Cosmo forcing his way through. "There you are," he said. "I've been looking everywhere for you. I thought you'd changed your mind about coming." He took her by the arm. "Let's go and dance." And then he became formal and cleared his throat. "I'm sorry. May I have the honour of the next dance?" He made a stiff bow and held out his arm. She smiled and finished off her champagne. She realized that she had been waiting for him since her arrival.

She saw Charles's disappointed face as they moved towards the dancers. "We might as well give the papers something to write about," said Cosmo.

She caught a glimpse of Chrissie's face. It looked strange. There was an odd glitter in her eyes and her mouth was wide open, her lips drawn back as if in a silent scream. But she forgot about her as she whirled across the floor in Cosmo's arms.

8

It was a new sensation for Georgia to be the belle of the ball, with everybody looking at her and, no doubt, wondering who she was; asking each other if they knew her family and saying she must be worth a few bob to have attracted the attention of Sir Cosmo. She could imagine the rumours that must already be circulating and the jealousy, perhaps even hatred, behind the hundreds of eyes that seemed to glitter spitefully at her as they swooped around the floor.

There were cameras flashing as they passed and, when the dance was over and they were working their way back to the bar, several perspiring men came pushing up to them and asked her for her name and could she tell them something about herself. There was quite a crowd forming in a circle around them, straining forward to hear her replies and she felt embarrassed – an imposter at the centre of so much attention.

Cosmo was standing close to her, but slightly to one side. She glanced at him and he nodded and smiled, seemingly delighted at the furore that they were causing. As she turned back, there was a blur of red beside her and a shoulder caught her in the breast bone, almost sending her flying. One of the reporters caught her before she could fall. He was staring, fascinated at the scene behind her. She turned to see Chrissie standing, hands on her hips, her face thrust into Cosmo's, who was looking at her with a puzzled frown.

For a moment there was silence. The whole room appeared to be concentrating on the drama, determined that no detail should go unrecorded.

Chrissie let out an ear-splitting scream. "How dare you do this to me, leading me on and making promises so I believed you and gave you what you wanted. I'm going to ruin you, you fucking fake." She turned to the sea of staring faces that surrounded them. "All that talk and do you know, he can't even get hard like other men, and then it's tiny, like a little pork sausage. He's a nance, if you ask me, the things he tried to make me do." She let out a howl of fury and swung her arm at Cosmo's head.

Cosmo caught her wrist and forced it back to her side. "Is anyone with this poor girl?" He addressed the crowd, but no one came forward except one of the reporters, who asked Chrissie her name. She flushed with triumph and turned to talk with him. They were joined by three other men with notebooks, all of them busily writing as she spoke. Someone took her photograph.

Cosmo had not moved. He was standing, apparently relaxed and unconcerned, as the circle around him started to break up and drift away in a mumble of whispers and half-suppressed sniggers; there were nudges and backward glances as people expanded up on and embellished all that they had heard. As Georgia approached him, she could see that there was sweat on his forehead and his face was pale and strained. She put her arm through his.

"What a bitch," was all she said and she reached up and kissed him firmly on the mouth. Then she took his hand and led him back towards the dance floor. He followed meekly behind.

She faced him at the edge of the floor. The band had started on the next dance; it was a waltz. "It's time for a bit of counter-propoganda," she said. She put her arms around him and pressed her body to his, grinding her pelvis against him and nuzzling her lips against the side of his neck. She could feel him responding to her, uncertainly at first and then his hands were running gently down her back and she could feel him hardening against her stomach. Chrissie had been wrong about the size, but it was impossible for her to prove it without provoking even more scandal.

After a while, Cosmo pulled away from her. "I don't think I can stand much more of this without disgracing myself, right here on the floor."

Georgia laughed and then blushed at her own lack of shame. "Let's go somewhere else. This place is too crummy for words."

The whole room was watching them as they left. One of the

reporters asked where they were going but Cosmo brushed him aside. He hailed a taxi when they reached the street.

"Where are we going?" he asked.

"How about somewhere dark and naughty. If we're going to make a scandal, it might as well be a good one." Georgia was surprised at herself. The stupidity with Chrissie and the reaction of the guests, those petty and vicious hyenas circling in wait for their prey to weaken, had brought to a head an uneasiness which had been churning inside her for several weeks. Away from her Aunt and her neverending lectures on life, gratitude and social attainment, the world for which she was being groomed seemed so trivial and grasping; so utterly pointless that, for the first time in her life, she was starting to doubt all that she had been so relentlessly conditioned to accept. The way that the pack had turned on Cosmo, revelling in his discomfort, when before Chrissie's spiteful little scene they were queuing to be his friend, just about summed up their worth and that of the world from which they came. Surely, she thought, there must be something else?

"If it's sleaze you want, I know just the place." Cosmo gave the driver an address in Soho, the area of narrow, teeming streets which sprawled between Leicester Square and Oxford Street. It was filled with nightclubs and restaurants, the streets packed with prostitutes and drunks, and seedy-looking men were everywhere, their sharp eyes ever on the look-out for the unwary passer-by.

The entrance to La Pourbelle was up a short and narrow alley which smelled of urine and vomit. There was a pair of legs sticking out from under a cardboard box. Georgia tripped over them in the darkness and a man's voice told her to watch where she was fucking going. The club was in a basement and there were two rough-looking men standing at the top of a steep flight of stone steps which led downwards towards the sound of loud jazz music and the babble of a noisy crowd.

Cosmo gave the men some money and went down the stairs in front of her. The place was packed. Most of the people were dressed in black: the women had black hair and black, heavily made-up eyes. The rest of their faces were a death-like white, so that they appeared to hang disembodied above their uniformly black clothing. The men wore polo neck sweaters and leather jackets. Couples danced together, casually but close, with a studied carelessness. Some of the women appeared to be drunk. They stared glassy-eyed into space, over the shoulders of their partners. There was a general air of determined depravity and contempt for the rest of the world that made Georgia feel silly and out of place in her pale pink chiffon

54

ballgown and skimpy white stole. She wished she could cover the bareness of her shoulders. As if reading her thoughts, Cosmo took off his jacket and slipped it round her. She glanced up at him gratefully and started to relax and look about her.

Most of the people were three or four years older than herself. A large number were foreigners; judging from the conversations she could hear, many of them were French. Cosmo bought them brandies. "Is this sleazy enough for you?" he asked. "This is Beatnik heaven here and they don't come much sleazier than that."

A man was sick on the floor close by, but everyone ignored him and the stench joined with the other smells in the room, making her feel sick herself. A woman came up to Cosmo and asked where he had been, but she didn't wait for an answer. Then she came back with a handful of purple, heart-shaped pills. She gave some to Cosmo, who gulped several of them down and then put three or four of them into Georgia's palm.

"What are they?" She was shocked. She had heard talk of Purple Hearts and Black Bombers, uppers and downers they were called, and Spanish Fly, which was used for sex. They were the pills most popular with a "certain type of person", as Lady Bacon was wont to say, but no one among her friends had ever admitted to taking any of them. She giggled nervously, unsure what she should do. Cosmo laughed at her and called her a silly goose. It made her frightened that he would think her childish. It would be too awful to lose him and her only contact with the world outside of the claustrophobic La Circle. She pushed the pills into her mouth and swallowed quickly, washing them down with a sip of the brandy. Nothing much seemed to happen.

Cosmo asked her to dance. It was a different kind of dancing at La Pourbelle, not the sort that you had to be taught; no steps or twirls or stiff backs gliding effortlessly across the floor. Hardly any movement at all really. Cosmo held her tightly to him, starting from where they had left off at the ball, grinding himself against her with his hands up under the jacket that he had lent her, digging at her naked shoulders, then unzipping the back of her ballgown, one hand holding her tightly round the waist and the other straying downwards, hovering at the top of her buttocks and slowly moving lower and lower beneath her underwear, until his fingers were stroking gently at the very top of her thighs.

She tried to pull herself together. With a great effort of will she pushed herself back from him. His fingers reluctantly fell away from between her legs. He looked down at her in surprise. "What's the matter?" He was genuinely puzzled and she found it hard to explain.

55

She just shook her head and sat down abruptly in an empty chair at the side of the dance floor. Then she started to cry, though she had no idea why she was doing it. Cosmo came and sat beside her. "Do you want to go somewhere else?" He was his old self, kind and polite, but a few moments before he had been something very different. She was scared and excited. He asked if she wanted to go home but she shook her head. She was not sure what she wanted, but certainly not to go back to La Circle and all the scandal and whispering that was bound to follow the incident with Chrissie.

Cosmo lived in two small and rather untidy rooms in Flood Street, just off the King's Road. He took two pills from a glass phial that was on top of his dressing table and she swallowed them obediently. She didn't ask what they were for.

They had gone straight to his bedroom – Cosmo had said that there was too much of a mess in the other room – and Georgia had agreed with him, although she knew that she shouldn't. There was a weak feeling in her stomach and a swirling confusion of sensation between her legs so strong that she could think of nothing else. She wondered whether it was because the pills were Spanish Fly, but it was too late to worry.

Cosmo came over to the bed and reached behind her. She had pulled up her zip as they had left the nightclub, but he carefully undid it once again keeping his body away from her and taking care not to touch her anywhere else. The top of her dress gaped open and he reached inside and released her breasts so that she was naked to the waist. Then he put his hands under her arms and pulled her to her feet. The chiffon folds of her dress sighed as they sank to the floor. Still apart from her, he put his hand between her legs and started to rub her, gently at first and then with increasing fierceness, pushing her back on the bed and starting to undress himself with his other hand. As if in a dream, she found herself helping him, tearing frantically at the front of his trousers, ripping the shirt away from his waistband, and then he was heaving inside her, and her blood was staining the sheets.

He woke her some time later. He gave her a coffee and then some more of the pills and soon she was squirming and screaming and begging him to stop and to continue, all at the same time; little shrieks of surprise punctuating her moans, until she sat, exhausted, on the side of the bed, her head clearing, as though from a trance.

Cosmo was lying half-asleep on the bed. She went to the window and was startled to see that it was already dawn. She glanced at her watch; it was all that she was wearing. It was five thirty in the morning. There would be an uproar at La Circle, when it was discovered that she had not returned. Perhaps it was already too late.

She started to dress. Her clothes were rumpled and, hard as she tried, her backcombed hair insisted on standing on end. Her eyes were bloodshot and, as the pills started to wear off, her head began to ache. Cosmo was no help. He seemed to be suffering just as much as she was, but he hadn't any of the problems that she was about to face. The thought of Lady Bacon waiting for her, and then Lady Pamela and, finally, her Aunt, all queuing up to tell her what they thought of her, was more than she could stand.

There was one thing of which she was certain, she felt no guilt at all about what she had done. In fact she was already looking forward to the next time. If Cosmo had not fallen fast asleep, she would have been ready to start again, even though she felt so terrible. She would have loved to spend the day with him, the two of them in bed together, with no one to interrupt.

Cosmo was lying, sprawled on his back. He was snoring gently. She pulled back the sheet and fondled his limp penis, pulling and tweaking in the hope that he would be aroused, but he only groaned and rolled over onto his stomach and, regretfully, she picked up her handbag and went towards the door. On the way out she saw the phial of pills. She opened it and put two of them in the palm of her hand. They were small, about half the size of an aspirin, dark green, and full of the promise of untold delight, although judging from the way that she was feeling, she should wait a while before she used them. She took them anyway; a souvenir of the night.

She felt nervous and conspicuous out on the street as she waited for a taxi. The King's Road was different at that early hour. The few people passing were in a hurry; some, like herself, hastening guiltily home, but most of them were working men, on their way to their jobs. A bus roared past. She could see the white faces inside turning in unison to watch her as it went by. Somebody shouted at her from the rear platform. She shivered and drew her stole more closely around her shoulders. They all knew what she had been doing. She started to feel ashamed, then she thought, they're jealous, that's all, they wish that they had been doing it with me. The idea made her feel much better and when the next bus passed, she looked at it with her head erect, laughed at the comments that came from inside, and gave a wave of her hand. The passengers gave her a ragged cheer. One of them made a gesture with a bent arm and closed fist. She had never seen it before, but it wasn't hard to work out what it meant. She was starting to enjoy herself in this new, liberated world, so far removed from the insincere formality of her life at La Circle and all that it stood for. It was just as well that a taxi arrived at that moment; she was having second thoughts about ever going back.

Had she but known it, the last thing that Lady Bacon had on her mind was making a fuss. One of her constant nightmares was that a girl in her charge would become pregnant or elope with an unsuitable partner or, worst of all, both. These things happened, of course, to other establishments, but never to La Circle. Not in any way that had been made public, that was, although there had been some very close calls indeed with girls being sent home suddenly and without real explanation, only that they "didn't fit in", or something equally vague. It was an important part of Lady Bacon's skills that she could spot a potential disaster before it had occurred, which was why she had acted so promptly by sending Chrissie Levinson home. And thank heavens she had. Word of the drama at the ball was already running through the ranks of the professional chaperones long before the arrival of the morning newspapers, one of which Lady Bacon was reading in the hallway as Georgia came through the front door. She had hoped that she would have been able to sneak upstairs to her room and at least get some sleep before she had to face up to the consequences of her behaviour. She gave an inward groan as she saw Lady Bacon waiting for her.

Lady Bacon stood up and rushed towards her, arms outstretched. "Oh, you poor girl," she cried, wrapping her arms around Georgia's head and pushing it protectively in the general direction of her bosom. She smelt of camphor and lavender and possibly a hint of gin. Georgia allowed her head to rest on her shoulder, wondering what on earth was going on, but grateful for the respite. Lady Bacon put her arm around her shoulders and led her down the corridor to her office. She seated her in an armchair, rang hard on the little handbell, and ordered tea for them both from the maid who appeared soon after.

There was a whole pile of newspapers on her desk, all folded neatly to the social column. She picked through them and handed one to Georgia. "You'd better read it, darling, and prepare yourself for a little shock. I blame myself for ever allowing that Miss Levinson anywhere near here, but how was I to tell, she was so well recommended." She sighed and shook her head. "But you mustn't allow it to worry you. We're all proud of the way that you behaved. It does your Aunt and Lady Pamela great credit and you mustn't upset yourself."

Georgia looked at the newspaper. Chrissie had certainly caught the headlines. There was a picture of her, face distorted in fury, as she tried to hit Cosmo, who looked startled but still dignified as he raised his hand to catch the blow. The angle from which the photograph had been taken made it look as if she were standing between the two of them. Lady Bacon handed across the rest of the papers. Both Tanfield's Diary in the *Daily Mail* and William Hickey in the *Express* had used the same pictures, with headlines ranging from "Deb Love Triangle" to "Battle at the Ball". They both carried extensive interviews with Chrissie, who was claiming that Sir Cosmo had promised to marry her and hinting that, because of that promise, she had allowed herself to be seduced — "in a weak moment", as her father had put it, when interviewed by telephone some time later. She wondered what story Chrissie had told her parents. Most ominously, Mr Levinson had said that he would be contacting his solicitor in the morning, although his daughter's honour was beyond price.

All the papers reported that after the event, Sir Cosmo had been seen dancing in a very intimate manner with the other young lady in the photograph, Miss Georgia Frayne, who had declined to make any comment.

Georgia groaned. "Has my Aunt been on to you yet?"

Lady Bacon patted her hand. "You've no need to worry, my dear. Lady Pamela and I have already had quite a little talk this morning and she is going to breakfast with your dear Aunt to make sure she understands."

Georgia was too tired to care. Lady Bacon told her to go and sleep for an hour or so in order to be at her best in case there was any follow up from the press. She was agog with excitement.

9

Lady Pamela lived by herself in a flat in Lower Sloane Street, not far from Sloane Square. It was a gloomy place, two rooms in a large Victorian house, with windows permanently shaded by white net curtains and the interior sombre with a mishmash of bulky furniture and the smell of impoverished gentility: a depressing mixture of lavender water and a decade of burnt toast. Few people had ever visited her in her home and those that had seldom returned, preferring to meet for tea at the Ritz or cocktails at the Connaught, or anywhere else they could think of, even if they would have to pay for it themselves.

Despite her air of self-confidence and her undoubted standing in society, Lady Pamela was a very nervous person indeed. She was only too well aware of the ease with which someone in her anomalous position could fall from grace. She made the bulk of her living by introducing into the society that supported her, a stream of young ladies, many of whom would have found its doors forever barred to them were it not for her sponsorship. This was all well and good, and her position was acknowledged and respected as providing a useful influx of new blood, and therefore money, into a scene that otherwise would not have been able to support itself. However, that same society relied upon Lady Pamela and her kind to act as a filter, ensuring that the wrong type of person was not admitted to its exalted ranks. Woe betide the sponsor who made an error and allowed the rustle of money to cloud their judgment. For society was a merciless and unforgiving mistress who would turn her stony face against those who abused her; and then that, as Lady Pamela knew only too well, would be that.

She shivered nervously at the thought. Society was not only her sole means of financial support, it was her whole life, and without its approval she would have nothing.

The newspapers were piled on the table in front of her. She thanked the Lord that Chrissie Levinson had not been one of her girls, it could so easily have been the case. She blessed Georgia for keeping her head. Things like that reflected well on everyone who was even remotely involved.

Eva was another matter. Lady Pamela looked for the hundredth time at her watch. She had been waiting impatiently since Lady Bacon's telephone call early that morning for the precise moment when, in her judgment, Eva Lubinski would be taking her calls. It was critical to the success of her plan that no one else managed to make contact with Eva before she did. She had no doubt that there would be plenty of people only too anxious to be the first to tell her the news of Georgia's publicity, along with all sorts of interpretations as to its significance, none of them complimentary. Once the wrong idea was implanted in Eva's mind, it would be extremely difficult for anyone to rid her of it.

There would have been no point in ringing earlier. Eva's levée was conducted to a strict and unvarying schedule that resulted in her being dressed and ready for the outside world at somewhere between eleven-thirty and midday, depending on the hour that she had retired. Anyone calling her before that time would find themselves talking to Druska which was worse than useless, even dangerous in matters of delicacy such as this; Druska's understanding of the English tongue was both erratic and inaccurate.

At half-past eleven precisely Lady Pamela picked up the telephone. Druska answered and, yes, Madame was receiving calls. Lady Pamela braced herself, waiting for Eva to come to the receiver. She was never sure just how much English Eva really understood, and how much was pretence. It was crucial that when speaking to her you phrased things in a certain way. Tone of voice was as important as the spoken word. Even if you thought that you had removed an erroneous idea, bits and pieces of it would keep cropping up for years after and sometimes in the most unexpected places.

"Hello." Eva's deep, almost masculine voice had no more than its normal overtones of mistrust and suspicion. Eva suspected the worst from any communication that she received. A letter, the origin of which could not be readily gleaned from the envelope, was always the subject of gloomy speculation and would be left for hours, sometimes even days before it was finally opened.

Lady Pamela took a deep breath. "Good morning, Eva. I hope I've not rung too early. It's just that I have received some really good and exciting news from Lady Bacon. Georgia has behaved herself beautifully in a very awkward situation and we are all very proud of her. Lady Bacon asked me to tell you how delighted we all are and what nice telephone calls she has been receiving after the piece in the paper, which I'm sure you have not yet seen." It had all come out in a bit of a rush, but there were no half measures with Eva. It was important to tell her everything in one go, rather than give her any opportunity to place her own, inevitably pessimistic interpretation on whatever she was being told. Once she started, Eva could embroider the most simple and innocuous situation into a high drama which, in the present case, could have disastrous and long-lasting results.

Thank heavens she only reads *The Times*, thought Lady Pamela. It was one of the few newspapers that had made no mention of last night's little fracas.

"I do not know what you are talking about."

"I know, my dear," said Lady Pamela, hastily. Not wanting to say any more on such a dispassionate instrument as the telephone, she continued, "That's why I thought that I might slip over and tell you the very good news in person."

Eva grunted something which Lady Pamela took to be assent. It was only a few minutes' walk to Eva's flat and Lady Pamela wasted no time in setting out. Who knew what telephone calls Eva would have received by the time she arrived and what damage they might have done. Thank heavens that she had managed to be the first with the story.

Eva was speaking on the telephone when she arrived. She was not saying very much, just grunting, until at last she said, "There are always people to spread dirty muck and I will know who these people are in the future. Everybody is very proud of my little Georgia and I am proud of her as well. When you understand the English people as well as I do, my dear Madame Beldofska, you will understand about these matters." She put down the telephone, without saying goodbye. "The old fool," she said, half to herself. Then she turned to Lady Pamela.

"Thank you for your call. I have already received three others since we spoke, telling me how sorry they are at my misfortune, and that they will stand by me in my hour of need."

She was heavy with sarcasm but worried at the same time. Lady Pamela would have felt sorry for her had she been English, but foreigners, even ones so dear to her as Eva, were beyond her understanding — always making a fuss and crying wolf so that when there was a little problem, such as the one they now faced, it was hard to have too much sympathy for them. She thought what a disaster it might be if one of those common reporters from the newspapers managed to talk to Eva, filling up her head with silly things and printing her answers without allowing for the fact that she was not British. She could see that she would have to do some discreet and careful coaching before that could be allowed to occur.

She had brought the pile of newspapers with her. She moved to sit beside Eva on the settee and, after giving a brief account of the night's drama, started to go through them with her, one by one and with great care, explaining every nuance that could possibly be misinterpreted so that Eva would be forearmed against future calls. There were going to be quite a few of those, that was obvious from the number of times the telephone rang while she sat there. At the first call, Eva had told Druska to say that Madame was engaged, but to tell her at once who the caller had been. Druska kept appearing in the doorway, saying that it had been Madame this and Countess that and once a Grand Duchess. She had no idea that Eva's acquaintance was so wide. She was quite impressed.

Halfway through, Eva had Druska pour them a drink. Pink gins, enormous ones, in deep-cut glasses, with a piece of ice and a crescent of lemon. The atmosphere started to relax after that and the second drink made all the difference; she could see that Eva really was starting to feel proud of her niece and the way that she had behaved. Lady Pamela made her escape before the mood could change. Daytime drinking did not suit Eva. She could become emotional and unpredictable after a while, making it hard to say good-bye.

Eva sat for a long time after she had left. She was still not sure how she should react to the idea of Georgia and her good name as the topic of public discussion. In the old days, any association with scandal, even as innocent as this appeared to be, would have had a disastrous effect on the future of any young girl, and Eva found it hard to believe that Georgia was entirely innocent in the matter. However she looked at it, her worst fears of sending Georgia away from her influence had been confirmed. There was little that she could do for the moment. Any move on her part would be seen by her circle of so-called friends as an admission that there was indeed something wrong. That would only set the gleeful rumours flying and do more damage to her own standing than if Georgia was allowed to continue unfettered. Perhaps the best thing would be to believe all that Lady Pamela had told her and pretend that nothing that was not completely normal had happened, or normal at least in modern England.

On the other hand, to leave Georgia to her own devices, without benefit of her Aunt's advice and direction, was absolutely unthinkable. She poured herself another drink before she picked up the telephone and dialled La Circle.

It was Lady Bacon herself who answered. She had spent the entire day hovering by the telephone in the optimistic expectancy that she would be contacted by a member of the press, and she had been disappointed. There had been two calls, from Tanfield's Diary and William Hickey. Both of them were anxious to contact Georgia and equally concerned that the other should not manage to do so. Lady Bacon had made vague promises to both that she would have Georgia ring them as soon as she was available. It would look bad to confess that she had no idea as to her whereabouts, for Georgia had paused only long enough to shower and change her clothes before she had disappeared out into the street, which had been long before Lady Bacon or any of her staff had been aware that she was going. Not that there was anything wrong in that. The girls had every right to go wherever they liked during their free time, in fact they were encouraged to be out and about – in all the right places of course.

So she told Eva that the dear girl had just gone out and how proud of her they all were at La Circle. Then she said how proud Eva must be to have brought up such a jewel, continuing in that vein until Eva knew that there must be something very wrong indeed going on with Georgia. She said goodbye rather abruptly and sat, seriously worried, wondering what she should do next.

After a few minutes she went into her bedroom and unlocked the drawer in the table beside her bed. She took out a small leather box. It was scuffed and worn and the brass bindings were dented with hard use. She reached for the key, hung permanently from a thin gold chain around her neck. She opened the lid and sat for a moment, looking at the thick, blue document inside. She lovingly, almost sensuously, ran her finger over its rough surface. Then she brought it out of the box and slowly unfolded it. She knew its contents by heart, but she nevertheless started to read it. The solemn legal phrases calmed and comforted her: *I, Eva Sophia Lubinski, being of sound mind* – her last will and testament, or the latest version of it, at least. There had been many others over the years. Even when she had been poor she had always had her will prepared, leaving the few objects that she owned to those on whom she counted as supports in her driving ambition for recognition and, more important by far, ignoring those who were her enemies.

This was the seventeenth will that she had made. She remembered the others in perfect detail. In a way they were the measures of her life. She wondered how many more she would have to make before her death.

She read on, engrossed in the inevitability of its legal phrases, and the power that it gave to her. It was her ultimate weapon and she used it to the maximum effect. Its presence underlined every argument that she might have, however trivial, with anyone who could conceivably imagine that they might benefit from her passing. To Milla it had been a constant scourge, to be brandished at every sign of rebellion, while to Georgia it had been used as both reward and incentive, frequently discussed and savoured when they were alone together. She would bring out the battered deed box and place it on the table between them, treating it with all the reverence that would be given to the Holy Grail itself.

It looked as if she might have to change it yet again. Since Milla's defection, Georgia had been the person who would inherit nearly all that Eva possessed, and that was a very substantial sum indeed. In the seventeen years since the death of her husband, the half a million pounds that she had inherited had grown by nearly ten times under her management. When it came to investment, Eva was very shrewd indeed.

She wondered why she did not have the same ability to handle her nieces. All she had ever wanted for them was the very best – and for their mother too, her half-sister Alexandra, after she had found her, half-dead and doomed to a life of misery in the refugee camp in Vienna. Eva slowly shook her head and her eyes misted. She could understand why Alexandra had needed to be independent after all that she had suffered. But why must her daughter be so tainted by her blood?

For bloodlines were everything to Eva. Lineage and breeding were all that counted in a world that had been made crazy by the war. Ancient families, dispossessed of their estates, begged in the streets while the scum of the gutters drove past in their Rolls Royce cars and sneered at their poverty. It was beyond belief that first Alexandra and then Milla should choose that poverty for themselves, rather than the life of ease and social acceptance that she had offered them.

She was fuming as she returned the will to its box and locked it back in the drawer. It was ironic that it was she, who had been so badly treated by her relatives in the Lubinski family, should be the one person who now had both the means and the desire to restore that family to its rightful position. It was doubly ironic that Alexandra and then her children, who had stood to gain most from her generosity, should have been the ones to resist her. There was something missing in their breeding, a weak link that was their undoing, and which left Eva with the entire responsibility for the future of their family.

Something told her that Georgia was going to disappoint her as well. She was her last hope and, if she was not up to the challenge, preferring to place her own, short-term pleasures ahead of her duty, then all was lost. Eva wrung her hands in despair. Then she went back to the sitting room and poured herself another drink. She was not beaten yet. Somehow or other her family was going to be restored to its greatness, and God help them if they stood in her way.

There was a light patter of rain against the window. Eva called to Druska to bring her mackintosh and galoshes. She walked up the road towards the Brompton Oratory.

It was quiet in the vast church, with only a few worshippers visible in the gloom. Eva knelt in front of a statue of the Virgin Mary. She knew that she would understand about families. There was a comfort in the smell of incense and floor wax and guttering candles. Kneeling there, she could have been anywhere in the world. It reminded her of her childhood, sitting in the village church, the noise of the wood hissing on the stove as she sat in the second pew with the senior servants, the major domo, the housekeeper, the head steward, halfway between the other members of the Lubinski family, who were in the pew in front of her, and the servants, several dozen of them, packed into the rows behind. She was so close to the family, and yet the gulf between them, represented by that single pew, might have been a million miles. Every Sunday she had prayed that some miracle would take place and the old Count, Tadeus Lubinski, would turn and beckon her to sit in her rightful place beside him, but it had never happened. She still felt the pain as she raised her eyes to the Virgin. But now the Count was dead and his estates were gone, and the only one left who bore his name was the daughter whose legitimacy he had so brutally ignored. Eva smiled grimly at the thought. How do you like that, Count Tadeus? He should have accepted her while he had had the chance. She hoped he realized that now.

10

The last three years had not been easy for Milla. It had been one thing to walk out on her Aunt and all the misery of her old life, but it hadn't been nearly so easy to find a place for herself in the real world that now confronted her. There were few jobs available suitable for a girl of her background, which her voice and bearing made impossible for her to disguise. She had tried to get work, first as a waitress and then in an office, but young girls of her breeding were not expected to take such lowly positions, and she was turned away so many times that she finally gave up.

She had neither the typing nor the shorthand skills which would have qualified her to become a secretary, or personal assistant, as girls of her class were normally called. As the small amount of money that she had saved from her allowance was quickly running out, there was nothing else but to take a job in a shop. Even then, her choices were limited, for only a certain kind of very proper establishment would ever consider a member of the gentry as a potential employee. The Matthews department store in Knightsbridge was one of those places. It provided a slender living to impoverished gentlewomen, allowing them to preserve the tattered remains of their dignity while rubbing shoulders with common shop girls and the other riffraff that went with their reduced circumstances.

Milla had gritted her teeth at the forced manners and ladylike pretensions which were a parody of the life from which she was trying to escape. She had avoided their company as much as she was able, but her own accent and upbringing had made it impossible for the other, less refined shop assistants to accept her, and she had spent miserable years as a lonely outsider until, just recently, she had been able to engineer her promotion to trainee manager, and a chance to start a career.

For a long time she had lived in dread that her Aunt would find out where she was working and arrange for her to be dismissed, in the hope that she would be forced to return to the flat in Pont Street and all the hatred and harassment of her former life. Twice she had seen friends of Eva in the distance as she had been running errands in the store, and once she had nearly bumped into Eva herself – and would have done so if she had not recognized Eva's guttural voice giving hell to one of the sales ladies, who was trying to convince her that her feet were a size larger than she was prepared to admit.

The experience had left her sick and shaking. For a moment she had instinctively moved to help Eva with her problem. It really had been silly of her, she knew, but the incident had left her feeling even more wretched and lonely than she had felt for a long time. She was furious at herself for her weakness.

She was taking her coffee break in the staff canteen, flicking idly through the pages of a newspaper that someone had left behind them, when she saw Georgia's picture. She did not recognize her straightaway; it had been over three years since she had last spoken to her sister or her Aunt, or had any contact at all with anyone from her previous life.

There was something about the girl in the picture that made her pause. She was standing tall, beautiful and self-possessed while another of her pampered breed tried to smack the face of an equally spoilt-looking young man – a chinless wonder, if ever she saw one.

She quickly scanned through the caption and, sure enough, it was her little sister. She laughed to herself. With any luck, Aunt Eva would be having a fit of apoplexy as she sipped her coffee. She looked at her watch. It would be happening about now. She wished that she could be a fly on the wall to see it.

The crowd in the cafeteria was thinning out and she drained her cup, tore out the article and hurried back to the cosmetic department, where she had been temporarily assigned as part of her management training. The great Matthews department store expected its trainees to be examples of punctuality as much as anything else, particularly if they were female. Women executives were still very much of a rarity in the male-dominated world of shopkeeping, and Milla's promotion from shop assistant had caused some shaking of heads amongst the older employees, and spiteful comments and some rather unpleasant innuendo from her contemporaries – brown nose and tart being a couple of the favourites.

They were not too far wrong at that, Milla thought to herself, but jealous that they did not have her abilities to ingratiate themselves with their superiors. She had earned her position the hard way and it had been a lot harder that any of them would ever imagine.

Her association with Mr Bramley had started several months before, soon after he had been promoted to the executive board, the committee that ran the day-to-day affairs of the huge store. He had spent his life working his way relentlessly through the ranks of the Accounts department until, by a series of manoeuvres both cunning and treacherous to those who had been his workmates for the past fifteen years, he had forced himself to the attention of the main board of directors. After that his carefully prepared line of flattery, subservience and self-promotion had done the rest, and now he was nearing the top of the ladder.

Milla had heard two of her superiors discussing his lightning rise one night in the locker room, several months before. She had been on the point of abandoning all the fine ambitions which had buoyed her up during the last few years of anguish before she could leave the lycée and her Aunt's home forever – which the hopeless reality of her lowly position in the shoe department had slowly worn away.

The two women, unaware that they were being overheard, had made no attempt to hide their contempt for David Bramley and the way he had behaved. It sounded as though they both had minor posts in the same department, and had first-hand knowledge of his duplicity, of his going behind the backs of his bosses, making them out to be lazy and antiquated, just serving time until their pensions were due, with no thought for the interests of the company.

Milla's mind had been racing as she listened to them. She found David Bramley and the way he had realized his ambitions totally commendable; she only wished that she had a similar opportunity. But, as a junior on the shop floor, she was the lowest of the low, with promotion dependant solely on time; however well she did her work, it would take years before she would get anywhere and even then, her prospects were extremely limited. She had wondered how she was going to meet Mr Bramley.

One thing that Milla had learned better than anything else in the nineteen years of her life was how to make herself attractive to men. The older they were the easier she found it. She was not a natural beauty, like her sister.

She was short and far too skinny for the tight blouses and full skirts that everyone was wearing. They made her look fragile and underfed. She was dark-haired too, which was another disadvantage, with straight eyebrows and a pinched, unhealthy look about her; quite unlike the picture of the blonde and robust Georgia that no doubt had all the silly shop girls gawping in admiration.

She knew very well that she was no raving beauty, but she was equally aware that she had an ability to attract pretty well any man who caught her fancy. It was a knack that she had: looking them straight in the eye, as if challenging them to come and get her, treating with contempt their pathetic efforts at courtship until, finally, they were grovelling for her attention, their masculinity dissolving as their lust increased. The few that she had allowed into her bed had soon bored her with their vain desire to be loved and wanted but she had used their presence to practise and experiment with the craft of sexuality until it was time to be rid of them; then she sent them away, most of them exhausted and a little afraid of her cold-blooded debauchery. Milla would smile quietly to herself. She was after much bigger game.

It had been easier to meet Mr Bramley than she could possibly have imagined. His first duty in his new position had been to make an assessment of the efficiency of the major departments and within a few weeks of Milla's overhearing the conversation in the locker room, it was announced that he would be spending some time in an examination of the very large shoe department and the one hundred-plus employees who worked there.

It was a task that was very much to David Bramley's liking. He knew that his experience so far had been strictly confined to the processing of numbers. If he were to go any further, he would have to prove his skills as a merchant as well. He was confident enough that his abilities and his knowledge of company politics would see him through. He was an expert at presenting the work of others as that of his own, and the higher he rose, the easier this was going to be.

Bramley was a man of medium height – unremarkable except for the premature baldness that made his head a shiny dome above a rim of hair that ran only just above the level of his large, pointed ears. To compensate, he wore his side-burns long and full so that they reached halfway down his cheeks. He favoured brown suits, with jackets one size too large for him, and long, draped lapels. His

71

too-tight trousers bulged over the top of sand-coloured suede chukka boots. He wore white shirts, usually with a red tie pinned to his chest with a fake-gold bar tie pin, and a little gold chain underneath. He swaggered as he walked, with his jacket open and his too-large shoulders swinging out of time with his legs.

Milla had spent the last few weeks learning all that she could about Mr Bramley. Age forty-five, he was married with three teenage children, a house in Surrey and a brand-new Jaguar to go with the job. It went without saying that his record with women within the four walls of the store had been spotless. It was an unwritten rule at Matthews that extramarital relationships were very unpopular indeed, and it would have been impossible to have reached his present level if there had been any suspicion of hanky-panky on the side.

Milla thought they would see about that. Luckily she was in one of her most slender phases. She wore a tight black skirt and snow-white blouse, and put on her most exotic perfume, Femme by Madame Rochas, which she only used when she had serious work to do. She arrived early that morning and was rewarded by being one of the few people present when Mr Bramley made his appearance. It looked good if you came in before the others.

Milla spent most of her days involved in unglamorous and back-breaking work in the stockroom, being allowed out only to deal with customers and have the chance to earn commission during periods when the department was short-staffed. Even then she had to share her extra earnings with one of her seniors. The sales ladies kept out of the stock room if they could possibly manage it, fearful of losing a regular customer and considering themselves far above the task of scrabbling through the tens of thousands of pigeon holes in search of the style, size and colour that their customer wanted to see. That was work for Milla and the other juniors.

It was the stockroom that interested Mr Bramley most of all. It was something that he understood – with numbers and neatness, everything in its place. He was sure that he would have no difficulty in finding enough things wrong with it to justify a major upheaval, thus showing his superiors what a thrusting new broom he was turning out to be.

It was a new experience for Mr Bramley, walking about on the shop floor, showing off to staff and customers alike what a knowing, dynamic person he really was: hearing people calling him "Sir", the men treating him with deferential respect and the women twittering and playing up to him. All very different from his life so far, stuck amongst the ledgers on the top floor, with only a few musty clerks to pay him any attention. He found it exhilarating, the start of the life for which he had been born.

It was the women who got to him most. The way that they fawned, hanging on whatever he said, looking up to him because he was a leader and going places. He wished he could be closer to them, let them get to know him better so they would see what a great sort of person he really was, in spite of the responsibilities of his position.

The small, dark girl looked very attractive indeed, standing at the end of the long, narrow passage that ran between the high banks of shoe boxes. He went up to her; there was no one else there for him to talk to at that time of the morning. The girl was obviously impressed to see him there, and she knew immediately who he was, calling him Mr Bramley and Sir, all in the first sentence, and following him around helpfully, answering his questions and bringing him a cup of coffee without being asked. She was a well-bred girl too, he could tell that from her voice. It was unusual to find a girl of her class working in a shop. The idea of being in charge of such a person was exciting. She was so different from the suburban ladies that were all he had ever known. In spite of her social superiority she was quiet and reliable, obviously dedicated to her work, and full of respect, which made him square his shoulders and swagger slightly as he spoke to her.

He wondered just how young she was. Old enough for what he would like to do to her, that was certain. He put the thought from his mind. There had been several occasions in the past when the urge had been too much for him and there had been brief affairs with ladies he had met in pubs – one-night stands most of them – and a flirtation with someone's wife at the Kingston tennis club where he had been a member of the committee until all the trouble and the incident in the car park. Her husband would have run him over if he hadn't moved so fast. But that had been the end of the tennis club and a devil of a job it had been to explain it all to Fiona, his wife, particularly as the lady had been her best friend. Still was, for that matter.

The whole trauma had put him off love for the last year or so; however, his new status, the power and the fast car and expense account and above all the thousands of employees who now had to look up to him, had made him forget about all that nastiness. There was no point in being a hero if there was no one to share it all with you. Fiona had gone funny recently. He suspected that she had heard something, some malicious bastard had been talking to her and quite recently too. They were like that in Kingston, jealous of his success and out to get him on anything they could. Two of his neighbours actually worked at Matthews although up until now he had seldom come across them. There was a big gap between the different departments; but now that he was a director they had better watch out. He was feeling sorry for himself. He had to break out from that suburban circle and live up to his new status, and if Fiona was not up to it, bad luck to her. He had outgrown her anyway, messing around with paint brushes and trying to make him feel small in front of her artistic friends, while he was working his balls off to keep her and the kids. Fuck it, he'd had enough.

He got to know Milla quite well during the next few days, nothing too personal, just the odd chat over a coffee when he felt like a break. She was always bright and attentive and he could tell that she was pleased to see him and flattered by his attention. Somehow it came out that she was between boyfriends and that she lived by herself. She had her own flat, not too far away – on his direct route home actually – so what was more natural than to offer her a lift one evening and for her to accept. There was a brightly lit little pub on the corner of the street where she lived, just off the Fulham Road, opposite the cinema. It was still quite rough around there, but it was all that she could afford. He asked her for a drink and she blushed and said that she would love that and he ordered two large scotches. His hand was trembling as he set down the glass. Outside the store, Milla seemed to have changed. How, he was not too sure, but there was a difference all right. She was more mature and definitely far sexier, sitting with her legs crossed so that he could see the top of her knee, and gazing at him with a look that he had never seen her use before.

Bramley thought that he had better be careful here. No point in rushing things when there was no need. He carried the drinks back to the table and she made room for him to sit beside her. Their conversation was confined to their workplace. She listened while he told her about his career, how he had started as a humble clerk and studied hard in the evenings until he had finally qualified as an accountant and so on and so on until he had reached about as far as anyone could be expected to go.

Milla was a good listener. She sat with her lips slightly apart, asking ingenuous questions at just the right moment, her admiration apparent in her voice – drawing closer to him as his story reached its climax until they were huddled together like two conspirators, which in fact they were, although each was involved in a very different plot.

Bramley's ego expanded as he talked. This was what life was all about. There was little point in success if there was no one with whom it could be shared. Shared properly, that is, with someone who could really appreciate the extent of his achievement and see him for what he had become, without the suffering and guilt of the past getting in the way. Suddenly he hated his home and his family. They were a ball and chain, holding him back forever from the life that he deserved, and was now his for the taking.

It was eleven o'clock and the pub was closing. They stood outside on the street. He hesitated, uncertain what to do. Milla had grown more and more attractive as the evening had progressed; her face was slightly flushed with drink and he was feeling light-headed himself, but cautious at the same time. He had enough of his senses left to know that the wrong move now could be disastrous, both for his future prospects with Milla and, more importantly, for his career. He had been wondering all evening just how innocent Milla really was. He knew that young girls were different today, more independent and sexually accessible than those of the late forties when he had done his courting – and there had not been too much of that. He had met his wife at a tea dance in Windsor, his local town, soon after his national service, and they had been married before he was twenty-one. He looked hard into Milla's eyes. They were almost violet in the streetlight. He wished he knew what she was thinking.

Milla was being cautious as well. Easy does it, she thought. No need to rush, there's plenty of time to hook you, my big-headed friend. She reached forward and took him by the hand, dropping her eyes demurely and thanking him for a lovely evening in a voice she hoped was choked with admiration and unfulfilled yearning.

Bramley gallantly raised her hand to his lips and Milla pressed it gently against her mouth, allowing it to linger for a moment before she reluctantly withdrew it and started to walk the few paces to where she lived. She turned at the gate and gave him a little wave. He was staring after her, as if deciding whether or not follow her. She made up his mind for him by hurrying up the front path and disappearing quickly inside. She peeped out of the window as soon as she reached her second-floor flat. He was slowly opening the door to his Jaguar. He glanced back at the house before he got inside and then roared off, with a loud revving of the engine and a clashing of gears.

Well done, Milla said to herself. She poured herself a glass of whiskey, which she drank as she undressed. She would go and buy some new underwear in the morning, black and sexy, and a new garter belt as well; Mr Bramley would like that.

11

It was a long time before Milla went to sleep. She lay in bed going over the evening, trying to remember everything that Bramley had said, how he had said it and his response to the questions that she had asked him. She tried to recall not only what he had said, but his tone, the expressions on his face, and then the things that he had not mentioned: his early life, his home and family and, above all, his wife.

His attitude towards her had altered from condescension to interest and then to the first flickerings of lust as the evening wore on, until it would have taken only the slightest encouragement on her part for him to be lying beside her at this very moment. And that would have been the last she would have seen of him. Worse than that, she would most likely have found herself being dismissed from her job a few weeks from now by one of her managers, who would never have known why or how the word had come down from above, but she would be gone all the same. Any protests or accusations that she could make would be discounted as spite. Mr Bramley would shrug his shoulders and say he hardly remembered the girl and that would be that. She was going to have to be very careful indeed.

The next morning she went about her work as usual. There was no good reason, as far as she could see, why Mr Bramley should visit her department. His work there was effectively finished. If he did make an appearance it could easily mean that it was because of her, but she would have to take care not to frighten him away. Driving her home and a not-so-quick drink were one thing, an act of generosity to a junior member of the staff, although even that would be frowned upon were it to be known. Matthews, like all institutions with predominantely female employees, was a seething mass of gossip and petty scandal and lifts home were a well-known lead in to other things – almost a standing joke.

If Mr Bramley was to seek further contact with her, it would be another matter entirely. He would have passed beyond the stage of a casual gesture of generosity and be making a very plain signal that he was looking for a much deeper involvement. It was a decision that he had to make for himself. Milla knew that the slightest sign from her that she was anything other than an adoring and passive little girl, waiting submissively for whatever was decided by the great god Bramley, would send him running in panic back to his top-floor office and she would have lost her chance forever. It was a waiting game, but Milla was a patient person and was not about to make a mistake.

It was the middle of the afternoon before Mr Bramley made an appearance. He had a clipboard with him and he immediately cornered the floor manager and started talking to him, pointing at the clipboard and flicking through the sheets of paper that it held.

Milla was working on the sales floor that afternoon. It was a Wednesday, normally a quiet period and a popular time for the senior salesladies to take their half-days. There were no customers in Milla's area and she was making herself appear busy by straightening up a display of rather boring flat-heeled court shoes. It was important that you always looked occupied, even if there was nothing useful for you to do.

Milla payed very close attention to her work, taking care not to allow Mr Bramley to catch her looking in his direction. At the same time, she tried to let him know that she was aware of his presence, posturing her body so that the outline of her breasts was towards him, and twitching her hips just a fraction more than was necessary as she turned. But all the time her head was down, intent on her work, careful to present a picture that she hoped was both seductive and submissive.

Bramley too had been thinking hard since he had said goodbye to her the previous evening. He was in a quandary. Common sense told him to leave well alone. Any further involvement with a sales-girl could lead to a rapid and premature ending to his career, with little prospect of his ever again finding employment that was any way comparable. On the other hand, where else was he to find somebody who could truly appreciate the extent of his importance and achievement, except among the people who worked beneath him? The greatly increased salary and irregular hours that came with his promotion gave him every opportunity to pursue an affair, but the brief experiences he had had in the past had been, if anything, almost degrading, and the self-respect that his new position demanded would not allow for that ever to happen again. Besides, it was obvious that Milla was an exceptional girl. She was well bred for a start, a true lady – he could tell that from her accent and the way she behaved. He wished he had found out more about her when he'd had the chance. Also, she was clearly attracted to him as a man, not just her boss, and understood completely his importance and the need for discretion. His mouth was dry as he watched her out of the corner of his eye, while he waited for the stupid manager in front of him to reply to one of his questions. He wondered if her breasts would be quite so firm and high if she were naked in his hands. He felt himself getting an erection at the thought. He dismissed the manager, saying loudly that he would have to look in the stock room for himself, so there could be no doubt about what he was doing. As he walked to the door, Milla disappeared from in front of the display. His heart sank. Now that his mind was made up, he was impatient to get started. He hoped she wasn't a prick-teaser, or perhaps he had miscalculated the whole thing and she was laughing at him behind his back, telling all her silly little friends so that the entire building would soon be ringing with tales of his indiscretion. He was sweating at the thought, but his lust and ego drove him on.

Milla was standing at the far end of one of the aisles. She was reaching up to a high shelf, so that the silhouette of her entire body was plain against the light. He moved silently towards her, but she must have heard him coming because she dropped her arms and turned to face him. She looked even more attractive than he remembered, not beautiful but with the promise of a deep almost menacing sexuality as she looked at him. There was a small smile on her lips and, for a moment, it frightened him in its triumph and knowledge, but then it was gone and she was looking at him in demure expectation, ready to do whatever she was told.

"Good afternoon," he said.

"Thank you very much for last night," Milla said. "It was very kind of you."

He could tell that she meant it. He said casually, as if he had only

78

just thought of it, "I'll be going the same way this evening, if you'd like a lift."

"I'll be leaving early," she replied, "but we could meet in the pub, if you have the time. I'd love to talk to you again, it was so interesting."

Perfect. Without knowing it, she had removed his final worry, being seen driving away with her from the executive car park. However innocent, it would be bound to attract comment if they were seen, which was very likely. "Okay then," he said, "how about six o'clock?" And so it was done. He had crossed the barrier. There was only one last chance for him to back out, just give her a quick drink and say he had to be going. He thought he would probably do that, but no harm in having a drink first.

Milla watched his face and saw the relief when she said that she would meet him away from the store. If she had needed any confirmation of his intentions, that was it. She wondered how he would approach the evening's task. It was going to be interesting. He would have to be cautious, inching his way forward, step by step, and she was going to have to allow him to set the pace. Any hint that she was playing a game of her own would scare him off, of that she had no doubt.

She took a bath and washed her hair as soon as she reached home. She changed the sheets on the bed, leaving them turned down invitingly, and turned off the overhead light. She lit a joss stick and left it to smoulder as she made up, going heavy on the mascara so that her eyes looked as large as she could manage, but soft on the lipstick – she didn't want it smearing all over her face, in the event that he grabbed at her early in the evening. She dressed simply in a black boat-necked dress with a long string of cultured pearls that fell down inside the front of her dress. She had paid particular attention to her underwear. She had bought a new set on the way home: a black lace nylon bra, half-cup, for the cleavage, with black knickers and garter belt, and flesh-coloured stockings with a seam up the back. She had almost bought an elastic waspie to accentuate her waist, but she had decided against it. It was too hard to take off in a hurry, and that was what the evening was going to be all about.

She stood looking at herself in the mirror. Perfect. Even her shoes were sexy, shiny patent leather with high heels and the front low-cut, so that you could see a hint of her toes. She took the contraceptives out of the drawer in her bedside table and hid them carefully at the bottom of the wardrobe. It was a risk, but French letters were definitely out of keeping with the image for tonight.

Bramley was already sitting at a table in a quiet corner of the saloon bar. He stood up when he saw her and half-raised her hand to his lips, but changed his mind and shook it instead, offering her a seat. She did not think he was a very attractive man. She hoped that no one she knew would see them. He was of medium height, with short legs and a head that was completely bald from forehead to crown but still thick around the sides, where it was slicked back, showing his large pointed ears. Like a garden gnome, she thought, smiling at him in sweet innocence and drawing her chair closer to his own, crossing her legs so that he could see up the back of her thigh. She said yes, she would love a whisky and just plain water please. When he came back she saw that he had bought her a double. She drank it quickly and accepted another. It would take several of them before they started to affect her, but there was no need to tell him that.

Bramley had already stopped off for a drink on his way to meet Milla. He had been tempted to forget about the whole thing, to keep on driving straight home and make some off-hand apology in the morning to put an end to the matter. But there was more to it than just giving up on an evening with a young girl from the shoe department. He knew that he would never have such a perfect opportunity in the future. Milla was straight out of his fantasies: she was young, attractive and well bred – everything that was lacking in his own wife and the several other women with whom he had briefly tangled in the past few years. The fact that she worked in the same organization as himself was a mixed benefit. There was no doubt that it added vastly to the danger of his discovery and disgrace but, at the same time, he would never be able to have a relationship in which the full extent of his power and position were an integral part unless it was with another employee. The thought of the total domination that this would give him over a sexual partner made him tremble. If he gave up now, he would be giving up forever, and his daydreams of the new, vibrant life that he had now earned for himself would be without meaning. Now was the moment and Milla was his for the taking.

It had seemed easy enough until she had arrived, and then he was not so sure. There was still a vast gulf between sitting in a pub, having a quiet drink – however damaging that might be were it ever to come out – and the next, irrevocable stage of physical contact. He had never thought about the next stage and how it was going to be accomplished. The thought that she might reject him had not crossed his mind until he was sitting beside her in the crowded pub. What would happen if she turned him down? It was an unthinkable idea. He would be the laughing stock of the entire store. Even if she told no one about it, he would never be sure. He could imagine the nudges and giggles that would follow him wherever he went until, inevitably, the tale reached his superiors. He had to be absolutely sure before he made a move. He stared hard at Milla, trying to divine some hint from her behaviour as to what her reaction might be.

The evening wore on. Milla wished that he would hurry up. It was apparent that Mr Bramley's capacity for strong drink was strictly limited, as was his ability to move things forward on the sexual front. She wondered what she should do. It was no good her grabbing at him under the table or asking him outright if he would like to take off her clothes. The only way to keep him was to make him feel that he had dominated her and seduced her and forced her to submit to his will.

"All this drinking is making me feel dizzy," she said. "Would you mind if we went back to my flat for a coffee? I have some brandy that we could drink." She had bought that on her way home as well, tipping a few inches into the sink so that it would look as though it had been there for a while.

She watched his face as she spoke. She could tell that he could not believe his luck, so that had gone all right. His conceit was still intact and he had no suspicion that it was she who was setting the pace.

There was a road to cross before they reached her front door. It gave him the chance to take her by the arm and she squeezed his hand tight against her. He had the sense not to let go once they were on the pavement; in fact, he hung on to her like grim death, pinching the flesh at the top of her arm, but she clenched her teeth and made no move to shake him off.

It was narrow on the stairs and he had to let go, but she stood close beside him as she fumbled with the key outside the door of her flat. She had rented it furnished, but it looked quite cosy in the dim light from the single reading lamp that she had left burning. She lit some candles on the low table that was in front of the sofa. There was an armchair, which she had pushed to one side before she went out. She had piled some magazines on top of it as well, so that no one could possibly sit down on it. Even so, she saw him eyeing it and quickly seated him on the sofa before he could do anything stupid.

He sat uneasily while she poured two very large brandies and then said that he had to go to the gents, just as she was going to sit down beside him. She remained standing until he came back, in case he went for the armchair again, but the visit to the bathroom had made him more relaxed and he sat back on the sofa and she sat beside him, close but not so close that he would think her pushy. She wished he would get on with it; any minute now he would remember his wife and say he had to go.

Bramley had been busy in the bathroom. His wife was the last thing on his mind. He had slicked back his hair, glad it was still thick at the sides. Bald men were meant to make great lovers – he had read that a few weeks ago. He wondered if Milla had read it as well. Then he put some of her toothpaste in his mouth, swilled it round with water, gargled quietly and spat it out. He straightened his tie and squared his shoulders. He looked stern and dynamic and he gave himself a smile in the mirror; he thought he looked dashing and surprisingly young to be a director, even if he was not on the main board. Not yet, but soon enough if he played it right. He was slightly fuzzy with drink and, for a moment, he wondered where he was, carried away by his dreams. Then he remembered and straightened his tie once again.

Milla was still standing up when he came back. He thought it all depended where she sat. It was too soon for her to be sitting on the floor at his feet, though that was a nice idea, but he would have to be very careful indeed what he did next. He would be asking for trouble if he just walked in and grabbed her and she resisted. The consequences were too horrible to contemplate. He felt like going home, but he knew he would be cursing himself forever after.

He sat down and, to his relief, she sat beside him. Body language – he wished he knew more about it. He had no idea what signals she was giving off. Then she crossed her legs, which he thought must be a good sign, raised her glass and said, "Cheers". Which could have meant anything. He saw that she had undone two of the buttons on her dress and he took a gulp of brandy before setting down his glass on the low table. He cleared his throat, turned towards her and took her hand.

Milla brushed her thumb along the top of his knuckles. Any passion that she had managed to whip up had long since gone. She pulled his hand towards her and, to her relief, the rest of him followed and he started kissing at her face and grabbing at her breasts, which she hated. She gave a slight twist to her body, bringing her legs forward so that her knees opened invitingly. He took the hint and stuffed his hand up her dress while she started to moan and say that he mustn't, slowly allowing her legs to open under the pressure, as if her passion was too much for her to resist. She hoped that she wasn't overdoing it, but he had reached the top of her stockings and was lost in the flesh of her thighs.

82

12

Milla had thought he would never go. She could see why he was so good at his work; once started, it was almost impossible to get him to stop until he had exhausted every avenue. Fortunately for her, his experience in bed was strictly limited, so that his experimenting had consisted only of sticking himself inside her and then twisting her about in a muscle-stretching tangle of limbs while she groaned and gasped and gave her best possible impression of a young girl overcome by the virility and expertise of her lover.

By the time he finally left her, it was well-past midnight. It was a good thing he had a wife or he would have been at her all night. She didn't know where she was the sorest, between her legs from his constant pounding, or in her throat – all that moaning had been harder on her larynx than she could have possibly imagined. She thought that she would have to be careful not to introduce him to any variations from the missionary theme. If he treated the other parts of her body in the same way, she would be a physical wreck. She hoped it was all going to be worth it.

Bramley raced his Jaguar down the motorway. He was light-headed with self-satisfaction. It was happening at last: the promotion, the car and now the woman to go with it; just as he had always dreamed that it would be. And what a girl Milla was turning out to be. He was going to have to teach her a thing or two but she was more than ready to learn. He smiled at himself, twisting the rear-view mirror and baring his teeth. It took a real lady to appreciate all that he had to offer, he could see that now. He had been wasting his time with all those lower-class scrubbers, messing around in the suburbs when he should have been up in the big city where he belonged. He was going to have to change all that, and quickly too.

He took the turn off and his mood changed as he passed the sign pointing to the Kingston Road. Another twenty minutes and he would be back in the middle of it all. He looked at the clock on the dashboard. It was one-thirty in the morning, the latest that he had arrived home for a very long time. He wondered what he was going to say, not only now but on all the other days to come, when he was going to be arriving at about the same time – or even later – or perhaps not coming home at all. Maybe he would get himself a flat in town.

His euphoria vanished as he entered the short driveway leading to the garage of the semi-detached, mock-Tudor house in which he had lived during the entire fifteen years of his marriage. It was the same as another twenty houses on the estate, all built in the 1930s and showing their age despite constant painting and repairs. It had been a good investment though. There had been one sold down the road for nearly £10,000 a few months ago. He would be rich if it were not for Fiona and the children. He felt guilty at the thought, but quickly put that aside. He had looked after them, hadn't he? What more could you ask? All the same, if he sold now, put them somewhere cheaper and used the money as a down payment, maybe he could manage the flat as well. The way prices were going up, it could be the wise thing to do. He'd have to work it all out, but the idea was sound, though Fiona wouldn't like it too much. Fuck Fiona.

The next morning Milla was still sore. She was in early to work, so that Mr Bramley would have every chance to make contact with her. She knew that today was vital to her plans. There was still the chance that he would decide enough was enough; he'd had his fun, and she would have nothing left for her pains but a sore throat. As the day wore on with no word from him, she became convinced that she had made a miscalculation but, at this early stage, there was little she could do about it. She could go around telling stories, how she had been propositioned or even raped, but that would be a paltry sort of revenge and probably end in her dismissal, with no permanent damage to Mr Bramley and his stupid career. Anyway, revenge was not what she had in mind. Blackmail was no use at all once the object had been exposed.

She was in a bad mood when she left the building that evening. She couldn't face going home right away and she had deliberately not made any other arrangements, expecting to be fully occupied with Mr Bramley. She went to the cinema by herself, something that she would not normally dream of doing, and it was nearly ten o'clock by the time she reached home. She recognized the Jaguar as she turned the corner.

Bramley was sitting at a table at the far end of the pub. He was looking miserable, but his expression turned to relief and then anger as he saw her enter.

"I've been waiting here since seven o'clock. Where were you?" he demanded.

"I have my own life, you know. I went for a meal with a friend."

"A boyfriend?"

"It's none of your business." Oh God, she thought, he's going to be the jealous type, always asking where she had been and accusing her of sleeping with everyone she happened to meet. At that moment she decided that her affair with Mr Bramley had better bear fruit very soon indeed if she were to continue.

Bramley looked surprised. She supposed he thought that she would be waiting for him, stark-naked on the bed, panting for more of last night's hammering.

"Well, you're here now, anyway," he said. He started to stand up.

"Where are you going?" Milla sat down at the table. He had made a big mistake if he thought she was going to go dashing upstairs with him, tearing off her clothes as she went.

"I'll have a scotch, please." When he came back, she saw that he had only bought her a single. So he was mean as well. She knew she was being impatient and would rush things too fast if she were not careful, but he was going to have to learn how to treat a girl properly or the whole thing would become even more sordid than it already was.

Bramley kept looking at his watch as she sat sipping her drink. She asked what the matter was and he said that there was a meeting that he had to attend later on and he hadn't realized that she would be so late. Milla wondered if his wife had been getting at him after coming in so late last night. What sort of person was she like to put up with that sort of thing?

Bramley was dancing with impatience as she finished her drink. She thought that it was time she gave in a bit. It was too early in the game to become really bitchy; too easy still for him to walk away.

So she said, "I thought you would be in touch with me sometime during the day. I never dreamed that you would expect me to be waiting for you. You know I'm very attracted to you – last night should have told you that – but I have no idea what you want from me."

"What do you mean?" He was looking at her, startled and suspicious. She thought, shit, I've upset him now, the booby. He really does believe that having sex with him should be enough for anyone.

"Don't worry," she said. "I don't expect anything from you. I know you're married and everything, but I have to know where I fit in – that's if I do fit in at all." She gave him what she hoped was a very serious look, thinking how she was going to make him pay for all this humiliation, and for feeling like a prostitute in letting him use her body. It had better be worthwhile in the end.

His face had cleared. His ego was back on top, although he was still wild to get her up to her flat. She stood up and he took hold of her arm, almost dragging her across the road. What a difference one day could make. He was talking about flats in Kensington and how he was going to move up to London during the weekdays – and they couldn't talk at work, it was too dangerous. All jumbled up, anything to get her to bed.

At least it was over quickly this time. It must have been the long wait, because he was hardly undressed before he was putting on his trousers again and looking at his watch. It was a Friday night and he said that he would ring her tomorrow, twelve-thirty sharp, and they would sort something out. She heard him thumping down the stairs and revving up that flashy car again as he rushed off back to his wife. Poor bloody woman, she could have him back in another few months, maybe sooner if things worked out.

The cosmetic department was on the ground floor. Management training meant the occasional class three or four times a week, and a vast amount of time standing around doing nothing but looking bright and alert and walking about in a brisk and busy manner if anyone that mattered came into view. It was better than carting loads of shoes around, but Milla was starting to become disillusioned with the whole idea of working for other people. It offended her to see the waste of both merchandise and man hours that was accepted as the norm. The thought of spending the rest of her life as one of the carefully coiffeured ladies who had made their way in the world of petty-minded male nonentities that formed the bulk of the management, was starting to appal her. She was starting to feel that on her own she would be able to walk rings round the retailing establishment, it was just a matter of getting the chance – and the money.

Bramley loved to talk about money: how much he would get if he sold his house – dumping his family in some hovel in Kingston, as far as she could see, while he bought himself a fancy place up in London. It was a move that, so far, she had managed to discourage him from making. It was the worst possible thing that could happen, as far as she was concerned.

Firstly, it would mean that she would have no rest at all from his confounded penis, which he insisted upon unsheathing at every opportunity, plunging into her for hours on end while she moaned and screamed how wonderful it was in order to stop him bucking even harder. Sometimes she felt like cutting it off while he was asleep; she could see how people were driven to do such things.

Secondly, she wanted to make sure that all his money was easily available. She was not sure how she was going to make him part with it, short of open blackmail which would be a dangerous thing to do. He might call in the police. It was not worth the risk. She was sure that a way would present itself in the end. It was only a matter of time. No one could say that she wasn't earning her money.

Apart from a half-day off in the middle of the week, Sunday was the only day that Milla had to be alone. Bramley had still not nerved himself to make the final break from his wife, and so he spent the day at his home in Kingston, playing head of the house and no doubt keeping up with all his suburban friends. Milla had few friends herself, but most of them were men and the thought of further sexual encounters after a week of Bramley's attentions was more than she could stand.

The photograph of Georgia had started her thinking about her sister and their childhood. Although there was no weakening in her hatred for her Aunt and all that she stood for, she could not help but feel a certain melancholy at the thought of her sister and her spoilt, carefree life amongst the cream of society, as she compared it with her own lowly position, training to serve the very people that Georgia counted as her friends, and sharing her bed with a vulgarian while Georgia danced with a baronet.

It was not that she was ashamed of herself; far from it. If you were going to make your way in the world, you must use all the weapons at your command. Her liaison with Bramley had already brought her out of the obscurity of the stock room. Soon she would be a junior manager and, with his influence behind her, could expect very quick promotion, perhaps even to buyer, in the next few years. Although, now that she was on the path to the top of the shopkeeping tree, it no longer seemed to be so important a goal. It would still mean a life of bowing and scraping and pleasing her superiors; playing all the little games that went with working in a big organization. Even Bramley, senior as he was, lived in terror of upsetting someone above him. The whole system was built on fear and favours. She thought bitterly that Aunt Eva would have gone a long way if she had been forced to turn her hand to a life of commerce, although she knew that her Aunt would rather starve than so degrade herself. And Milla felt degraded as well.

The Sunday after she had seen the picture of her sister, she was wandering aimlessly through the streets of South Kensington, drawn by her isolation to the area of London where she had spent most of her childhood. It was around midday and the streets were full of well-dressed, prosperous-looking people on their way home from High Mass at the Brompton Oratory. Aunt Eva had always insisted that she and her sister attend the same Mass. It was more of a social ritual than a religious service for the thousands of emigrés who had made their homes in the neighbourhood; an informal clearing house of information and scandal and general keeping in touch.

She stood in the entrance to the tube station, watching them pass; hating them as a part of Eva and her childhood, but somehow drawn to them in her loneliness. She was only half surprised to see the Prince walking towards her. He had aged considerably in the three years since she had last seen him. His suit was shabby in the bright daylight and he looked seedy and out of tune with the smart crowd around him. She was startled by his deterioration. Without thinking, she stepped forward and touched him on the arm.

The Prince was surprised by at the sight of her. He looked quickly round, as if he was afraid that someone he knew would see them together. She had never used the confession that she had forced him to sign. She had torn it up years ago, fearful that it would be discovered by her Aunt.

"Don't worry," she reassured, "I'm not going to bite you." And put her arm through his. "Where are you going?"

The Prince recovered his composure. There was a hint of his old charm as he replied, "Miss Milla, excuse me, it was a shock seeing you so suddenly. Does your Aunt know that you are in the neighbourhood?" He glanced round again, fearful that Eva would be standing nearby, watching them. Her Aunt had that sort of effect on those who depended upon her.

She laughed. "Let me take you to lunch. It's time you and I became friends; after all, we've known each other so long." Perhaps that was not the most tactful thing to say, stirring up memories of the past. After his unfortunate lunch years ago, the Prince had taken great care to keep as far away from her as he could possibly manage; avoiding ever being alone with her and looking acutely nervous in her presence. He must have lived through a nightmare; it almost made her feel sorry for him. She was tempted to tell him that the letter no longer existed, but she decided against that. It was stupid to give away an advantage for no good reason.

She could see that the Prince was torn between the prospect of a free lunch and the demands that she might make upon him. The free lunch won. They went to an Indian restaurant, halfway to the Earl's Court Road. It was unlikely that any of her Aunt's friends would visit such a place. It was popularly supposed that Indian curries were made from stray cats and there was a theory that you should always ask to see the kidneys of the animal that you were eating because cats' kidneys were different – although how, no one ever seemed to remember.

The Prince was still nervous, even in the relative safety of the restaurant. She ordered him a large gin and tonic and then another, and a bottle of Frascati to go with the meal. The Prince drank a lot of the cold white wine. He was not used to eating curry and the dishes they had ordered were very hot indeed; after a while, the sweat was running into his eyes and the spice had made his lips start to swell. He moaned gently to himself as he ate, but ploughed on determinedly to the end.

The meal was a disappointment to Milla. She had expected at least to hear something of her Aunt and Georgia, maybe some hint of the scandal at the ball and her Aunt's reaction, but the Prince was in no shape for polite conversation and she had to put him in a taxi once the meal was over. He was complaining that his stomach hurt.

All the same, the sight of him had brought back memories that were both unsettling and depressing. Memories of her Aunt and her eternal moralizing. She still hated her and the misery that she had caused but, at the back of her mind, she knew that in some ways her Aunt had been right. There was a barrier beyond which it was both wrong and demeaning to pass. Georgia could do what she liked with her baronet and it might be wrong, by old-fashioned, prewar standards anyway, but her own calculated seduction of a man so low down the social scale as Mr Bramley was something very different, close to outright prostitution if she allowed herself to think about it. She gritted her teeth. It was too late to have any regrets. If she was to be a whore, it was up to her to make sure that she was paid handsomely for her services.

She went back to her flat and sat, staring out of the window. There was a bottle of brandy on the table, compliments of Mr Bramley. She raised her glass in a toast. Make the most of it while you can, my little man.

13

The Count owned a large apartment on the boulevard Haussmann. It had several bedrooms, a huge salon for entertaining and a withdrawing room for the ladies. Eva explained all this to Druska as they explored their new home. They had arrived in Paris in the late afternoon, exhausted from the five-day journey and relieved that they had finally reached their destination.

It was clear that it had been some time since the apartment had been occupied. The curtains were drawn and the furniture covered by big white sheets; everything was covered with a layer of dust and Druska threw up her hands in panic that she would be discovered in such a place and be blamed for the mess that it was in. She immediately went to the kitchen and emerged with a mop and duster, cleaning frantically until Eva told her to stop.

They unpacked their battered suitcases and made up their beds. The linen smelt old and mildewed, but they were too tired to care. Eva chose the second-largest bedroom. It had a big bed with a feather mattress, a deep red velvet canopy and a dressing table with a stool and two armchairs, all covered in the same material. There was a bathroom with a connecting door and she lay back in the hot water and took stock of their situation.

They had plenty of money, more than she had ever imagined in her life. The Count had given her a leather wallet, with the Lubinski

91

coat of arms emblazoned in gold on the front. Inside there were several thousand francs; a great wad of thick, crinkling notes that Eva had hidden in her underwear as soon as she had been unobserved. There was also a letter of credit for another fifteen thousand francs — which Eva was to present to the bank that handled the Count's affairs — and a long letter to its director which, the Count had said, was to be delivered the moment she arrived.

Apart from that they were absolutely alone in the great city, with no idea what they should be doing and no one to ask. Eva shivered in excitement. She put on her best dress and went to look for Druska. There was a servant's room beside the kitchen and some tiny bedrooms leading from it. Druska had established herself in the smallest of them and was already cleaning the stone-flagged floor of the pantry.

"Come on Druska. There's no need to do that now. Put on a dress and let's go and see outside."

Druska shook her head. "If Madame pleases, my duty is in here. There is so much to do to make this place as Madame would wish."

Eva looked at her sharply, wondering if she was making a joke, but Druska just stared back at her, waiting for her command. Eva smiled and put her arms around her. "You do what you think is right. Let's make a list of all that we need and I'll go and have someone deliver it right away."

Druska beamed in relief. She thought how lucky she was to have such a good mistress as Mamzelle Eva.

Eva visited the bank the next morning. She was shy and nervous as she stood in the marble hall that echoed with the footsteps of important-looking men in long black coats with velvet collars, and long canes with gold handles. They came and went with an assurance that made her feel like a shabby serving girl which, she realized with a shock, was exactly what she was.

She stood for a while against a wall, waiting for one of the imposing men behind the wire grille to be unoccupied. Finally there was a lull in the constant parade of customers and she made her timid approach. She had discovered that the French she had learned from Monsieur Ribot was inadequate for all but the most simple requests, although she could understand well enough what others were saying to her. Without speaking, she passed the Count's letter through the bars. The clerk stared at her suspiciously. Then he glanced at the envelope and told her to wait, in case there was anything to be returned. She moved away from the counter and retreated back to the safety of the wall.

She waited for ten minutes, wishing that she could leave, but there was no sign of the clerk. Then a side door opened and the clerk appeared. There was another man with him. He was tall and dignified, wearing a black frock coat with a knot of ribbon in the button hole. The clerk looked round the hall and she shrank back against the wall, terrified that he might see her, but it was too late. He was pointing her out to his companion. They both advanced towards her. The man in the frock coat bowed and taking her hand, raised it to his lips. "Mamzelle Lubinski, what a pleasure. Your father has written to me the clearest instructions that I should be of all assistance to you during your stay in our city. It will be my pleasure to do so. Please do not hesitate to call on me for anything that you feel you might need." As he spoke, he was escorting her through the door at the side of the counter and seating her in a chair in his grand office. He told her the details of the handsome allowance that the Count had made for her and left to prepare some papers that she had to sign. She had hardly heard anything that he had said. He had called her Mamzelle Lubinski, and she could think of nothing else. The Count had finally given her his name.

The director returned and placed the documents in front of her. She signed "Eva Lubinski" with a flourish. The director wondered why she was crying as he showed her out. He sighed to himself. They were emotional people, these Poles.

She raced home, eager to share her happiness with Druska, but Druska was not impressed. She had drawn back all the plum-velvet curtains and removed the dust sheets, revealing tapestry-covered furniture with ornate gilt woodwork, armchairs and chaises longues and marble-topped tables with silver candelabras. The daylight showed the wallpaper, its designs picked out in gold, and the curved ceiling with faded cherubs fluttering above an enormous crystal chandelier. Druska's face was flushed with effort and pride.

"I hope Mamzelle finds everything to her satisfaction," she said, dropping a curtsey. Mamzelle said that she was delighted. She felt like giving her a hug, but she could tell that it would spoil everything. In her new position of housekeeper, Druska must be treated with respect.

They were happy in their new roles. Eva went for walks around the neighbourhood, opening accounts at the butcher and greengrocer and any other shop that she thought might be useful. Sometimes in the evening when no one would see, Druska would come with her, although she was always glad to reach home.

They had been by themselves for almost a week and Eva had already exhausted the possibilities of the neighbourhood, walking further and further afield, discovering the delights of the Champs

Élysées and wandering for hours, staring at the wonders in the department stores and the shops in the Rue de la Paix. She knew that her clothes were old and out of style, but she could not nerve herself to face any of the *vendeuses* who lingered behind the doors of the dress shops and stared at her contemptuously through the windows.

At three o'clock on the first Sunday after their arrival there was a knock at the door. Not just one knock but a series of quick, nervous little pecks, as if a bird were trapped on the other side. It was a shock for them both; they were becoming accustomed to their isolation and, besides, as there was no one that they knew in Paris, who could it possibly be?

As usual, Druska was dressed in the formal wear that befitted a servant of her new station. There was a cupboard full of uniforms that were used by the servants when the Count was in residence and Druska made sure that she was always wearing the outfit correct for the time of day and the task in hand. It was the hour for serving tea and Druska was in a black dress with a white lace apron and a little lace tiara perched on top of her head.

Eva had just returned from another walk along the Champs Élysées. She was depressed. For the last week she had been one of the crowd, alone and anonymous, always passing by cafés full of smartly dressed Parisians, the women happy and laughing and the men sleek, sophisticated and always attentive. She knew she was dowdy and plain with her peasant's clothes and her hair done up in tight little plaits around the top of her head. No one gave her a second glance. She knew that she must do something about it, but where was she to start?

Druska was flushed with excitement as she went to open the door. Eva assumed that it was a tradesman who had come to the wrong entrance. She went into the drawing room and stood looking out of the window, wondering how she should fill the rest of the afternoon.

Druska returned. There was a visiting card in her hand. She was stuttering with pleasure. "Mamzelle, there's a grand lady here to see you." She gave Eva the card. It read, "Madame Lilianne de la Reve", with an address that Eva knew was not far from their own.

Druska showed the lady in to the room. She was small and brittle, wearing a long and bulky chinchilla coat and a blonde cloche hat that came down low over one eye. She had shiny grey silk stockings and grey, kid-skin shoes. The hand that she held out was wearing a tight glove made from some filmy material. She was the epitome of all the ladies that Eva so much wanted to emulate.

"What a pleasure to meet you," said the lady. "Monsieur le

Comte has written to me about you." She fumbled with the clasp of the small bag that hung by a chain from her shoulder, and pulled out a letter. "He has asked me to look after you here in Paris until his arrival, but I have no idea when that will be. Your father is a very unpredictable man." She shrugged and smiled, as if Eva would know all about that. She took off her coat and threw it carelessly over a chair. Eva could see her initials monogrammed on the silk lining. She was wearing a soft, knitted dress the same colour as her hat. It clung close to her body, emphasizing her small, high breasts.

Druska was making signs to her from the doorway. Eva asked if Madame would like to take something and the lady said to call her Lilianne and perhaps she would take some champagne, the day was very hot. Eva looked inquiringly at Druska, who nodded vigorously and left the room.

Lilianne sat down. She looked hard at Eva for some time and Eva stared back at her, taking in all the details of her clothing and jewellery, wishing that she could be as beautiful and worldly and in command of herself.

"Your father, who is a very dear friend," Lilianne began, "has asked me to instruct you in the ways of Paris and the world of which you are going to be a part. I think you will be a credit to him, once we have bought you some pretty clothes and done something about this." She leaned forward and poked disparagingly at Eva's plaits. "Those really have to go. I will make an appointment right away with my hairdresser." She looked around. "Where is your telephone? Don't say you don't have one. I will order one for you as soon as I go home. Life is impossible without one."

She talked on and on, sipping at the champagne and insisting that Eva join her. "A lady who doesn't drink has no place in modern society, she is just too boring." She slipped in other pieces of advice while she talked, bringing the Count into the conversation every few minutes, saying how close they were and how much she was in his debt, although she did not say why. After an hour or so, Eva's head was reeling; she would have to practise more with the champagne, but she hung on to Lilianne's every word. When the champagne was finished Lilianne took her leave and arranged to collect her the next morning. She kissed her fondly at the door. "You are a dear girl, just like your father. I can see so much of him in you." The thought seemed to upset her and she was dabbing at her eyes with a silk handkerchief as she said goodbye.

Eva decided to have some more practice at the champagne. Druska was reluctant to join her, especially in the drawing room, so they compromised and sat in the kitchen, sipping at the wine and discussing their guest.

Eva was enthusiastic, overwhelmed by her new friend and the prospect of entering the world from which she came. Druska was less sure; there was something about Madame Lilianne that was wrong, what it was she could not say, but she stuck doggedly to her opinion, until Eva became annoyed with her and went to her room.

Exactly seven days later Lilianne gave a soirée to introduce her protégée to the civilized world. She was so delighted with the results of her work that she could not wait to show Eva off to her friends from the haut monde, as she constantly referred to it. She delighted in telling Eva that she was the duckling who had become a swan and then, in the same breath, warning her to be careful of all the gentlemen she was going to meet and to do absolutely nothing without confiding in her beforehand.

Eva could hardly believe the change in herself. As she walked down the street she was no longer one of the crowd. She could see men turn their heads to look at her, and some of them were very attractive men indeed. Her hair was drawn back in a chignon, just like Lilianne's. The hairdresser had called upon her the morning after her first visit and Lilianne had followed him soon after, supervising every detail, making sure that the lemon rinse did not make her too blonde, and examining the size and shape of her ears in great detail before deciding how much of them should be revealed.

It had been the same in the dress salons. They had spent the best part of three days trying on and comparing countless outfits before Lilianne had decided upon Eva's wardrobe; the shoes and accessories had taken up the rest of the week. Eva was exhausted by the time it was over.

There were about thirty people at the soirée. Eva stood in the doorway looking at them. She had just arrived and she felt gauche and out of place amongst the sophisticated crowd who were standing in murmuring groups, with waiters carrying trays of champagne flitting between them.

Lilianne saw her as she arrived and rushed forward to greet her. Linking Eva's arm in her own, she started a tour of the room, introducing her to the other guests as they went. Eva thought it interesting that the men were all counts and grand dukes or chevaliers at least, while the women were, without exception, simply madame, with not a hint of a title between them; nor did they behave like gracious ladies. They were hard-eyed and possessive of the men around them and greeted her with frozen half-nods, or else ignored her, turning their backs towards her and engaging in animated conversation with their neighbours as Lilianne approached.

The men, too, despite their titles, did not treat her with the quiet respect that she had seen during her brief visit to Warsaw. They were considerably more familiar than she would have thought to be proper, eyeing her in a way that she did not like. She thought that it was because the French treated women differently. She had heard that French men had a way with women. The ladies were also different and were sometimes sharp with their escorts. Some wore skimpy clothes – with very bare shoulders and deep cleavages, which were almost indecent. Eva was quite shocked.

One of the men appeared to be a particular friend of Lilianne. He was tall and inclined to fat and there was a dark tinge to his skin. He had black, greased-back hair and a thick black moustache. He had also taken a considerable amount of drink and spoke French loudly with a thick accent that was hard for Eva to understand. His name was Anzar, but everyone called him Pasha and treated him with respect.

After a while he came up to Lilianne and asked her to introduce him to her new friend. He made a great show of kissing Eva's hand and then he patted her on the cheek and said, "*ravissante*" several times and patted her again. He put his arm around Lilianne and started to fumble with her buttocks in full view of all the guests, although nobody seemed to be surprised. Lilianne blushed and looked furious but she appeared too embarrassed or frightened to tell him to stop. It made Eva feel very uncomfortable. She had liked Lilianne but that was no way for a lady to behave; not the sort of lady that she was going to be. She wondered if the Count realized what sort of a person Lilianne really was. She waited until her hostess was occupied at the other end of the room and slipped away. One of the men tried to follow her and it was fortunate that a taxi was passing as she left the house. He was standing in the street, looking after her as she drove off.

14

Druska was waiting for Eva when she arrived home from the party. She took one look at Eva's face, went silently into the bathroom and started to run the hot water. Eva sat on the edge of the bed and wondered what it was that the Count expected her to do. She knew that she had little experience of the world, but she had seen enough of society and the way that it behaved — both in the castle and during her brief stay in Warsaw — to realize that Lilianne and her friends were very different from the well-bred ladies and gentlemen who had been entertained by the Lubinski family.

It was an end to the euphoria that had buoyed her spirits during the few weeks since the Count had finally recognized her as his daughter. The tears were running down her cheeks as Druska came out of the bathroom. She sat down beside Eva and put her arms around her, rocking her back and forth as if she were a child. They fell asleep, side by side on the huge bed, with its four ornate posts and tapestry canopy.

It was still dark when Eva woke. She shivered and wrapped herself in a silk dressing gown that she had found in one of the wardrobes and stood looking out of the window. It was raining outside, a fine drizzle, and the street was filled with early risers, scurrying to work beneath opened umbrellas. Eva wished that she could be amongst them, with somewhere to go and a purpose in life and friends and loved ones waiting for her at the end of the day. Her loneliness was a physical pain and she hugged her body in her anguish.

She could hear the rattle of cups as Druska prepared the morning coffee. At least there was one person who relied upon her and, for both their sakes, she knew that she had to be strong. She dressed quickly and went into the kitchen. She put her arms round Druska and gave her a kiss. "I was tired last night, and not myself. Today we are going to start on a new life. We will take our coffee in the salon and make a plan for our future." She hoped she sounded more confident than she felt. Druska looked happier anyway, which was one good thing.

The telephone rang as soon as they reached the salon. Druska jumped up to answer it which was a relief to Eva, who had no idea what her grand plan was going to be. It was Lilianne on the line. Eva was surprised that she was awake so early; she had thought the party would have continued until very late indeed.

Lilianne's voice was croaky and hoarse, as if she had a cold. She sounded relieved when Eva spoke to her. "We were all so worried when we realized you were gone. Pasha wanted to go and search for you. It was all I could do to stop him going round to your home." I'm sure it was, Eva thought, and it would have been even harder to get rid of him once he arrived, something which had no doubt been on Lilianne's mind as well.

"Is there anything the matter?" Lilianne's voice had taken on an unattractive whine. Perhaps she was worried that the Count would be displeased if his daughter were upset.

Eva decided to be in no hurry to make friends. She sounded cold and distant as she replied. Before she spoke she heard a man's voice asking Lilianne what the time was and telling her to go back to sleep. It sounded like Pasha, thick-tongued and guttural. Lilianne lowered her voice and asked if she might visit her in the late afternoon.

Eva said, "Very well, Madame," in her steeliest voice. She was relieved to have something to do and time to think before she did it. If only she could handle Lilianne properly, it might still come out all right.

"Druska, this is going to be a very important visit, and we must prepare ourselves so that everything is as it should be. Madame Lilianne must not have the impression that we are two children, alone and helpless in the world. I think she has been presuming altogether too much, and we are going to correct that. We will serve cocktails so that she will see that we are women of breeding."

Druska looked doubtful, but Eva picked up a copy of a magazine

99

she had been reading that gave recipes for such things. Most of them seemed very complicated, with a great many ingredients of which she had never heard, so she settled for dry martinis and sent Druska to the grocer for gin and vermouth and some lemons, olives and a sack of ice.

They spent most of the afternoon mixing and tasting to make sure it was just right, until Eva fell asleep and Druska had trouble waking her in time to change. It was as well that Lilianne was late.

She looked terrible when she finally arrived. Her face was heavily powdered and her cheeks were bright with rouge, but she could not disguise her bloodshot eyes and the puffiness of her skin.

She sank with a sigh into an armchair and said how tiring it was to give a soirée, even one so modest as last night's. Druska was standing at the sideboard behind her and she rolled her eyes, so that Eva had to force herself not to laugh.

Lilianne became far more cheerful when she was offered a cocktail. She sipped cautiously and then swallowed it down and Druska hastened forward with another. They spent a while in small talk and Lilianne became quite emotional about her troubles with Pasha, whom she said was very rich and well born but who was from the East and sometimes found it hard to pick up the ways of Western society. Eva sympathized and said how difficult that must be.

She thought it was about time that the conversation turned more serious. Lilianne and her problems became boring quite quickly and she was glad that Druska had not rushed forward to replace her second martini. She wanted Lilianne with her wits about her.

"Last night's party and all the interesting people that I met made me think that it is time for me to find a husband, while I am still young" – and also a virgin, she could have added, but there was no need for that; Lilianne seemed to catch her meaning at once. She thought it was a marvellous idea and became quite excited, making a list of eligible men that she knew, and some that she had only heard of from other people, but she wrote them down as well because you could never tell.

She gave Eva a long lecture about love and marriage and how they should never be confused, because husbands were hard to find; love could come later, and as many times as a lady found convenient. It seemed good advice to Eva and she thought of Andrzej and swore to herself that, although impossible, her love for her half-brother would sustain her for the rest of her life.

Even after including every man Lilianne could possibly think of, and some that she marked as outsiders, for she loved the races and saw the whole affair in terms of a sporting contest, the list in her little alligator-skin notebook was not very long. It appeared that eligible men were few and far between that year, but Lilianne said that beggars couldn't be choosers and she would see what she could do. It was not a very hopeful ending to the conversation.

The doorbell rang twice which meant that the concierge was telling them there was someone at the door to the street, and Lilianne said that it must be Pasha, coming to collect her. She seemed in a hurry to leave and said no thank you very firmly when Eva asked if he would like to join them.

Eva had the feeling that she was trying to keep Pasha away from her. Maybe that would encourage her friend to find her a husband as fast as she could. It was an amusing thought. Druska helped her to finish the martinis and they went to bed early. Druska was already worrying about Mamzelle's trousseau.

It was the sort of project that Lilianne adored. Meddling in the lives of others was what she did best and Eva had only to wait until the next afternoon for her first meeting with a potential husband.

The Marquis de Saint George was an older man, as mature and sophisticated as Lilianne had described him; also childless and with the misfortune of having had a wife in a lunatic asylum for the past several years. He was of impeccable breeding, with a house in Paris and an estate somewhere in Provence, as well as the fortune that went with such grand possessions. Eva had been surprised and impressed that Lilianne had been able to arrange for such a suitable escort in so short a time.

He called for her at twelve-thirty the following afternoon and they drove to a restaurant close to the Opèra. He had a Hotchkis town car, with a grey-uniformed chauffeur who saluted her as he held open the door. The Marquis most certainly appeared to be all that her friend had described. He was tall and thin with a hooked nose and watery blue eyes, well-dressed in a formal morning suit with a winged collar and a grey silk cravat fixed to his shirt by a diamond pin.

He did not say very much during the drive, just asking her if she had another engagement for the afternoon and grunting when she said that she had not. As Lilianne had instructed her, she was wearing a simple white dress made of calico, with white silk stockings and a broad-brimmed straw hat. She had worried that she might appear too young for such a refined gentleman, but Lilianne had laughed and said that there was no fear of that.

She had caught the Marquis taking sidelong glances in the direction of her legs and had taken care that her skirt stayed well down over her knees. She would hate him to think that she was forward.

He was not quite so prepossessing when she looked at him from her seat across the table. He was older than she had thought. His hands trembled as he tore at a bread roll and a piece of crust became stuck to his moustache, making her want to lean over and brush it off. He was not very much of a conversationalist either; in fact he was rather vague and seemed to have mixed her up with someone else, saying how pleased he was with the agency and would she give his best regards to Madame.

She ate sparingly and refused a second glass of wine, which was the right thing to have done – the Marquis said he hated girls who were drunk, which had happened to him before and ruined his entire afternoon. He seemed to drink more than enough himself, and his hands increased their trembling as the meal wore on; his face became red and he started to twitch in his seat. It was an uncomfortable sort of meal, but Eva thought that the Marquis must be embarrassed; looking for a wife was bound to put a great strain on a man.

As they were waiting for the dessert, he leaned foward and started to stroke her arm, mumbling that she was a pretty little thing and was she going to make an old man happy? She had already decided not to marry him; there was something about him that made her flesh creep, but she was too polite to tell him to his face. She thought she would leave that to Lilianne.

He called for the bill as soon as the dessert was served. She was about to stand up when he reached over the table and took her by the hand. "I prefer to take care of the details first," he said. She felt him push something into her hand. Looking down, she saw that it was a little wad of money. "Count it first, my dear. I'd be disappointed if you thought I was being ungenerous. There are a few rather special little things that we are going to be doing together this afternoon, and I want you to be sure I am paying enough."

Eva was confused for a moment and then she became furious, throwing the money down on the table and storming out of the restaurant. She was more angry with Lilianne than she was with the Marquis and furious with herself for being so stupid as to be there in the first place.

She had calmed down by the time she reached home. She looked at herself in the bathroom mirror, wishing that she had counted the money. It would have been nice to know how much he had been prepared to pay for her services. There was always that to fall back on, she supposed.

She rang her friend, and told her what had happened. She had

expected at least an apology, but Lilianne thought that the whole
thing was terribly funny. It was hard to get her to stop laughing and
Eva could hear Pasha laughing too, as he realized what had happened
from Lilianne's one-sided conversation. Lilianne said that she was
going to make it up to her right away. She had arranged for her to
have dinner with the son of a lady that she had met at a party a few
weeks ago. She was a very rich lady and one day her son would be
very rich as well, but he was still young and needed the love of a
strong woman to help him mature.

Henri du Boeuf collected her that evening in his shiny, drophead Delarge Roadster. He was a handsome young man, though
not as young as Eva had expected. He was tall, with a slender,
athlete's body and black curly hair which blew becomingly in the
wind as they drove with the roof down across the Pont Neuf and
on to the Left Bank. It had been noisy in the car and impossible to
talk, but Henri had smiled at her several times and she was starting
to look forward to the evening, glad of the chance to put the Marquis
out of her mind forever.

They stopped outside a small and obviously popular bistro, where
Henri was greeted as an old customer. They were shown to a table
at the back of the room, cut off from the others by a high-backed
banquette. Henri insisted on sitting beside her. He did not say very
much, occupying himself with building a little castle of slices of
baguette, using tooth picks to stick them together and tearing some
of them in half to make them fit.

She pretended to be interested for a while, but the table was soon
a mess, with breadcrumbs everywhere. The waiter wanted to brush
them up, but Henri wouldn't let him; he was worried that his castle
might be damaged. There was a pitcher of wine on the table and
Henri poured them both a glass, but he put it down awkwardly and
it spilled all over the crumbs, making a sort of pink paste which was
very unattractive.

They had steak au poivre and he was silent while they ate, but
very attentive, passing her the salt and ordering some more wine.
Some of the crumbs had fallen on her skirt. Henri started to brush
them off, using first his napkin and then his bare hands, brushing
everywhere, all over her body, even where there were no crumbs at
all. He seemed to enjoy this very much and he put his arm round
her and started to fondle the side of her breast, pushing his hand
down the front of her dress.

She grabbed his fingers and tried to pull them away from her,
which made him roar with delight, as if it were the best game in the
world. He put his hand over her mouth and, half standing, pulled

her legs upward, so she was lying along the length of the banquette. Then he pulled up her skirt, drooling with glee, and plunged his hand between her thighs.

She struggled furiously to hold him off. She was too embarrassed to call out and risk being discovered in such a position. The place was full and noisy and she dreaded the thought of all those people staring at her distress. Henri fumbled with his belt and his trousers fell down to his ankles. His underwear followed and he flung himself on top of her, his knee prising apart her thighs and his weight half crushing the breath from her lungs as he thrust down on her.

There was a lighted candle on the table. Her left arm was free and she gently reached out until it was in her hand. She forced herself to relax, raising her other arm and drawing Henri towards her. She ran her fingers along the cleft of his buttocks and he grunted with satisfaction at the success of his courtship and moaned out something she couldn't understand as his hands tore at her underwear. She opened his buttocks with her right hand and plunged down with the lighted candle.

It must have been more painful than she had imagined. The rest of the room fell silent, shocked by the terrible scream as Henri leaped to his feet and stumbled round the corner of the banquets into full view. His trousers were still down by his feet and he tripped and fell across a table, where his penis encountered a plate of very hot tripe à l'oignon that had just been served to a lady from Nîmes. This time his shriek was truly terrible and he collapsed writhing and screaming onto the floor.

There was a lot of shouting and people peeping at Eva over the top of the banquette, but she had adjusted her clothes and was sitting, blank-faced and innocent, so the people went away. As she left she could see Henri lying in a corner. His trousers were still around his legs and some kind person had placed some ice between his buttocks to take away the pain. They were half covered by a white linen napkin.

There was silence as she left, but she could hear the noise rising behind her as she went into the street.

15

Pasha had arranged the trip to the races at Longchamps to celebrate her reconciliation with Lilianne. Eva had been going to ring her early the following morning, but it was Lilianne who rang her first, asking what in the name of heaven had she done to that poor young boy? His mother had spent the last half-hour on the telephone, screaming and shouting about how Eva had ruined her loved one, causing him a psychological trauma that would take years of love and affection to heal. How could Eva had been so wicked and irresponsible after all that Lilianne had done for her, introducing her to all the best people for no reward, except rude telephone calls so early in the morning that she was still half asleep?

Eva had said a few words as well, all about being introduced to retarded rapists and perverted old men, who were the only people someone like Lilianne would ever know. They had both slammed down the receiver at the same moment and there had been a silence between them for the next five days, until Pasha said that it had gone on long enough and called on Eva personally in an effort to make peace.

Eva had been very glad to see him. She had been bored and listless without Lilianne to amuse her, cut off from the rest of the world and taking out her frustration on Druska, which she knew was not fair.

Lilianne seemed equally delighted to see her. She said that Henri and his little accident had become quite famous in Paris society, the cafés were still buzzing with the tale, everybody asking who the girl with the candle was and making up crude jokes at Henri's expense. She insisted that Eva told the whole story as they drove out of the city in Pasha's Duisenberg Tourer.

They were all of them helpless with laughter by the time they arrived at the course. It was a bright autumn day and Pasha had brought a picnic with champagne and quails' eggs and little larks in aspic. They sat on the grass beside the track and Eva thought that it was the happiest day of her life.

After lunch they went for a stroll to the paddock to view the horses for the first race. It was a smart crowd, the men in tweed suits and soft hats and the women wearing long, diaphanous dresses and romantic, cartwheel hats. Pasha was using his binoculars to survey the crowd in the stand behind them. He suddenly grunted and tapped Lilianne on the shoulder. "There's a man up there whom I've been trying to see for the last two weeks. He's a banker called Jack Powers. He's had a proposal of mine for over a month, about a factory I'm trying to buy in Silesia, and I need his answer quickly or the deal will fall through. I think we'll stroll up there and just bump into him by chance. You ladies might come in very handy indeed."

Pasha pointed out Powers to them as they stood at the top of the huge grandstand. He was a neat-looking man, with white hair and a very straight back. He was standing by himself in the middle of the excited crowd. Pasha said he hoped that she had left all her candles at home, he could not afford to upset Mr Power. Eva was about to make a rude retort but Pasha had taken Lilianne by the arm and they were moving away from her. She was in no hurry to catch up with them and they had been talking with Mr Powers for some minutes by the time she approached. Mr Powers did not appear to be ecstatic at their presence. She could tell that he was barely being polite and Pasha was hopping from foot to foot, trying to find an excuse to prolong their conversation. Lilianne was standing beside Pasha, laughing frantically at something that he had just said and looking at Mr Powers in the hope that he would start laughing too, but his face remained polite and impassive, as if he was waiting for them to go away.

Pasha seized on Eva with relief as she arrived, pulling her forward and making a big fuss of introducing her, saying she was the daughter of Count Lubinski, and then standing back and making out that they were all honoured by her presence. Mr Powers bowed over her hand and said he was pleased to meet her. To her surprise, he was an American. He was the first American that she had ever met and she told him so, which seemed to amuse him. He asked her how she was enjoying her stay in Paris and whether she had been there long. Pasha seized on his interest and invited them all for a glass of champagne. To her surprise, Mr Powers agreed and they found themselves a table on the balcony at the top of the grandstand.

Mr Powers said please call him Jack and toasted Eva when the champagne arrived; she could see Pasha starting to relax. Then Mr Powers asked her if she would help him place a bet; she might bring him good luck. She saw Pasha smiling encouragingly at her, so she said that she would be honoured and they went down to the ring. Jack asked her how she came to be in Paris and she said that her father had sent her, not lying but not telling the whole truth. She was enjoying being a grand lady and was afraid he would have no more to do with her if he knew the secret of her birth.

Lilianne and Pasha were gone when they returned to their table. She didn't want to spoil Jack's afternoon, having to drag her around wherever he went, so she said she would go back to the car; the others were bound to be there soon. But Jack insisted that he should come with her, and there was no sign of her friends when they arrived.

Jack said that it looked as if she was stuck with him and she took his arm and said, "Don't be silly." He smiled and asked if she would like to go back to the paddock. They spent the rest of the afternoon together. She felt comfortable and secure with Jack. He was the first older man she had ever really spoken to – you couldn't count the Marquis – and she found herself talking about things that she would never before have dreamed of discussing with a stranger.

Jack was a widower; his wife had died five years earlier. He had two daughters, both older than herself and both of them married and living in America. He had chosen to live in Europe; after his wife had died, there had been nothing left for him in the United States and he had come to Paris as head of the European branch of a Washington bank that was owned by a good friend.

That reminded Eva of Pasha, and she said how disappointed he would be to have missed them; he had so wanted to talk to Jack about his deal.

Jack looked at her thoughtfully. "How much of a friend are you to Pasha?" he asked.

"I'm not really. It's Lilianne who is his friend." She had already told him how Lilianne was looking after her while she waited for her father to arrive.

He started to question her about her childhood in Poland. She had skipped through it briefly, earlier in the day, telling him only that she was a Lubinski and making up a story about her life in the castle, but now he wanted to hear it again, listening seriously to her replies and asking other questions that were hard for her to answer. She started to have an idea that he did not believe her and could feel herself becoming flustered, but then he stopped questioning her and said it was time to go if they were to miss the traffic after the last race.

He asked if she would have dinner with him. They stopped at a restaurant in the Bois de Boulogne. They were quiet and relaxed together, almost old friends. He casually asked her an innocent question about Warsaw and she could no longer stand the evasions and half-truths with which she had been disguising the shame of her origins.

"You might as well know this now," she said. "I can't stand the secrecy any longer, even if you never want to see any more of me. I have not told you the whole truth. The Count is my father and I am a Lubinski, but he was not married to my mother. I've been sent away from the castle, and I can never go back. No one but Lilianne knows the truth and she is trying to help me as best she can."

Jack looked at the young girl, red-faced but defiant, her head held high, daring the world to sneer at her shame. He reached out his hand and placed it gently on her shoulder. "You are not alone any more. I am going to look after you for as long as you will allow me." He kissed her softly on the lips and she let her head lean forward until it was resting on his shoulder. She felt secure as his arm went around her.

They were married two weeks later, in a side chapel of the church of the Sacré Coeur in Montmartre. Pasha gave her away and Lilianne was maid of honour. After the ceremony they all went to a bistro near the Bastille and Pasha became drunk and asked Jack why he wouldn't put money into his factory in Silesia. Jack became angry and said that Pasha was a fool if he thought that Hitler would stop with Czechoslovakia; Poland was next and the British would be powerless to stop it.

Eva was horrified. She knew vaguely that there were big problems with Germany, but they were far away and of no concern to her. The thought of Poland being invaded reminded her of Andrzej and the terrible danger that he might have to face.

She had done her best to put Andrzej out of her mind since she had left the castle. At first it had been relatively simple. The excitement of her journey and her new life in Paris had deadened her pain so that it had become no more than a dull ache, always at the back of her mind, but bearable if she did not allow herself to think about the hopelessness of her passion. At those unguarded moments, when it would take her unawares, she would dream of a miraculous day when it would be revealed – though how she had no idea – that her mother had lied and the Count was not her real father. Then she would take Andrzej in her arms and be with him for ever.

Meeting Jack had forced her to abandon her fantasy. She had found a comfort and security in his presence that she had never known before and she was determined to be a good and faithful wife to him, even in her dreams. She cursed Pasha and his drunken meanderings. If he had not brought up Silesia and his stupid deal, there would have been no mention of Poland and she would have been just another young girl, nervous on her wedding night and worried only about her husband and what it would be like when they were finally alone together.

She felt a deep depression settling over her. The wedding vows that she had taken so willingly only a few hours before now took on all the horror of a sentence to a life without hope of happiness. She did her best to fight against it. She was too fond of Jack to allow anything to spoil his wedding night, but the joy had gone out of her. Later, when he lay beside her, she was stiff and numbed, and after he had finished his lovemaking, she could no longer hold back her misery and she wept hysterically, with her head buried against his chest whilst he soothed her and finally calmed her so that she fell asleep in his arms. He assumed that it was the loss of her virginity that was causing her tears.

She was still huddled against him when she woke during the night. The moonlight was falling on his face, and she stared at him for a long while, swearing to herself that she would never betray his love and kindness, no matter what the future might bring.

Two days after her wedding, Germany invaded Poland and Great Britain declared war. The newspapers were full of tales of the heroism of the Poles as they fought in vain to halt the German advance. Their equipment outdated and their army ill prepared, it was over almost as soon as it began. She read, with shocked disbelief, of the suicidal charges of the cavalry, imagining Andrzej lying crushed and broken as the tanks rolled across his body.

It was impossible for her to hide her distress, but Jack imagined that it was the natural grief of an exile whose homeland was being destroyed. He did everything in his power to make her happy, bringing her little presents and flowers and treating her gently as he would a child, comforting her in their bed at night, subjugating his own obvious sexual desire to her unhappiness. She knew that she should feel guilty at the way that she was treating him, abusing his kindness while she yearned for Andrzej, but it was beyond her strength to throw off the melancholy that engulfed her.

Three weeks after war was declared, Jack came home and announced that he had been instructed to move to Geneva, where the bank was going to make its headquarters until the war was over. They had been given only one week to make the move.

He travelled to Switzerland the following morning, leaving Eva and Druska to pack the essential belongings that they were to take with them. The bulk of their possessions were to be left behind. No one believed that the war would last very long, perhaps six months at the most, and Jack fumed at the panicky people in Washington, whose unnecessary pessimism was causing them all such inconvenience.

There were still some of their belongings left at the Count's apartment in the boulevard Haussmann. They went over there to collect them the following morning. The concierge waved to them from her window as they entered the house. There was a letter for Madame. A foreign gentleman had left it for her, not two days before. Eva thought that she was going to faint as she saw the handwriting on the envelope. It was from Andrzej. She ran up the stairs, leaving Druska far behind, and locked herself in the bathroom. Her hands were trembling as she tore open the envelope. The note inside said simply:

Dearest Eva,
  I am in Paris for a short time only. I am longing to see you and pray that by some miracle you will receive this before I must leave. I have only this address and no other way of finding you. I am at the Hôtel du Dragon in the street of that name, and I wait in hope that God will bring you to me.
                    Your loving Andrzej.

Eva was ashen as she came out. Druska was standing in the bedroom. She gasped in alarm as she saw her mistress but Eva brushed past her and ran to the front door. She paused before she opened it. "There's someone I must see at once. It's more important to me than anything else in the world. We'll tidy up here tomorrow and you go home by yourself." She saw the surprise and worry on Druska's face and ran back and kissed her cheek. "Don't worry about me, I'll be back as soon as I can." She ran down the stairs, before Druska could ask her where she was going.

The Hôtel du Dragon was in a small street on the Left Bank. There were some soldiers leaning against the wall outside the front door. Their uniforms were creased and dirty and one of them had his arm in a sling. Her heart leaped as she saw from the ribbons on their shoulders that they were from the same regiment as Andrzej. The men stared at her with dull eyes as she approached them, but came to life when she spoke to them in Polish and one of them asked if by any chance *Pania* had a cigarette she might spare, as they had no money and the Captain had already been generous enough, paying for their food and lodging from his own pocket although even his money was starting to run out.

"Is it Captain Lubinski who is paying for you?" She held her breath for the answer and the men nodded. They told her that he was inside in his room, resting from his wound. The foyer was dingy and there was no answer as she hit the brass bell on the top of the counter. Then she heard footsteps coming slowly towards her down the wooden staircase, and a pair of feet in battered riding boots came into view round the corner of the balustrade. She knew it was Andrzej as soon as she saw them, and she walked quickly to the foot of the stairs.

They stood for a moment, looking at each other and then he gave a sigh of happiness and opened his arms. She wrapped her own around his neck and they clung together. She pulled back her head and kissed him on the lips. She felt his passion responding and it was hard for each of them to pull away.

She took him by the hand and led him out to the street. He left brief instructions with his men and she flagged down a taxi. They sat close together, neither of them speaking on the drive to the boulevard Haussmann. She could sense the caretaker staring after them as they went up the stairs to the apartment. "I was here two days ago," said Andrzej, "just sitting in that armchair, holding a blouse that you had left behind and feeling your presence. I thought that would be as close as I would be to you for a very long time. There is a Polish brigade being formed in Lyons and we have orders to leave tomorrow, early in the morning. I had given up hope of seeing you."

They were standing in the centre of the salon. There was no sound except for that of their own voices. They were suddenly embarrassed, almost frightened at being alone together, with no one to interrupt them, nothing between themselves and their passion. Andrzej was standing, awkward and ill at ease, and it was Eva who moved

111

forward and pulled him to her. She knew that she would live with the shame and the guilt of their lovemaking for the rest of her life, but there was no power in the world that could possibly stop her.

It was cold at the Gare de Lyons the next morning. It was still before dawn when they arrived. A silence had fallen between them during the last hour that they had been together and they had lain naked on the bed, side by side, with only their hands touching, each facing a different reality as the time came for them to part. Andrzej had talked of their future together once the war was over: how they would return to Poland; the life they would lead, back in the castle; the children they would have and the unending delight. She had agreed with all he had said; anything to make him happy and keep at bay the terrible truth of her sin. They held each other at the station before he kissed her and walked away from her through the barrier. He turned and waved to her once and then he disappeared into the crowd of soldiers on the platform. Her body ached as she watched him go, longing for his return and at the same time dreading the terrible consequences that would follow.

She walked in a daze through the dark streets. Already it was hard to remember last night, as if she were waking from a dream. Then she thought of her husband and his trust, betrayed and trampled over forever, and of the lies and deceit that lay ahead of her. The burden of her guilt was too much to face and her mind withdrew from its horror. She was weeping hysterically by the time she reached home and Druska called the doctor, who gave her a sedative and said he would come back the next day.

She was still in bed when Jack returned two days later and they delayed their journey to Switzerland until she had recovered. It was several weeks before she was well enough to travel.

16

Georgia had taken a quick shower and changed into a brown tweed coat and skirt and a beige polo-neck sweater. She hated the idea of Lady Pamela and her Aunt's tête-à-tête over their gin and tonics, discussing her behaviour; her Aunt's reaction would be the same, however much Lady Pamela praised and explained how proud they all were of their darling little girl.

She thought it was amazing what losing one's virginity could do for a girl, although this would be the first thing her Aunt would accuse her of, and she'd probably demand a doctor's examination as she had once threatened Milla. She was tired of being a good girl, spending her life pleasing her Aunt and now Lady Bacon, whilst Lady Pamela hovered nervously between them, twittering and soothing and making out that everything was for the best.

Cosmo was dressed when she reached his flat. He was surprised to see her, and not nearly as pleased as she thought he would be. He was wearing a dark blue formal suit and an Old Etonian tie over a shirt with thick blue stripes and a starched white collar. She sat on the bed while he checked his wallet and wound his watch.

"Where are you off to?"

"To see a man about a dog." His answer was brusque, almost rude and she wondered if he had, indeed, only been after one thing, as her Aunt had always warned.

She must have pouted or given some other sign of her displeasure because Cosmo turned on her and said, "I'm tired of you debs and your stuck-up ideas and rich families. I've told you that I've got to make a living, and that's what I'm trying to do at this precise moment. I'm going to an important meeting with some powerful people and I can't afford to be late."

Georgia opened her blouse and taking his hand, placed it on her breast. "Let me come with you. I might be very good at business, for all I know. I could be a big help to you, entertaining your clients and hanging about like your assistant, taking notes and saying yes and no and calling everybody sir whenever they look at me."

She put her other hand against the front of his fly. He was already hard. She gave a cry of triumph. "You see, you can't do without me."

Cosmo gently disengaged his hand from inside her bra and she rebuttoned her blouse, all the time staring into his eyes.

"I'm sorry, my love," he said, "I really am. I'm flat broke; I can't even pay the rent on this crummy place, let alone eat. It would be great if you came with me, but the people I'm seeing are pretty odd types, and you're not going to like them at all. Are you sure you want to come?"

As they climbed up a narrow flight of stairs off a Soho street where she had never been before, Georgia was not so sure that she should have said yes. The stairs were laid with a new red carpet and there were two men on the small landing on the first floor trying to get it to fit around the curve of a desk which was set diagonally across one of the corners. There was not much room for the four of them. Cosmo asked if Mr Gallo was around and the men shrugged and pointed towards the double swinging doors behind them.

It was dark inside and it was a few moments before her eyes could adjust. There was a postage-stamp dance floor to her right, with two tiers of seats around it and a small stage at the end. The room was L-shaped, with a bar against the far wall and a few tables and chairs scattered around it. The red wallpaper and carpet and subdued red lighting made the place feel decadent and rather spooky, especially entering it from the bright daylight as they had done. Georgia felt uncomfortable and slightly unsafe.

There were two men sitting talking at one of the tables. They turned their heads at the sound of the doors opening and then one of them stood up quickly. Georgia thought that he looked very dangerous indeed. He was a short man with slim hips and very wide shoulders beneath his sharp suit. He had thick, curly hair, cut short, and a close-cropped beard, pointed and piratical in the dim light.

The other man stayed seated. He was fat and bald and wore an open-neck shirt. There was a small white poodle asleep on the floor beside him.

Cosmo went over to them and they all shook hands. Then he introduced Georgia. He was rather awkward, quite unlike his usual, confident self. The thick set man was Mr Gallo, whom Cosmo called Mike, and the other was Mr Malinski, who said nothing at all while Mr Gallo shook her hand and asked her how she was. His accent was foreign, slightly guttural. He spoke rather fast.

He said to the other man, "This is the fellow in the newspaper today, the one I was telling you about." He seemed very pleased with himself. Looking at Cosmo, he said, "How are you going to fix us up with some of that when we open up? Those friends of yours are just up our street. It's class that we're selling here." He pinched Cosmo on the cheek, making him wince. Georgia was surprised that he put up with it. Then he put his arm round Cosmo's shoulders and said that he was a real gentleman and a knight, as well as his personal friend. It seemed as though he was trying to impress the balding man who just sat there, looked at Cosmo, and asked, "How much you paying him?" as if Cosmo were not there. Mike said that they were just going to get round to that.

The balding man stood up. "Give the girl a job, too. She can take the hats or somethink. Five bob a night and tips, that's what she's going to get." His voice was flat and without emotion. On his feet he was round and unhealthy-looking, with a big belly and small, pointed feet. He jerked the dog on its lead and walked out of the door without saying goodbye. Georgia had wanted to say something nasty about him, but he had frightened her and she kept quiet.

As if apologizing, Gallo said, "He's having a rough time collecting his rents; it's worrying him." But he said no more about him, as if that was enough. Cosmo nodded. He was very subdued.

Gallo was much more cheerful, now that Malinski had gone. He went to the bar and poured them all drinks and sat beside Georgia when he came back. She could sense him looking at her legs. She pretended not to notice, but it was rather exciting. She could tell that Cosmo didn't like it.

Gallo asked her if she would like a job in his club. He said it was going to be a very "U" place – Mr Malinski and he had put in a lot of money to make sure that it would work. She would go a long way in the club world, he could tell. He put his arm around the back of her chair as he spoke. Cosmo looked furious but kept quiet. She thought it was amusing to see him so jealous, particularly of a common sort of person like Mike.

She explained that she was at finishing school and Mike, pulling a piece of newspaper from his pocket, looked at her and laughed, saying that she was much more beautiful than her picture. Then he turned to Cosmo and said, "So how much do you want me to pay you?"

Cosmo went red, even puce in the light. He glanced at Georgia and she could see that he wished he hadn't brought her along. But he said, "Well, I thought five pounds a week and ten shillings a membership."

Gallo looked at him. "You're joking. Five pounds a week and a commission as well. Tell him he's crazy." He appealed to Georgia. "He'll make more than I do and that's not right."

She could see that he was enjoying himself. If he owned all this, the money would mean nothing to him, but it meant an awful lot to Cosmo. He was blinking and fidgeting and hating himself for being in this position, hating her as well because she knew about it.

"I don't think that's too much," said Georgia. "Not with all the work he'll have to do and all the people he knows."

Gallo gave in straightaway. He squeezed her shoulder, saying he would never argue with a lady and asking whether Cosmo knew what a very special girl he had because, if not, there were plenty of people who would like to take care of her.

Once they were outside, Cosmo wouldn't talk to her, walking off down the street as if she weren't there. She followed behind him, but not too quickly. She was thinking about what Mike Gallo had said. Maybe she could earn some money working for him. The thought made her feel much better. At least there was a chance that she could get away from her Aunt if Eva really turned the screws.

Then she started to worry being away from La Circle. There was a taxi passing in the street and she hailed it. Cosmo would have a shock when he turned round and she wasn't there.

When she arrived at La Circle, there was a note on the board to ring her Aunt. Things would only become worse if she delayed. Her Aunt became unpredictable after lunchtime cocktails and it was already late in the afternoon.

Druska answered and said that Eva had gone out. Georgia had not rung home since she had started at La Circle, it had been agreed that although she was only just down the road, it would help her to mature more quickly if she stayed out of contact with her Aunt. It had been Lady Pamela's idea and she had been surprised that Eva had agreed, but she supposed that Lady Bacon would make sure that her every move was relayed back.

It was good to talk to Druska again and, for a moment, she felt herself weakening. It would be only too easy to do whatever her Aunt wanted. She told Druska how much she missed her but Druska was funny on the other end. "Miss Georgia, you don't do anything to upset your Aunt," she said. "She has suffered very much for everybody all her life and it will break her heart if you are bad."

It was a new idea, her Aunt suffering for other people, and Georgia dismissed it as just Druska's Polish sentimentality. After all, she was getting old. It was a relief that Eva was not at home. At least she had made the effort to contact her.

There was a cocktail party on the programme for that evening. She had forgotten about it. She had not intended to go, but now she was too keyed up to spend the evening alone. She was sure that Cosmo would telephone later on and she did not want to be there when he called. She had not thought about him since she had left him on the street and as she changed into a simple black dress and prepared herself to go out, she kept pushing him out of her mind.

She wondered if she had been a fool to go to bed with him. She had no one to blame but herself and she knew that she would do the same thing again as soon as she could. Perhaps that was why she was going out tonight. She took a long look at herself in the mirror. For God's sake, she thought, calm down. She was becoming exactly the sort of girl that everyone she had ever known since she was a child had done their best to prevent her from being. The excitement tingled at the nape of her neck. Maybe they were the ones who were wrong.

The party was in St James's Square. It was a quiet night on the social calendar and there was a cluster of taxis unloading guests on the pavement. It was unusually crowded inside, people milling about, bumping into each other and spilling their drinks, and everybody shouting at the top of their voices – the sound a high-pitched angry howl that was frightening as you drew close. She braced herself and plunged into the middle of it, certain that in a few minutes she would be surrounded by people she knew.

She saw Cosmo almost immediately. He was forcing his way towards her. He looked angry and she turned her back and started talking to a young man with whom she had danced several nights before. It was no good. Cosmo came barging straight up to her and rudely pushed between them, blocking out the young man with his body and thrusting his face close to hers.

"Where the hell did you go to?"

"It's none of your business."

"It is my bloody business. I don't like people running away from me in the street."

"I expect that happens to you a lot."

Cosmo took hold of himself before the whole thing became a farce. She liked him for that. He laughed and said, "I'm sorry. It was my fault, but Gallo and his spooky friend are so ghastly, and I felt really bad getting you involved."

She put her hand on his arm, "I don't think they're that bad, though the bald one is a bit much. Offering me five shillings wasn't very flattering, I must say."

They both laughed and the tension went away. "Let's go somewhere else," said Cosmo. "It's bedlam in here."

Then Cosmo said he was broke and they would have to go to a pub. Georgia had some money and offered to pay for them both, but Cosmo became annoyed at her for suggesting it. It was unthinkable that a woman should pay. It was the first time that Georgia had really thought about money. It had always been something that was there, not to be wasted or ignored but there all the same, a part of life. The real money, the stuff she had been taught to worry about, was in her Aunt's will. That was another matter entirely. For as long as she could remember the will had been the ultimate threat; to be excluded from its miraculous benefits would be a punishment against which Hell itself would be a blessed relief.

They went to a pub down by the river on Cheyne Walk. It was a quiet place, with only a few young men – from the City, judging by their conversation – and some working men playing darts in the Public Bar. It was a letdown after the noise and excitement of the party. She felt deflated and the two large gin and tonics that were all Cosmo could afford did nothing to restore her spirits. She wondered if Cosmo had brought any pills with him. She was not ready for a quiet night.

Cosmo started to knead her thigh under the table and then he took her hand and rubbed it against the front of his trousers. He was standing up. Until their visit to the Soho club, she had thought of little else but having sex with him, but now she found his demands annoying, even insulting. How dare he think he was going to get her to bed after a couple of drinks in a pub. It was as though they were already engaged.

"It's too early for that," she said, "let's go somewhere else."

Cosmo just shrugged and said that his money had run out, and suddenly she became impatient with him. She was starting to see that her Aunt and Lady Bacon were right about money; there was no fun with a man who didn't have it. It looked as though Cosmo was going to be a waste of time.

"What about your friends in Soho?" she asked. "I thought their club was having their opening bash tonight."

Cosmo raised his eyebrows. "I didn't think you liked those people."

"It's better than nothing. At least it's free and you should be there if you're going to work for them. It would be odd if you weren't."

She could see that Cosmo was not too happy with the idea. He took hold of her hand again and started to pull it towards him, but she stood up. "You don't own me, you know. I hate to be pawed about in public. Perhaps you'd like to do it to me on top of the bar, so everyone can have a look?" She thought it might be fun and was horrified at herself for even having the idea.

Cosmo was very sulky. "Well, okay," he said. "Just for a while then." He stood up and she could see that the front of his trousers was still bulging, but she ignored it. She went out into the street and called a taxi before he could change his mind.

17

There was a crowd standing outside the door of the club and the stairs were packed tight with people trying to get in. Cosmo tried to force their way past but a big man in a tight-fitting dinner jacket said, "Watch it, cocker!" and asked him if he wanted a poke in the mush. Cosmo was furious, but had the sense to keep quiet. There were several other big men around them. It turned out that they were all friends, making jokes about things that Georgia couldn't understand and roaring with such laughter that she could tell they had all been drinking before they arrived. Their women were a tough-looking lot as well. They were all much younger than the men and dressed in stiff, shiny dresses with hair lacquered in the beehive look, which was something Lady Bacon had forbidden as common and not for young ladies. They smelled very strongly of perfume and sweat and they gave Georgia hostile stares as they moved slowly forward towards the top of the stairs.

There was a tough young man in a blazer standing in front of the doors and another one, thick-set with huge shoulders and curly blond hair, behind the desk. Everyone was showing them invitation cards before they were allowed into the club. The big man who had been so rude to Cosmo said that he had left his at home and his friends all said that he was telling the truth and started pushing the young man in the blazer, calling him names because he wouldn't let him in. The young man started to get annoyed and his friend came out from behind the desk and they both started pushing back. The man in the blazer hit someone in the head and cut his hand, which made him furious. Then he butted another man in the face so that there was blood all over the place and Georgia started to become frightened. Cosmo was standing as far from the fracas as was possible, with the crowd pressing behind him. He was white and scared and she could see that he would be no use at all.

Two of the men pulled knives from their pockets, ones that flicked open so that you could hear the blades snapping into place. The rest of the crowd fell silent, giving them room as they inched forward with the knives held out in front of them. The two doormen watched them as they came. They were both frightened, she could tell, but they were standing their ground, their eyes fixed on the knives. At any moment there was going to be a tragedy. Georgia knew that she must do something to help, but she found herself watching with the rest of the crowd, hypnotized by what was happening.

The two glass doors swung open and Mike Gallo appeared. He put his hands on the shoulders of the doormen, pushing them gently to one side. He looked smart in his dinner jacket, with a scarlet cummerbund around his waist. He stood there, smiling easily at the two knife men, who were looking white and shocked at the sight of him. "It's not that sort of club," he said, "you boys had better go and play somewhere else." Georgia saw that his eyes were not smiling at all.

The men started to shuffle their feet. Their knives disappeared back into their pockets and they hung their heads. One of their friends said, "Sorry Mike. No hard feelings, mate. We didn't know this was your gaff."

"No hard feelings," said Gallo. "Just put the word out and save me some trouble."

There was a mumble of agreement and someone said, "Ta, Mike." The men started to go back down the stairs with their girls tailing along behind. A man in the crowd said to his girlfriend, "That's Mike Gallo. He'd have fucking killed them if they'd caused any aggro."

Georgia saw Cosmo from the corner of her eye. His colour was coming back as he pushed himself to the front and clapped Gallo on the back, saying, "What gutless scum. They soon ran when somebody stood up to them." He placed himself beside Gallo, as if he had been there all the time, and looked fiercely at the crowd on the stairs. The young man in the blazer laughed in an unpleasant way. She could see that he was going to say something rude to

Cosmo, but Gallo grabbed him by the arm and whispered into his ear and he laughed, more relaxed. The crowd started to move towards the doors.

Gallo was turning away when he saw Georgia standing against the wall. He ignored Cosmo and waved to her to come forward. The crowd parted, respectfully, to make way for her. He shook her warmly by the hand and asked her how she was and would she join the party at his table? She thanked him very much, saying that she'd love to, and followed him into the club. She could sense Cosmo coming in behind her.

She could hardly recognize it as the same place she had visited that morning. It was packed full of people, with waiters rushing about with trays of drinks, and a three-piece band playing on the stage. There was an air of excitement and anticipation, and laughter came from all round the dimly lit room. Gallo led her to an oblong table which was raised up on one of the platforms so that you could see the stage and the dance floor above the heads of the crowd. There were several others already seated at the table: two quiet, Eastern-looking men at one end, and an older man with white hair whom Gallo introduced as Lord Monahan, and who stood up as he shook her hand, saying how delighted he was to meet her. There were two other tough-looking men and their ladies, whom Georgia thought looked like tarts, but they were all very nice to her and said "Pleased to meet you" as if they really meant it. They made room for her to sit down beside Gallo, at the head of the table. Cosmo was left hanging about without a chair. Georgia pretended not to notice. She was ashamed of him and the way he had behaved, doing nothing while the poor doormen were risking their lives, and then making out to Gallo that he had somehow been involved.

She turned to look at Gallo. Close up he was much younger than she had thought, probably not much older than Cosmo. She wished that she knew more about him. The way those violent men had suddenly caved in at the sight of him was both impressive and terrifying. She wondered what he had done to deserve such respect.

There were bottles of champagne in ice buckets dotting the length of the table and Gallo reached forward and poured her a glass. It was very good champagne – Dom Perignon, by the shape of the bottle – and gulping some down, she started to relax. She saw that Gallo was not drinking alcohol himself, just sipping from a glass of iced water as his eyes darted around the room. Suddenly he gave a grunt of annoyance and asked her to excuse him for a moment. He started to move towards the bar, making slow progress through the crowd as people said hello to him and shook him by the hand.

She looked around at her fellow guests. Cosmo was looking miserable at the other end of the table. He had found a chair from somewhere, but as nobody had moved to make room for him he was perched on the very corner, with passers-by bumping into his chair every few seconds. It was hard to be sorry for him. He looked up at that moment and saw her glance. She could see that he was still angry at being ignored as he stood up and started to come round to the empty chair where Gallo had been sitting. She thought that would be a very silly thing for him to do, but he was too late anyway. Someone sat down in the chair before he could reach it, leaving him to skulk back to his seat.

Georgia recognized the smell of the cologne even before she turned her head to see Mr Malinski sitting beside her. She was disappointed, but she smiled hello. Malinski grunted and bent down to pick up the white poodle from the floor beside him. He sat there, fat and perspiring, while a waiter appeared and poured him champagne. The waiter stayed, standing attentively behind him, looking ill at ease, nervously fingering his bow tie and cleaning his nails with a fork he had taken from the next-door table.

Gallo came back and shook Malinski warmly by the hand. He did not appear at all upset that his chair had been taken and squashed himself in beside her. Malinski leaned towards him and said something she couldn't hear. Then Gallo stood up and asked her to change places, so that she was between the two men. She could tell that Gallo was unhappy with the arrangement. She was also beginning to see that however important Gallo might be, Mr Malinski's influence was even greater. It was a frightening thought. There was something about Malinski's quiet assumption that he was going to be obeyed that was far more terrifying than the rough, brawling men who had caused trouble at the entrance. The rest of the room seemed to be treating him with respect as well. Suddenly there was no one bumping into them at the table and she could feel her neighbours grow quiet, watching them covertly as they spoke in murmurs, anxious not to attract attention.

She decided to enjoy herself; Malinski was no concern of hers. Nevertheless, there was a pall of caution over the entire table; even Gallo appeared strained and watchful beneath his apparent high spirits. After a while he asked her if she would like to dance. She could feel Malinski watching as they went towards the floor.

Gallo was light as a cat. She could feel the hardness of his shoulders and the swell of his bicep as his arm went around her waist. They danced in silence for a few minutes, other couples moving away from them, taking care not to get in their way. Gallo pulled her close to him and made as if to bury his face in her neck. She was surprised at the crudeness of his approach; she had expected something better from him. He must have sensed her thoughts, because he gave a low laugh. "Excuse me," he said. "I'm not trying anything on – not yet that is. I just wanted to tell you something, but it's got to stay between the two of us, you promise?" She nodded her head, uneasy about what he was going to say. He dropped his voice even lower. "Watch out for Malinski. He's a business partner of mine, that's all. He has a bad reputation with women and I'd hate it if anything happened that you didn't like. I won't be around the whole time tonight, I have to run the club. I'll see you home later on, so don't go accepting any lifts." He straightened up and started to lead her back. She was disappointed that their dance was over so quickly. Cosmo was glaring at her as she reached the table.

There was another girl sitting in Gallo's place. There was nowhere else for Georgia to sit but between the new arrival and Malinski. The girl said her name was Linda and she was a personal friend of Joe's. She pointed at Malinski as she spoke, so Georgia would know who she meant. She was a blonde girl, wearing a green dress in a sleazy fabric that shone even in the low light, emphasizing the whiteness of her deep cleavage. She had gigantic pearl button earrings, and tight-fitting, elbow-length satin gloves with vulgar rings and bracelets worn over them. She had a common, suburban sort of accent and lifted her little finger so that it was rigid as she raised her glass, which was something that she was to do often during the course of the evening. All the same, she appeared to be a friendly sort of girl, and with Gallo having left to attend to his business, Georgia was glad to have someone to talk to besides the menacing Malinski and Cosmo who, she could see, was still sulking at the other end of the table.

She glanced at her watch. It was already after midnight and waiters were bringing cut-glass bowls full of ice with silver tubs of caviar buried in the middle. The blonde girl said that she had been a friend of Mr Malinski's for about six months and he was a very nice man, once you got to know his little ways.

She asked if Georgia smoked and, lighting a cigarette, passed it to her before she could refuse. Out of politeness, she took a puff and realized at once that it was marijuana. She was going to hand it back but Linda said that it was all right, she had plenty more. Georgia knew that she shouldn't, but she took another hard pull and felt the drug start to reach her. Why not, she thought. She was starting to feel angry with Gallo for leaving her. It would serve him right if she did start to pay a little attention to Malinski. He couldn't be all that dangerous in the middle of a room full of people, however bad his reputation was.

She had another glass of champagne – she had lost count how many she had already drunk – and then Linda reached into her handbag again and brought out some pills, saying that she might as well wash them down as the night was still young. She repeated that several times and Georgia could see that she was becoming a little woozy. Then Linda reached across and took Mr Malinski by the hand, saying yet again, "The night's still young, ain't it Joe?"

Georgia thought that Malinski would be angry at the familiarity, but he sipped his wine and nodded, starting to stroke Linda's hand with his thumb. It was a very fat thumb, white with a long, manicured nail. It moved slowly, like a gorged slug. It was repulsive and made Georgia shudder as she watched. As Linda leaned forward, she pressed up close to Georgia; she could feel Linda's breasts pushing against her arm. For a moment she thought that Linda was rubbing herself against her and she pulled away as far as she could against the back of the banquette. She looked sharply at Linda, who stared back at her with blank eyes, and she decided that she was mistaken.

The room was becoming boisterous, with the women as loud as the men. They were all screaming and shouting and pawing at each other. The dance floor was wet with spilt drink and a girl fell over as she watched. The girl sat there looking dazed, her legs stretched out in front of her, while the other dancers crowded round, pointing at her and screaming with laughter. There was no sign of her partner and Georgia saw Gallo beckoning to one of the doormen, who shouldered roughly through the packed bodies and pulled the girl to her feet. Her head lolled against his shoulder as he looked round for someone to claim her, before giving up and dumping her in an empty chair. The girl's head fell forward on to the table and she lay with her arms hanging by her sides.

It was a disgusting sight and Georgia was glad when Linda said, "Let's get out of here. These pills are doing nothing for me and Joe has some goodies in his car which we're all going to try." Malinski must have heard her, because he stood up at once. Linda pushed at Georgia to follow him. She felt her legs wobble as she walked behind him down the stairs, but Linda put her arm round her waist, so she was all right. There had been no sign of Gallo as they left and Cosmo had disappeared as well. It would serve both right that she had gone off without either of them.

It was a relief to be out in the fresh air, but her legs were still weak and she was grateful to Linda for holding on to her. They leant against the wall while Malinski went to find his driver, who should have been waiting in the doorway. Linda was holding on to her very tightly and Georgia thought it was time for her to go home. She looked at her watch, but the dial danced in front of her eyes and she gave up.

There was a taxi unloading a latecomer in front of them and as she started to go towards it Linda held her back. "Where do you think you're going?" she said. Her voice was high and forced and she clung onto Georgia, pushing her back against the wall. "Don't you start wandering off now, darling. He'll fucking kill me if you're gone when he gets back." Georgia wondered what she meant but she was feeling very, very tired and it didn't seem to be important; besides, Linda was a nice girl and it was kind of her to hold her up. She was sure she would fall over if she let go.

A long black Austin limousine pulled round the corner and, to her relief, Malinski was waving to them from a back window. The chauffeur came round and opened the door. He was a rough-looking man to be driving such a fine car. Malinski leaned forward to help her as she reached the curb. She could feel his pudgy hands around her waist as he pulled her down beside him. There was a fur coat on the seat beside her and instinctively Georgia put out her hand and fondled it. She lifted a sleeve and rubbed it against her cheek, feeling the rich softness on her skin. She heard Malinski chuckle beside her. It was a sneering, self-satisfied sound that made her drop the sleeve at once, ashamed that she might have shown a weakness that she did not feel. "You like mink, do you, darling?" asked Malinski. "You might just get lucky and find yourself owning that, if you behave yourself that is."

There was obscenity in his voice and she would have left him sitting there and gone straight home, but Linda got in at that moment and sat on one of the jump seats, facing them. There was a compartment in the door and Linda reached inside and came out with a small black box. "Here's just the thing we all need to cheer us up," she said, as if she was going to make a pot of tea.

18

She was cold. She reached down in search of the blanket but gave up as Druska started to shake her awake. It was light outside, time to wake up, but she was so tired. She groaned, "Just a little bit longer, please Druska." Her pillow was gone and the bed was hard as stone; Druska was hurting, the way she was squeezing her arm. She became fully awake, conscious of a strange face and a man's voice asking, "Are you all right, miss?"

Georgia's eyes came into focus. There was a policeman bending over her and a little crowd of strangers, mostly men, in a semicircle behind him. There was the flash of a camera, weak in the morning light, and the pavement was rough and uneven beneath her hand. There was a dustbin beside her that smelt of fish. The stench and the voice of the policeman were suddenly very important, realities she must not lose, vital clues to be retained.

The policeman helped her to her feet. He was fumbling at her waist and she started back from him in alarm. She had a brief recollection of other hands tearing and probing. "Cover yourself, miss, they're all looking at you." She looked down in disbelief at her own nakedness. She was wearing a strange coat. It was an expensive coat, made of mink. She wondered who the owner was. It reached nearly to her ankles. She could see its darkness against her naked legs and the white of her belly as she looked down. She

127

slowly drew it about her, looking hard into the eyes of the policeman as she did so, desperately wanting to do the right thing.

The feeling was coming back to her legs as the policeman took her by the arm and led her through the group of people that surrounded them, but her five-inch stiletto heels still wobbled as she walked. There were others hurrying to see what was happening and the end of the narrow street was blocked by a mass of bodies that parted as they approached. There was the sound of a siren in the street beyond and a police car drew up beside them as they reached the curb. She was grateful for its warmth as she sat in the back seat and the door closed out the rest of the world.

The car tore through the early morning emptiness of the Soho streets, and she sat back against the soft upholstery, her mind vacant except for a feeling of horror and impending retribution so severe as to be beyond belief. Then the sound of the engine and the feel of the fur against her legs brought back vague, disjointed memories of the previous night. She remembered the girl in the shiny green dress kneeling in front of her and the back of the blonde head as it burrowed between her parted legs; the clashing smell of cologne and stale hair lacquer as the man beside her pulled her down to his small, flaccid penis.

Her stomach started to heave; the police car came to a jolting stop, and someone held her head as she was sick in the gutter. She felt slightly better as they continued their journey. One of the policemen had got in beside her. He was worried about her, using his handkerchief to wipe her face, pulling the coat tight about her and making consoling noises, as though she were his own daughter. She clung on to his hand, wishing that he was her father, longing for someone to put their arms around her and tell her that everything would be all right.

"Chin up, miss," the policeman said. "We're nearly there now and you'd better get hold of yourself. There's going to be a lot of people asking you questions in a minute, and if I were you, I'd be careful how I answered. If you like, I'll call your dad and tell him to come over. You're going to need someone to take you home." Georgia shook her head. She felt like crying but there was an emptiness at the back of her head that blocked all emotion.

There was another crowd at the front of the police station. "There's no back door, miss," said the constable. "We'll have to make a dash through this little lot, I'm afraid. It looks like someone has had a tip-off. I can see a few reporters and cameras. We can hide your face, if you like."

Georgia shook her head. There was something so ignominious in

128

the photographs she had seen of people scurrying into police stations with blankets over their heads. It was almost an admission of guilt and all their friends would recognize them anyway, so what was the point?

The policeman lent her his comb and she tugged at the tangle of her hair. There was nothing to hold the coat together and it was difficult to get out of the car and keep her hands in the pockets as she clasped it about her. The policeman pulled her upright, his hand on her arm. She held her head very erect as she crossed the pavement, taking care not to wince as the cameras flashed close to her face, ignoring the babble of questions that followed her to the big wooden door that was being held open for her.

At first she had to sit on a bench with three women and a drunken man, who sat staring straight ahead of him, occasionally breaking into snatches of song. It was always the same one: "Sugar in the morning, sugar in the evening . . ." He would peter out, sitting with his face blank, as though it had been someone else who had been singing. Nobody paid him any attention.

Then a policewoman took her to a small, bare room at the end of a long corridor. She was a big, tough sort of person and Georgia expected the worst. She was told to sit at one of the two chairs facing each other across a scuffed wooden table. There was no other furniture. The policewoman left her by herself for a few moments before returning with a mug of steaming tea. She offered Georgia a cigarette and sat silently while she sipped the scalding tea and smoked with deep, nervous drags.

After a while the woman pulled out a notebook and said that it was question time. Her voice was weary, as if she knew that answers were going to be hard to come by and Georgia felt sorry for her. It must be a rotten job.

She said that she had no idea how she had come to be found naked in a Soho back alley, and no memory either as to where she had been earlier in the evening – nothing at all, in fact, except her name. As she spoke flashes of what had happened continued to come back to her: the club and Cosmo sitting angry and alone at the end of the table; dancing with Gallo; his warning. Oh God, if only she had listened to him. She kept silent, frightened that if she said anything else she would be involved in even more hateful scandal. Remembering how everyone had been so afraid of Malinski, she became terrified of what he might do to her if she mentioned his name.

The policewoman asked for her address. Georgia hesitated, uncertain as to what to say. She dreaded being returned to her Aunt in her present state. She could imagine the trauma that would take place if she arrived at her door escorted by a policeman and wearing only a mink coat that belonged to a stranger.

Lady Bacon was not going to be too happy either, at her return, but at least her reaction could not possibly be as bad as that of her Aunt. Reluctantly she gave the address and telephone number of La Circle. The policewoman looked at her in surprise. "One of those debs are you?" She sniffed and there was an immediate change in her attitude. "Well, you'll have no trouble then. Daddy will take care of everything, I have no doubt." She closed her book and went out of the room. Georgia would have liked to call after her, to have explained that it was not like that, but the moment had passed and she sat for what seemed a very long time before the door was opened again and another woman told her that there was someone waiting for her and she could go home.

Georgia was surprised to see Lady Pamela standing in the ante-room, amongst the drunks and prostitutes who seemed to be a permanent fixture. Lady Pamela looked out of place and horrified at her surroundings. She held a handkerchief to her nose and stood with her back erect, staring at the clock above the counter that ran down one side of the room.

Georgia had expected that whoever came for her would bring some fresh clothes, but Lady Pamela was empty-handed and was clearly shocked as she saw her approach.

"Where on earth are your clothes?" came her first question. Then the full meaning of Georgia's situation seemed to strike her. She blanched and made as if to put herself between Georgia and the rest of the world.

"Oh dear," she said. "You're going to catch cold if you walk about like that."

Lady Pamela had her car parked down the street and Georgia waited in the doorway while she went to fetch it. There was a glass panel in the wooden door and she could see that there were still one or two men who looked like reporters standing around outside. It was hard to believe that they were waiting for her and she had half convinced herself it was someone else they were after, when Lady Pamela honked her horn outside and she opened the door to cross the narrow pavement. As soon as she appeared, the men sprang forward and started shouting, all asking questions at the same time, so it would have been impossible for her to answer them even if she had wanted to. There were more of them than she had thought and they blocked the way to the car and she had to push through them. There was no sign of a policeman to help her. She was starting to see that being a deb was not the most popular of occupations.

Lady Pamela jerked away violently once she was safely inside. Georgia looked back, but there was no one who seemed to be following them. They drove in silence for a while, away from the West End and back towards the more genteel streets of Knightsbridge. Lady Pamela took a sharp right turn into Hyde Park and pulled up under a tree. She stopped the engine and turned to look at Georgia.

"I don't know what we are going to do," she said. "I promised your dear Aunt that nothing would happen to you and now look at the mess you have made. How could you, after all everyone has done for you? Letting them down like this is a very, very wicked thing and one day you will be sorry for all the unhappiness you have caused."

Georgia felt like getting out of the car. After all, she was the one who had been abused, not Lady Pamela or Eva. Then she remembered her lack of clothes and thought better of it. "There's no point in sitting here," she said. "We might as well go back to La Circle. I need a bath and some clothes."

"You just don't understand, do you?" Lady Pamela was shaking with frustration at her stupidity. "La Circle is out, the Season is out, and every decent person in society is out, for ever and ever. Lord knows what your Aunt is going to say."

"Why? Doesn't she know yet?" Georgia was starting to understand the reason for Lady Pamela's concern. "You mean that nobody has dared to tell her?" It would have been funny, but Lady Pamela was so clearly distressed that Georgia felt sorry for her: "I suppose I will have to go and tell her in the end. Don't worry, I'll make sure she knows that it's nothing to do with you. How can it be your fault? You had no idea what I was going to do — nor did I, if it comes to that."

Lady Pamela took her by the hand. "I know you are a good girl really and I'm sorry I was annoyed. You can come home with me and wait there while I collect your suitcases. Then we can work out how we are going to tell your Aunt."

Georgia said, "I'll come with you and pack my things." But Lady Pamela did not think that would be a very good idea.

It was lonely in the flat, nothing to look at but pictures of its owner: yachting at Cowes, curtsying at Ascot, and a picture of the old king with Lady Pamela in the background. Not much to show for a lifetime in society. She felt thankful that she at least was never going to be in the same situation. She couldn't now, even if she wanted to. It was a comforting thought.

It was after midday when Lady Pamela returned. She was nervous and would not allow Georgia to help her lift the cases from the car, telling her to stay inside, out of sight. Georgia gathered that there had been more trouble when she had reached La Circle. She was anxious to find out what had happened, but Lady Pamela did not want to talk about it. She went to the sideboard and poured herself a large glass of whisky and then, as an afterthought, another for Georgia. She offered it to her as if she were a fallen woman which, in a way, Georgia supposed she was.

It was a relief to have a bath and put on her own clothes. She chose a tweed skirt and a snuff-coloured twin-set and a soft, low-slung bra to go underneath. She put on her sensible lace-up shoes and a string of pearls around her neck. She combed out her hair and allowed it to hang down her shoulders, with a brown velvet headband to hold it in place. She removed the bright coral varnish from her nails. She was almost unrecognizable as the girl in the mink coat.

They were discussing Aunt Eva and how best to break the news when they were interrupted by the telephone. Lady Pamela jumped nervously and went to answer it. Georgia could tell it was her Aunt on the other end by the way Lady Pamela rolled her eyes and took a long gulp from her glass. It was a one-sided conversation and it was quickly over. Lady Pamela was white as she returned to the table. "It's in all the evening newspapers," she said. "Someone rang your Aunt and she is angry with me for not telling her, and she is absolutely right. I don't know what came over me. I was hoping that it would all blow over and you and I could make up some little story, but now I can see that I was a fool even to think of that for a moment." She was close to tears and Georgia put her arm round her shoulders. It was unfair that so many people were going to be upset by her misfortune, or stupidity, whichever way you cared to look at it.

It was a silent drive to Pont Street. There were no reporters on the pavement and nobody to help them with the two heavy suitcases which carried most of her worldly possessions. Druska opened the door. She looked scared and her eyes were red. Her face lit up when she saw Georgia and she ran forward, hugging her to her chest and rocking her as she had done when she was a child. "My poor little darling," was all she could say, time and time again, and Georgia hugged her back, feeling the love flow through her.

Druska wordlessly pointed to the door of the sitting room and Georgia nervously entered. Aunt Eva was sitting at one end of the sofa. There was an empty tumbler on the table beside her.

The two of them stood in the doorway. Georgia thought it was ridiculous, two grown English women standing in fear of such a tiny little foreigner as her Aunt. It was the first time she had thought of her Aunt as a foreigner. It made her uncomfortable. It seemed such a petty thing to do after all the care Eva had taken over her upbringing.

Eva looked hard at Lady Pamela. Her eyes were an unblinking, icy blue and her lips a thin, hard line against her white face.

"Why do you bother to say you are my friend," she said. "You take my lovely girl away from me, clean and beautiful and pure as the snow, and you bring her back like this?" She thrust the paper towards them. There was a blurred picture of a figure lying against a wall. It was naked from the waist down and an artist had filled in a little cloud at the join of the legs. Indistinct as it was, there was no mistaking Georgia's face against the light-coloured pavement.

Eva threw the paper onto the floor. "In the gutter. My girl is in the gutter because of criminals like you and that Lady Bacon with the big mouth for telling lies." She hissed the last sentence and then she exploded. "Get out of my house and never, never come back here." Lady Pamela was white-faced as she turned on her heel. They heard the front door close gently after her.

"It's not her fault." Georgia had blurted it out before she realized it. Eva stood up and walked to the table full of drinks. She turned and went back to her seat, beckoning Georgia to sit beside her. Georgia was surprised to see that she had poured a drink for her as well. Eva handed her the glass and raised her own. "To us both," she said, and took Georgia by the hand. "I don't want to know all the details, just that you're all right." She looked hard into her eyes. "You have made big trouble for yourself and it's going to get much worse before it's over. I've been sitting here thinking what is best. If you stay in England they are going to hound you and make up stories until you are branded forever as the girl in the mink coat and no one will ever forget. I cannot allow that. It will be the end of you. People will keep on telling you that you are bad, until in the end you will believe them and that will be that. I've rung an old friend in Nice. She runs a guesthouse there of some sort. She was a fool when she was young, but maybe thirty years have taught her a lesson. She's expecting you tomorrow and there's a flight booked for you, early, through Paris, so no one will know where you are going." She drew Georgia to her and kissed her on the top of her head. "You have made a bad start and I blame myself for letting you go away. Let's spend the evening together and tomorrow you will start again."

Georgia was weeping by the time she had finished. She fell asleep on the sofa, with her head resting on Eva's knee. She had never seen her Aunt like this before, but then she had never been in trouble either.

19

Milla had finally managed to install David Bramley in his new flat. It had not been easy. Once the first glow of conquest had died down, he had turned out to be a mean sort of a man, petty and spiteful in his dealings with those he thought below him. He had been quite content to use her own small two rooms as his base in London, always promising that next week he would talk to an estate agent and then finding excuses for why it had to wait.

One day she had come home to find that he had arrived ahead of her and there were two suits in her wardrobe and his socks and underwear in one of her drawers.

The sight of Bramley's clothing, dumped without asking amongst her belongings, served as a warning that she was in danger of allowing her status to slip from "light of my life" to "bit on the side" in the David Bramley game plan. It had made her very angry both at him and his boorish presumption, and at herself for allowing it to happen. It was still too early in their relationship for her to apply the full extent of the pressure that she planned eventually to use on him. She was starting to wonder if a career in shopkeeping was really what she wanted after all. There were other, far less degrading, ways of making your fortune.

It had been fortunate that she had caught the eye of William Piggot. He was considered to be on his way to the top of the management tree and although still one rung lower than Bramley he was far too senior for her lover to brush him aside.

Willie was several years younger than Bramley, a nice, well-educated man, with a flat of his own in South Kensington, and a Jaguar SS100 sports car with a drophead that made all the girls wriggle and give him arch looks as he came roaring past them on his way to work. He was just the sort of young man to make a normal girl delighted if he fell for her. At first Milla had ignored his advances — he had not quite yet reached the stage where he could influence her career — but she had taken care not to upset him; you could never tell what might happen a year or so later.

Piggot's attention had come at exactly the right time. He was such a well-known young man about town that the "no fraternizing with the staff rule" quite simply did not apply to him at his present level in the company. Milla took pains to have him collect her in the evenings right outside the staff entrance, and they would go roaring off down the street in his open-top sports car, the other girls fretting and fuming as they watched them go.

She knew that word of her new conquest would soon get back to Mr Bramley but, even better than that, on the third time Piggot collected her, she had seen Bramley watching them drive away. He was standing on the pavement with a red face and furious look in his eyes. It was an evening when she knew that he and his wife had to attend a dance at the local tennis club. She could imagine him sulking his way through the evening, perhaps even slipping away to ring her flat to see if she were home. It added spice to her own evening and she allowed Willie to kiss her after dinner, drive her to the car park overlooking the Serpentine, and push his hand halfway up her skirt before she stopped him. She felt sorry for him — the state he was in — but she had decided to play the virgin, and it was just his bad luck.

The telephone rang several times that night, the last time at two o'clock in the morning. She could imagine Bramley sneaking downstairs in his slippers while his frowsy wife tossed and turned and wondered what was happening. Surely she must suspect something by this time. Bramley seldom reached home before the early hours and his excuse of working late must have become threadbare during the three months that they had been lovers — although love was not the word she would use.

The next morning Bramley was hammering on her door at seven o'clock. He looked terrible, as if he had been up all night, and there was a nasty nick on his upper lip where the razor blade had slipped. Altogether a very satisfactory state of affairs.

136

He could not bring himself to ask her where she had been and she had no intention of telling him. He paced up and down the small sitting room, red-faced and glowering, while she prepared herself in the bathroom. She was tempted to make an appearance wearing only high heels and stockings, something that she knew would make him slobber, but she knew that now was the time to get certain things straight between them.

She was demurely dressed in the standard black shop assistant dress when she re-entered the room.

"This has got to stop," she said, "your coming here whenever you like, even when I am out. If I'm going to be your girlfriend, I expect to be treated like one, not just a piece of fluff for your convenience. I have a life of my own to lead and I'm going to enjoy myself, whether it's with you or someone else."

She poured him a brandy. It was early in the day, but by the look of him, he needed one. He was not used to women who spoke their minds and it took some time and another brandy to cushion the shock. Then he started pawing at her and calling her his darling, fumbling her hand against him and moaning that he couldn't live without her. It was an altogether disgusting exhibition and what was left of her respect for him quickly disappeared. But it showed her how to handle him, and she promised to see him that night.

He rang her at lunchtime. His voice was hoarse and he sounded as if he had been drinking. He asked her to meet him straightaway, at a pub near Notting Hill Gate. He said to take a taxi; he would pay for it. She could see that he had been drinking all right as soon as she arrived, but there was a look of triumph about him. As soon as he saw her, he dived into his pocket, produced a sheet of paper, and told her to read it. It had the name of an estate agent across the top and the details of a nearby flat, in one of the side streets off the Bayswater Road. She hardly bothered to look at the print. There was a price at the bottom of the page: £7,500 for a twenty-one-year lease. At least he was not trying to fob her off with some cheap rented place, and you could buy something really nice for that sort of money. So she smiled and said how marvellous, and later, as he proudly showed her round the empty rooms, she allowed him to lift her skirt as she leaned back against the kitchen sink. He heaved and grunted and thought himself one hell of a fellow, she had no doubt, but it was a step in the right direction. He had taken the day off and wanted her to spend the afternoon with him, but she said that it might look suspicious if they were both absent at the same time. Now that this stage of her plan was over, she could not wait to get away from him.

She had promised to return to the flat that evening. When she arrived he was asleep, flat on his back on the carpet, with a bottle of whisky, half drunk, beside him. She went out and bought some coffee and did her best to make him sober. It would be too bad if he did something stupid and lost his job before the rest of her plan was complete.

He was too drunk even to want to play around with her and she put him in his car and watched him drive away. He was going very slowly, wavering slightly from side to side, and she hoped he wouldn't hit anyone on the way home. Then she forgot about him and rang Willie from a phone box down the road. Anything to get rid of the taste of Bramley. She was starting to feel dirty every time she thought of him. She decided to give it another month and see what happened, but it was going to be a month that he would remember.

There was a group of salesgirls clustered around a newspaper in the canteen. They were tittering and nudging each other and one of them asked her what she thought of that, pushing the paper along the table towards her. The headline read: MINK COAT MYSTERY. DEB IN THE GUTTER. There was a photograph underneath.

She recognized Georgia at once: the profile of her upturned nose and blonde hair outlined against the pavement. Her long, naked legs were sprawled in an angle of abandon along the length of the gutter. Milla again felt the surge of jealousy that she thought she had outgrown. She had spent her childhood fuming against the injustice that had given her sister a look and bearing that made her instantly popular with whomever she met. Life was so easy for her, with people praising her for the slightest thing and making up excuses for her if she did wrong.

Milla looked hard at the picture. It was only too easy to imagine how her sister had managed to find herself passed out on the pavement. In her entire life no one had ever said no to her. Everything had come to her so easily, without any effort of her own except to stand there and look appealing and wait for good things to happen.

Milla thought of her own struggles, first with her Aunt and now the scheming and humiliation with Mr Bramley, the necessity of allowing him to use her and her body just to take the next miserable step forward.

"She's got the same name as you, miss." One of the girls was grinning at her and she shrugged and said, "So she has." She handed the paper back to its owner and finished her coffee, forcing herself to look relaxed and in control. After all, it had nothing to do with her.

As soon as it was lunchtime she went to a newsstand and bought a copy of all the daily papers. Georgia was front-page in most of them and Fleet Street had obviously given the story its full attention. There were quotes from a Lady Bacon, who said that she had never been so surprised in her life, and from Lady Pamela, who had stood up for Georgia and told the reporters to mind their own business. They had tried to talk to Aunt Eva, but she had been "unavailable for comment". Milla wondered why she was not feeling elated at the embarrassment that her stupid little sister had caused. Instead, she felt sad and sorry for her Aunt. However badly Eva had treated her, she did not deserve this public shame. She wished that she knew how her Aunt was reacting to the catastrophe. She had half a mind to ring her up, but that would look as if she were crawling, so she decided to do nothing for the moment. She thought of the Prince. She would ring him when the excitement had died down; maybe he would know what had happened.

Things had changed between Mr Bramley and herself since he had his new flat. She had taken care that he would not forget her friendship with Willie Piggot, going out of her way to flaunt it on every possible occasion. Bramley had changed as well, becoming more demanding of her, as though his purchase of the flat had put her in his debt. He had been annoyed at first and then insulted at her refusal to move in with him and had taken to calling round unexpectedly to her rooms in Fulham, hanging about in the pub on the corner if she was not at home. He was drinking too much as well and when she did allow him to touch her he was rough and selfish. Quite often he was unable to climax, which annoyed him even more and he would sulk for days, sending notes of complaint to her department manageress about minor details that he knew would cause Milla unnecessary work and perhaps a rebuke.

He was starting to turn his attention to Willie as well. Willie was finding himself increasingly criticized by Bramley, and blamed for minor mistakes that frequently had little to do with him. Bramley would send him unpleasant memos, with copies going to other directors of the company. Nothing too serious, and always written so that Willie had no real cause to make a formal objection, but they were starting to add up and Willie could feel a change coming over the way that he was being treated by his superiors. Bramley was a past master of the poison pen. Willie had no idea why he was being persecuted and Milla was too jealous of their friendship to tell him. She was terrified that he would despise her for her cold-blooded relationship with Bramley.

She was puzzled by the way things were going between them. Willie was the first man not to try to tear her clothes off at every opportunity. They spent most of their time in the cinema or in out-of-the-way pubs and little bistros, sometimes bumping into his friends, all of whom seemed to be young, interesting and creative, working hard to establish themselves, usually in businesses of their own. They were a new and unsuspected part of life to Milla and she found herself enjoying their company and starting to dread her encounters with Bramley and his stuffy, hidebound world.

Listening to them talk about their hopes and problems had given shape to Milla's plans. Before meeting them she had been concerned only with rising to the top of a world that she had hated since she was a small child. There was little difference between working in a department store, or any other large business suitable for a girl of her situation, and the life she had led under the domination of her Aunt. There were the same barriers of class and breeding; there were still the right sort of people and those whom it would be considered a betrayal of your social status to have as friends. Everything that you did, from your accent to the way you held your tea cup and ate a boiled egg, was prescribed and catalogued as evidence of your birth.

The world was divided into the upper class and the rest; the U and the Non-U, according to the best-selling book that was read with apprehension by a very much larger part of the population than would ever admit to it. They studied its instructions and agonised over such niceties as when to pour the milk into your tea and the exact placing of the cutlery on a plate.

It had been a terrible life with Aunt Eva, made worse by the fact that as a foreigner she did not have an inherent grasp of the fundamentals of polite behaviour, as would someone who had been brought up within the system from birth. As a result Eva was not only fanatical in her observance of these funadmentals, but frequently incorrect in her application.

Milla had grown up to hate the class to which she had been born and to which she felt doomed to belong for the rest of her life. Until she had met Willie and his friends, she had known of no alternative world to which she could escape, and she had no other thought than to rise to the top of whatever tree she could find and place herself forever beyond the pettiness of her Aunt and everyone like her.

Her new acquaintances were from every class and background that could be found, drawn by the common bond of creative thinking

140

and a desire to make their lives around it. She had been shocked at first when Willie had introduced East Enders and people from provinces like Liverpool and Manchester as his friends. They had greeted her in their different accents and even laughed at her own, mockingly doffing their caps and calling her Lady Milla when they thought she wasn't listening. They were suspicious of her as well, she could sense that, waiting for her to put them down and watching carefully for her reaction to their ideas. She had soon learned to keep silent and listen. It was no hardship; she knew that she had so much to learn.

The more Willie and his friends became a part of her life, the harder it was for her to face up to Bramley and the demands that he was increasingly making on her. He must have bought a dirty book from somewhere because his lovemaking was starting to abandon any pretence of affection and he was forever devising new and humiliating things that he insisted on doing to her.

Willie was feeling the pressure as well. Bramley was now waging a thinly disguised hate campaign against him. Some evenings he would be really depressed and spill out his problems to her, still puzzled as to why he was being picked upon. The more it went on, the harder it became for Milla to confess the truth. She agonised over what she should do, knowing that she was betraying her friend, but unable to find a way out that would keep their friendship intact.

She knew that she must finish with Bramley, once and for all, but now it must be in such a way that he could no longer take his anger out on Willie — perhaps even causing him to be sacked and in a way that would make it impossible for Willie to find other work. It was easy, at Bramley's level, to start rumours of dishonesty which would ruin Willie for the rest of his life.

20

It was Bramley's own demands which gave Milla the opportunity she had been waiting for. She had arrived, reluctantly, at his apartment one evening, a week or so after her first meeting with Willie's friends. Bramley had been lying on the bed when she entered. He was wearing a new dressing gown of printed silk and from the look of him he had been waiting impatiently for her arrival.

There was a gift-wrapped box on the bed and he handed it to her as soon as she came in to the room. Inside was some sort of leather harness and a black silk blindfold. There was a pair of handcuffs, shiny and evil, at the bottom of the box. She could imagine what horrible things he was planning to do to her.

She slowly put the revolting things back in the box. Bramley was looking at her strangely from the bed. She wondered what pornographic book he had been reading to give him this idea. He had little imagination himself. Be careful how you handle this, she thought; you mustn't lose him now, after all that he has done to you. But the idea of submitting to him and the filth that would follow was more than she could face.

"It's too much, jumping at me with all these things you want me to do," she said. "I need time to think about them. I can't just arrive here, not knowing what's waiting for me and you expecting me to be in the mood right away. We're going to have a new rule here.

You write to me first, before you want me to do something as far-fetched as this. Then we are both going to know what's happening. It will be more exciting that way." As soon as she said it, she realized what it would mean if Bramley agreed, but surely even he would not be so stupid as to put in writing all the dirty things that he wanted to do to her.

Bramley thought it was a marvellous idea. He put away the box and its contents and immediately went to his briefcase, anxious to get on with the evening's entertainment. It's not going to be that easy, my foul-minded friend, she thought. She went to the front door. "You can put it through my letter box, later on." She was out of the door and running down the stairs before he could attempt to stop her.

The next day was a Sunday, a day that Bramley always spent at home in Kingston, no doubt playing the family man and showing off to his neighbours. Milla wondered if he had any friends to whom he could boast of his little bit of crackling up in London. If not, he had better hurry up and find some while he still had the chance.

She was in a grim mood by the time she reached home. There was a letter from Bramley stuffed through the front door. She took it upstairs and made herself a cup of coffee before she opened it.

As an exercise in obscenity it wasn't up to much, full of dirty words and crudely expressed ideas with a couple of child-like drawings thrown in to make the point. The most important part was the signature, which was written, clear and bold, across the bottom with the flourish that Bramley had developed since his promotion. She breathed a deep sigh at the sight of it. Her days as a sex toy were over. She sat for a long time, staring at the letter while she worked out how best to use it.

In the following few hours she cleared out her flat, throwing away anything that she did not absolutely need, and packing her things into a suitcase. There was not much to do. She had very few possessions and the case closed easily over everything she owned. She had only just paid a week's rent and she left a note for the landlord, explaining that she had been forced to leave in a hurry and would not be back. She took a bus going north and booked into a cheap hotel in the area around Paddington station. She told the clerk that she would be staying for about a week.

It was evening by the time she was settled, about the same time that Bramley would be taking his dog for a walk and ringing her from a telephone box, somewhere well away from his house. She wondered why his wife had still not suspected that her husband had another lady, but perhaps she already did and no longer cared. Maybe he had tried the handcuffs and blindfold trick on her first, in which case she was probably looking for a lawyer to handle her divorce. If she thought she was going to get Milla in court as co-respondent, she had missed her chance.

She rang Willie. He had been trying the number of her flat, off and on, for the last few hours and was relieved to hear from her. He said that her line had been engaged twice when he had tried it. Bramley must be working himself up into a sweat.

Willie's call gave her another idea. It would be better to keep her dealings with Bramley at as long a range as possible. She went back to her flat and sat in the emptied room, waiting for him to call. It was after nine o'clock, a late hour for the residents of sleepy Kingston, but she had no doubt that his lust would find a way. He might even think he was going to give her a quick handcuffing and a bit of sado on his way to work in the morning – have himself a flying start to the day.

It was half an hour before he rang. From the noise behind him, he was in the local pub, perhaps bragging to his friends about the little girl waiting to do his bidding. In a way, she hoped that was the case; it would make the shock of what he was about to hear just that much harder for him to take.

"I've been ringing you all evening," he said. "I expect you to be waiting in the future."

"Oh yes!" she said. "Why would I do that?"

He was slightly taken aback, but he must have decided to ignore her tone. "I'm going to pass by early tomorrow, about seven o'clock. I'd like you to wear those things I bought for you last week." He must have meant the stockings, suspenders and six-inch stilettos. She had thrown them into the dustbin earlier in the day.

"I am afraid I have some bad news," said Milla. "Someone else has seen your letter, in fact he has taken it away and put it in a safe place. He doesn't seem to like you very much, this person, and he is going to start showing it around if I can't get him to give it back."

There was a silence at the other end. His voice was higher when he spoke, disbelieving and frightened and, above all, shocked.

"This person," she continued, "is going to want £20,000 before he gives the letter back, and he is going to want it next week." She wondered how he was going to find twenty thousand in a hurry. She hoped she had not asked for too much, but twenty thousand was what she was going to need, and how he came by it was Bramley's worry and nothing to do with her.

"We've got to talk." Bramley was almost whining now, as he

started to realize the depth of his problem. He was going to have a rotten night. Milla smiled at the thought.

"I'll ring you tomorrow afternoon in your office," she said. "Let's say three o'clock. You'd better have something very definite to tell me. The man who has your letter has taken a dislike to you, for some reason I can't understand, and I might have trouble getting him to accept any money at all if he has to wait too long. He really is a very nasty man and it's a great pity he got hold of the letter in the first place, don't you agree?"

"You blackmailing little bitch," said Bramley. He was going to go on, but Milla interrupted.

"I'm in as much trouble as you are. Why on earth did you put my name on your filthy bit of paper? The man says he'll show it to my Aunt if I don't go to bed with him, so we're both in the same boat and it's up to you to get us out of it."

She put down the telephone. It was ringing again as she quietly closed the door and went towards the stairs.

The next morning she rang in and said she was sick. Then she rang Willie, telling him the same thing, but saying she would be better by the evening and arranging to meet him. She spent the rest of the day with a pencil and paper, doing calculations involving £20,000. It was amazing what you could do with a bit of capital.

At three o'clock she called Bramley. She was put through to his secretary, who said that Mr Bramley was out for the afternoon. She went in search of a photostat machine and at last found one at the Great Western Hotel, beside Paddington station. She was worried that the clerk would take a peep at the contents of the letter but he was in a hurry for his tea break and made her six copies without even glancing down. She went to a Post Office from where she mailed it to his wife. There would be some fun over the breakfast table, if Bramley spent the night at home.

There was nothing more she could do for the moment. She imagined Bramley would be waiting for her at the flat she had abandoned. With any luck, he would run into the landlord and have a problem explaining his presence. He had been very stupid not to be there for her call. She supposed he thought that it would all go away, but the drawing she had posted to his wife should make him think twice. She thought of trying him at his flat in Bayswater, but decided to wait for the post to do its work. There was plenty of time.

Willie was nervous when they met. He had already had a large whisky by the time she arrived and he quickly had another one, and then another, as they talked. She had asked him what the matter was as soon as she had sat down, but he said it was nothing and changed the subject. She let it go for a while, talking about nothing very much, waiting for him to calm down before she started to tell him her big idea, but the drink only seemed to make him more agitated and she became annoyed.

"I don't know what's the matter with you. If you'd rather be with someone else, for God's sake go; if not, I'm going. I can't stand you being a martyr." She stood up, but he held her by the arm and said he was sorry. Bramley had been after him all day, sending his memos and almost accusing him of negligence over a little mistake that an office junior had made, so small that it made next to no difference. "He's been after me for weeks, as you know, but today he changed gear. I've seen it before, when he wants to get rid of someone. It's sickening to watch, even when it isn't aimed at you."

Milla decided that now was the wrong time to tell him her idea. She just said that she was going to leave her job quite soon, as she had an idea that was going to take off. Willie didn't pay much attention to her. He was much too tied up with his own problems. He only laughed, saying, "Have you come into money?" before he started to go on about Bramley and what a shit he was – until she had heard enough and said she'd see him tomorrow.

She went back to work the next morning. She arrived a few minutes after the others, not wanting to be alone. It was as well that she did. Bramley walked across the salesfloor as soon as she arrived. He did not see her for a moment. He was looking angrily about him, his face flushed. As soon as he saw her he came straight towards her. "I need to see you," he said, grabbing her by the elbow and forcing her towards an exit that was seldom used.

Once in the corridor outside, he spun her round to face him. "How dare you involve my family in your filthy game?" He was almost snarling in his anger, shaking her so that her head snapped from side to side. "I want that letter back, now." He seized her handbag and turned it upside down on the floor. Although they were in a seldom-used part of the building, he was taking a tremendous risk of being caught with her in such a situation. He still thought that he was going to be able to bully her into giving in and admitting that it was she alone who was the blackmailer.

"Maybe you'll feel differently when you read the paper tomorrow morning," she said. "I warned you that my friend had a very short temper when it comes to people like you." She tore herself away from him and stuffed her possessions back into her bag. He was

146

staring after her as she went back on to the salesfloor. She wondered what she was going to do next.

It came to her during her coffee break. She rang the Prince who, fortunately, was at home. She arranged to meet him at lunchtime, at Green Park tube station.

21

Milla wished she hadn't made that stupid threat about the newspaper. The last thing she wanted was for the whole thing to become common knowledge, with Bramley losing his job and blaming her in public, ruining her scheme before it had even started. But she could see that she would have to think of another approach if Bramley was to take her seriously, or else they could go on forever like this – with her threatening and Bramley trying to bully her and nobody getting anywhere at all.

The Prince had been an obvious choice as an accomplice; he would not be too surprised at the moral depths to which she was prepared to sink in her quest for capital, which would save her from all the shock, disbelief and probable rejection she might face if she were to approach someone else, Willie for example. Another plus was he did not know that she had long ago destroyed the incriminating letter she had forced him to sign, scared that her Aunt might discover it amongst her belongings.

The Prince looked even seedier than when she had last seen him. He was wearing a dark blue, pinstripe suit that was shiny at the elbows; the turn-ups of his trousers were worn and she could see where he had snipped away the loose ends. His face was thinner, almost gaunt, and she could smell the alcohol as he bent to kiss her hand. In bright daylight he could be taken for a tramp, which was all to the good, Milla thought, as they passed the entrance to the Ritz. The Prince looked hopeful as they passed the colonnaded front of the grand hotel, but Milla quickly put herself between him and the entrance and nudged against him as he veered towards the revolving doors. The doorman looked relieved as they passed.

There was a pub round the corner and the Prince fitted in well with the raucous crowd of salesmen and office girls giggling and pushing along the length of the polished bar. She found them a table in a corner and the Prince sat down at once and said that he would like a large brandy, please. Milla thought she might as well buy the same for herself; it had been a tiring day.

As she had thought, the Prince did not appear either surprised or horrified at the idea of a little blackmail. In fact he was grateful that she had included him in her plans. Not that she told him all the details – there were some things that she would rather he didn't know – but she had to mention the handcuffs and the letter and a few other things as well and it wasn't too difficult for him to fill in the rest. She was surprised what an expert he appeared to be on the subject, asking her detailed questions and becoming quite animated as the second glass of brandy did its work. Then she decided that he was spinning the whole thing out in the hope of a third and she had better put a stop to it while he was still capable of speech.

There was a telephone box back by the tube station. Milla told the Prince to turn his back while she dialled first the number of Bramley's flat and then, getting no answer, his home in Kingston. If the Prince knew how to contact Bramley, he might have some bright ideas of his own, like going freelance on her and ringing Bramley at all hours, demanding the price of a drink or a hot meal and spoiling everything in the process.

There was an answer from Kingston. She listened, making sure that it was Bramley on the line, and then gave the instrument to the Prince. He grasped it the wrong way round and there was a moment's confusion before he could start as she had instructed. He was quite good, once he was under way, although his accent was almost unintelligible as he tried to disguise his voice.

"Mr Bramley, Miss Milla has been very silly," he said. "She has left your filthy letter in a place that is not very safe and somebody has picked it up, which is unfortunate for you both."

He turned his head, anxious for her applause, and she gave him a nudge in the small of his back, to make him pay attention. She held her ear close to the telephone, trying to hear Bramley's reply, but she could only pick up an angry buzzing from the other end.

"There's no need to be rude," said the Prince. "It will only make me ask you for more money for your little note. At this moment the price is £20,000, that is if I am paid by tomorrow evening. If not, it will go up by £200 each hour — which will be very expensive — so I think you will pay quick, no?'

There was another angry splutter from the telephone and the Prince said, "You should think about all that before you do dirty things to such a nice young girl. I will ring you again at high noon tomorrow to tell you what you are going to do next." He put down the phone with a look of triumph and nodded confidently at her. "Okay," he said. "All is well. I told him where he gets off and tomorrow I will collect. You tell me the number and I'll take care of everything; then we go and have some champagne."

It annoyed Milla that he thought she was an idiot, giving him Bramley on a plate whilst she sat at home, waiting for the money to be dropped through the letter box. She stared hard at the Prince and the forced smile of good fellowship slowly faded from his face. He shrugged, and for a moment she thought that he was going to turn nasty and start to make a fuss, but instead he asked if she could let him have five pounds in advance; he had come out without his wallet. She gave him thirty shillings, telling him to meet her in the tube station at Knightsbridge at eleven-thirty the next morning. It was stuffy, nose to nose with him in the phone box, and she was glad to get out into the evening air.

She took a bus back to her hotel and changed into a skirt and blouse. She rang Willie, who was home, and told him that she had moved from her flat to temporary digs without a phone. She didn't want anyone to know where she could be found until the money was in a safe place. Even then she would have to be careful. Bramley would never forget what she was doing to him, his punctured pride would see to that, and given a chance he would try for his own back at the earliest opportunity.

Willie asked her out for a meal, but she said she was tired and that she would see him tomorrow. She needed to concentrate on the day ahead.

There was no sign of Bramley the next morning and she had no excuse to visit the executive floor to check if he was at work. She went to lunch early, at eleven o'clock. There was a crowd of shopgirls waiting to pass the guard on the way out. It was lucky she had a few minutes in hand; it looked as though the store was having one of its periodic security checks. She could see the girls in front of her opening their handbags and a manageress whom she didn't know rummaging half-heartedly through their belongings. As she moved closer she was shocked to see Bramley standing half-hidden by an open doorway, just behind the manageress. His eyes were fixed on hers and he gave a vicious little smile as he caught her glance.

These snap searches usually happened once or twice a month and were treated casually by both management and staff. It was true that occasionally some particularly stupid or careless person was caught carrying home goods that did not belong to them, but there were so many safer ways that stolen merchandise or money could be spirited out of the store that the whole exercise was regarded as a waste of time and the girls normally submitted good-naturedly to the inconvenience.

Today's search seemed to be even more lackadaisical than most. So, despite Bramley's presence and the look on his face when he caught sight of her, Milla was shocked when the woman in charge seized her by the arm and pulled her from the crowd, forcing her through the doorway where Bramley had been standing and pushing her up against the wall. There was another woman from the person-nel department standing inside the room and both women started to turn out her bag on to a table.

Bramley was standing a few yards away. He looked sick when they found nothing that was suspicious and made a gesture with his hand. The two women ushered her into a small alcove and told her to take off her clothes. Milla thought of refusing or at least putting up a struggle. Then she thought of Bramley's sneering face and of the Prince, who would be arriving at the tube station in a few minutes and whom she could not depend upon to wait for long. It was obvious that Bramley had set the whole thing up, probably accusing her of some crime and hoping that the search would turn up the incriminating letter, which he would no doubt have grabbed before anyone else had a chance to read it. It was a desperate move on his part; he must have finally realized the seriousness of his problem.

She stepped out of her dress and before they could stop her, she slipped off her underwear and stood stark naked for a second before she stepped out into the main room and twirled around, her breasts thrust out in front of her. Bramley's mouth gaped at her in surprise and the two women rushed out, clucking at her behaviour and telling her to cover herself up. Milla pretended to see Bramley for the first time. She gave an innocent little shriek and ran behind one of the women and dug her fingers into her shoulders, keeping her between herself and Bramley. The woman screeched in pain and Milla started to scream as well, pointing at Bramley, asking who the dirty old man was, how dare they let him peep at her. Then she burst out crying and said that she would tell her boyfriend, who was a judo black belt and didn't like men looking at her even when she had all her clothes on.

Bramley stepped forward in a fury, but the two women started screaming at him as well and one of them screamed very loud indeed, as Milla's hands were twisting at the flesh on her shoulders. Bramley swung on his heel and tried to retain his dignity as he walked to the door, but it was a pathetic attempt. The women were very upset and told her to put on her clothes. One of them lent her a handkerchief and the other was wriggling her shoulders and moaning how much they hurt.

It was all over in ten minutes and Milla was hardly late at all when she met the Prince. She had written out everything he should say on a piece of paper and she made him go over it several times before she dialled the number of the direct line to Bramley's desk. The Prince's breath had not improved overnight, but he was wearing a much smarter suit, charcoal grey with a thin, light-grey stripe. It was no longer an embarrassment to be seen with him in the street.

Bramley answered and she handed him the receiver, taking care that it was the right way up. The Prince said, "Well, is the money ready?" and she could hear Bramley's voice in reply. The Prince looked very pleased at what he was hearing and kept on saying "yes" and "excellent", nodding at her the whole time as if everything was going as they had planned. Then he said, "See you tonight, Mr Bramley, six-thirty at the Green Man, and you'll have a white flower in your button hole." He beamed at Milla as they left the telephone box. "Everything in order. I'm meeting him tonight."

Milla had listened helplessly to the end of his conversation with Bramley. If she had not been trying to convince Bramley that she had nothing to do with the affair and the Prince was blackmailing them both, she would have snatched the telephone or at least given the Prince a kick on the ankle to make him tell her what was going on. Now it was too late.

"Everything's most certainly not all right," she said. "I told you to meet him in the park, so that I could keep an eye on you, make sure there were no tricks." She didn't add that she was as worried by what the Prince might do with £20,000 in his hands as by any last-minute stunt that Bramley might think up, even though she had offered the Prince ten per cent of the money. Two thousand pounds could buy a lot of brandy, but you could never tell with Princes, or so Machiavelli had written and she had read his book several times.

The Prince was hurt. A public house was the most natural place in the world in which to conduct business and the Green Man was an establishment well known to the sort of people with whom he was no doubt accustomed to mixing. Milla had never been there herself; it was not that kind of place.

She was uneasy the whole afternoon. Bramley's attitude that morning had been foolhardy in its defiance; it was too abrupt a change for him now to be agreeing to everything that they had demanded, only ten minutes after he had arranged for her to be searched. But that was why she had involved the Prince in the first place, to make sure that whatever Bramley might attempt, she would not be involved. For all she knew, he might be desperate enough to go to the police, in which case, anybody showing up that evening would find themselves in jail. She still thought it was unlikely that Bramley would be fool enough to do that, not now that he knew there was more than one person involved; but the Prince would not suffer in silence if he were caught and she suddenly felt certain that it had all gone wrong. She left the sales area and went to a public telephone on another floor, but there was no answer from the Prince, although she tried him several times during the course of the afternoon.

She could not leave the store until six o'clock, when she took a taxi to Belgrave Square. The Green Man was in a mews close by, but by the time she arrived it was already six-twenty and she was frightened of entering the place in case the police were watching it. She had given the Prince the original copy of the letter to exchange for the money, but Bramley would know from the drawing she had sent to his wife that she had taken at least one copy. It was impossible that he would be so stupid as to hand over £20,000 to a stranger, and then hope for the best. She was in a panic now, but there was nothing that she could do. There was a bench at the corner of the mews and she sat down to see what would happen.

She didn't have long to wait. There was no sign of the Prince, although several men passed her on the way to the pub. One of them asked her if she was waiting for someone, but she ignored him and he went away. She assumed that the Prince had arrived early, probably at opening time, which would have given him an hour of drinking before Bramley arrived. She hoped he would remember why he was there.

Two men passed her at six-thirty-five. There was something about them that was different from the others she had seen. They were big and purposeful in their walk. They had broad shoulders beneath their dark suits and as they turned the corner she saw that one of them had a white flower in his button hole. She knew at once what was going to happen.

She sat, frozen in her seat, as the man with the flower came out of the door and she saw the Prince behind him. He was clutching a large leather attaché case to his chest. The second man followed him and they took hold of the Prince, one on either arm, and pulled him to the far end of the mews. She strained to see through the gloom but they had disappeared into the darkness. There was silence, and then the clatter of a dustbin lid. The two men suddenly came walking quickly past the light from the bar window. One was straightening his tie and the other had the briefcase under his arm. She shrank back as far as she could, frightened to move, and they went by, not ten yards from her. One of them was laughing.

She waited while she counted to a hundred and then walked after them. She had some notion of seeing where they went, but there was a car waiting for them. She heard the doors slam before it drove away and was lost in the traffic in the square. She walked to Hyde Park corner and dialled 999 from the telephone outside the hospital. It was the least she could do for the Prince, but it was hard to feel sorry for him. It had been his own fault.

22

There was still an hour before she had to meet Willie in a coffee bar in Notting Hill Gate that was popular with his creative friends. She walked up Park Lane and started down the Bayswater Road, hardly conscious of what she was doing. She was feeling the same unbearable sense of claustrophobia that she had felt during her years with her Aunt, and that had finally caused her to cut herself off from her family.

Bramley, in the way he had treated her when they were lovers, never considering how she might feel, always assuming that he knew best, ignoring her except when she was needed to gratify his ego, had behaved to her, in his way, in almost exactly the same manner as her Aunt. All either of them wanted from her was that she be there — willing and submissive, waiting like a lap dog — for their next command.

Even under the threat of certain ruin, Bramley was refusing to take her seriously, treating her as though she were having a fit of childish tantrums and riding roughshod over her, having her stripped and searched and then sending bruisers to beat people up.

There had been moments in the last few days when she had wondered whether she was right. Perhaps blackmail was going too far, even if it was her only chance to get away from the stifling world of the Establishment and do something on her own; create a world for herself where she and she alone was in control. As she walked, she felt a huge sense of relief. Bramley and his mean bullying reaction had driven away forever any guilt that she might have felt. She was still furious as she approached the coffee bar, but now it was a cleansing rage that concentrated her thoughts and determination towards the one goal. Her independence was more important than anything else, no matter how much damage she caused on the way.

She was still early and Willie had not arrived. A boy and a girl were sitting at one of the grey, formica-topped tables. She had met them briefly before. The boy was called Fizzy and had recently left the Royal College of Art, where he had studied Fashion Design, and the girl, Wanda, was a textile designer. Everybody said that they were very good and would go a long way. She asked if she could join them until Willie arrived and Fizzy waved her to a chair. "You work in a department store," he said. "Perhaps you can tell us what we need to get the buyers to take us seriously?" She could see that he was only half joking.

"Why, what's the problem?" she asked.

"It's the same old problem that everyone else has, if they don't want to become a commercial hack: designing frocks for mail order, two sleeves and two darts and the hem three inches below the knee or else it won't sell, or so everyone says. It's hopeless trying to be different, unless you work in Paris and even then you need lots of money, which means rich partners. That's okay if they leave you alone, which they do out there because they respect design, but here they think they own you, so it never works out."

Wanda nodded and said, "That's why this country is so hopeless when it comes to fashion, or anything else creative for that matter. Design is just a dirty word here."

Milla was glad to think about a subject that did not involve Bramley and what she had to do the next day. She thought that she might learn something useful from Fizzy and his friend. They seemed to be as anti-the-Establishment as herself, although for very different reasons. "I'd love to see your work," she said. "Perhaps I'll be able to talk to one of the buyers at the store. You never know what might happen."

Willie arrived at that moment and Fizzy and Wanda were eager to take them both back to their home. They seemed delighted to have an audience and came on heavily to Willie when they realized that he was senior to Milla. Willie listened politely but she could see that he was none too pleased to have his plans for the evening interrupted.

The two designers lived in three small rooms in a narrow street

156

parallel to the Portobello Road. The streetlamps were far apart and several of them had been broken, so it was dark and slightly spooky as they got out of Willie's car. Milla was still shaken by the violence in Belgrave Square and was starting to wish that they had not come to this gloomy neighbourhood. She was surprised that anyone would choose to live there. It was a place to be avoided, with tales of black men and beatings and people being robbed in the street; even the police kept away, patrolling occasionally in groups of two or three and keeping to the wider streets whenever they could.

There was an off-licence on the corner and Fizzy suggested that they bought something to drink. He pulled a half-crown from his pocket and said he was broke, but Wanda said that he had more money than she did, so Willie had to pay. It didn't stop Fizzy asking for whisky and, as Wanda said she only drank Drambuie, it cost Willie almost a pound by the time they were finished, but he was too nice to object.

There were two black men on the street corner as they crossed the road to Fizzy's front door. It was the first time that Milla had seen a black man close up and she looked curiously at them, taking care that Willie was between her and them. They appeared harmless enough, but Wanda and Fizzy had grown quiet and they all hurried through the front door and up the narrow stairs to the flat.

Milla was surprised to see that they slept in separate rooms. She had assumed that they would be living in sin, which was becoming a popular thing to do, although she would never dream of it for herself. She could see no point in tying herself to one man. Which reminded her of Bramley, so she had a drink of whisky and did her best to put him out of her mind.

The flat was full of bits of fabric and the walls were covered with drawings of textile designs. Fizzy kept his own drawings in his room, which was locked. Creating a big fuss about opening the door, he made them promise that they would tell no one about what they were about to see. It was an anticlimax when he did let them in. There was not very much, after all the build-up, just a few drawings on the wall and a portfolio on the bed with several dozen more.

Fizzy poured himself a glassful of whisky and settled down to talk. It was soon clear that he was prepared to go on all night, discussing himself and his ideas, cursing all the people who had rejected them, while Milla and Willie sat, nodding agreement and Wanda chimed in every now and then, saying what a genius Fizzy was and how she had designed her prints just for him.

After about an hour, Fizzy was becoming drunk, making wild

157

statements and saying how people were going to be sorry about the way they had treated him. It was a relief when Willie looked at his watch and said it was getting late. It still took over half an hour before they could finally leave. Fizzy had finished the whisky by that time and was starting on the Drambuie. He appeared to be insulted when they said they had to go, and they could hear him calling them toffee-nosed bastards as they went down the stairs.

They were silent as they drove away. It was nearly midnight and Willie said he knew a place down the Earl's Court Road that would still be open. As they drove, Milla thought about Fizzy and his problem. He was the first designer she had ever met. "Are they all like that?" she asked.

Willie thought for a moment. "More or less," he said. "They don't all drink quite as much, but most of them think that the world owes them a living. It's the fault of the colleges really, filling them up with ideas so that when they leave and find it's not like that at all, they're disappointed and start hating everybody. Fizzy is a fairly typical case. He'll probably wind up driving a bus in another couple of years."

Milla knew that she should feel sorry for Fizzy and all the others like him. Wait till I get hold of the money, she thought; there must be thousands of Fizzys in London. I'll find some who aren't as stupid as he is, and then we'll see what happens. Then she thought, why put up with all the bother, soothing yet more egos for the rest of her life? She might as well do it herself. It must be easy enough, if idiots like Fizzy and Wanda were meant to be so marvellous. She still didn't know how she would do it, but she was sure that she would think of something. But first she had to deal with Bramley. She found herself looking forward to the next day.

She woke up early and had a coffee at a working man's café down the street. She ran over her plan time and again, working out all the dozens of things that could be wrong. It was very risky, but she had to bring Bramley begging to his knees, hit him hard and finish him off before he had a chance to recover.

She arrived at the store at the usual time and went about her work, careful to do nothing that would seem unusual or might draw attention to herself. It was the timing that would be critical if she were going to succeed.

The way the staff breaks worked, there was always somebody out of the department; sometimes at least half of them were away. There were coffee and lunch breaks in the morning and a tea break in the afternoon, so there was a constant coming and going in the staff areas, particularly at lunchtime when everybody wanted to spend time out of the building, if only to take a walk in the fresh air.

Milla took her morning break late, so that it was almost time for the first shift to go to lunch. There was a brief hiatus of about five minutes before the lunchtime rush started. The staff canteen was on the top floor, reached by a lift reserved for staff use. Beyond the lift there was a stone staircase, running the full height of the building; it was the main fire escape and seldom used. There were notice boards in both the lift and the canteen, and another, the one most looked at, on the ground floor beside the staff exit.

Milla lingered until the canteen was empty. She took a copy of the letter from her shoulderbag and pinned it to the notice board, right in the middle, where no one could miss it. She had cut out her name from the top and Bramley's from the bottom but apart from that, there it was in all its obscenity.

She walked briskly to the lift and pressed the button. She had given herself thirty seconds for it to arrive. Any later and she would leave it and take the stairs. She was lucky, it came at once, and she pressed the button for the next floor. As the doors closed she whipped another letter from her bag and fixed it to the lift notice board. There was no one waiting as the door opened and she dashed out and down the staircase to the ground floor. She paused to catch her breath at the last landing and peeped cautiously round the corner. Three girls came out of the staffroom and walked towards the exit. They said something to the guard and he went with them, out on to the street. She walked down the remaining few steps and it was done. She darted back to the stairs and walked up to the second floor, where she was working. Nobody noticed her as she slipped into the stockroom. There were over a thousand girls working in the store, and she guessed that nearly half of them would see the letter during the next ten minutes. It was going to be an interesting afternoon.

It took about five minutes for news of the letter to reach the salesfloor. She saw two of the girls whispering in a corner and soon they were joined by a third. She wandered casually over in their direction. One of them looked up and saw her. Pink-faced and embarrassed, she blurted out, "Did you see it, miss?"

"See what?" Milla hoped that she was looking innocent, though it was hard with her heart pounding at the storm that she had unleashed.

"The dirty letter, miss." The girl giggled and looked away, but one of the others broke in. "He wanted to tie her up and whip her and then he wanted —" but her companion gave her a push and told

159

her to shut up. Both of them were red in the face and bursting to tell their friends, yet obviously shocked and unsettled at the idea of these filthy goings-on, particularly in such refined surroundings.

By the time Milla went for her tea, the whole canteen was buzzing with speculation. Everyone seemed to know for certain whose names had been cut from the letter, and the whole place was screaming with laughter as people made up names and pairings.

A far as she could tell, the letters had been removed almost at once, but their contents had been passed on and embroidered upon until they were already part of a legend.

There was another search on the way home that night. Once again, Bramley was standing in the background and the same manageress was opening the bags. Bramley was pale and tight-faced. He stepped forward as soon as he saw her and asked if he could have a word. He did it quite well, she had to admit, stopping her in front of a hundred others, out in the open so that no one could possibly suspect. Even if they did, with the amount of rumour flying round no one was going to take it seriously.

They walked outside on to the street. She felt calm, now that the moment had come. "That's far enough," she said, as they reached the corner that led to the car park. The street beyond was quiet and badly lit and she had no intention of taking a chance on his good behaviour.

He was quivering with fury as he turned to face her. He put his hand into his breast pocket and pulled out a thick brown envelope. "It's all there, you little bitch. Twenty thousand. You have ruined me and my family and I've half a mind to kill you. If I ever hear from you again, I promise you I will."

Milla put the money into her bag. She laughed and said, "It would be an awful waste of money if you did. I've already thought of that, after what happened to that stupid old man last night. If anything should ever happen to me — even if you have nothing to do with it — the newspapers are going to have the letter, only with the names still on it this time. You had better pray that I don't have any accidents. It might even be worth your while to get me a bodyguard, to make sure that I'm all right."

She thought he was going to hit her, but he turned on his heel and walked away.

She gave in her notice at the end of the week and found herself a smart flat in Prince's Gate. If she was going to be a businesswoman, she had better look the part.

Willie couldn't believe it when he heard that she was leaving. He

160

was more upset than she had thought possible. He took her out for lunch and asked her what she was going to do; she told him that she had been left some money and needed time to think. He had never even tried to kiss her since she had rejected his first advances, but now he asked her to go for a walk in the park with him. There was something on his mind.

It was nice in the park. The leaves were starting to fall and the air was clean, with the slight tang of a bonfire to underline the approach of autumn. They walked by the Round Pond and Willie held her hand. He told her that he loved her and that he wanted her to be his wife. She was terrified that he would go on his knees in front of everyone, so she quickened her pace and he walked beside her, his eyes on her face. She wondered why he had to spoil everything. After Bramley, the thought of being handled by any man, even one so gentle and loving as Willie, made her cringe inside.

She said no to him, as kindly as she could, telling him that there was no one else and that she hoped he would always be her friend. His face was white as they walked back to the car. She said goodbye and kissed him on the cheek. She felt desperate and lonely as he drove away.

23

Jack died on New Year's Eve, 1944. Eva was beside him at the end. She had been with him for every moment of the three weeks he had spent in hospital since the tumour had started to eat away his brain. He had appeared to revive at the last moment and for a while they had held hands and been close, closer perhaps than they had ever been during the five years of their marriage. He had asked her not to cry over his passing and told her how happy she had made the last years of his life.

He had turned his head to look at her, grunting from the effort as the tubes that hung from him resisted his feeble strength. His eyes held hers with a desperate urgency and he clasped her hand tightly, as he asked, "Have I made you happy, my darling? I have tried, but it's something that I will never really know."

She laid her head on his chest, softly, so that he would not feel the weight. She could not face his gentle stare, nor could she lie to him when she knew that very soon he would know the truth. She wept into his shoulder and felt the heaving of his body as he strove for breath. His hand patted her shoulder and he died with her name on his lips. She knew that she had failed him, even at his last moment.

She was grateful that the war made it impossible for his daughters to attend the funeral. She knew that they were bitter at their father's marriage and she had dreaded their eventual meeting. They were bitter too that Jack had left her his entire estate, valued at over half a million dollars, and invested in blue-chip stocks and bonds, their certificates neatly filed and deposited in the vaults of his bank.

It was not long after the quiet funeral in the cemetery overlooking the lake that Eva realized the difference between the young, obedient wife she had been and the wealthy and highly attractive widow she had now become, her attraction enhanced a thousandfold by the fortune she now owned.

Long before the socially acceptable period of mourning was over she was bombarded by notes and telephone calls from all sorts of men, most of them claiming to be old friends of Jack. After offering their condolences, they would either ask her to meet them, or claim that Jack had owed them money – often quite trivial sums – expecting her to honour the debt.

She soon stopped answering the telephone herself and Druska became an expert at filtering her calls until the word must have spread that the widow was not worth pursuing and they finally died away. It had made Eva think, though. Think about how her life would be once the war was over and she could leave the bourgeois boredom of Geneva and return to Paris.

For the last five years she had studied the news of the war, tracing the progress of the various Polish units, searching for any indication of where Andrzej might be. It was an impossible task. The Polish forces had been so fragmented that there were Poles involved in every area of war and, isolated as she was in the tranquillity of Switzerland, it had been impossible to keep track.

She returned to Paris in the autumn of 1945. Although it had been liberated in the previous year, the city was still very far from normal. Traces of the German occupation were everywhere, and the city was filled with refugees from Eastern Europe, all of them seeking news of their families and trying desperately to survive in the new world in which they were strangers. The streets were full of foreigners, wandering, shocked and aimless, trying to adjust to their new lives.

They moved back to the apartment near the Parc Monceau. It was late in the evening when they first arrived. Eva left Druska to unpack their luggage and hastened round to the boulevard Haussmann. The shortage of petrol meant that there were few taxis and, as she hurried through the streets, she felt a new energy. It was as if she had been released from a cage and now, at last, she could start her true life, shape her own destiny, free from the need to please anyone else but herself.

The house was dark and the once-smart front was shabby, with peeling paint and cracked plaster. The hinges were broken on one of the huge oak doors that led to the central courtyard. Inside, the house was silent, although there was a pile of leaves swept into a corner and a broom leaning against a wall.

The apartment was as she had left it five years before. The bed was unmade and she could see the impression of Andrzej's head on the pillow, with that of her own beside it. There were two wine glasses in the sink, and an empty bottle of Dom Perignon on the draining board. There was a towel on the bathroom floor, lying dank and rotten with mildew where it had been carelessly thrown. There was a single, white bone shirt button on the floor beside it, which she picked up and held in her palm. She touched nothing else and sat for a while in an armchair, staring at the bed as her mind wandered around the apartment, reliving that night five years ago. It was as though he was in the apartment with her and twice she looked round quickly, thinking she had heard him behind her.

It was midnight when she walked slowly down the broad stone staircase. As she went across the courtyard there was a sudden tapping on the window that guarded the entrance. A pane slid open, and peering into the gloom she could see the faint outline of a head. "Who's there?" She recognized the croaky voice of the concierge. "I am Eva Lubinski," she replied and there was a rattling and wheezing as the concierge unchained her door and emerged, squinting at her through the darkness.

"Is it really you, Madame?" The woman was shocked to see her. "After all these years, I thought you were gone for good." She shook her head in disbelief. Eva thought the old woman seemed disappointed to find she was still alive.

The woman plucked at her sleeve, insisting that they should have a drink together to celebrate old times. She went back to her room and returned with two glasses of Pernod, which was a drink Eva hated, but she gulped half of it down as she listened to the woman's rambling reminiscences of the war. That was one of the bad things about being in Paris, Eva thought; the way everyone insisted on telling you about their life under the Boche and how terrible it had been. It became very boring after a while, as very little seemed to have happened, except a shortage of food which was only what you would expect.

She was only half listening as the woman rambled on with the usual set of complaints; she seemed to be particularly annoyed at the price of veal. Eva was on the point of making her excuses when the concierge said, "The gentleman came back only the once. He left you a note. I still have it somewhere." She dragged herself back into her room and Eva could hear her rummaging around, cursing to herself as she knocked a glass onto the floor.

There was a drumming in Eva's head as she waited. It was five minutes before the woman returned. She had a crumpled envelope in her hand. There was a smeared circular coffee stain across the front, but she recognized the handwriting immediately. She felt her knees buckle and the woman screeched in alarm and brought a chair so that she could sit down, but Eva thanked her and said she would be back in a few days. She wrote down her address and left it with the woman, telling her to give it to anyone who might ask.

There was a café down the street that was still open. She ordered a coffee and sat staring at the front of the envelope. Then, making up her mind, she quickly opened it. The writing blurred in front of her eyes and she had to hold it up close before she could read.

The note was dated October 1944. It said:

My Dearest,
I am in Paris for two days and I will spend the whole time looking for you. This is my first stop and I am leaving this note in the hope that there will be another miracle and you will return while I am still here. I am staying at the same hotel, L'hôtel du Dragon, and I will be constantly checking there to see if you have made contact, although I have little hope. The concierge tells me that you have not been seen for three years and I pray that you are safe. The war will be over soon and I will be back to stay with you forever. When that happens, I will leave a note for you at this address. I will love you always and live only for you.
Your devoted Andrzej.

She read the note a hundred times. Imagining Andrzej standing in the courtyard as he wrote. She wondered what she had been doing at that moment when her lover was so desperately trying to reach her, but her life in Switzerland had been so bland and uneventful that it was impossible to recall. She knew now that she had made a terrible mistake in leaving Paris; she should have stayed, waiting for Andrzej to return. She sat in the café until it closed and held the note in her hand as she walked back to the Parc Monceau. Her dread increased each time that she read it. It was over a year since the note was written and six months since the war was over. Surely he would have been back before now, if it was in any way possible?

She spent the next weeks haunting the offices of the many organizations that had sprung up and whose task it was to trace the millions of homeless people who wandered western Europe in search of their loved ones. The remnants of the Polish army had been dispersed all over the world. Those that had been lucky enough to survive, and also to escape from the Russians, were housed in camps that spread from Great Britain to the United States and news of who had survived and where they were was infrequent and often incorrect. Everywhere there was confusion and untold grief. The agencies were packed with refugees, stunned and half-demented by their loss, begging and pleading with the overworked and helpless staff to aid them in their misery.

It was useful to be rich. Eva had discovered that early on in her search. She had found a young Polish boy who worked for the Red Cross. He was a nice young man and made no disguise of his pleasure in helping *Pania* Lubinski, particularly in view of the little bundles of francs that she slipped into his hand at their daily meetings. She thought that he was her best chance of penetrating the vast mass of official papers, the interminable lists of names that changed sometimes three times a day as new information was added, until it was a matter of pure luck to come across the name that you sought.

Eva was determined to leave nothing to chance. The thought of Andrzej and what might have been if she had only thought to tell the concierge of her whereabouts, spurred her on to consider and examine every detail she could uncover. She knew that somewhere amongst this confusion there had to be the information that would lead her to her lover.

It was three agonizing months before there was any news. The Polish boy was looking out for her when she arrived on her daily visit to the Red Cross. He waved excitedly at her and came out from behind the counter. They went out to the calm of the street. He had a piece of paper in his hand.

"Pania Lubinski," he said. "I don't want to raise your hopes, but this list came through late last night. It's from the Koenigsberg Camp, just outside Vienna. There was a Lubinski admitted there only two weeks ago. See, I copied it down: A. Lubinski." He handed her the paper and stood back, his face serious. "Don't be too disappointed if it's not the man you're looking for." But Eva was already running down the street.

The camp was on the edge of a forest, some five miles out of the city. There was a row of wooden huts, half-hidden by the fir trees, cut off from the rest of the world by a high mesh fence. It was bitterly cold and there was no sign of life apart from the thin wisps of smoke rising from each hut.

There was an American soldier guarding the gate. He looked at her passport and seemed surprised that Mrs Jack Powers, an American citizen, should speak no English, but he showed her to a bare waiting room in a wooden hut at the other side of the compound. Another American, a clerk, appeared after a short wait. He seemed impressed at the sight of a smart and beautiful woman in such a dreary place. She explained the reason for her visit and he went out, returning with a list of names in his hand. He said yes, there was a Lubinski still there and would she wait while he made some inquiries. He was polite but offhand, clearly uninterested in the fate of just another wandering Pole. She waited, her mind in a ferment of expectation. She heard the footsteps of two people echoing on the wooden floor as they came towards the room where she was pacing up and down, nearly weeping in anticipation.

The door banged open and she stood, frozen in her tracks as a woman came slowly into the room and stood, crouched against the wall; wild, red-rimmed eyes, staring at her from under a mass of lank and greasy fair hair that fell uncombed and matted across her face. The clerk followed her into the room. "Here we are, Ma'am." He consulted his clipboard. "Alexandra Lubinski. At your service," he added as a sarcastic afterthought. The woman looked frantically about her, as if seeking an escape.

There was a table and two chairs in the centre of the room and Eva sat down heavily. Her disappointment was too much for her to bear and she put her head on her arms and wept.

The clerk said he would go and get her a glass of water and left in a hurry. He had seen too many of these tearful reunions and wished he was back in Brooklyn where he belonged. He thought that the newcomer was a looker though, if you liked that type. He imagined how it would be if he brought her home; okay he would bet. He decided to give them half an hour to get over the excitement before going back. That was the trouble with Polish women, they were too emotional for his taste. It must be murder being married to them, but he supposed the men were used to it by now.

Eva gave herself up to her grief. She lost count of time as she sat, with her head in her hands and her shoulders shuddering with the shock of her disappointment.

She felt a touch on her hand and looked up. Her sleeves were soaked with tears. The woman was sitting at the other side of the table. She had lowered her face so that it was only inches from her own. "Eva? Eva? Is it you, Eva?" The woman was staring into her eyes. She started to stroke the sleeves of Eva's fur coat. It was a brown sable that had been a present from Jack. Eva suddenly felt ashamed of its opulence as she looked at the tattered shawl that the woman was clutching about her shoulders. She leaned forward and brushed the tangled hair back from the woman's forehead. The skin was red and chapped from exposure and the face was lined with suffering, but the eyes and nose belonged to her half-sister. There was no doubt.

The eyes were staring at her, wild and fearful, like those of a lost child. Eva stood up and took off her coat. She gently draped it round the thin shoulders. She could feel the bones, sharp beneath her hand. "Yes, Alexandra, it's Eva, here to look after you." She spoke almost reluctantly, as if fighting against the responsibility that was being forced upon her; but she was a Lubinski, and the family must look after its own. She knew that God was punishing her for her sin. She wondered if his punishment would ever end.

24

It was two days before the bureaucratic process could release Alexandra into Eva's care and even then she had to spend an hour being interviewed by an English psychologist. He tried to explain to her that rehabilitating her half-sister was not going to be as simple as the shopping trip down the Rue St Honoré followed by a hot meal at the Café Lipp with which she had been planning to celebrate their return.

The psychologist, Dr Frayne, had spent some time with Alexandra when she had been first admitted to the camp. He had managed to find out part of the story of her survival, from the time that the Lubinski castle had been razed by German artillery, causing the deaths of the Count and Countess and most of their retainers, until she had been discovered by the advancing allied troops, alone and starving, in a Hungarian hedgerow. Since then she had been passed from camp to camp until she had finally been sent to Koenigsberg.

It was known from another survivor that she had been a member of a group of partisans and had actively engaged in operations against the enemy. Someone else had said that they recognized her from the Warsaw uprising, although they had heard that she had been killed by a mortar shell and were surprised to see her still alive.

Dr Frayne said that he was telling all this to Eva so that she would not underestimate the task before her, if she were to be responsible for her sister's welfare.

Eva listened for as long as she could but the place was too much like a prison for her to linger and she was impatient to get out of there and back home to Paris. She was fearful that there had been news of Andrzej and that she would miss him once again if she were away for too long.

She bought Alexandra some new clothes in Vienna, just enough for her journey. The shops were dull and empty of all but the most basic items. She would buy her a new wardrobe as soon as they returned.

It would be strange, being alone with her, their positions reversed. Now it was Alexandra who was dependent on her sister for everything she needed. The food that she ate and the bed in which she would sleep were all provided by Eva, and her bounty could be withdrawn at her slightest whim.

She glanced sideways at Alexandra as they left the camp in the hired car. She wondered if she realized just how much things had changed between them during the last few years, but her sister sat staring nervously out of the window. They passed a column of prisoners of war as they approached the city. There had to be a special reason for them to have been detained for so long. As they came closer she saw from their uniforms that they were from the SS. Alexandra was terrified. She flung herself to the floor of the car and tried to pull Eva down on top of her. She was whimpering with fright. It took Eva the rest of their journey to the railway station to calm her, but even then she was nervous, and in the dining car that night she caught her sister hiding one of the bread knives under her skirt and had a difficult time persuading her to put it back.

Druska was out of her mind with joy when Eva arrived back to the apartment with Alexandra beside her. She recognized her immediately and curtsied and bobbed her head as though they were still living in the castle. She appeared to be quite shocked when Eva did not give Alexandra the big bedroom that she had so briefly shared with her husband and she sat at the head of the table that night, making it clear that she expected Druska to serve her first, as head of the household.

It was not that Eva wanted Alexandra to feel uncomfortable or unwelcome, but she could see that she was going to have to establish the new way of doing things right away. It would save a great deal of unpleasantness later on.

Alexandra was oblivious to what was going on around her. She seemed overcome by the sudden change in her surroundings, hardly believing the luxury in which she found herself after the deprivation and constant fear she had known for so long. For the first month she was reluctant to leave the apartment, spending hours in the kitchen with Druska, just sitting and watching her as she did her work. Whenever she tried to be of help Druska would shoo her away, scandalized that any daughter of the House of Lubinski should so debase herself.

Eva spent her time haunting the offices of the various refugee agencies, but to no avail. The Polish boy had disappeared from the Red Cross office when she returned there the day after she arrived back from Vienna, and she had found no one else to take his place. The crowd of refugees was slowly diminishing as time wore on, many of them, in despair giving up all hope of ever seeing their loved ones again, vanishing into the world outside to start their own lives amongst strangers.

Eva, too, was starting to feel the strain of her daily pilgrimage. The emotion and hope that had kept her driving forward for so long was starting to drain her of her natural strength and she no longer had any real expectation that her search would be rewarded.

Her search had brought her into contact with many members of the Polish colony now establishing itself in the city. They were a strange mixture, the blood of old families mingling with upstarts and imposters, all driven together by desperation and loneliness, by desolation at the loss of their fatherland which, it was now clear, was never going to be returned to them. Many had chosen to go back and risk their lives at the hands of the Communists rather than be forever strangers in another's land. Eva thought that many of those who remained should have gone with them. They were incapable of adapting to their new circumstances, hating the French and their independence as they would the people of any other country that gave them a home.

None of them had news of Andrzej. There was a major who thought he had heard of him at Monte Cassino and another who had seen him in Normandy, though where he could not say. But there was no news of him since he had written the note at the boulevard Haussmann, and she could find no one who could help her.

However, there were plenty of people, men mostly, who were willing to try. There were very few young and attractive Polish women with large fortunes, who were unmarried and living in Paris. In fact there were very few Poles who had any money at all. Most of them had lost everything they owned when Poland had fallen, and even those who had nothing to start with blamed either the Germans or the Russians for their present predicament. Eva was in danger of being swamped by telephone calls asking her to dinners, for which she knew she would have to pay, and requests to discuss grand ideas for businesses, which were poorly disguised attempts to borrow money against the day when Poland would be liberated.

She very soon grew tired of the constant harassment and decided that it was useless to continue her search. Instead she paid for a daily advertisement in all of the newspapers, asking Andrzej to contact Eva, and leaving a box number for the answer.

At first it drew all sorts of replies, sometimes over a dozen a day, but even they tapered off to a trickle after a few weeks and she slowly had to admit to herself that it was in the hands of the Lord whether she would ever again hear from her beloved.

She could feel the melancholia wrapping its black tentacles around the edges of her mind. With all real hope of finding Andrzej now gone, there was no point to her life. There was nothing for her to do and not even the struggle for existence to occupy her. She could feel herself slipping into a depression which she knew, if it was allowed to take hold of her, would last forever. She knew that all around her there were those who had already succumbed. The shock of their new circumstances had proved more than they could endure and either they had ended their own lives or they could be seen walking the streets, careless as to their appearance, existing in doorways and under bridges, living with their tragedies locked inside them, their minds barricaded forever against all contact with humanity.

Eva knew that it would be only too easy for her to join them. For several days she stayed in her room, refusing to eat and hardly sleeping, slipping into the netherland from which there was no return.

One morning she woke from a doze to find Alexandra sitting on the side of the bed. She had hardly spoken to her sister since bringing her home. She had been too intent on her search to want any distractions. Alexandra was looking much better. She had put on some weight, her hair was glossy, and there was a hint of colour in her cheeks since she had taken to going out with Druska as she went about her errands.

Alexandra saw that she was awake and gave her a hesitant smile. She clutched her arms around her body and started to rock herself back and forth, all the while watching Eva, as if she were frightened of her reaction. Eva sat up and started to go towards the bathroom. The movement startled her sister who stood up as well and came to stand in front of her. She put out her hand and timidly touched Eva's hair, ready to flee at the first sign of displeasure. There was a desperate urgency in her eyes that made Eva stand still. Alexandra opened her mouth and Eva could see that she was fighting for the right words. Finally she managed to speak. "Please don't leave me," she said. She dropped her hand and stood there, waiting for Eva's reply. Eva opened her arms and her sister crept forward between them, and they hugged each other for a long time. Eva felt the desperate need as her sister clung to her, and the depression lifted from her brain as she realized that to one person, at least, she was life itself.

"Come along," Eva said. "It's time you were better. Let's go and have breakfast and plan our day." She felt the life come into her sister's body as she spoke. Druska was beaming at her as she came into the kitchen. She put her arms around the two of them and hugged them to her.

It was another six months before Alexandra was well enough to take care of herself, and it had not been an easy six months for any of them. Sometimes Eva despaired that her sister would ever be completely normal. She had picked up certain habits during the war which were just not acceptable to Parisian society. There was the problem with the dustbins, for example, which would keep cropping up when least expected and made a simple walk down the street into a potential embarrassment, particularly if it were somewhere smart, like the rue de Rivoli or the boulevard St Germain. There were people that you knew who would remark on the sight of a Lubinski groping amongst yesterday's slops in search of Lord knows what succulent morsel. It was a habit Alexandra had acquired during the months of starvation that had followed the Warsaw uprising, when she had lived in hiding, daring to come out only at night, with the refuse of the day her sole hope of nourishment.

Even after six months and much animated discussion after every little lapse, Alexandra would still look longingly at each dustbin that she passed, growing restless and ill at ease at the thought of the unknown delights she was missing.

In fact food was a major obstacle on the path to Alexandra's rehabilitation. Apart from her obsession with dustbins, she was a determined hoarder of anything that was both edible and accessible. Neither Eva nor Druska had suspected that there was any cause for alarm until one day when Druska decided that the sheets for the whole apartment should be washed a day earlier than was usual. Alexandra had always insisted on making her bed and cleaning her room herself, and it was the first time that either Eva or Druska had had cause to enter there since her arrival. Alexandra was on a visit

173

to the dentist at the time, and Eva had gone with her to make sure she didn't get lost on the way.

As soon as they returned she could tell by Druska's face that something was wrong. She said nothing until Alexandra had gone to her room. Then she asked, "What's the matter? You look as though you're going to burst."

Druska came up close to her and glanced around to make sure that Alexandra was nowhere near. "Her room is full of food. I thought everything was going down too quickly, things like jam and potatoes, and four whole packets of coffee in one week. It's all in her bedroom, hidden everywhere you can imagine, under the mattress, Lord knows how she can sleep, and the bathroom cupboard is packed. I think that one of the floorboards is loose, but you came back before I could be sure. There's something far worse, though. There are things there that I've never bought in my life: a whole smoked ham and a sack of rice, things that can only have come from a shop, and she has no money to pay for them." Druska rolled her eyes and shrugged her shoulders in horror. It was beyond her imagination that an aristocrat such as her beloved Alexandra could possibly be a thief. "Will you speak with her, madame?"

Eva thought for a moment. "I don't think so, not just yet. She's not stealing because she's a thief. It's all part of the same problem as the dustbins. I had no idea that it was so bad and talking to her might make it even worse. Just keep a watch on her until I think of what we should do."

It was new territory for Eva. She realized that there was very much more wrong with her sister than she had ever imagined. She was frightened of what Alexandra might do if she just walked in and confronted her. She might even run away if she thought that Eva was angry with her. Perhaps it was best to do nothing and hope that in time whatever was driving her to do these strange things would go away.

It was the incident with the Algerian that made Eva change her mind. Paris was still full of the flotsam and jetsam of the war, but now only the riffraff was left – people who would have difficulty in settling down under any circumstances.

The streets were full of them, begging and borrowing and telling stories of their wartime exploits to anyone with enough money for a drink who would listen to them. A woman had to be careful walking in the streets after dark, but Eva never thought there might be danger when she went with Alexandra for an after-dinner brandy in a café close to the Champs Élysées, less than a kilometre from their apartment.

The man was slightly tipsy. They could see that as they strolled towards him on their way home. They were in a side street that was usually busy with people taking a short cut through to the park but now, as they walked towards him, it was empty.

The man stood on the corner of the street. He was weaving slightly as they approached so they crossed the road to avoid him. They could see him out of the corners of their eyes as he moved to cut them off. She could feel Alexandra tensing beside her and was about to say something to calm her when the man increased his speed and was suddenly standing in front of them. Close up, he did not seem as drunk as Eva had thought. He looked muscular and dangerous as he reached out his hand towards her bag. She instinctively clasped it against her and the man gestured angrily and slipped his hand into his breast pocket. She felt a movement beside her and Alexandra stepped forward. Eva put out her hand to pull her back, frightened that she would come to harm. There was a sudden gasp in front of her, but her sister was in the way and she could not see what was happening. Then Alexandra stepped aside and she saw the man on his knees. There was blood pouring from his throat. He coughed and fell on to his face.

There was a knife that she recognized in Alexandra's hand. Druska used it to peel the vegetables, but she had been complaining that it was nowhere to be found. Alexandra bent down and took hold of the man's tie. She used it to wipe the blade of the knife, which she then slipped inside her dress. It went somewhere below her left arm. She turned and beckoned to Eva and they walked hurriedly out into the crowds on the boulevard Haussmann. Alexandra was calm and detached, as if nothing unusual had happened and Eva found it difficult to know what to say.

She put a call through to the camp in Koenigsberg that night and asked for Dr Frayne. There was nothing else she could do.

25

Georgia stood in front of the racks of newspapers at London Airport and thanked the Lord that her flight would be called within the next half-hour. Her picture was absolutely everywhere; all the dirty papers had her on the front page and even *The Times* had a headline, halfway down with a note that there was a picture inside. They were all using the same photograph. It had been taken outside the police station and she was looking very haughty and dignified, only it was easy to see that she had no clothes on under the mink coat and the way the policeman was holding her arm made her look like a spy or a murderer and rather spoiled the whole effect.

She thought that it was asking for trouble, standing in front of her own picture, even if she was wearing her hair in a bun and large dark glasses. It was unlikely she would be recognized unless someone was suspicious, which would be the case if she stood there much longer.

There was a line of telephone booths along one wall and she went over to them, more from want of something to do than with any idea as to who she should ring. Standing in the booth, she had to do something or it would look even more suspicious, so she opened her address book and thumbed it through, wondering who she should call.

It was hard to decide. She didn't think that Lady Pamela would be too pleased to hear from her, and neither would Cosmo, for that matter. She had only just said goodbye to her Aunt and didn't want to go through all that again. Although she had been super about everything, she would keep warning her about men and the things they could make you get up to, if you didn't watch out. Not that her Aunt knew anything about it, Georgia thought; with her experience of the world she probably still thought babies grew under gooseberry bushes; but she meant well, she had to give her that.

Gallo's name was scrawled across the top of a page and on an impulse she dialled him, not expecting him to be at the club so early in the day. He answered the phone himself and she suddenly felt awkward talking to him after what had happened. She nearly cut him off, but then said, "Hello, Mr Gallo. This is Georgia Frayne. I'm ringing to thank you for a lovely evening." She didn't know what else to say. It wasn't Gallo's fault that she had been drugged and probably raped and made to do all sorts of things that she couldn't remember. In fact, he was the one who had warned her, but she had been too stupid to listen.

"I was looking at your picture when you rang," he said. "It doesn't do you justice, but your legs look nice, sticking out of that coat. I'm sorry it happened to someone like you, and with people you met in my club. I hope you won't hold it against me."

It was great of him to put it that way. No "I told you so's", or "served you rights"; nothing to make her feel that she had been an idiot, although she knew she had been.

"I'm going away for a while," she said. "I just hope that you won't get into any trouble if the police start asking about what I did that night."

Gallo said that it was kind of her to think of that, but he didn't think the police would be all that interested, not if she was going away.

"Would you like to know where I'm going?" she asked. "Perhaps you could let me know if it all turns nasty. I'd hate to come back at the wrong moment."

"Okay. If that's what you want." He didn't seem too keen, which was a disappointment. She had rather hoped he would have shown more interest than that, maybe say that he'd come down and see her in a couple of weeks, but she could hear her flight being called and had to hurry to give him her address.

Madame de la Reve owned a pension on the outskirts of Nice. It was not very big, about a dozen rooms in an old house which was built around a stone-flagged courtyard. It was mid-afternoon when she arrived and there was a maid clearing the remains of a large lunch, obviously for several people, from a table set outside, close to a wall entirely covered by a flowering vine.

The maid helped her with her suitcases and asked if mamzelle would like some soup. Georgia declined, but accepted a glass of wine instead. The maid said that Madame was taking her nap and would be down in an hour, so Georgia took a walk around the neighbourhood and stretched her legs. Apart from a café on the corner, the place seemed dead. There was a cat asleep in a doorway and two dogs lying panting in the shade of a jacaranda tree, for it was a hot afternoon even for the end of August, and that was more or less that. She could see a thin strip of sea from the end of the street. It looked far away at the bottom of a long hill, with the roofs of the city stretching out between. If her Aunt wanted her out of the way, she had chosen the right place for her to go. She wondered how long she would have to stay.

When she returned, Madame de la Reve was sitting at the table, drinking a *citron pressé*. She jumped up and kissed Georgia on both cheeks, saying she was a beautiful girl and just like her mother. She crossed herself when she said that, spat over her finger, which she said was for luck, and then told the maid to bring some wine.

Madame de la Reve was quite a shock, not at all the sort of person that Georgia had expected. She was tall and skinny with thinning hair, bright red and spikey so that you could see a pink patch on her scalp where the dye had come off. Her lined face was dead white with powder and her cheeks thick with rouge. Her lipstick was smeared along the top of her upper lip, making her mouth big and crooked, and there were red stains all round the rim of her glass and on the cork cigarette tips that were piled up in the ashtray.

Madame de la Reve was having a good look at her at the same time. "You are much more mature than your Aunt described," she remarked. "I thought you were going to be a young and gawky girl, all knees and elbows, simpering in the corner at the sight of a boy. It's very nice to have you here, an unexpected pleasure to be sure, but a beauty like you is not going to be leaving anywhere in a hurry without a very good reason, and a sudden desire to learn French is not good enough, whatever your dear Aunt would like me to believe." She drank her wine and poured herself another. "But Eva never did have a very high regard for my intelligence."

Georgia was still feeling exhausted from her night on the pavement. Whatever drug they had given her was still washing around inside her and the wine was making her sleepy. She asked to be excused and went to her room. She didn't wake up until early morning, but by then she was feeling back to normal and impatient to get out and about.

Madame de la Reve was already having coffee in the courtyard and Georgia joined her as soon as she had washed. She had put on a short, pink gingham dress with a matching scarf which she tied at the tip of her chin, like Brigitte Bardot. She had bought it by post a few weeks before.

Madame de la Reve – she said to call her Lilianne – was already fully made-up, in much the same way as she had been when Georgia had first seen her. This morning she was wearing a white blouse with a frilly front, and a fluffy bright pink angora cardigan, with the wool brushed so that it stuck up all round. Her skirt was frilly as well, with a purple print and a wide belt. From a distance she looked twenty years younger than she did close up.

There was a bottle of aspirin beside the coffee pot and Lilianne said that she was having one of her headaches. There was a bottle of brandy on the table and she poured a little nip into her coffee as she spoke. "I have arranged for a young man to show you around the town this morning. His name is Roger Testu and he lives with his mother down the street. He's the same age as you, but not quite mature, so I hope you're both going to like each other." She did not seem to be too optimistic about the prospect. "In fact, looking at you this morning, I have a feeling that he is going to like you very much indeed, so please remember two things that might make both our lives much easier. Firstly, he is the only boy around here who owns a motor scooter, and it's a long walk to the town. Secondly, I have to live here after you are gone and his mother is a person whose friendship I would like to keep. I hope I make myself clear enough?"

Georgia said that she was very clear indeed and thought what a ghastly time she was going to have if she wasn't careful.

A man came out of the front door and joined them at the table. He was fat and balding with a frizzle of greasy curls slicked across the top of his suntanned head. He was wearing a towelling bathrobe which had once been white but was now a yellowy grey, with a stain that looked like red wine on the front. He walked very stiffly, with his back erect and a great bulge right above his waistline, as though he were wearing a corset, for the stomach below was flat.

He bowed low over Georgia's hand as they were introduced. Lilianne said that he was a Pasha in his own country, which was the same as being a Marquis in France, only grander because there were fewer of them now. The Pasha sat down beside her and she could see the veins, purple and fat below his dark olive skin.

He said that it was a pleasure to have such an enchanting guest and it would be no trouble at all if she would allow him to show her the town — maybe a visit to the casino and a supper later on. He poured himself a brandy and sipped at it thoughtfully. The front of his bathrobe fell open and she could see that he was wearing a faded pair of baggy underpants, so baggy that when he made a sudden move she was looking right up the inside of his leg. She thought it was an accident and looked quickly away, but he was watching her closely and she was suddenly not so sure.

Lilianne told him to be careful in front of a young girl who was Eva's niece as well, and he covered himself hastily, at the same time asking her if she had been to St Tropez, where there was a beach especially for ladies to bathe with their tops off. Though men were allowed on there as well, it was all in the best of good taste.

Lilianne said that it was disgusting, what they allowed people to do, and no one was going to catch her with her top off, running about on a beach. Pasha nodded and said he thought it was disgusting too, but he just had to mention it as Georgia was a guest. He put his hand on her thigh, and said that he hoped she had not taken offence. Lilianne stood up at that moment and he took his hand away quickly, before she could see.

He asked how her dear Aunt was, and said they had all been friends a long time ago, when they were very young. He had always thought that Eva would go far in this life and events had proved him right. He said that he had gone far once, but the war had made him come back again and he had never tried it since, preferring to live a quiet life with his friends. Then his stomach gave a rumble and he said he should be going. Lilianne poured herself some cognac, no coffee this time. She said that Pasha had lived a very hard life, always working and meeting the best people, and it was he who had introduced Aunt Eva to Jack, which was just as well for all of them, as it had turned out. She explained that it had been difficult for a person like Pasha during the war. People from the Levant were sometimes confused about which side they were on and it had led to some terrible misunderstandings when the Germans had lost.

Georgia was not sure what one could say to that. It was a relief when Roger Testu arrived on his Vespa a few minutes later. He was a nice-looking boy, but dressed up like an English gentleman, in a navy-blue blazer with brass buttons and an open-necked shirt with a cravat. He had a briar pipe which he pulled out of his pocket as soon as he stopped. He was tallish and skinnyish with a long, pointed nose and a polite smile which he used the whole time. He kissed both their hands and said "Enchanté" when they were introduced. He reminded her of a stuffed dummy, but she remembered what Lilianne had said and gave her best smile, saying how kind he was to show her the sights.

She clung on like mad when they drove off, with Roger revving the engine and slamming in the clutch, leaning the scooter over on the bends so that he nearly hit a lorry and had to stop suddenly. People were jeering at him from the pavement and one of them called him *"un sale cochon"*. He went very pink and drove even faster until she got off at some traffic lights and told him that she would walk home if he didn't slow down.

It was better after that and he drove her down the boulevard des Anglais, which ran along the beach, and they stopped and had an ice cream and looked down from the promenade at the heads of the lunchtime customers in the restaurants. She told Roger that she was hungry, thinking he would suggest that they went down and joined them, but instead he drove to a square where they sold salade Niçoise in big bread rolls. It tasted very good, but that was not the point. She wanted to sit in a smart restaurant with nice, adult people all round her, not perch on the back of a scooter, chewing at a huge lump of bread with oil oozing down the front of her gingham dress.

Roger seemed to think that buying her a sandwich entitled him to a lot more besides. He stood up close to her as if he wanted to lift up her skirt, which she thought very gauche in broad daylight with the square full of people. She wouldn't have let him do it anyway, even if it had been somewhere private. She had grown out of young men, she decided.

Roger showed her the University where he was a student. It was closed *pour des vacances*, and the café where he had lunch with his friends was closed as well; *les vacances* again. Then they went to visit his best friend, Michel, but he had gone to St Tropez and his mother said that he would be away *pour le weekend*. She gave Georgia a nasty look and said something about English girls which she didn't understand.

They drove past the casino on the way home. She made Roger stop, although he said he was late and sulked as they walked past the café and the ladies' orchestra playing Volare for all it was worth. It was disappointing, once they had climbed up the wide, stone staircase. The first room they came to was full of tourists; they had passed their coaches parked below in the street. They were all playing a game that was a sort of roulette, only very simple, with far fewer numbers and big, heavily marked squares where you put wagers so there would be no arguments when the tourists lost their money, which they all seemed to be doing. Some of them were

English and she wondered if you could buy the London papers in Nice. She was keen to leave and headed up another flight of steps to the casino proper, where there were smart people going in and out wearing evening dress, although it was still early.

Roger said that they should go home but she became angry with him following her about the whole time, telling her what to do. They asked for her passport at the door and said that she was too young, but she could go in with an adult. She made Roger show them his identity card, but he was too young as well, which just about summed it up, as far as she was concerned.

She was furious on the way home. There was nothing for her in Nice and the thought of months of Roger and his scooter was a nightmare she was not going to endure.

Roger was randy when they got back to the pension, which gave her an idea. She let him come close to her in the courtyard and gave him a big French kiss; he seemed to like that, being French himself. She thought he was going to do himself damage, the way he was groaning and rubbing his thing up against her, so she stepped back and said, "Not here. Not in Nice. Let's go to St Tropez tomorrow, and we'll see what happens." She allowed him to mess around with the front of her dress for a minute, to give him the taste, and he said he would see her at eight. She ran her hand up the front of his trousers, to make sure he wouldn't forget.

26

She could see that St Tropez was going to be her only chance to escape. The thought of spending the next few months in Nice, with Roger and his little friends pawing at her all day and Pasha probably having a go in the evenings, was worse than going back to London, which was what she had decided to do, if today did not work out.

She had taken trouble to look as appealing as she possibly could. She was wearing very brief white shorts, with an ice-pink cotton shirt knotted round the waist so that it showed a good stretch of her midriff. She had a pink-and-white polka dot handkerchief around her hair which was piled on top of her head, white ballet shoes, and a big straw basket holding her two-piece bathing costume, her make-up bag and her purse. She just hoped that after all the trouble she had taken there would be somebody worthwhile to see the result. She had no intention of wasting it on Roger, that was certain.

He arrived at eight o'clock, revving up his stupid scooter in the quiet street and peeping the little horn when she did not appear. He had obviously also taken some pains to dress up for the occasion. He had on a striped, matelot tee-shirt, navy-blue canvas trousers and navy espadrilles with white socks. They all looked as if they were brand-new. With the white yachting cap on his head, he looked like Popeye as he puffed at his pipe, and she was glad that there was no one to recognize them on their journey.

He leapt off his scooter when he saw her and jerked it back on to its pedestal. Then he came scampering over to her, giving her a big kiss, as though they were already lovers, and started to run his hands down her back, right there, out in the street in broad daylight. She dodged away and went to stand by the scooter, Roger following after her. He was already crestfallen that she had not responded to his advances. She could see that it was going to be quite a day, keeping him keen so that he got her to St Tropez, without allowing him to mess her about on the way.

It was a long way, much longer than she had thought, and Roger kept wanting to stop every ten minutes. Either he felt like a coffee, or his bladder was full and he couldn't wait, or he would swerve off the road to show her the view and start pawing at her and moaning that he loved her, trying to get her to go with him into the strip of pine trees that lined the road.

At last they arrived at a highway where it was impossible to stop and he had no choice but to wind up his engine and keep going, while she clung on behind him with the wind tugging at her clothes and the dust going everywhere, making her skin itch and her eyes water behind her sunglasses.

All the time there were expensive, flashy-looking cars roaring past them, the smoke from their exhausts making her cough and the wind of their slipstream causing Roger to swerve and wobble. The passengers looked smart and condescending as they went by, turning their heads and giving them smug glances. She was beginning to get furious at the whole miserable charade and wished that it would stop. She imagined how it would be if they had an accident, in which Roger's neck was broken, leaving her standing, unscathed by the roadside, for someone to stop and pick her up.

There was a white Rolls Royce with an open top that drove beside them for a while. The two men who were in it were waving and shouting and asking her if she wanted a ride. She would have given anything to have got in with them but Roger kept shouting curses at them and waving his finger in the air so that in the end they accelerated and disappeared around a bend. She could happily have killed Roger.

It was nearly three hours before they arrived. She was stiff and aching and her arms and legs were sore from the sun. Roger was very proud of himself for completing the journey as they sat in a café across the road from the port. He ordered an orange juice and was shocked when she asked for a large whisky. He started to count his money in front of her, opening the padlock on the effeminate leather handbag he carried slung over his shoulder, fumbling around inside until he could find it. She hoped he had more in his pockets, because there didn't seem to be much there.

She had thought that the town would be busy but Roger said that everybody was out on the beaches, which were some way away and not worth visiting because they were too crowded and it was impossible to be on your own. He had a stupid expression on his face when he said that, like a dog waiting for its reward. He would be wagging his tail in a minute, which was exactly what she didn't want. It was lucky she hadn't told him to get lost as soon as they had arrived. She had not reckoned on the beaches being so far away.

It was quite a problem to get him to take her there. He said that there were much better places up in the foothills, where there would be no one at all, and started rubbing her back again, trying to slip his hand down the inside of her waistband. She gave him a big kiss and rubbed herself up against him, putting her hand on the front of his trousers, which made him jump back with a shout. It seemed that it was all right for him to do it to her in front of everybody, but not the other way round. He began sulking again, starting up the bike and gunning the engine so that a cloud of smoke floated down the line of tables. An Englishman called him an arsehole and told him to fuck off. Roger went very red and said something about English pigs, but he waited until they were moving before he did it.

There was a car park behind the beach but Roger said that only tourists paid for that sort of thing and left his scooter on the grass verge by the entrance.

She had expected it to be the same sort of beach as they had in England, with everybody lying wherever they liked, but this one was different, divided up into sections, each one fenced off, with cabins and sun beds, and beach boys running about serving drinks. They were full of people and most of the girls had bare tops, walking around as though it were perfectly natural. It was a shock to see them and she didn't think she would do it herself, not with Roger peeking at her the whole time, panting and moaning and trying to touch her up.

Roger said that only tourists paid to go on the beach and that it was much quieter if they walked right down to the other end. There were some sand dunes where nobody went.

She said that she was a tourist and wanted to be like everybody else. She marched up to the gate and Roger was right, it was very expensive to get in. He counted his money again and said that he would not have enough to buy petrol. He was very annoyed and started to walk away. She opened her purse, paid the attendant and slipped inside one of the cabins. She had a glimpse of him running back as she closed the door.

She changed into her costume, debating for a moment and then deciding that she was not ready to emerge topless, not if Roger had decided to pay to get in. He might be waiting outside, ready to pounce as she came through the door, trying to push her back inside and take her standing up in the tiny cabin, with half the beach knowing what was going on.

There was no sign of him when she came out. There was a beach boy ready with a thick, white towel, which he put over a sun bed at the water's edge. She gave him a few francs and he bowed and said, "if there is anything that mamzelle would like . . ." He was smiling as he said it, not wanting to upset her if she took his meaning in the wrong way, and she smiled back and said thank you very much. He was a good-looking boy and she could feel the stigma of Roger and his infantile ways starting to fade. She lay back and relaxed in the sun.

It had been an exhausting journey and she was half nodding off when she heard a shout and a scuffle close by. The beach boy and Roger were struggling, ankle-deep in the water, or rather Roger was struggling as the beach boy held him by the scruff of his neck and pointed him back in the direction of the car park.

She saw his head turning towards her and she closed her eyes, pretending to be asleep. She could hear him shouting her name for a while but when he was silent, she looked cautiously around her. Most of the sun beds were occupied and the sight of the women made her feel tacky and out of date. They were all wearing the briefest of bikini bottoms and their naked breasts were bronze, the same colour as the rest of their bodies. They had blonde streaks in their hair and she saw two of them wetting their manes at the water's edge which, she thought, must have something to do with it. She decided to try for herself, feeling out of place as she stood up. Her two-piece costume was baggy and shapeless compared to the others and she sat down again, defiantly undid the back of her bra and looked down at her naked breasts. They were dead white in the sunlight, making her feel even more self-conscious as she stood up once again. She folded down her waistband as far as she could and felt slightly less of an outsider as she stood in the water, feeling her nipples contract as the waves lapped over them. She wondered how she was going to get back to Nice.

Bertrand Delpine had been watching the blonde girl since she had arrived on the beach. He had seen the little boy who had escorted her trying to prevent her from entering and his pathetic attempt to get past the surveillance of the beach boys. He didn't blame the youth from trying to keep the girl to himself. He would have no chance at all once she was allowed on the loose. The beach was full of good-looking, sophisticated men who would be only too glad to take her off his hands. Himself, for example. He looked down with satisfaction at his sun-browned, muscular body with its curly black hair and the gold cross and chain glinting in the bright light.

It was fortunate for the girl that he was different from the others. He had a feeling that this was going to be a lucky day for them both. He had spent the years since Vadim had discovered Bardot searching for an unknown face and body he could mould into another overnight sensation. There was a quality about this girl: her square shoulders, the proportion between arm and waist, her breasts and the curve of her buttocks, her long, coltish legs which made his mouth dry at the thought of lying between them; it all added up to the girl he had been looking for. It was time for him to act before one of the others leaning on the bar beside him or lying by the water, their eyes on the lookout for fresh meat to revive their appetites, tried to move in ahead of him – which was going to happen any minute as the girl emerged from the sea and stood on the sand with the water running down those milk-white breasts.

His film director's eye was working out camera angles as she walked back to her sun bed. Her face was already almost perfect. Set on a long neck it had the full lips, high forehead and short, upturned nose and wide-apart eyes that were essential for his purpose.

He stood up and put his finger inside the front of his tight briefs, bunching up his testicles to emphasize the bulge, and slicked back his short, heavily greased hair. He put on his aviator sunglasses with the mirrored lenses and finished off his margarita, feeling the salt from the rim of the glass sting his lips. He popped a pill into his mouth and started to walk across the sand. He had forgotten how hot it would be and his head swam with the pain and perhaps the tequila. He had to dig the sides of his feet deep into the sand to avoid the burning heat, so that his approach was awkward and crab-like. He was glad that the girl was looking out to sea.

Georgia was wondering what she was going to do next. She was not short of money, that was one good thing, but it was still going to be difficult to get back home, stranded as she was miles from anywhere. She supposed she could always hitch a lift; maybe Roger would still be hanging around, although she would rather walk than have to face another journey on his scooter.

She felt the sun bed shake as a body thumped down onto it. She looked round quickly, thinking that Roger had somehow found a way past the beach boys, but the man beside her was a very different matter indeed. For a start, he was a man, mature and good-looking, and very sure of himself as he smiled at her surprise. "Pardon mamzelle," he said. "The sand is roasting my feet and I am desperate for some beautiful lady to come to my rescue." He took her hand and placed it on the sole of his right foot. It was a very strong and attractive foot and Georgia felt herself tingle as she touched it. He introduced himself and she told him her name. He was surprised that she was English. He said he would never have guessed it in a million years; she was so elegant, with a beauty hard to define, but which set her so very far apart from all the rest. He waved his hand scornfully around the beach as he spoke and Georgia thought that it was happening at last. It looked as though her nightmare of a journey was going to be worth it after all.

Bertrand asked her whether she had taken her lunch and if she would be so kind as to join him. It was the least he could do. She was going to refuse, she was sure that was what Lady Pamela would have advised, but then she thought that she was being silly. It was no good wanting to be part of this glamorous world and then turning down such an attractive man, so obviously in his element. Just talking to him had stopped her feeling a gauche and naïve outsider. Her memories of Roger and his motor scooter were fading to the back of her mind.

There was a little restaurant on the beach, close to the cabins. The tables were set outside on the sand, each one with an umbrella against the blazing sun. It was odd, sitting down to eat with a strange man, her naked breasts swaying in front of her, but all the other girls were doing the same thing and she would only appear prudish if she tried to cover herself. She had been watching his eyes, but they had never flickered downwards, so she assumed he was used to bare bosoms at the table and she felt more comfortable and relaxed.

They ordered freshly grilled fish and he asked her if she were an actress, but casually, so that it did not sound as if he were shooting a line. She told him that she was there to learn the language and he said how well she spoke French already. She was flattered, even though she knew that he was lying. She asked him if he was in the theatre and he said not really, he made films. She could see him waiting for her reaction so she said how interesting that must be, not wanting him to think that she was impressed.

There was an interruption just then as someone called her name from beyond the fence that separated the beach from the scrubland beyond it. It was a high, mesh fence and she could see Roger waving at her from the other side, dancing up and down in his efforts to attract her attention.

Bertrand noticed as well and asked if it was her boyfriend. As she told him about Roger and what a nuisance he had become, he leaned over and said, "Excuse me." He pointed to her right breast, where a drop of mayonnaise had dripped from the salad. He reached over and removed it with his finger. She felt it brush her nipple as he scooped it up, and then he put his finger in his mouth and sucked it, looking at her the whole time until she blushed and dropped her eyes to her plate.

Roger's shouting stopped after that and over the ice cream Bertrand asked her if she would have dinner with him. Perhaps they could go shopping first; he would like to buy her something to wear. She knew what Aunt Eva would have said, but times were different now and her Aunt was a long way away.

Bertrand had an Aston Martin in the car park – British racing green, with a drophead and electric windows. She sank back in the leather front seat and thought how much she hated poverty. She had put up with almost a whole day of it and that was enough.

Roger's scooter was still parked at the exit. He must have been following them, because he came running towards them as Bertrand pulled out. He was waving his arms and ran right in front of them, so that Bertrand had to swerve in order to miss him. The wheel of the Aston caught the side of the scooter, and she heard it fall over. When she looked back it was flat on the ground and its front was all twisted. Roger was trying to lift it up.

27

They inched through the narrow, crowded streets of St Tropez, stopping every so often while Bertrand talked to a whole string of glamorous-looking people, all of whom seemed to be his very close friends, judging by the way they all kissed him, men and women alike. Everyone in the streets was very brown, and dressed in casual but expensive clothes, and there was an air of excitement and expectation, as if something big were going to happen any minute. It was like one huge film set, with a cast of thousands crammed into the short and narrow street facing the port. On one side there was a row of cafés, their tables jamming the pavement, and on the other were the luxury motor cruisers of the very rich, moored sterns into the street, their occupants lolling in studied ease, sipping their drinks and studiously ignoring the hoi polloi who milled about on the quayside.

Bertrand had an apartment that faced the port. It was at one end of the street, above a boutique that jutted out across the road so that from the upstairs you could see both the boats at anchor and the full length of the crowd below. The flat was reached by a flight of stone stairs, crumbling with the wear of centuries.

Bertrand poured her a glass of white wine and she sat on a narrow balcony with rusting, wrought-iron railings while Bertrand went to change. The swarming crowd was really rather frightening when you saw it from above. She had the feeling that everybody was looking at everybody else, and that if somebody slipped the others would fall on him and tear him to pieces.

When he came back, Bertrand was wearing a white suit with a white shirt open at the neck, and a different gold chain – shorter, so that it showed against his tan. He looked smooth and sophisticated as he gave her a kiss on the cheek. It was very casual, not like Roger slobbering all over her whenever he could, but cool and relaxed as if there were no hurry and he was confident that things would happen in their own good time. It made her shiver, but she had no idea why.

He said that they must go and buy her something to wear for the party. "What party?" she asked, thinking that she should look as if she were in control.

"Whatever party we decide to honour by our company. There may be dozens of them, for all I know." He smiled at her, very much at ease, his head thrown back, challenging her to question him further. She shrugged and let it go and he took hold of her hand and pulled her up from her seat. "Let's leave," he said.

The boutique downstairs was called Maximillian's and Max, the owner, said he had been a friend of Bertrand's for years. He was German, short and stocky, with blond hair, a very deep tan and flashing white teeth. He sat with Bertrand at the front of the shop, leaving her to try on whatever she felt like, but watching her as she did so, giving her compliments on how nice she looked. It was a small shop, crowded with customers, so that the two girls who worked there were running round hanging up dresses and telling people prices. It was a very expensive shop but the customers didn't seem to be worried about how much they were spending. Some of them had men waiting for them in the doorway, and they all seemed to know Max and Bertrand.

She picked out a white dress with a halter top that showed off her back and shoulders. She would have looked better if she was as brown as the others, but the day on the beach had already given her skin some colour; in fact she was starting to feel quite sore.

She changed her clothes in the shop. Max said she should have new shoes to go with her dress and she chose a pair of gold sandals with gold thongs that wrapped around her ankles. Max said to leave her old ones behind the counter; she could pick them up in the morning. She was going to say something – after all, who said that she was going to stay overnight – but Bertrand took her by the arm and said they had to leave. Max said he would see them later, and they walked through the crowd to a restaurant at the other end of the street. She felt much easier amongst all those people now she was wearing her new dress and had Bertrand walking beside her, waving to friends as they went.

The restaurant was outside on the pavement, two lines of tables with blue tablecloths, running edge onto the street. It was packed with still more beautiful, suntanned customers, identical to all the others roaming outside. There was a whole group of them crushed round a table at the far end. They all waved to Bertrand. He went over and started shaking hands and kissing them; everyone was smiling and laughing to show they were having a good time. They all crushed up even more, to make room for them.

There was a space for her between a blonde woman of about thirty, which was old in comparison to the other girls, and a dark, wiry little man with short-cut hair, slightly curly and slicked back from his forehead. They were both English. The man was older than the woman, probably around thirty-five. He obviously thought a lot of himself and gave his opinion about everything in a rather high and querulous voice, as if the world were against him and he couldn't understand why. All the others listened to him whenever he spoke, the men with serious faces, nodding and agreeing with him as though what he said was important; the girls all nodding as well, squirming their shoulders so that he would notice.

He didn't pay much attention to her at first, when Bertrand introduced her around the table. He was talking to the girl on the other side of him and didn't bother to look up. She was worried that being English they might have seen her in the papers but from the sound of it they had been away for at least two weeks, so that was all right.

It was strange that there weren't very many young men about, hardly any in fact, as she looked around the table. There hadn't been too many in the street either, although the girls were all about her age, some of them even younger by the looks of them and the stupid things they were saying, though nobody seemed to mind.

One of the men asked Bertrand how his film was coming along and that started them all off talking about how talented he was and how it was a shame that Dino had pulled out at the last minute. Somebody thought that Dino was in big trouble because he was not an artist and would go down one day for millions. They all agreed that it would serve him right.

From the way they were talking, it sounded as though Bertrand was very talented indeed. One of the men mentioned Vadim, saying that he was over the hill, latching on to every young girl he could find, thinking he was going to discover another Brigitte, but they all left him soon enough, when they found out what a sham he really was.

They asked the man next door to her what he thought. They called him Gerald and were all very respectful. The table hushed as they waited for his reply.

Gerald sat back and said that he really hadn't thought about it very much, there were too many so-called geniuses about who cost people money in the end. He preferred bricks and mortar himself; although, with the cost of money these days, even that was not as good as it was.

Bertrand look a bit miffed at that. He said that it was lunatics like Vadim who were giving French film directors a bad name, which was something that he was fighting all day long and which made life very difficult, but Gerald had lost interest. He turned to Georgia, said he gathered she was English and asked what she was doing there?

She was about to answer when Bertrand shouted down from the other end of the table that she was not to tell Gerald anything at all about what was going on, as it was still a big secret and he didn't want anyone to know until he was ready. It was very confusing, but she smiled and nodded and tried to look mysterious. Gerald put his arm round the back of her chair and leaned up against her, pushing his thigh against hers. He started to tell her about his yacht, which was anchored just down the road, and how you could land a helicopter on the top; which he hoped she would come and watch some time. Then he took a business card from his pocket and told her to read it, leaning back and watching her face, so that she had to look impressed, although she had never heard of the London Property Co. The card said: *Gerald Rankin, Chairman*. She tried to hand it back, but he said she could keep it. She stuffed it down the front of her dress. She had been going to leave it on the table but she didn't want to appear rude, even though he was a smarmy little man and she wished he would stop trying to get off with her.

She was glad when the meal was over and she could get away from him, but it turned out that they were all going to a party on his boat. Bertrand took her aside as they walked back through the port. He took her to sit in a café and ordered cognacs for them both. He said that he had not meant to spring this on her so quickly but, as she could see, he was a film director, and a very serious one, with a lot of respect from those in the business. He thought she might just have what it takes, if she were prepared to work hard and do what she was told.

Georgia was expecting to go to bed with him anyway, in fact she was quite looking forward to it, so there was really no need for him to shoot her such a big line. But it was quite flattering really, and she went along with it. Why not, if it made him happy?

Then Bertrand said that there were one or two things that she should know before they went to the party. First of all, Rankin was a very rich man indeed, and a new friend; he was extremely interested in Bertrand and his talent and was going to finance his film, if everything went well. Then Bertrand took her by the hand and said it was not always easy being a film star, as Bardot would tell her when they were introduced. It would be as well if she was as nice as possible to Gerald, because people with money liked to be friends with their stars. He hoped she would remember that.

She was starting to be a bit disappointed in Bertrand. She wondered just how nice he meant her to be. She was going to ask him when Max sat down opposite them and it was too late. They had another brandy and Max brought out some pills, which they all took. She didn't want to be naïve by asking them what they were.

It was a big boat, open at the back with a long narrow cabin where a table with flowers and bottles of drink stood against a wall. Bertrand pointed out the older woman who had been sitting beside her at dinner. He said not to be too nice to Gerald when she was nearby. She was called Rilda and she was Gerald's wife. She was not as sophisticated as French women and sometimes became quite upset if girls paid Gerald too much attention.

It was starting to become rather boring at the party. The men were doing all the talking and the girls were just standing around, pouting and looking sulky as they helped to pass around cigarettes with cannabis in them. Everybody made a great fuss about smoking them, holding them cupped in their hands and sucking in the smoke with silly expressions on their faces, hoping that the others would notice. Georgia's French was not good enough to understand what they were saying, even when they did try to talk to her, so she wandered off by herself, hoping someone would suggest they went on to a nightclub – anywhere else where there would be some men of her own age.

She heard Gerald's whiny voice asking her what she was doing on her own and whether she would like to have a look around the boat. He had a sneaky sort of expression that put her on her guard, but she thought that she had better do what Bertrand wanted, so she said that that would be nice, thinking there wasn't much he could do to her with all those people so close by.

It was really rather pokey downstairs. Just a narrow corridor with three or four small cabins leading off it containing bunk beds and not much else. He left his own cabin until last. He called it the state room and was very proud of it, opening the door with a flourish and insisting that she come inside and try out the bed. It was quiet down there and the noise of the party was very faint. She felt her flesh start to creep, but she sat on the bed just to please him, and standing back, he asked her what she thought of it, waiting for her answer.

She hadn't noticed at first, but it did feel a bit different, hard and soft at the same time. He told her that the mattress was filled with water, which was a brand-new concept. She could tell she was meant to be impressed from the way he spoke, so she said it was very nice. She was going to stand up when suddenly he pounced on her and started to fumble at her front, saying that he thought she would go a long way as an actress and he might just be interested in doing something with Bertrand and his film. It would mean that they would be seeing a lot of each other, as he would like to help her career. He had a mean little face close up, with squinty eyes and a hooked nose. She could tell he would say anything to get her clothes off and she was going to push him away when there was a noise behind him and Rilda was standing in the doorway, looking at them.

She had a carving knife in her hand. The blade was worn where it had been sharpened and she held it in front of her so you could see that her hand was trembling. They were all still for a moment. Georgia was glad that she was fully dressed, although her skirt had become wrinkled up around her waist and she made a movement to pull it down. It was a mistake doing that, because Rilda lunged forward and the knife caught Gerald in the thigh, which made him scream. Georgia rolled to the other side of the bed and as she did so, Rilda stabbed again and there was a most awful swoosh as the water started to come spurting out of the mattress. Gerald stopped screaming and started to try to find where it was coming from. He was furious at Rilda and kept shouting that she was a dirty bitch and could she see what she had done? He seemed to have forgotten about his leg, but the blood was still coming out and mixing with the water, giving it a pinkish tinge.

Rilda stood looking for a second. Then she turned and ran out of the cabin and up the stairs, back to the room with all the guests. They could hear her screaming as she went and there was a tremendous splash and a lot of shouting from above. Bertrand came running down, saying she had jumped into the harbour and Gerald went limping up the stairs after her. He was groaning and clutching his leg.

Bertrand was absolutely furious with her. He said he had warned her about Rilda and she should have known better, trying to get off with Gerald while she was around.

There was a tremendous commotion when they went back to the party. Everyone was on deck looking for Rilda and there were policemen on board, with boats all round, shining their lights on the water. There was a blue light from an ambulance that was coming for Gerald, but the quay was thick with spectators and it couldn't get through. The rest of them had to wait there for hours, answering questions, and Bertrand told her not to say that she had come with him; she had done enough damage already.

28

It was five o'clock in the morning before they allowed her to leave
the police station. There had been a lot of fuss and bother on the
boat, with people jumping into the water trying to find where Rilda
had gone to and a big crowd on the quay. All the tourists from the
cafés along the front were pushing and craning their heads, pointing
at the guests who were being allowed off the boat, one by one, after
they had been questioned by the police.

Bertrand had been one of the first to leave. Georgia had watched
as he spoke to the police and at one stage they had turned to look
at her and she thought what a shit Bertrand had turned out to be,
telling tales and dropping her right in the mess when all the time
she had been doing exactly what he had asked of her.

But it wasn't only Bertrand. There had been several other guests
pointing at her as well, so it was no great surprise when the police
asked her to come with them and she was led through the dense
packed throng and past an ambulance inching towards the boat
with its horn blaring and lights flashing. Nobody was paying it any
attention. It would be some time before Gerald reached the hospital,
which served him right, the way he was groaning and carrying on;
saying he had no idea what could have happened, when all the time
it was his fault for trying to get his hand up her dress when they
had hardly met. He was a repulsive little man.

It wasn't much better in the police station. It was packed with people, all shouting and pointing at each other, so it was hard to know who the prisoners were until they were taken off to the back where the cells were.

Nobody seemed that interested in her once they had taken her name and address and found out she was English, the same as Gerald and Rilda. In fact they seemed to find the whole thing a bit of a joke, as if foreigners didn't count, and she was left by herself in a corner. Somebody bought her a cup of coffee from the bar next door.

It looked as if Gerald never reached the hospital. He arrived about half an hour later, still hobbling and holding on to his leg. There was a bandage wrapped several times around his thigh. The bleeding seemed to have stopped, although there was a stain on the bandage and he was still moaning whenever anyone came near. There was nowhere for him to sit and the people in the chairs along the wall were not going to move for him, so he had to stand in the middle of the crowd, hopping about and cursing, being bumped from all sides.

In the end he was taken to a side room and that was the last she saw of him, although she could still hear his whiny voice rising above the din.

Soon after he had left the room, they brought in Rilda. You could tell that she had been in the water. Her hair was all bedraggled and her clothes were creased and still damp in parts, sticking to her as she moved. You could see that she had taken off her underwear, or perhaps she hadn't been wearing any in the first place, which was a mistake on her part as her body didn't look very good if you saw too much of it.

The police were very angry with Rilda and so was a man in an apron who had come in with her and who kept on shouting that she was a thief. It seemed that she had been sitting in one of the cafés for quite a while, watching everybody as they searched for her. She had been drinking brandies all the time but she had no money to pay for them, which was why she was in the police station; she had tried to leave and the man in the apron had spotted her.

She just stood in the middle of the room with them all bellowing at her, shrugging her shoulders and looking into the distance as if it wasn't happening. There was a crazy expression in her eyes, but you couldn't blame her for going potty, stuck with a little jerk like Gerald. God knows why she didn't leave him.

The police said Georgia could go soon after that and she walked towards the port, back to Bernard's apartment. The streets were empty, with only a few derelicts picking through the debris of the evening. She kept in the light of the streetlamps. It was spooky, so quiet after all the people only a few hours before.

There was no light in Bertrand's windows, but she went up the stone stairs and knocked loudly several times on the door. She could have sworn that there was a noise from inside when she first knocked, but there was nothing after that. She could imagine him squatting on his bed, waiting for her to go away. He was probably blaming her for spoiling his plan. She felt like leaving him a rude message, but there was nothing to write on.

There was a narrow side street leading away from the port. She crossed a square where the gravel crunched under her feet, and came to a long road that looked like the one she had driven down on the back of Roger's scooter. It was a pity that Bertrand had ruined it. She would have been very pleased to see Roger's stupid face at that moment; it was a long way back to Nice.

There was a small group standing on the pavement some way down the street. The sun was coming up over the rooftops and as she drew close to them she could see that they were locals. The women were dressed in long black skirts with black blouses and shawls, and the men looked as if they were going to work in the fields. They all huddled together as she approached and gave a communal grunt when she asked if this was right for the bus to Nice. She assumed that it was and stood beside them, but they seemed embarrassed by her presence and mumbled amongst themselves, ignoring her completely.

It was a long bus ride, almost four hours before she reached the terminal in Nice. The road ran by the sea, winding along the coast line with little villages dotted along the route and no sign of tourists. It would have been lovely to have driven that way, swishing by in an open-topped tourer, but the bus stopped for anybody who waved from the roadside and she fell asleep after a while. She was stiff and sore when she finally got off, and her head felt absolutely terrible.

She took a taxi from the terminal and made it stop at the end of the road, hoping that she could sneak into her room and at least have a shower before she had to confront anyone. But Lilianne was sitting, having coffee with Pasha when she walked into the courtyard and there was no way of avoiding either of them.

They both leapt up at the sight of her and Lilianne came rushing towards her. She put her arms around her and hugged her while Pasha came panting up behind, saying how worried they had been and blaming Roger for abandoning her.

"I wish I had never introduced you to that dirty little boy,"

Lilianne said. "His mother was in here screaming, early this morning when we were all asleep, saying that you had tried to rape her baby and had wrecked his scooter when he tried to stop you. She called you a prostitute, going off with older men and baring yourself in front of everyone until Roger didn't like to look, the little halfwit."

Pasha said he had told them all how the place was full of naked women and next time he would go as well, to make sure that nothing happened. Lilianne told him to shut up and he went back to the table and poured himself a coffee; it was still too early for brandy.

She excused herself and went up to her room. It was evening before she woke up.

As usual Lilianne and Pasha were sitting downstairs in the courtyard. It was before dinner, so they were drinking Pernod; they saved the brandy for after the wine. They were not quite as jolly as they had been that morning, but subdued and worried; avoiding her eye. There was a copy of the evening newspaper open on the table and Pasha passed it to her without saying a word. She was on the front page. She couldn't believe it. She had only been there a few days and it had happened again. There was a picture of her which must have been taken as she was leaving the boat because there was a policeman on either side of her, and another picture next door to her own of Gerald and Rilda sitting at a restaurant table. They couldn't have been expecting to have their picture taken, because it looked as if they were having a row. The headline said something about a "Triangle Anglais". She didn't bother to read the rest.

Lilianne and Pasha were looking at her. They seemed to be nervous. "Have you told my Aunt about this?" she asked. She had a feeling that Aunt Eva would not be quite so forgiving this time. You couldn't blame her. Twice in one week was a bit much.

"No, we haven't," said Lilianne. And Pasha said that it would be better if her dear Aunt did not have anything else to worry her; God knew that there had been enough trouble in her life already. They both seemed relieved when she agreed that it would be inconsiderate to bother Aunt Eva with any more bad news. She thought they were scared stiff of what Eva might do if she found out.

The following three days were the most boring she had ever known. She spent the time dragging round the town and along the promenade, wondering what to do next. Most of the people were very old and the younger men all looked like Gerald, and behaved like him as well, sidling up to her when their wives weren't watching and making stupid suggestions. Many of them were English and would become annoyed when they discovered that she was English, too - as if she had been leading them on, trying to make a fool of them. After the second day she stopped going near the front and wandered around the back streets, but the same sort of thing happened, only this time the men were French and they became annoyed when she told them to push off.

She had seen Roger the day after she came back from St Tropez. He had been standing by the bus stop, his suitcases beside him on the pavement. He pretended not to notice her and stood staring straight ahead until she was right beside him. He was very nervous and said that he was not to talk to her anymore as his mother was cross with him over the scooter, which was going to cost 500 francs to repair. He blamed it all on her, which was only right as it was her fault. The bus came at that moment and she was unable to tell him what she thought of him, so she put her tongue out at him as it drove off, which was about the most exciting thing that had happened for days.

She had more or less given up any hope of finding anything to do when she walked home on the afternoon of the third day and saw Bertrand's car parked outside the pension. He was sitting inside, talking to Pasha and Lilianne. He was wearing a dark suit and a white shirt with a navy tie. He looked very proper and correct and rather smarmy as he jumped up and started kissing her hand, saying how he was just talking about her career with Monsieur and Madame; showing them his press cuttings of all the other beautiful girls with a certain, indefinable look that he had made famous in the past. She thought he was joking at first, the way he was laying it on, but he was deadly serious and so were the other two. They were looking through the big album full of press cuttings which he must have brought with him.

Pasha was very excited. He said that they were not going to stand in her way; a man like Monsieur Bertrand could be the making of a young girl. He would be happy to visit her when she was a star, because he had always felt that he should have been a film-maker. Lilianne told him to be quiet, but nicely this time in front of Bertrand. She said that they would allow her to go with Monsieur, just for two days at first, to see how she got on. She was going to have a hotel at Bertrand's expense and a chaperone for the evenings.

Georgia looked hard at Bertrand but he nodded his head vigorously and said "*absolument*" several times.

She packed quickly, before anyone could change their minds.

It was quite a difference, driving to St Tropez in Bertrand's Aston Martin. He rather spoilt it by revving the engine and trying to do racing changes, tearing past all the other cars and blowing his horn the whole time. Then he tried a four-wheel drift and went off into the grass and all the cars passed him, blowing their horns and pointing. He was very upset. They took the back way, after that.

She was surprised that he really had booked her a room in a hotel. It was an old pension overlooking the port and close to where he lived. They dropped off her bag and went straight to his apartment. He had not said much during the journey but now he sat her down at a table and produced a legal-looking piece of paper from the next-door room. He placed it in front of her and unscrewed a Mont Blanc fountain pen, handing it to her with a flourish and indicating that she should sign at the bottom, where there was a large cross marked in pencil.

She ignored the pen and started to read. The document was written in French, using long words that she had never seen before. She struggled through it while Bertrand sat down opposite her. He started puffing out his cheeks and making impatient noises with his mouth. It was no good, she could hardly understand a word. He became angry when she asked him to translate, saying that it was perfectly normal for an agent to get half the earnings of a young starlet. She would be nowhere at all if it were not for him and he was surprised at her ingratitude, which he had not expected from her. In the end she signed it, just to shut him up. She could always say he forced her to do it and besides, she was under twentyone, which would surely count for something if it ever came to court.

He relaxed after that. He took the document next door and she could hear him lock it up in a drawer. When he came back he said there was something that they had to discuss before they went any further. It seemed that the film depended entirely on Gerald and his money. Bertrand said that Gerald was very interested in her and her career and it was going to make a big difference, now that she was under contract.

There had been no sign of Gerald's boat when she had looked round the harbour, but Bertrand said that he had moved it to Cannes so that there would be no more trouble from Rilda who, being English, was very unsophisticated and naïve; besides, the police would lock her up if she tried any more of her games in St Tropez. He said that Gerald would be down in the next few days, maybe even tonight, now that he knew she was here and he, Bertrand, was relying on her to do the right thing.

If he thought she was going to have Gerald playing around with her just so that he could make his film, he was in for a shock, but she was hungry and she thought it would be better to get him to buy her a dinner before they had a row.

They went back to the same restaurant with the blue tablecloths. The people at the table were about the same as well. It was hard to say if they had been there the other evening, but it made no difference. The men did all the talking while the girls – who were all much younger, about the same age as herself – sat listening to them, pretending to be amused and sometimes making coy little comments which the men ignored.

There was an American girl sitting opposite her who was different from the others and seemed as bored as she was. Her name was Karen and she was statuesque, with long blonde hair and a tight black dress in a shiny fabric that showed her shoulders and most of her bosom. There was a small satin pouch hanging round her neck that rested on the top of her large pointed breasts.

She said that she was going to the bathroom and Georgia said that she would come as well; anything to get away from the table. When they were in the ladies' room the girl said she was going to take some horse before she passed out with boredom. She asked Georgia if she would like some as well. Georgia said: wasn't it dangerous? and the girl replied, not if you only popped your skin. She had been doing it for months and it was no problem at all if you kept away from the veins.

She had a syringe in her bag and filled it from a glass phial that she took from the satin pouch she wore round her neck. Georgia hated anything to do with needles and injections but the girl showed her how to do it so that it didn't hurt and she was right, because you hardly felt a thing if you squeezed hard enough. Georgia felt quite dizzy afterwards but the girl said that it was usually like that the first time, so she didn't worry about it.

It did the trick, though. The evening went past really quickly after that and she could hardly remember going to bed. She was relieved that there was no one beside her when she woke up in the morning. She thought she could remember Bertrand saying that Gerald wouldn't like it if she was playing around, though she had no idea what that had to do with him.

29

Eva had agonized for hours before ringing Dr Frayne. She knew that she had to contact someone who could be of help to her sister and she also knew that to call in a local psychiatrist would mean Alexandra's arrest. No French doctor would take responsibility for a murderess walking free in the streets, no matter what oaths of secrecy they had sworn. It was just not the way things worked in France.

It was a letdown when her call finally went through and she learned that Frayne was no longer at the camp and no longer in the Army at all. His demobilization had taken place within a few days of Alexandra's leaving the camp.

She was desperate to find him, but there was nothing that she could do until the next morning except keep a close watch on her sister and plan how Druska and she were going to handle things until she could find the doctor.

She told Druska what had happened as soon as Alexandra had gone to her room. There was no point in sparing her from the knowledge of the terrible thing that had been done; in fact, it was essential that Druska and she should share everything that they could discover about Alexandra if she were to be saved.

Practical as ever, Druska immediately collected all the knives in the apartment and locked them in a drawer in her bedroom. Then she came back to the drawing room and sat opposite her mistress, staring at her with worried eyes, waiting to be told what to do.

Eva was in a quandary. She was terrified that too close a watch on her sister might stir a further outburst of the unknown torment that lurked in her mind. If she felt that her freedom was threatened, she might even run away from them and disappear into the street, leaving a trail of bloody corpses behind her until, finally, she was cornered. What might happen then was too terrible to consider.

At best, she would be taken to an asylum from which she might well never be released, no matter what her state of mind might eventually become. French institutions were notorious for such things, with sane people committed by accident and never seen again — driven to real madness by the conditions under which they were kept.

At worst she would be shot dead in the street while fleeing from her pursuers.

The two women sat for hours, discussing how they were to behave and what they should do to keep Alexandra under a strict watch without alarming her in any way. Eva knew that it would be impossible to keep up such a pretence for very long.

The next morning she started early, ringing every organization she could think of who might know where Frayne could be contacted. Both the Red Cross and the Royal Medical Corps were very polite and completely unhelpful. She tried the camp at Koenigsberg once again, and spoke to the corporal whom she had met on her first visit. He said that the Captain had always talked about London and what a time he was going to have once the war was over, so she made a list of the London hospitals and rang them all during the course of the day. Often it took over two hours for the operator to make even one connection. By the end of the day she had covered them all. None of them had heard of a Dr Frayne.

Druska had been with Alexandra throughout the day. It had been easy in the morning because there was plenty of housework for her to do, and it gave her an excuse to stay at home. Alexandra had said that she had a headache when she woke up, but by the middle of the day she was ready to go out and there was nothing that Druska could do but go with her. Eva was on tenterhooks until they returned, but nothing unusual had happened so they both relaxed. It was almost impossible to believe that the horror of the previous night had really occurred.

As a last resort, Eva asked the operator for a list of numbers for all the Fraynes in the London telephone book. There were dozens of them and she could see that it was going to take most of the night to ring them all. But she was lucky on the third attempt. A woman's voice said, yes, her son the doctor was at home, and then she heard Frayne's voice asking what she wanted.

It was dangerous to use the telephone to tell the whole story. She explained who she was and how the doctor had warned her that her sister might be far less well than she appeared. Then she said, "Doctor, if you imagine the worst thing that could have happened, the very worst, you will understand that I can say no more and why you are the only person that I can turn to."

Her voice was trembling as she made her plea and Frayne was touched by her desperation. He did not remember the patient among the thousands of poor wretches who had passed through his hands, but he most certainly recalled the svelte and beautiful woman who had been such an unusual visitor to the camp in the woods. Besides, he was finding it hard to settle down in London after the upheaval of the war and a trip to Paris and the small fortune that the lady was offering was more than enough to set him on the boat train from Victoria station the following morning.

Eva met him at the Gare du Nord. They sat in the café in the station where she ordered cognacs; she waited until they had arrived before she started to speak. She was eyeing the Englishman as they waited. He had thick, dark hair and was quite short, but with a big chest and shoulders. She was still not sure if she could trust him, but she had no choice. He watched her as she told him all that had happened since Alexandra had left the camp: the dustbins, the hidden food and last of all, the knife. He knew how the story was going to end and cursed himself for not diagnosing the depth of Alexandra's illness whilst she was under his care, although he knew how impossible it had been to deal in any detail with any but the most obvious cases of acute disturbance. Nevertheless, she had been his patient and he had let her down. But if she had anything of the character of her sister, sitting calm and determined in front of him as she recounted the terrible event, then he would have more than enough good material upon which to start his work.

Hesitantly he reached out and touched Eva's leather-gloved hand. "Don't worry any more than you have to. Your sister has an extreme case of a very common reaction to all the ghastly things to which she has been exposed. It is very possible that she will be cured and, if I am not able to do so, there are other, more highly experienced doctors to whom you can go."

Eva felt like weeping as his strength and certainty lifted a great part of the helplessness that had been weighing her down.

Alexandra showed little surprise at Dr Frayne's arrival. Eva explained that it was a part of the conditions under which she had been released so early from the camp and that the doctor would be with them for a few days. Alexandra smiled and said that it was nice to see him again. There was no suspicion in her eyes and she seemed genuinely glad when she discovered that the doctor knew even less of Paris than she herself did. She promised to start showing him the sights the next morning.

It was going to be a slow process, Frayne could see that after their first walk together. They had bought a guide book and had spent the morning strolling along the Champs Élysées, starting at the Arc de Triomphe and slowly making their way down the slope until by lunchtime they were close to the rue de Rivoli, stopping for a sandwich at a café in one of the side streets. It was a sunny day and they sat outside at a table on the pavement. Alexandra was happy and relaxed, with no hint of the terrors that he knew were lurking around the edges of her mind.

They settled into a routine, each day visiting a different section of the city, sometimes going for hours without exchanging a word as the relationship between them grew and Frayne cautiously started to probe behind the brittle façade with which Alexandra had learned to disguise the seething violence within her. It was going to be a long, perhaps neverending task. The more he delved the deeper he found the roots of her sickness to be.

There was no doubt that she was enjoying his company, they could all see that. She was a different person from the sad and tormented girl who had left the camp in Austria. Eva and Druska were so delighted at her progress that they had no eyes for the condition of her physician. If they had watched, they would have seen a change in him as well, for Dr Frayne was finding himself becoming altogether too involved in his patient despite the barriers professional etiquette prescribed.

But there was something else to occupy Eva's attention. Alexandra and Frayne had been on their daily outing, about a week after his arrival, and Druska and she had been alone in the apartment when there was a single ring on the doorbell. It was unusual for there to be a visitor at the front door without notice from the concierge and they looked at each other in alarm, both fearing that the police had finally arrived. It was common knowledge that they had been asking questions around the neighbourhood since the body of the Arab had been found.

Druska went to the door and Eva sat in the drawing room, trying to look calm and composed and rehearsing once again all the answers she was going to give.

There was a burst of voices in the hall and the sound of sobbing. Before she could move, the door was flung open and a strange woman stood weeping on the threshold. She gave a scream when she saw Eva and ran towards her with her arms outstretched. Eva took a step backwards in alarm. The woman was tall and thin with a weather-beaten face and tattered, prewar clothing; her hair was hidden by a faded scarf. She looked most definitely unhinged, the tears running down her face and little screams coming from her throat.

The back of a chair prevented Eva from further retreat and she was swept up in a welter of boney ribs and stringy shoulders. It wasn't until the stranger started kissing at her in a frenzy of joy that she suddenly realized who it must be.

"Lilianne? It can't be!" She had given up all hope of ever seeing her friend again. There had been no sign of her, or any of her circle, in their usual haunts, and her apartment on the rue George V was occupied by a family of Rumanians who had told her that they had been living there for the last thirty years. Rumanians did that sort of thing.

It took a while to calm Lilianne down and a large glass of cognac before she was able to speak. She was vague as to where she had come from and what she had been doing since they had last seen her at the beginning of the war. She said that the war had been very hard on Pasha and she had suffered terribly because she had stood by him. No one realized how difficult it was, being a neutral. It had been all right at first. Silesia had been taken by the Germans and Pasha's factory had made metal things to use on their tanks; nothing that killed people, not guns or shells but the part of the turret that made it go round. They had lived in Silesia because it was safe and they had visited Paris a few times for Pasha's business. Everybody had been so pleased to see them, and grateful to Pasha for doing them favours with his friends in the Wehrmacht. Then things had become different and very confusing if you were a neutral, with both sides saying that they were winning and nobody knowing who to believe. They went back to Paris to escape from the Russians but someone must have said bad things about Pasha when they could see that the Germans had lost, and they had been forced to leave quickly, before something happened.

She was crying the whole time she was talking and Eva could not help but feel sorry for her. It looked as though she had lived the last few years in the hedgerow, which was punishment enough for someone like Lilianne.

Druska had brought her another brandy, a smaller one this time. She rolled her eyes at Eva over the sideboard.

"How is Pasha?" Eva asked. "I hope he's with you." Lilianne put her hands to her mouth and said that she had forgotten all about him. He was sitting downstairs, waiting for her to come back.

Eva went to look out of the window and Druska moved to stand beside her. There was a tramp sitting on a bench on the other side of the road. He was wearing an old and baggy camel-coloured coat and there were two brown paper parcels on the bench beside him. Druska said that she would go and get him and Eva was left alone with her friend.

"Listen, Lilianne," she said. "As long as you haven't caused anybody to be killed, I am your friend, no matter what you have done, but there's someone staying with me, my sister from Poland, who has suffered terribly at the hands of the Germans and there's a doctor with her who was an officer in the army until a few weeks ago. If either of them were to find out that you were a collaborator, it would be the end for you. They would report you at once and my sister might do something even worse. Do you understand?"

Lilianne was watching her as she spoke. She looked startled by Eva's vehemence. "My little Eva," she said, "how you have changed. Don't worry, I'll do nothing to upset anyone and I'll talk to Pasha. I've such a problem with him. He just cannot see that he has done wrong and he keeps on saying stupid things that make people suspicious. I have to take him a long way from here where nobody knows us, or one day he will say something and that will be that. They are still shooting people without trial in the country. There are hundreds of others like us in the city and word gets around about what is happening."

They could hear Druska returning with Pasha. He looked a wreck as he stood in the doorway. Eva ran to him and gave him a hug. She led him to a chair and Druska poured him a full glass of brandy. He sat back and sniffed it, all the time without saying a word. He raised it to his lips and toasted them. There was a hint of the old, debonair Pasha as he bowed to each of them, but there was a tear in his eye as he sipped at his drink.

Eva had realized how impossible it would be for them to stay with her as soon as Lilianne had finished her story. They would never be able to hide it from Alexandra for long and she feared what effect the introduction of two collaborators into the household would have on her sister. They might both be found dead with their throats cut one morning, if the truth were to come out. She had thought of the apartment in the boulevard Haussmann. It was still there, untouched since her night spent with Andrzej. She had tried to stop going there, knowing that it was useless to live in the past, but she had not had the heart to disturb it. It was there as a shrine to her lover and as a perpetual reminder of her terrible sin. She knew that the time had come to wipe clean forever the wicked spirits with which it was infested. She decided that she would move them there at once; Alexandra would never know that they existed.

Even now the sudden thought of Andrzej brought tears to her eyes. Perhaps at that very moment there was a person offering him sanctuary in their home. She prayed that he was alive and in safety.

30

It was not possible to move them straightaway. Eva and Druska had drifted diplomatically into the kitchen, to discuss what should be done. They were only gone a few minutes, but when they came back Lilianne and Pasha had both fallen fast asleep. The brandy and the unaccustomed comfort, the relief at being amongst friends after so many years of suffering and vigilance, had left them both snoring, open-mouthed and rather smelly, so that Druska had to open the windows to let some air in.

They were still asleep when Alexandra came home. She was very excited at the sight of the two tramps sprawled in the salon and terribly impressed that Eva should have such friends. She said she could hardly wait to talk to them; there was so much that they must have in common. Eva had to take Frayne aside and tell him that it would not be a very good idea, as her friends and their story could only be detrimental to her sister's state of mind. He appeared to be quite startled at their presence and nodded in relief when she suggested that they both took themselves off to the cinema. There was an English film with Laurence Olivier and Vivien Leigh showing on the Champs Élysées.

Druska went on ahead of her to make the apartment in the boulevard Haussmann ready. It was the first time she had been there since Eva's marriage. The same concierge tapped at her through the window as she entered through the front gates. She was old and decrepit and it was sometime before Druska was recognized and allowed to pass. The woman called after her as she started up the stairs: "Tell Madame that there is still no sign of her young man. If you ask me he's gone off with someone else." The old hag cackled maliciously at the thought. Stupid old woman. Druska had always loathed her. She would never forget the way she had treated them when they had first arrived from the castle in Poland.

The mention of a young man set her thinking. She would never forget the night, just after Eva's wedding, when Mr Power had been in Switzerland and her mistress had disappeared for the entire day and the night that followed. She had sat up waiting for her, finally falling asleep at dawn, and she would never forget Eva's face when she had at last come home, white and lined with strain, as if she had looked into the eyes of death itself. Druska thought that Eva had changed from that day onwards. It was as if all the joy had been crushed out of her. Overnight she had aged, become hard and practical, with an ever-present overtone of sadness as she drove forward along her own, private way from which everyone else was excluded. Druska thought that the existence of this young man could explain many of the things that had been worrying her for the past several years. She wished she knew who he was.

The apartment was already looking bright and clean by the time Eva arrived with the others. She had been dreading the thought of her shrine being disturbed, but already all traces of her night with Andrzej had been obliterated. She thought Druska had given her a strange look when she entered and sometimes she felt Druska's eyes following her as they bustled about, making beds, airing blankets and clearing away the last traces of the grime of seven years. There was plenty to do and enough to concern her without worrying about Druska's mood so she ignored her as they went about their work. After a while she left them all to get on with it and went to one of the nearby department stores to buy some clothes for Lilianne and Pasha. Dressed as they were, it would be impossible for them to go anywhere to buy clothes for themselves.

She had bought them a bottle of the finest cognac as a welcoming present and they were sitting opposite each other on two ornate Louis XV chairs in the grand salon. The bottle was between them on a carved Chippendale table, as she and Druska said goodbye. They had still not changed into their new clothes.

Druska was silent on the way home. The apartment was still empty when they arrived. Druska hesitated in the hallway. She put her hand in her pocket and then held it out, palm open, in front of

Eva. Her eyes were fixed intently on the floor. She said, "I found this in the apartment. It was under one of the pillows. It must have been there from before the war."

There was a ring in her hand. She waited for Eva to take it from her and then she turned and went down the corridor towards her room. Eva looked at the ring. It was a gold signet ring and, from its size and weight, it had belonged to a man. She peered at the crest that was etched into the black stone. Her heart told her what she would see before her eyes could distinguish the soaring eagle that had been the symbol of the Lubinski family since the mists of time began. She ran to her room and sat, holding it in her hand, turning it round, feeling its weight and the roughness of the crest against her cheek. Andrzej would never have parted with his heirloom by accident. She knew that he had left it there for her, expecting her to return to the apartment after they had said goodbye at the station. She would have found it waiting for her, as a token of his love and the future that he had planned for them both.

She took a gold chain from her jewellery box and hung the ring round her neck, tucking it beneath the front of her dress. She would wear it forever, or until her lover returned to claim it.

She did not see very much of Alexandra for the next week. Frayne seemed to have organized her daily routine so that they were nearly always out together on some expedition to the countryside or on a trip to a museum or a concert; and Eva was delighted that her sister appeared so happy in his company. She congratulated herself on her decision to track down the Englishman. It was obvious to them all that whatever he was doing to cure her sister was having the most encouraging results.

Whenever she and Frayne were alone together, she would question him on the progress of his patient and he would tell her that it was early days and there was still a long way to go before he would be able to judge the extent of her progress. So she sensed nothing unusual when, one morning, he asked if he could have a word with her in private. The breakfast room had been cleared and they sat facing each other across the empty table. It was then that she noticed that the doctor, usually so definite and sure of himself, was flushed and awkward, staring at the tablecloth and twisting his hands as though he were a child with a confession to make.

She still felt no reason for alarm when, hesitantly, he started to speak. "What I'm going to say will give you every right to be furious with me. If you decide to dismiss me or even report me to the association in London, I will fully understand, but . . ." He hesitated and stammered with his face going even redder and his hands twitching. "I am in love with your sister and she is in love with me." He went on hastily, before she could interrupt. He wasn't to know that she was speechless with surprise – and annoyance as well, as her mind started to clear from the shock. "The real problem is, how real and lasting is Alexandra's love for me? You may well say I have abused my position. It's common for patients to transfer undue affection to their doctor and she is very sick indeed; and in my opinion, will continue to be so for a very long time, perhaps even for the rest of her life. That makes it even more important that I should look after her. I swear that nothing wrong has happened between us and if you tell me to go, I will leave at once. I just beg you to think and not act hastily."

Eva stared at the green baize tablecloth. It was unforgivable for him to have become involved with her sister – and yet, he was an honourable man, or he would not have come to her. It would have been only too easy for him to have said nothing. She was sure that, as a psychiatrist, he could have persuaded Alexandra to do whatever he liked. She felt the signet ring hard against her breast. Who was she to stand in the way of happiness, even if it were not to last? Her entire life was contained in that one night of love and she counted herself more than fortunate to have experienced it, even if it had to last for the rest of her time on earth. There was a noise outside the door and she knew that Alexandra was listening and she called out to her. Her sister was red-faced as she entered, but her eyes were shining; happiness and anxiety mixing together as she stood waiting for Eva to speak.

Eva felt like an old woman as she looked at them. It was hard not to be jealous of their joy. She fought back the bitterness that she could feel rising inside her. She found it difficult to speak. She stood up and embraced her sister. Alexandra clung to her. They were both sobbing, though neither knew why. "Be happy while you can, my darling," Eva whispered. The ring pressed against her again as they hugged and she felt as though her heart would break.

Eva would have preferred it to have been a quiet sort of a ceremony, rather like her own: just a few friends, a nice lunch afterwards and some handfuls of rice to see them off. Unfortunately the Frayne family had been of a different mind, pointing out that their son and his bride were going to make their life together in England, as well as all the inconvenience of shipping the hundred guests from London to Paris, not to say the cost and the damage that would undoubtedly be caused to the health of Mr Frayne, senior, who had a condition which nobody was meant to discuss.

After three weeks of whinging letters, full of implications and double meanings that she could not understand — even when Frayne read them out loud to her, although they appeared to be plain enough to him — she decided to damn the lot of them. She agreed, with very bad grace, that the ceremony should be held in London. She had lost a certain amount of respect for Frayne, and had none at all for his parents and their emotional blackmail. He had been visibly upset as it became increasingly clear with every cloying letter and telephone call, that he was not going to be allowed to make up his own mind on the matter. Anyway, there were only the three of them. There was no one else in Paris that she would want to invite to such a family occasion, except for Lilianne and Pasha, and they were reluctant to go anywhere outside the safety of the apartment. In fact, their obvious terror at being discovered had set Eva to thinking that there was something more to Pasha's wartime activities than a simple, opportunistic collaboration with the conquering Nazis. But then she had decided that there were certain things it was better not to know.

Even after Eva had agreed to the wedding being held in England, there seemed to be no end to the stream of meddlesome queries from London. Mrs Frayne had obviously decided that her son was marrying beneath his station, and that his bride and her family, being Polish, could not be expected to understand the genteel niceties of a civilized wedding. The mail was full of instructions, loosely disguised as helpful suggestions. They covered everything from the quality and amount of the champagne, and the address of the local church where the Frayne family had worshipped for at least ten years, to the name of the nearby assembly rooms, where, it was assumed, she would wish the reception to be held.

The way the letters were written made it clear that it was Eva who was going to be paying for the festivities. The more she read the more her spirits sank. The Fraynes didn't even live in London, but in some little suburb several miles outside. It was silly: she had never imagined that Frayne was an aristocrat. She had never really thought about his family at all. He was such a strong and straightforward type of man, and clever as well, that she had had no doubts about him making a successful career. And her sister was so obviously dependent upon him, not only for her happiness but for her very sanity, that she had banished all her half-formed dreams of restoring her to her true heritage as a Lubinski and had wholeheartedly given the approval to their union.

Now she was not so sure. It was one thing marrying a young and good-looking commoner with a bright future in front of him, but another matter if his family were intent on dragging him back to their own bourgeois level. The Lubinski lands and fortune might be gone, but the blood lived on. She was not going to allow that to be debased without a struggle.

She had taken to visiting the cathedral of Notre Dame, not attending Mass or any formal service, but going there when the vast building was quiet and silent except for the shuffling of feet in the side chapels and the occasional flurry of a group of tourists gawking their way through the echoing gloom. One day she had fallen into conversation with an English priest, a Father William Ganning on loan from the Jesuit community of Farm Street, in Mayfair, in the centre of London. He was exactly the sort of person who would know all the right things that would have to be done to ensure that her sister started her new life in a way befitting one of her breeding.

Father Ganning had been the correct choice, there was no doubt of that. The Jesuits at Farm Street saw themselves as clergy to the upper end of their Roman Catholic flock and the priest threw himself into the launching of the Lubinski name with an enthusiasm that would have been both surprising and gratifying to anyone less cynical than Eva. Her experience since the death of her husband had brought her to realize the power that her fortune had given her, although this was the first time that there had been occasion for her to use it.

They had travelled to London several weeks before the date of the wedding and the priest had joined them soon afterwards. Eva established herself in a large suite at the Connaught Hotel, just down the road from Farm Street. They started their campaign immediately, the priest arranging for her to lunch with an old friend of his family, a Lady Pamela Berry, who had only recently finished the Season herself and who, together with her brother, knew everybody who counted in London society.

Lady Pamela was exactly the sort of person that Eva had been hoping to meet. She was well born and well connected and had no money or mind of her own. Perfect for Eva's purpose. Within a few days she had more invitations to cocktail parties, lunches and weekends in the country than she could have attended in a whole year. One thing was certain, the Lubinski side of the aisle was going to be overflowing with grand people on the day of the wedding even if they were all friends of Lady Pamela. There would be no doubt in anybody's mind which family was lowering itself by the union.

Alexandra was far too happy to be bothered by social niceties. The contrast between all that was happening to her now and her sufferings during the war was almost more than she could grasp

216

and she spent the days in a whirl of delight, grateful to her sister for all the marvellous things she had made happen. Frayne found himself swept away in her joy. He, too, was overcome by the unexpectedness of his new situation. Eva's sudden assault on the London scene had changed him overnight from a young man of relatively humble origins and prospects to a friend, if not yet a member, of the Establishment. There was already talk of a private practice in Harley Street and he was meeting plenty of potential patients every day. He wished that his own family were slightly more pleased with his sudden elevation.

They had visited the Frayne family at the end of their first week in London; Eva had wanted to assess her own social strength before the encounter. They had swept down on the quiet suburban street on the outskirts of Epsom, in Surrey, in a large black Daimler limousine with a uniformed chauffeur who opened the door and ushered Eva to the gate of the small front garden. She stood back and looked at the street. The line of houses stretched, uniform and dismal, as far as she could see. It was a Sunday and there were men washing their cars in the front of their garages and some of the gardens had ponds, with little gnomes standing stolidly beside them. It was much worse than she had thought.

Rupert came running down the front path to meet them. He looked cowed and nervous, with all his usual self-confidence vanished in the presence of his family. Eva was suddenly furious with him for threatening to drag his sister down into his wretched little world. She sniffed loudly and strode up the path. "Over my dead body," she muttered to herself as she passed him.

There was a small, pebble-glass window in the front door, and the hall, more of a passage really, was cluttered with cloth coats and umbrellas. The sitting room, or lounge, as Mrs Frayne liked to call it, was filled with ornate, highly polished furniture and there was a three-piece suite swathed in loose covers of floral chintz which matched the curtains. There were other curtains made of white netting set tight against the small windows. They made the room dark and gloomy, even though the sun was still bright outside. The mantelpiece was full of photographs of rather ugly-looking people, standing stiff and unsmiling, as though scared of moving and spoiling the picture. The remaining space was so filled with standard lamps that it was hard not to bump into them as they were shown to their seats. There were glasses of warm, slightly sweet sherry, that had already been poured and were awaiting their arrival.

The lunch was less of a success than even Eva had expected. There was an instant antipathy between herself and the Frayne family that

217

grew worse as the meal progressed. Mr Frayne was a bank manager and nearing his retirement. He had prided himself all his life on the values by which he conducted himself, and the home that he had made for his family. His wife saw herself as a loyal and long-suffering woman who had dedicated her life to the wellbeing of her loved ones and had succeeded in her task in spite of all of the terrible and unfair privations that the war had thrust upon her. She had a deep mistrust of foreigners, particularly women, who she saw as immoral by nature and scheming in their dealings with men. The sight of Eva and Alexandra, sleek and immaculate in their smart, Parisian suits and little pillbox hats, confirmed her worst fears: they were plotting to capture her son, luring him away from all that was good and righteous for some secret and selfish purpose, far beyond the imagination of all decent people.

Afterwards, Eva had to admit to herself that she had behaved badly, but the sight of their self-centred smugness had been too much for her. All the same, perhaps she shouldn't have upset them quite so much, sneering at everything and saying what a pity it was that the war had ruined Mr Frayne's career, and that it was the same in France, with people being forced to live in the most humble surroundings, far beneath their station, and forced to exist on scraps and charity – this as Mrs Frayne had been proudly producing the Sunday roast, the highlight of her week.

She had managed to unload several other barbs along the way, climaxing in the news that the wedding was now going to be held in the ultra-fashionable church at Farm Street, with a reception at the Connaught to follow, and would the Fraynes mind keeping their invitation list as short as possible, there was only room for three hundred in the chapel; she was sure they would understand.

Frayne was to travel with them back to London. It was a silent journey. He appeared dazed at the way things had gone.

Eva summoned Alexandra and Frayne to her the moment they were back in the hotel. She was sitting at the table in the dining room of their suite. There was a pile of documents before her and she looked grave and determined. They sat down in front of her, wondering what else could possibly have gone wrong.

Eva waited until they were seated and then she said, "I have been thinking a lot about your future and it has been worrying me very much." She addressed herself to Frayne: "I have a duty to my sister and our family. She and I are the last ones to bear that name. Frankly, you are, as yet, unable to provide any sort of suitable existence for someone of her birth."

Alexandra suddenly butted in, rising furiously to the defence of her lover, but Eva stopped her with an imperious wave of her hand. Alexandra was silent. She knew better than to stand up to Eva when she was in this mood.

Eva continued as if her sister weren't in the room. "I've decided that I am going to give you a wedding present that will enable you to live as is expected of a Lubinski. There is a house in Kensington that I went to see yesterday. It will cost £15,000, but I am prepared to buy it for you as a gift, if it meets with your approval, of course."

It would be years before Frayne could afford such a house. He started to acknowledge her generosity, but she held up her hand. "In addition, I have formed a trust which will pay my sister not less than £5,000 a year for as long as she lives. I want to make sure that she has her independence." Again, it was an astonishingly generous gift and both Frayne and Alexandra stood up to embrace her, but she motioned them back to their seats.

"There is one further matter to which I want you to agree. I pray that it will never happen, but we must be prepared. If anything terrible were to happen to you both, and you were to die leaving children behind you, I want you to make me the legal guardian of those children. I have had a document prepared." She slid a sheet of paper across the table. They were too grateful to her to think of hesitating; anyway there was no reason why they should refuse.

Eva asked Druska to pour them all drinks. She toasted their happiness and watched them relax, the unpleasantness of the day forgotten. She thought she had handled that very well. There was nothing else she could do at the moment. She would wait and see how the marriage turned out before she tackled the problem of changing their name. She was glad that, so far, she had not been forced to use the contents of her will as a lever. She could save that for later.

219

31

Eva had been bitterly disappointed at the way she had lost touch with Alexandra and her family. Apart from an annual visit to London and her attendance at the baptisms of the two girls, she had seen little of them in the five years since their marriage. It was not as though they were deliberately trying to avoid her, she was quite sure of that. Alexandra wrote to her regularly and Frayne was always genuinely pleased to see her whenever she arrived, always thanking her for the wonderful start that she had given them and attributing the success of his growing practice to her influence and the friends that she had directed to him in the early days. She supposed that it was just that they had a life of their own to lead, and Paris and her world were a long way away.

She kept an eye on them though, making sure that Lady Pamela called on them regularly and waiting impatiently for her reports on their progress, wanting to know about their friends and connections and, most important of all, about the two baby girls and the influence that Grandmother Frayne was having on their upbringing. She supposed it was impossible to stop any contact between the older members of the Frayne family and her nieces, but she could sense that their influence was always there, jealous and self-centred, undermining all the momentum that she was able to give during her own brief visits.

It was both frustrating and infuriating, sitting in Paris while that miserable woman and her husband had a clear field. She often thought that she should move to London to be closer to them all, but she sensed that the time was not yet right and that somehow her presence would do more harm than good. Frayne was doing too well in his career to make either her will or her cheque book an effective force.

Eva was due to pay them another visit and had just returned from the travel agent when she answered the telephone to hear Lady Pamela's broken voice telling her that there had been a terrible car crash and Alexandra and her husband were dead. The two little girls were alive but in hospital, and Lady Pamela didn't know what she should do.

It was strange how Eva felt as she put down the telephone. The grief would come later, she knew, but all she could think of was the two children and her duty – or was it opportunity – to bring them up in the way that befitted their lineage.

She left Paris with Druska that night, and arrived in London in the early hours. She sent Druska to the Connaught, where she had booked her usual suite, and took a taxi straight from the airport to the hospital in the suburb of Ealing where the two children were being cared for.

Lady Pamela was waiting for her outside the ward. On Eva's instructions she had brought her own doctor with her. He was a man who was well known for the impressive names in his care, frequently appearing in the society columns in the company of his famous patients. As the two little girls were only shaken by their experience and would have been released the next day, he had little trouble in obtaining their immediate discharge. There was an ambulance outside and a nurse already waiting for them when they reached the Connaught. Possession being nine-tenths of the law, Eva had no intention of being at a disadvantage should the Frayne family choose to challenge the legality of her guardianship.

She would never forget the funeral. She had arranged for the service to be held at Farm Street. She had already received a letter from a lawyer acting for the Fraynes, demanding that she handed over the future of the children into their hands, quoting all manner of reasons, mostly insulting to herself, why they should be taken out of her care.

They had ignored each other at the church but it was a different matter at the graveside. There had been a very upsetting incident when Mrs Frayne had tried to lure the older girl, Milla, away from her. Georgia was still a babe in arms, so there had been no trouble with her, but Milla was already four years old and it was natural that she would prefer to be with her grandparents. She knew them much better than she knew Eva. She had been seeing them at least once a week for as long as she could remember and Eva had expected that she might cause some sort of problem at the funeral, but even so, when it came it had surprised her. Milla had kicked and screamed and fought her furiously, scratching and biting in her efforts to reach her grandmother. It had been all both Eva and Druska could do to drag her back to the limousine that was to take them to the hotel.

After that there had been a bitter and protracted battle between lawyers and a final appearance in front of a judge before the matter was settled. Eva had been forced to undertake that the children would be brought up in England and that the Fraynes would be able to visit them on a reasonable basis.

It had always been as though Milla had never forgotten the scene at the graveside. Young as she was, it left a scar on her mind that Eva had been unable to erase. She had tried hard enough, setting up a luxurious home for them in the best area of London, sending her to one of the best schools it was possible to find and, at first, showering upon her all the attention and love that a little girl could possibly want. She spent hours each day telling her about her ancestors and breeding and how she had to be worthy of her heritage.

But meanwhile, that wicked old woman was using the time the judge had so stupidly given her to brainwash the child against Eva, mocking her foreignness and grand ideas, as she called them, and insisting that Milla was a Frayne and should be proud of her third-rate, suburban blood. Milla would come home full of stories about obscure Frayne relatives: Uncle Martin, who had been a soldier in the War, although he had never actually been abroad because his legs had not been up to it; and Auntie Millicent, who used to play the piano until she had done something silly with an American on VE day and had been sent away up North to get over it. There were other Fraynes as well, with less illustrious careers, but all of them, according to her grandmother, were the salt of the earth and the backbone of England, and far superior to feckless, foreign emigrés, however grand they might think themselves.

Every time Milla returned from a day with her grandmother, she seemed to go out of her way to tell Eva all the spiteful, malicious things that had been said about her, solemnly sitting in front of her and reciting, word for word, in her young and innocent voice, the litany of insults and innuendoes, until Eva would be writhing with fury, prepared to throttle them all for their smug, suburban pretensions. Sometimes there was a tone of inflection in Milla's voice that would make Eva look at her very sharply indeed. It was as though the little girl was not quite so naïve and simple as she would like to pretend, and was secretly revelling in the rage and upset she was causing. Eva would find herself inventing reasons to avoid being at home when Milla returned from one of her visits with the details of the day still fresh in her mind.

Try as she would, Eva was unable to break through the barriers with which Milla had surrounded herself, and as Georgia grew older Eva began to fear that she would become infected with the same perverse and sullen resistance. The thought both frightened and infuriated her. As she began to lavish attention on the golden-haired little girl, Milla's role increasingly became that of the wicked sister in all their games.

It was not that she abandoned Milla. Physically she was still cared for as she had been before, but Eva's feelings towards her had become frozen and shallow. As long as she behaved herself and brought no disgrace upon her sister or the family name, Eva made no attempt to instruct or influence her, or to have any contact beyond what was necessary to conduct their daily routine.

Druska watched the change in her mistress and her heart ached for both Eva and Milla. The little girl reminded her of Eva when she had first been brought to the castle, stubborn and determined to have her way, whatever the obstacles. She even looked like Eva, dark and slight of build, with a steeliness of spirit that was impossible to break. Once she had tried to speak to Eva about it and had recoiled from her anger. It was the only time in her life that her mistress treated her unkindly and she was too frightened ever to raise the subject again. She spent hours in her room, with the candles alight before the statue of St Stanislaus, praying that they might be reconciled. Her own attempts to befriend Milla were met with a cold rebuff. In Milla's eyes she was just another of her Aunt's minions, sent to torment her.

At least their Grandmother had not proved to be the constant, nagging problem that Eva had feared. She had tried all right, for the first year or so, ringing up at awkward moments and threatening to involve her solicitor if she were not able to see the children right away. It had been Milla whom she was after, of course. The baby was still too young to be responsive to the insistent, self-pitying barrage of outrage and disparagement with which she attempted to win Milla to her side.

There was one good thing that Eva could say on Milla's behalf, the brainwashing had not worked; in fact it had exactly the opposite effect from what her grandmother had intended. Even as a child, Milla had no time at all for losers. She dreaded the weekly visits to Epsom, the constant moaning tirades against her Aunt and the terrible, cloying sympathy for herself – forced to spend her life with such a monster.

One day, she could take no more. Her grandparents came as usual to collect her for yet another interminable day of recrimination. The sight of them, standing on the pavement, their faces already twisting into the long-suffering look they adopted in her presence, was just too much for her. Mrs Frayne put out her hand to brush back her hair, an annoying habit she had which was usually accompanied by some cutting little remark about how Milla was looking, and Milla quite deliberately took the hand and placed it in her mouth. Then she bit down on it, as hard as her young jaws would allow.

Eva had been watching her departure from behind a curtain in the drawing room. Druska was standing beside her. They heard the screaming before they realized what had happened. Mrs Frayne was jumping about on the pavement, holding onto her hand and trying to slap Milla's face at the same time. Mr Frayne was coming round the side of the car. They could see by his face that he was unsure how to handle the situation. Milla was standing, stiff with defiance, refusing to duck from the blows that were being aimed at her.

It was Eva who recovered first. "Quick Druska, run down and get hold of Milla. If that woman hits her again, I'll have to go down myself and do her some damage." She would have continued, but Druska was already gone. Eva saw her arrive on the pavement and clasp Milla to her, putting her own body in front of her and catching a nasty blow from the infuriated women as she did so. Then she heard the front door slam shut and Milla was standing in the doorway. Her body was rigid and she was shaking with passion, fearful of what was going to happen to her and expecting to be punished heavily for her behaviour. She and Eva stared at each other, eye to eye, for a few moments and then Eva smiled. "If you're that hungry," she said, "trying to eat up your grandmother so soon after breakfast, Druska had better make you a snack."

It was as close as they were ever going to be. Eva felt like hugging her and Milla's eyes filled with tears, but the moment passed and nothing more was said between them. Neither of them would ever forget those few seconds for the rest of their lives. They would both wonder what difference it would have made, if only one of them had made a move towards the other.

* * *

It was a strange life in the flat in Pont Street. Eva busied herself with her social contacts: the Prince and Lord Harley and Lady Pamela were constant visitors and there was a whole group of less-favoured friends who came and went, falling in and out of favour, depending on Eva's moods and the political shifts and twists that were the daily bread of all those in her circle. There were suitors as well, and not all of them totally unacceptable. There was a lord who was madly in love with Eva for over three years until he gave up and found a wealthy American lady to help him to pay the taxes due on his inheritance. There was also a dashing and still reasonably young artist who was making a name for himself – for what nobody was quite sure; he said he was very fond of her indeed and wrote her long letters. And there were several more who fancied their chances with the still attractive widow. Eva ignored them all, seeming to go out of her way to mock their attentions, keeping herself as an icy model of propriety, far above the need either to conquer or be conquered.

Her friends all asked themselves, why? Surely she did not intend to spend the rest of her life as a widow, with no man in her bed to keep her company. Some said that she should not wait too long; the day would come when even all her money would not buy her a partner, not one that any right-thinking person would want, so she had better get on with it while she had the chance. But these were unkind people whom Eva had upset, and some who had felt slighted when she refused their attentions. They were not the sort of person on whose opinion you could rely.

Only Druska knew why Eva was waiting. She would kneel in front of her altar and pray to the Lord for Eva's forgiveness. She would pray, too, for the children and the life they were leading. Growing up together in the same household, but in two separate worlds: Georgia receiving all the love and attention, and Milla left alone to fend for herself, a part of the daily life in body alone. Druska would look at her and wonder what was going on in her head, what thoughts and emotions were hidden beneath the hard-set little face.

Milla just counted the years until she could leave home. At one stage she had thought she might go to art school. She spent hours every day alone in the kitchen, or in her room when Georgia was out, and she found that drawing was something that absorbed her, made her forget her shame and frustration at being trapped in a world that was so bleak and so foreign, waiting for the sound of her Aunt's guttural voice to put an end to her dreaming. She had mentioned it one day, mustering her courage but letting it slip out casually, so her Aunt wouldn't think that she really cared. Eva had said that it was no place for a lady, only common people and people who couldn't do anything useful went to art school. And that had been the end of that. She knew better than to show a weakness to Eva.

It had been all right with her sister when she was very young. Milla had no time for toys but Georgia had fascinated her. She would spend hours dressing her up and playing with her, as if she were a doll. Georgia would sit there placid and uncomplaining; even in those days she was eager to please.

Eva would become very angry when she caught Milla doing it, and until finally she was made to promise that she would never touch her sister again. Not that she had any intention of keeping her word. She continued as before, until one day she went too far and gave Georgia a haircut. She was surprised what a difference it made to her looks and there was no point in denying it when she was accused. After the terrible row that had followed she decided it best not to do it anymore.

It was terrible, having to be dragged round with her sister. Eva insisted that she went on all the outings and holidays, attended the same parties and did all the same things as Georgia. She said that it was a part of her education and she couldn't sit alone in her room all day, just staring at the wall. She would turn into an idiot if she did that too much. All Milla wanted was to be left alone with her dreams.

The big trouble started during her last term at school. She was sixteen and more than ready to go out into the world and look after herself. She had done well in her exams, too well in fact, because Eva decided that she should be a doctor, like her father, since she had done very well in science and maths. It was a shock to Milla, who had spent years counting the days to her freedom, when Eva casually made up her mind that she should spend another seven years dependent upon her Aunt for her daily existence.

She had been too numb to say anything when Eva had told her. She had gone to her room, knowing they would all be going out in a minute. She waited until the house was empty and packed up two bags with her dearest belongings. She had thought of doing something dreadful before she left, like setting fire to the drawing room, or Eva's bedroom, something that would mean she could never go back. But when the moment came and her suitcases were by the front door, and the flat was silent and empty and at her mercy, she found herself crying instead.

She had left a note lying in the hallway. It had said very little, just that she was going away to lead her own life and please, not to waste time trying to find her as she would never return. There was nothing of the years of torment and despair, of the numb unreasoning hatred of the world and its unfairness that had started at the death of her parents and had fixed itself on her Aunt, the symbol of all the harsh injustice that had disrupted the happiness of her childhood.

Eva was furious when she discovered the note. She said that she was an ungrateful little slut and that she would be back soon, they would see, crying and asking forgiveness. But at the back of her mind she knew that it was over. Milla would never come back to her, of that she was certain. She went to her room and sat on her bed. She wondered how she had allowed it to happen, starting to realize the extent of her failure. But now it was too late.

32

Georgia didn't know why she wouldn't let Gerald touch her. It was probably to spite Bertrand, to teach him a lesson for all the nagging and the lectures she had to put up with. He was always telling her what to do and how to behave if she was to be a star, so that quite early on she decided that she couldn't really care less what became of her, as long as she did not have to go back to Nice and all that boredom. Her Aunt was becoming restive as well. Lilianne had stupidly given her the number of Georgia's hotel in St Tropez. Now she could ring her up in the middle of the night and there would be hell to pay the next day if she weren't there.

Sometimes she wasn't quite so sure about Bertrand and his film. It all seemed a bit far-fetched, if you really thought about it, making her into a star overnight and Gerald stumping up millions so that they could all be rich and famous – and just because Bertrand used to hang around with Vadim before he was famous, and she looked a bit like Brigitte Bardot – or so Bertrand said, although she couldn't see it herself, even if she half-closed her eyes when she looked in the mirror. Anyway, the late nights meant that she no longer went to the beach, and the fading suntan and the puffy eyes that seemed to go with the drugs were starting to make her look old and used up. She thought that Bernard had better get a move on, before Gerald went off her and the deal was all up. She had no illusions about winding up in bed with him sometime, but it was going to be an expensive bit of fun for Gerald if he had to finance the film to get at her body, and she knew that Gerald was a lot smarter than that. She took care to keep well away from him, in spite of Bertrand's urgings. She had no qualms about going to bed with anyone, but there was something repulsive about Gerald and his creepy assumption that his money would make him irresistible. She had a feeling that some day she was going to be dumped – and Bertrand along with her, if he was not very careful.

The whole thing was becoming a pain and several times she was about ready to go back to London, but just when she had made up her mind, there had always been something to stop her. It was usually Bertrand who managed to prevent her leaving, he and the American girl. Karen had turned out to be quite a friend of his, much more than she had let on at first, and Georgia sometimes wondered if it really was an accident, the way she had given her the first prick of heroin – although she had been right at first about the effects.

She had felt super the next morning, with hardly any hangover, so she had taken some more when they had all gone to a party the next evening. Only it hadn't been so good that time and she had wound up with a man who had wanted her to do some very odd things to him. She could remember that part, but what had happened afterwards was still a blur and the bits she did remember did not make her want to think too much about it.

Bertrand had been angry when she came home after that occasion. It had been about lunchtime and he looked as though he had been pacing up and down for hours outside her hotel, waiting for her. That had been the first time Gerald had been in town. Bertrand had stayed in her room until she had showered and changed and then they had rushed off to meet Gerald for lunch at one of the restaurants on the beach. Gerald thought the restaurant had atmosphere, but she could tell that he was only there to look at the bare breasts. They were waggling all over the place and he could hardly eat his lunch.

That had been the first time she had gone funny when Gerald had tried to touch her up. It had become a matter of pride after that: Gerald with his tongue hanging out and Bertrand beside her, urging her on, kicking her under the table or pinching her hard on the bottom, depending on where they happened to be.

They would have terrible rows afterwards, with Bertrand accusing her of sabotage and letting him down. She quite enjoyed it when he started to plead with her, saying how much he needed her and

229

asking what he had done to deserve this, when all he had ever wanted was to make her a star. She thought he really believed that Gerald was going to give him millions of francs to make his film and all that was stopping it was the fact that she wouldn't go to bed with him. She thought she knew Gerald's type better than that; he was a mean little man and although he might have the hots for her, he was just the sort to put it away afterwards and push off without even a thank you.

She had tried to explain all this to Bertrand the second or third time Gerald had been over from Cannes and she had sent him away with his pants still bulging, but he had started shouting, telling her that he would pay her back for all the trouble she was causing. He had stormed off, leaving her wondering what he meant.

She had forgotten all about it until the evening, when she was expecting Karen to come round to the hotel to have a little skin popping before the evening began. After a while, when Karen had been over an hour late, Georgia, nervous and angry with her for not showing up, had gone out on to the port to look for her. It had not been nearly so crowded as the season was almost over and some of the cafés and boutiques had already closed for the winter. She found Karen almost at once. She was sitting at the first café Georgia had passed; it was almost as if she were waiting for her.

She had just shrugged her shoulders when Georgia asked where she had been. She said that there was nothing for her that night. Georgia had become really angry in her disappointment, almost shouting; asking her what she meant by springing it on her like this at the last moment and what did Karen think she was going to do for the rest of the evening?

Karen looked uncomfortable and told her that she shouldn't have upset Bertrand because he was the person she got it from and tonight he had only given her enough for herself. Georgia had thought, all right, you bastard, if that's how you want to be, and had gone and found someone else who wasn't so mean, winding up in bed with him in the end. She had been quite proud of herself really, teaching Bertrand and Karen a lesson like that and finding someone so quickly, so that she didn't need them any more. Bertrand had been very sorry when she came home the next day. He had apologized, saying he would never shout at her again, and Karen had come round as soon as he had left and had given her a big shot. She had put it straight into a vein this time, choosing one on the inside of her thigh, so the mark wouldn't show.

She still would not go to bed with Gerald. It had become an absolute phobia with her now, not being able to stand him, but he seemed to be keener on her than ever, and it was hard to make Bertrand understand why she wouldn't do it. As he said, she had been to bed with everybody else and he couldn't see the difference, it wasn't as if he were expecting her to marry Gerald; he had a wife already, as she well knew.

Then, one day the season was all over and everybody was gone. Gerald was back in London and Bertrand said that he was going there as well. Her Aunt had stopped ringing her late at night some time ago. Georgia had made up some tale about the switchboard closing down at seven o'clock so that no calls were put through to the rooms. She paid the night watchman a few francs every day to stick to the story. She didn't think that her Aunt really believed her, but there was nothing much she could do.

Eva sent Lilianne and Pasha over one day. It was lucky that Karen had just left her and she was feeling at her best. She bought them lunch and Pasha had been disappointed that the beaches where the girls went topless were so far away, but Lilianne had been relieved. She was worried that he might have a heart attack if he saw too much of it, after talking about it for so long. Georgia had been sorry to see them go. She had tried to call after them to ask if she could go with them. She ran round the corner, but they had already gone.

That night Bertrand told her that he was leaving the next day and asked what she was going to do. It was a shock that he didn't want her to go with him; she had taken it for granted that he would.

He drove her to Nice the next morning; he was going to the airport anyway. Gerald was giving him a lift to England in his private plane, and it was not too far to the pension. He dropped her off at the end of the street and gave her a glass phial of heroin as a goodbye present. It was nice of him to do it, but it was not going to last very long and everyone she knew who could get hold of it had gone off for the winter.

She was feeling rather desperate as she walked up the road. Even Roger would be back at the University, although he would be the last person she would ask. As usual, Lilianne and Pasha were sitting outside in the courtyard. They were wearing cardigans and jumpers; the weather was getting colder and it would soon be quite nippy. They were so pleased to see her that they became weepy and they all had some brandy to calm themselves down.

Lilianne said that Eva had been ringing almost daily. She was terribly worried so she and Pasha had told her things to cheer her up, as though they were seeing Georgia every few days and knew exactly what she was doing. They thought it would be a good idea if she were to ring Eva and perhaps it was time for her to go home.

Eva was there to meet her at the airport. It was lovely to see her and she was so delighted that Georgia was home, she didn't ask all the questions Georgia had been dreading. Druska was almost in tears when they arrived back at Pont Street and it would all have been so nice and cosy, except that the phial was almost used up.

It was completely empty after she had given herself a bracer the next morning. She had given a lot of thought to when she should use up the last of it, but she was feeling strange, being back in London again, and she decided that she should be at her very best if she were going to start ringing people up and get her life moving again.

Once it was gone, it was hard to think of anything else but where she was going to get some more. She was sure it was easy, once you knew who to ask; it was just that most of her old friends were not that sort of people, and you could be in trouble if you said something to the wrong person. There was only Cosmo who came immediately to mind and she would rather not go running straight back to him if she could avoid it; he would only start to get possessive if he thought she had no one else.

There was always Gallo. She was not too sure how he would react if she arrived on his doorstep, panting for a fix. Not that it would be too much of a shock to him. In his kind of work, he must know hundreds of people who could help her find a new source of supply; perhaps he had some himself, although thinking about him, she rather doubted that. He was the type of person who might not approve of that sort of thing, and she would hate to put him off her before they had a chance to get to know each other. She had thought of him quite often in St Tropez, wondering what he would make of it down there, with all those people out to enjoy themselves the whole time. Perhaps he would like to open a club there and she could run it for him. It would make a good excuse to talk to him, anyway.

Gallo seemed pleased to hear her voice. He asked her how she'd been and she told him that she had stayed a while in St Tropez and had become very close to the club scene out there. She had paused after that, hoping it would interest him and he would ask her to tell him more about it, but he said nothing very much after that, just that it was nice to hear from her and he hoped she would visit the club. He was getting ready to say goodbye, so she had to tell him that she had an idea that she wanted to discuss with him, right away

232

if possible. He became interested at that and asked when was convenient for her. She felt a fool, asking, "How about now?" But he didn't seem to see anything wrong and they arranged to meet for lunch.

She wished there had been a bit more left in the phial; she could have done with a booster before she set out. Her aunt asked where she was going and she told her she was seeing a girlfriend. It annoyed her, having to explain her movements, but she supposed Aunt Eva had a right to be concerned after the last time she had been out on her own in London, even though that was months ago and she was a different person now, far more mature and in control. She thought that her Aunt would never believe all the things that she had been up to while she was away; she was so old-fashioned and out of date.

Eva watched her go. There was something wrong about her, something furtive and rather desperate, as though she had a deep and disgraceful secret that she was frantic to hide. Lilianne and Pasha were the worst liars she had ever met and she had years of practice in drawing them out. She had almost wanted to believe all the rubbish they had been telling her about Georgia, what a fine actress she was going to be and the special school she was attending in St Tropez. The south of France sounded to her very much like Deauville and Le Touquet just after the war. It was not hard to guess what sort of friends a beautiful young girl was going to make. She just hoped that Georgia would change, now that she was back in London, and settle down to the sort of life suitable to someone of her breeding.

Wearily, Eva rubbed her temples. Breeding didn't seem to matter very much any more. The papers were full of young people whose only claim to fame appeared to be the lowly circumstances of their birth. She comforted herself with the thought that it would be a passing fad. The Lubinskis and their peers had survived for a thousand years and they would still be going when all these little upstarts with their old mothers in carpet slippers in the street and their drunken fathers sitting on their doorsteps, were back in the gutters whence they had come.

Eva was surprised at her own bitterness, but it was as if everything that she had held important and struggled to achieve, first for herself and then for the two girls, were no longer of any account. There had been an article about Milla and that disgusting shop she had opened in one of the papers a few days ago. She had been too ashamed to read it, but all her friends had rung to congratulate her; even Lady Pamela had been impressed. It was infuriating that all this had to happen at just this moment. If only it could have waited another thirty years.

The pain was nagging at her stomach again and she went into her room in search of the pills the doctor had given her. She would have to get some others, because these were not doing any good.

Gallo was even more attractive than Georgia had remembered. There were now two extra floors above the club and he had met her at the reception desk on the first floor. She was surprised to hear the noises of a busy office coming from the door behind him.

"I'd no idea you had such a setup," she said. He laughed and made some deprecating joke, saying that he did a bit of building work on the side as nightclubs were a very risky business and few of them lasted for very long. She was impressed, all the same, although she had never thought of him as a business man and it made her feel rather nervous, bringing up the subject of dope to someone who looked so straight and together as he did in the daytime. It made her realize that she had only met him twice before and that he might be very different from the person she had imagined.

It was too late to worry about that. She could feel herself becoming jumpy and depressed. There had been hardly anything in the phial when she had woken up, and she knew that she was going to need some more pretty soon or she would start to feel absolutely ghastly. She thought that she could easily become addicted, if she were not careful.

33

It was nearly five o'clock by the time Georgia left Gallo, and she was starting to feel frantic. There was only Cosmo left now and she had better pull herself together, or she would make a mess of that as well, and then where would she be?

She thought she had been wrong about Gallo after all, the way he had taken advantage of her like that, becoming all righteous and sensible afterwards just because she had asked him if he could find something to fix her up. She had explained to him that it was not really a habit and she didn't always have to do it, but it was a very emotional thing, coming home after such a long time, and she wanted something to help her get over the shock.

He had simply not listened to her, but had gone on and on about what a terrible thing it was and all the bad ends it could lead to, just as if she were a real addict and couldn't stop taking it whenever she felt like it.

She had been stupid to wait until he had done what he wanted before she asked him. You could bet it would have been a different story if she'd tried it earlier. Yes, my darling; no, my darling, and a whole bottle of the stuff by the side of the bed before she could cross your legs.

There was a telephone down the road and, thank God, it was working. She rang Cosmo's home number without much hope, but there was a woman from an answering service who gave her another number, which seemed to be some sort of a shop. They weren't too keen to let her talk to Cosmo at first, asking her name several times and what company she was from until finally they were satisfied and Cosmo was on the line. He gave a big shout when she said it was her. He said he had thought she might be a creditor, because he'd had a lot of those ringing up recently and they were becoming a bore. Then he asked where she was and would she like to come over; he was dying to see her. He gave her an address off the King's Road.

She had never seen a shop like it. It was in a side street, not far from Sloane Square, and she would have missed it completely if she had been driving past. As it was, she thought she must have come to the wrong place. There was no name on the front, just a big painting of a pink teapot covering the entire window so you couldn't see what there was inside.

Cosmo must have seen her dithering on the pavement, because he came rushing out and gave her a big hug and a very mushy kiss on the mouth. He was a surprise, as well. He was wearing an old-fashioned army jacket, scarlet, with a high collar and brass buttons down the front. His hair was long and shaggy and he had the beginnings of a little goatee beard. He bowed deeply and ushered her inside. "Welcome to the Teapot," he said. She could see he was very proud of himself and his shop, so she said "super" a few times. She couldn't afford to upset him, but she didn't know what else to say.

It was even stranger inside. The whole place was full of dark drapes printed with exotic designs, with matching pillows all over the floor and a platform at one end where Cosmo went to sit, cross-legged like a buddha. He beckoned her to come and sit beside him. There was a smell of joss sticks hanging over everything and a smell of something else that she thought must be pot, judging from the name of the shop. She wished she had decided to visit Cosmo first, without wasting all that time on Gallo.

Cosmo brought out a tobacco tin and rolled up a joint. It helped quite a bit, taking the edge off her nerves so that she was able to relax for a while. There were two other people who worked in the shop, but you could tell that Cosmo was the boss. There was a girl called Belinda who was dressed up like a gipsy, with a big bandanna round her head and long blonde hair straggling down her back. She looked smelly and unwashed but you could tell that her family was okay from the way she spoke. She was annoyed to see Cosmo being so friendly and kept on flouncing about, tripping over the cushions, so you could tell she was stoned.

There was a man as well who worked in an office at the back. His name was Hugo and Cosmo introduced him as Lord Hugo, but they didn't talk about that anymore. He was wearing a normal sort of business suit. Cosmo said it was good for getting credit, which was important when you were starting up, and Hugo was in charge of the money.

It looked as though Hugo was having a bit of a problem. He kept looking at his watch, saying they were late and were going to mess everything up in a minute. He didn't say who "they" were.

Georgia couldn't see very many clothes hanging up in the shop. There were two long dresses in plain ecru cotton with high lace necks and pearl buttons down the front, and a black silk jacket, with heavy gold epaulettes and gold piping, was draped over a dressmaker's dummy in the centre of the room.

She asked Cosmo where the rest of the stock was and he said they didn't do stock, just made things to order for very special people. The jacket was for Wilfred, of Wilfred and the Wonderboys, who were on at the Palladium the next week. He was going to wear it for the show. He was coming to collect it in a minute, and another one like it, only in red. He looked at her, waiting for her to be impressed, and she said, "Oh, wow." A lot seemed to have happened while she had been away.

Hugo said, "Where are those fucking designers? He'll be here any time and he won't pay us without the other jacket, which they're meant to have brought here last night. I told you it was a mistake to give them a cheque, not that it will do them much good unless Wilfred coughs up."

Georgia suddenly felt desperate. It was impossible to concentrate any longer on what they were saying. The pot had only made things worse and her stomach was aching so much that she thought she was going to be sick. She knew it was the wrong moment, with all of them worrying about money and people turning up, but she couldn't wait any longer. She supposed she hadn't realized how used to taking it she had become. She'd have to cut down, once she was settled.

She moved up very close to Cosmo and whispered in his ear. She tried to make it as casual as possible, saying she needed something a lot stronger than the pot as it had been a rough day, and she wondered if he happened to have anything handy to keep her going.

Cosmo gave her a curious look and, for a moment, she thought that he was going to say no. Then he called out to Belinda, in a very loud voice: "How are we fixed for the hard stuff? Our friend here needs a little something to help her along."

Georgia was furious a the way he told everybody that she had a problem. It sounded as if she really were on the hook, sitting there gasping to get herself fixed, when in fact she wouldn't have needed anything if there had been more left that morning – at least not until much later on.

She could hear Belinda grumbling as she went through to the little kitchen that led off a corridor running from the shop to the rear exit. The refrigerator door slammed and Belinda came back with a glass bottle, much bigger than the phial Bertrand had given her, and half-filled with a clear liquid. There was enough in there to last her for a week, but she knew it was a bad sign if she was worrying about what was going to happen tomorrow. She should be grateful, for now, that she had come to the right place.

She stood up and tried to walk as calmly as possible towards Belinda. She must have hurried a bit at the end because Cosmo shouted, "Whoa! There's plenty more where that came from." She slowed down and Belinda reluctantly handed over the bottle. She had brought her own syringe with her, in case her Aunt searched her bedroom while she was out.

She went past Belinda and locked herself in the loo. She could feel her veins burning in anticipation as she unscrewed the cap. The mixture must have been much stronger than what she was used to: she felt like passing out as soon as she had taken it. She sat on the edge of the seat, her skirt still around her waist, until the feeling went away. She would have to start putting the needle somewhere else soon. The scars on the inside of her thighs were starting to show – if you knew where to look.

There were two newcomers when she went back. A boy called Fizzy and a girl called Wanda. She could hear Hugo telling Belinda to get rid of them before Wilfred, the pop star, arrived. It seemed as though he wanted to keep them apart, but they were in no hurry to go.

Wanda was a dark girl, with thick black hair, long and braided like a Red Indian squaw. Her dress was like a Red Indian's as well. It was a rusty brown, long and full, and she wore a woollen wrap around her shoulders which looked as though she had knitted it herself.

Fizzy was high on something and very pleased with himself. He was long and thin with a hooked nose and a feather stuck in his blond, matted hair. He had on a loose-fitting shirt and tight trousers and carried a leather bag in his hand. He asked Cosmo if he had any weed to spare and appeared grumpy when Cosmo said that he hadn't and he had to open up his bag to use some of his own. He

238

said he couldn't wait to meet Wilfred and his band and see how he looked in the jackets he had designed.

Hugo came out of the office. He said that Wilfred was going to be very late and there was no point in Fizzy and Wanda waiting, but just then a car pulled up outside – she couldn't see what it was – and suddenly the shop was full of people, at least it seemed that way because it was so small. In fact there were only four of them: Wilfred, who was short and skinny and wearing a jacket very like Cosmo's, a girl called Vikki, and two nondescript men wearing business suits, who looked worried and in a hurry to go.

Vikki was wearing the shortest skirt Georgia had ever seen, more like a low-worn belt than anything else. It was just as well she was wearing tights, otherwise everybody would have been looking right up her crutch as she sat down, sprawling across one of the cushions. She had long legs and was wearing a skinny knitted top with a polo neck and high armholes with no sleeves. It showed off her flat little breasts. Her hair was dark, cut short at the back with a long front piece, brushed flat across her forehead and then down in front of her ear, framing one of her cheeks. She had a tough, painted little face, with huge false eyelashes, caked and heavy with mascara. She came from somewhere in the East End, judging by her voice, which was high and whining as she kept on interrupting whatever anyone said.

It was a surprise to see Cosmo being so nice to her, treating her like royalty and opening a bottle of white wine especially for her while all the others were drinking whisky. Georgia refused a glass for herself; it was too early for drinking. She was starting to feel really good now. Her body had relaxed and the dizziness had been replaced by a sense of lightness and wellbeing, as though her spirit were floating slightly above and to one side of her body and she was looking down at herself and all the others in the room.

It had suddenly become very noisy. Fizzy was strutting up and down, sucking at his joint and explaining to Wilfred how he had felt designing the jacket, and then going outside and coming back with the other one he had made, showing off the high, pointed collar and nipped-in waist. He kept saying, "It's great to meet you, man," slapping Wilfred on the shoulder every time he said it and going on about how the vibes were right between them and all the marvellous things he was going to do, now that they had met. Wanda was having a go as well. Every time Fizzy stopped talking to take a pull at his joint, she would start up about how she played Wilfred's music all night long for inspiration when she was designing, and all the fabulous fabrics that she was going to do for him. Fizzy would shut her up as soon as he was ready to start talking again.

Georgia had gone to sit on the platform and Cosmo came over to join her. He was looking really fed up, and she could see from the looks on their faces that Hugo and Belinda were fed up as well. She asked Cosmo what the matter was. He said, "That sneaky bastard is trying to cut us out, so Wilfred will go straight to him in the future and we'll lose him as a customer. That's the trouble with designers, they can't see why anyone else should make any money out of their work, even though they wouldn't have any work in the first place if it weren't for us."

It was obvious that Vikki hated to be out of the picture for very long. She started whining, saying that she needed something to cheer her up. Cosmo whispered that that meant she wanted some dope, which was why they always had to keep so much in the refrigerator. It was all part of the service and was becoming a serious problem because of the overheads.

He stood up and said that he had just the very thing for her. Wildred said that he was feeling a bit choked himself so the three of them went down the corridor. She could hear the refrigerator opening and closing and there was silence in the room until they all came back. Wilfred was staggering slightly but he didn't want to sit down.

One of the men in business suits looked at his watch and said they were getting late for rehearsal. He took out a cheque-book and went over to a table in the corner. There was a big smile on Hugo's face as he went into his office and came back with what must have been the bill. She could feel Cosmo relaxing as well, as the man started to write out the cheque. Even Belinda was looking pleased and she came and sat beside Georgia, whispering that it was about time too, she was three weeks late with her wages; but she was very friendly when she said it, and offered Georgia one of her cigarettes. Then she stood up again and took the jacket from where it was hanging and started to put it into a big paper shopping bag with a large pink teapot printed on the front.

Vikki was back on her cushion. You could tell she was in no hurry to get up. She started whining that they had only just got there and why wasn't Wilfred going to try on the jackets and show them all what he looked like? Fizzy thought that was a super idea and he grabbed the jacket away from Belinda and held it out with flourish. Wilfred turned round and backed into it with his arms out, while Fizzy slipped it on.

You could tell there was something wrong straightaway. Wilfred gave a little grunt and suddenly Fizzy's face was serious. There was a loud ripping noise and one of the sleeves came away at the

240

shoulder, then the other one tore and Wilfred was standing, looking like a tramp, trying to see behind himself to find out what had happened.

Vikki gave a scream of laughter and said, "It doesn't fucking fit." She was very pleased at her joke and repeated it several times, rolling about so much that she slipped off the cushion and hit her head on the foot of a cheval mirror that had been painted pink to match the teapot in the window.

· · The businessman stood up from the table and put the cheque-book back in his pocket. He said they had better be going. He helped Vikki to her feet and the other man opened the front door as Fizzy struggled to get what was left of the jacket off Wilfred's back. It seemed to be stuck. Nobody had said anything, apart from Vikki, and she had more or less said it all.

Fizzy was standing with the bits of the jacket in his hands as Wilfred followed the others out of the door. He appeared to be surprised that they were all leaving. "Don't you like it?" he shouted after them. He sounded plaintive and annoyed, as though they were playing a dirty trick on him.

Wilfred stuck his head back through the door. "It's no fucking good if it don't fit, mate," he said, and the door closed behind him, leaving Fizzy standing with his mouth open.

Cosmo took a swig from the bottle of whisky. "There goes two weeks' takings, thanks to you two wonderful people." He went and sat down on the platform.

Fizzy said that it wasn't his fault if it had been a little tight. It was meant to be tight; that was the look; it was Wanda's fabric that was too weak and it shouldn't be used for men. Wanda said, "I like that. You knew bloody well that it frays easy. You should have double-stitched the seams." She was screaming by the time she had finished. It looked as if she were doing a little war dance at the same time.

"Well," said Hugo, "it looks as if we are going to have to have our cheque back, seeing how Wilfred doesn't want the stuff, and I can't say I blame him after what happened."

There was a cunning look on Fizzy's face. "Not on your nellie, you're not getting it back. I've been to all the trouble of making those jackets and Wanda had to pay for the fabric. I can put the whole lot right in a couple of days, a week at the most. You're not going to pull a fast one on me, just because I'm a designer. The cheque's in the bank and that's that." He was defiant and self-righteous and Wanda was wiggling with indignation beside him. She said they were all fucking crooks.

"Good luck, if that's what you want," said Cosmo. "The cheque's going to bounce anyway. We were waiting for Wilfred to pay up so we could cover it. Now, if you would be so kind to leave us alone, I have to talk to my partner about getting out of all the shit you have just dropped us into."

Fizzy started squealing that Cosmo couldn't do that. He would call the police, and what about all the cheques that he had written, thinking that Cosmo's would be okay? He'd done one for a tenner in the pub and the landlord would send round some of his friends if it bounced. But Cosmo just ignored him, and Belinda started to turn out the lights, so Fizzy had to leave and Wanda went with him.

When they had gone, Cosmo said, "I have to take my hat off to your sister, the way she kicked them out almost before they had started. She may be a bitch, but she knows what she's doing."

Georgia stared at him. She had told him almost nothing about her sister when they had first met, and she had been so involved in her own problems that it had been months since she had last thought about Milla. "What do you mean, my sister? How does she come into it?"

Cosmo looked surprised. "I thought everyone knew about Milla. She's in the papers the whole time. She's making a fortune with that shop of hers. We'll drive past it in a minute. She'll be packed out, even this late in the evening."

It was a strange feeling for Georgia, Milla being a success. It made her think that perhaps she was missing out on her life, but she was feeling too good to let it worry her for long.

34

They drove past Milla's shop as they left. It was still open, despite the lateness of the hour. Cosmo stopped the car and they stood outside, peering into the dark interior. It was hard to see anything at first, just the vague shapes of customers as they moved between the clumps of bright-coloured clothing hanging from clusters of tall, Victorian bentwood hat stands. There were matching feather boas and felt hats, and little, quilted bags with long gold-coloured chains hanging amongst the clothes, all in apparent disorder. The whole shop had an air of vibrancy and excitement, despite the dim lighting and dark-painted walls. There was a high ceiling, with purple-painted concrete beams, and she could just make out the shapes of the black plastic ivy hanging down in great, surrealistic swathes from out of the gloom.

There was a long counter at the back of the shop with two girls serving customers. There was a large, black till at one end and another girl standing behind it. There was something familiar about the way she moved and with a shock, Georgia realized that she was looking at her sister. It was almost impossible to recognize her as the same, grim-faced, rather dowdy girl that she had for so long been taught to regard as her enemy. She looked slender, almost skinny, her breasts fashionably flat, doll-like in her tight-fitting dress. Her once pudgy face was thin beneath her geometrically-cut hair, her long fringe brushing against thick, black false eyelashes. It had been her eyes which Georgia had first recognized. The heavy make-up accentuated their glacial blue irises, whose look had so terrified her as a child. She watched, transfixed, as Milla moved out from behind the counter, shocked by the shortness of her skirt and the long skinny legs beneath. Her aunt had always mocked those legs as knock-kneed and spindly, but they made Georgia feel that her own long, well-fleshed limbs were heavy and awkward. So much had changed in the short time she had been away.

Milla looked towards the door and, for a moment, Georgia thought that she had been spotted by those implacable eyes. She knew that it was impossible for her sister to see her in the dark of the street, but she backed away nervously and pulled at Cosmo's arm. She was suddenly frightened of her sister, as though they were back in their childhood.

She felt secure again, once they were in the car. She said, "Well, I can't see why you think she's so wonderful, with a dirty little place like that." She knew that her voice sounded strained.

Cosmo said, "Don't you believe it, she's a sharp one, your sister. There's a big change happening here, with all the kids born after the war leaving school and getting jobs. Fashion and shopkeeping is a whole new game and everybody is trying to cash in on it, opening boutiques all over the place but charging the same sort of prices they've been doing for years.

"Milla was different. She bought designs from people like Fizzy and made them up cheaply so all the little dollies could afford them, and when the designers didn't like their stuff being sold so cheaply, she told them to fuck off and started to do it herself. It looks as if she was right, judging from the way Fizzy and that idiot Wanda messed us up tonight. I sometimes wish I'd had the same ideas. There's always some problem dealing with pop stars. Most of them are ignorant or conceited, usually both, and it's very tiring chasing after them the whole time, telling them how great they are, so as not to upset them."

He was silent for a while after that and they had a meal at a bistro in Kensington. She felt exhausted afterwards and she knew the dope was back in the shop. Anyway, it would look bad if she started to ask for more. He dropped her in Pont Street and they arranged to meet the next morning. There was no one awake in the flat. It was a lot later than she had thought.

Aunt Eva was waiting for her when she finally emerged from her room the next morning. Georgia had been awake since six o'clock. She had tried to go back to sleep, but had felt absolutely rotten, as

244

if she were coming down with a really severe flu, and she spent the next two hours twisting and turning and sweating a little, which she supposed was the fever. She had arranged to meet Cosmo at midday, but that was a long time to wait and she felt a bit better after she decided to go and meet him early. She dressed quickly and thought she would just slip out without disturbing anybody, so it was a shock to see her Aunt standing in the hall when she left her room.

Eva inquired if she would like some breakfast, and then took a closer look at her and asked whether she was feeling all right. The way she said it made Georgia impatient. She was no longer a child to be bossed about, but she held herself in check. She was just not up to a row. She had never really had one with her Aunt. The idea frightened her, the more she thought of it. It would be terrible if she fell out with her, in the same way Milla had, and had to go out and fend for herself. Even in St Tropez she had often thought of her home and how it would always be there if things became too much for her. She dreaded the thought of being left entirely on her own, with no one to love her if everything went wrong.

She wished she could tell Eva all the bad things that had been happening to her since she had been away, but she knew that she would be shocked and then angry and she couldn't stand that, not when she was feeling so ill.

She gave Eva a kiss on the cheek and said that she had an appointment and had to fly. Eva hugged her. "Georgia," she asked, "you would tell me if anything was wrong?" Georgia laughed and said of course she would, and kissed her again. Her Aunt stood at the head of the stairs and watched her as she went out. As Georgia walked down the street, she felt as though she were still being watched from one of the front windows.

It was not far to Cosmo's shop but she was panting by the time she reached there and her legs were like lead. It was only nine-thirty and Hugo was opening the door as she arrived. He did not appear too pleased to see her. For a moment she thought he wouldn't let her come in. There was a pile of letters on the floor and he took them into his office. She could see him opening them through the door. She sat on the platform and wondered what time Cosmo would arrive. She didn't like to ask Hugo. He was frowning at the letters and she could tell that he didn't want to be disturbed. She had been going to ask him if she could have a little go at the bottle in the refrigerator, but with the mood he was in she was sure he would say no.

It was ages before Cosmo came in. He only had time to wave to her before Hugo called him into the office and they started going through the letters, talking together in low, serious voices. Cosmo looked worried when he came out, although he tried not to show it. "Belinda has left," he said, "and we were wondering if you would like to help out for a while. We can only afford three pounds a week, but it would get us out of a mess, and you might even enjoy it."

Georgia said she would love to, just for a while. She didn't want to appear too eager, but she would have done it for nothing to be near the bottle of dope. She said she was feeling a bit under the weather this morning and could she have a little pick-me-up before she started? Cosmo nodded and she could hardly wait to get to the refrigerator.

There wasn't much shopwork to do. No customers all day and she was on her own for most of the time. Hugo and Cosmo went out, leaving her by herself. She thought she was going to be bored, but the phone kept ringing with people asking for money and some of them became rather nasty when she said that there was no one to deal with them. Two men came round in the afternoon and asked for Hugo. They said they had arranged a meeting with him and were furious that he wasn't there. As they left, she thought she heard one of them tell the other that she was stoned, which was absolute rubbish; although she had taken another trip to the fridge because she couldn't go out to lunch. Hugo rang a couple of times to ask what was happening. He just grunted when she told him about the two men, and the second time he said she could go home early. She took a trip to the kitchen before she left.

She was in very good form when she reached home. Her Aunt was out but Druska told her that there had been a telephone call for her from a Monsieur Bertrand. He had left a number where she could ring him back. The phone rang just then and Druska said it was the Frenchman. It was clear that she had taken a dislike to Bertrand.

He was all over her, asking how she was and telling her of all the trouble he had been to, trying to find her. She had to come immediately to meet Gerald, because the film was all on again now that he had found her. Gerald was as keen as ever and she was going to be the star, just as Bertrand had always promised, only this time she was going to have to be nice to Gerald in a big way, because now he was ready with his money and there would be a better chance.

After the last injection, Georgia was ready for anything. Not that she trusted Bertrand and his enthusiasm. He was probably just as far from getting Gerald to invest his money as ever, but she could see that Cosmo and his shop were not going to last and it was about time she met some new people. All her old friends would still be worrying about coming-out parties and who they were going to marry and anyway, she didn't think she would be too welcome after all those pictures in the newspapers.

They met at Trader Vic's, a bar in the Hilton Hotel which had opened whilst she was away. It was the sort of place you would expect someone like Gerald to think was fun; it was new and flashy and very expensive, with phony little beach huts to try and make you think you were in the South Seas.

Gerald hadn't changed much since St Tropez, except that he was wearing a suit and had two young men with him who said they were his personal assistants. They seemed to spend their time making sure that he was treated with respect. They had both jumped up when he arrived and one had pulled back a chair for her next door to Gerald, whilst the other asked her what she wanted to have. There was a card on the table with a list of fancy drinks with stupid names. One of them was meant to have a pearl in it, so she ordered that and Gerald made a snide joke about it being a real one someday. He looked very hard at her as he said it, and everyone at the table seemed to understand what he meant. It was as though she was a call girl, earmarked for his amusement.

It was really degrading sitting there with all the others assuming that she was going off with Gerald, so she turned her attention to one of his assistants, who was sitting on the other side of her. He said his name was Martin. He was a tall, smooth young man, with wavy blond hair slicked down with grease, and a public school accent. He told her he had been to Harrow, as if that was enough for anyone. His companion, Nigel, looked just like him, with a dark suit and a striped shirt with a stiff collar and club tie. Gerald seemed to like to surround himself with smart young men; it probably made him feel important and let everyone see how far he had come.

She reached under the table and rubbed Martin's thigh. He started to fidget and tried to pull away. There was not much room at the table and he couldn't go very far. She swivelled round to face him, leaning forward so that the front of her dress fell open and he could see right down to her navel. It was fun, watching him trying to ignore her, and she became quite carried away by the game, pinching the inside of his leg and then grabbing at the front of his trousers. She was getting through to him, she could feel that all right.

Bertrand insisted on talking to her, although he could see she was busy. In fact he was bellowing above the noise of the music, using French so that the others wouldn't understand. He was really frantic, saying she was behaving like a tart and that it was Gerald who should be getting all the attention. The drink was not mixing too well with the heroin. She had taken quite a stiff jolt before leaving the shop, to make sure the effects would last. But there was a fresh glass in front of her, and she used her free hand to drink it down. She was starting to enjoy herself, watching all the shocked faces as they stared at her. She reached out and grabbed hold of Gerald as well. Now she had the two of them, but Gerald was not as worked up as Martin. He was flabby and rather small and she must have snatched at him harder than she had meant, because he gave a shout and tried to push her hand away.

Bertrand came round the table. It was surprising how fast he could move. He seized hold of her by the flesh beneath her armpits and squeezed very hard, which was a very mean thing to do. The pain made her eyes water and she had to let go of Gerald and Martin as he pulled her to her feet.

The rest of them stood up as well and they all went in a body to the lifts. Gerald was limping and had trouble keeping up so they had to slow down for him. Nobody said anything on the way up to the top floor and when they arrived at the penthouse suite, where Gerald appeared to be staying, Bertrand took her straight to a bedroom and threw her onto the bed. He called her a *putain* and slapped her across the side of her face, but she could hardly feel it. It made her laugh, the way he was carrying on, first shouting and then pleading, telling her to be nice to Gerald or he would be ruined, getting her a glass of water and mopping at her face where her make-up had run. She felt like having a sleep but he kept on shaking her and a waiter must have brought some coffee, because he made her drink several cups, until she felt sick and he had to help her to the bathroom. She felt a bit better when she came out.

Bertrand made her fix her face. He stood beside her as she did it, like a warder in a prison, telling her to hurry up in case Gerald left. Before they went back into the living room, Bertrand pulled open the front of his jacket. There was a phial and a needle in his inside pocket. He said he would give her some later, if she was a good girl. It made her want some right away but he said no, she had to be nice to Gerald first.

Gerald was sitting on a long sofa. There was a low coffee table in front of him, piled high with legal-looking papers. Bertrand guided her to the sofa. He told Gerald that she was very sorry, but she had been taking penicillin for an infection and the drink had gone to her head. Gerald was alarmed by the thought of an infection and Bertrand had to make up a story that there was something wrong with her ear.

Bertrand stood in front of the table. He was hopping from one foot to another, looking expectantly at Gerald. Georgia could see that one of the documents on the table was folded, waiting for a signature. Bertrand took a fountain pen from his pocket and hovered, waving the pen in Gerald's direction, but Gerald ignored him. He yawned and said that it was too late for any more business and he would see Bertrand in his office in the morning. Bertrand looked very upset, but he put away his pen and wished them goodnight. He was looking into her eyes when he said it, frowning, as though he was trying to tell her something. It was not too hard to imagine what it was.

"Don't you have something for me, before you go?" she asked. Bertrand looked embarrassed and said that it was next door and she had better come and get it. He didn't want to pull out dope and hypodermics in front of Gerald; it would spoil the romantic atmosphere.

Once they were in the bedroom he took her by the shoulders and said he hoped she was going to be sensible. She nodded and promised that she would, anything to get hold of the dope. She could see that he didn't trust her, but he gave it to her anyway; there wasn't much else he could do. She went into the bathroom and gave herself a shot. There was still some left for later on. When she came back, Bertrand had gone and she was left alone with Gerald. He was almost rubbing his hands with anticipation as she sat down beside him. She had pulled her skirt up to the top of her thighs, as she did so. She might as well get it over with quickly.

She was still sitting on the sofa the next morning when she woke up. It took a while to remember how she had got there and she finished off the rest of the dope while she worked it out. She thought that Gerald must be really pissed off with her, after all the trouble he had been to, to have her pass out on him before he could get started. She had checked herself all over, and she was nearly sure that he hadn't touched her at all.

The telephone rang as she was leaving. A woman asked her if she was staying in the suite and she said no, it belonged to Gerald, which was stupid of her, she supposed. The voice had been rather muffled, but she was sure it had been Rilda's. Gerald's evening was going to turn out even worse than he could imagine.

It was ten o'clock by the time she was home. She had no choice but to go there. She simply had to change her clothes. Eva was waiting, as Georgia knew she would be. It looked as though she had been crying. Georgia would have loved to comfort her, but there wasn't much she could say that would do any good. She made up an excuse, saying she had stayed with a friend. She didn't expect to be believed but at least it avoided telling the truth.

Eva said that she was very worried about her health. She had looked terrible since coming back from France, and she would like her to see a doctor as soon as she could arrange an appointment. Georgia had heard that doctors could tell if you were taking things that you shouldn't. She shrugged and said that there was nothing the matter with her and anyway, Eva would be pleased to know that she had a job, which she had started yesterday. Now she had to run, because she was going to be late.

She hated to see the hurt in Eva's eyes as she turned away, but she had her own life to lead, and that was that.

35

Gallo was curious to see what Georgia's sister would be like. He had been annoyed and slightly ashamed with himself ever since he and Georgia had gone to bed. It had been several months ago but he still felt embarrassed at the way he had so nearly made a fool of himself, believing that he had scored a conquest and half-inclined to fall for her heavily, only to find that she was desperate for drugs and playing him along as a potential source of supply.

Gallo hated drugs, as he was coming to hate the nightclub business and all the inhabitants of that dim, semi-legal world who made up the bulk of his customers. It had been okay whilst he was young, a half-educated tearaway from the backstreets, but he had learned a few things since then, not too much maybe, but enough to make him see that there were better ways to make a living than pandering to shady men and flashy women, running around being nice to everyone in case he upset the wrong person and wound up one morning in a concrete mixer on an East End building site.

There was a mob from north London who had been pestering him for months, fancying their chances at the posh life and offering him a fair price for his share of the club. Malinski wouldn't be too pleased to have them as partners, but he was tired of Malinski and his little perversions and the mob had said they'd take care of him, as part of the bargain. The do planned for Milla would be his last night in the business. He would be glad when it was over; it was tiring running a construction company all day, after a night in the club.

He had nearly turned down the man from the mail-order company who wanted to celebrate their signing up of Milla by giving a bash for the press, but his curiosity was too much for him. He would never again have the chance to meet a lady like Milla, a famous designer and Georgia's sister as well.

He had no idea what to expect, but the slim, intense girl, with the hard eyes and stern-set jaw, was so far removed from her sister that it was hard to believe they were related. She had arrived at his office at ten in the morning to discuss the arrangements for the party. He had expected her to be elated at signing the deal with the mail-order firm. It was worth a great deal of money for not much work, or so he had read in the papers. It must be a big break for a girl who had only recently started. He knew what it was like when you were running a business.

There was a man who came with her whom she introduced as Willie. He was tall and well spoken, a nice enough fellow, but a bit of a drip in comparison to Milla. She seemed happy to let him do the talking, but it was easy to see that she wore the trousers. It was the way that he kept looking at her whenever there was a question.

When she did speak, there was electricity. She had a force that caught your attention, but it was as if she could only be bothered to use it when she had to, which was not very often, the way the meeting went. It was quite clear that they knew exactly what they wanted; they had costed it out and knew down to a penny what he should be charging. It was his last do anyway, so he wasn't too greedy.

He said a few things, just to get her reaction, and once he annoyed her. She flashed him a look and Willie stepped in to cool it all down before she could get started. Gallo had thought for a moment that he was in for a blasting. He felt sorry for Willie, living with that all day long, following her around like a puppy. But the guy seemed to like it, so maybe there was more between them than just business. He found himself thinking what she'd be like as a girlfriend. He wondered if she knew what had gone on with her sister.

It was lunchtime before they were finished. It was a big enough deal to make him polite, so he asked them if they were hungry. Willie said they had to get back to the business, but Milla surprised them both by saying that she would stay. It was plain that Willie didn't like it, but there was nothing he could do but be on his way.

Gallo took her to a restaurant in Soho. They were sitting down

252

before he remembered that it was the one where he had taken Georgia a few months before. It made no difference and he had been there with other ladies since then, but he would have rather been somewhere else, all the same.

Milla didn't say much at first, asking him about the club and how long he had owned it, and he explained that he was selling out in a few days and told her about the building business and the money to be made in conversions. She came alive at the mention of money. It was amazing how much she knew, for a young girl. Not that she seemed greedy, just interested in business, and he found himself talking as he would to an investor, only without all the tension of doing a deal. The meal flashed by and he was sure she was enjoying herself – there had been plenty of chances for her to cut it short – but then he remembered her sister and how she had played it, and he started to wonder what she was after.

It came at the end, when they were drinking their coffee, but even then it was an afterthought, and he wasn't sure if it was the only reason she had stayed.

"Oh, by the way, you may know my sister," she said. "There was a bit of a fuss after one of your parties. Her name is Georgia and she was all over the papers. Perhaps you remember?"

There was no point in saying he didn't. He had been in the papers as well when the police had come asking questions, and it had been rather nasty for a couple of days. They had threatened his licence if he didn't co-operate. He had managed to convince them that he knew nothing about it, but it had been very unpleasant while it lasted, with the underworld waiting to see if he could keep his mouth shut. It worked out fine in the end, when nothing had happened and the word had gone out that he was okay. He'd been packed out with villains from that day onward, which was good for business. There was nothing like a few gangsters to bring in the punters.

So he said that he remembered it very well and he hoped that she wouldn't hold it against him. There was no telling what people got up to at the end of a party and not all his members would be welcome at the palace.

It was the first time that he had seen her laugh. She said, "I'll bet they wouldn't, Mr Gallo." She looked at him through the smoke of her cigarette. She said she had to be going as she was late for a meeting, but there might be a favour that she would have to ask from him, but strictly for business, should the moment come. She said she would know by that evening and could she contact him if she needed his help? He said that it would be his pleasure. After all, what else could you say to a lady when you had just bought her lunch? He wondered what sort of trouble she was in. It had to be nasty if she needed him. He found himself hoping that she would come back.

It was busy in the club that night, and they were short-handed. One of the bouncers had not shown up and the other one said he had been bitten by his girlfriend while doing something he shouldn't, which would have been funny if they hadn't been so rushed. Gallo found himself having to help out on the door on a couple of occasions when the going got rough, and he had taken a kick in the ribs from a sailor when he was fully employed in ejecting his mate.

Things settled down around midnight, when the drunks from the pubs had all given up, and Gallo was able to have a drink for himself, something to calm the pain in his ribs. He went to the bar and ordered a scotch. The cabaret was starting out on the dance floor, which would give him a break of over an hour. He was glad that his life as a club owner would soon be over. It was making him old before his time.

There had been no chance to think of anything very much in the last three hours and Milla had gone to the back of his mind. It was a shock when he heard her voice behind him: "That was a terrible kick in the ribs." She slipped onto a chair at the bar beside him. She was totally different from the way she had looked in the daytime. Her black hair was long, curling across the top of her very white, slender shoulders. She was wearing a dress that was shiny and filmy and showed off the curves of her body beneath.

It was more than her look that had changed. Her face was relaxed, there was a smile on her lips, and her eyes glittered as they watched him, bright but inscrutable, like a cat's. He said, "I didn't see his mate in the corner, and when I did, it was too late." He laughed and the movement made him wince.

Milla looked concerned and put her hand on his. "How bad is it?" she asked. He realized that her voice was different as well, deeper and warmer, not like the tough-bitch tone of the morning. He could still feel where her hand had touched him, even though it had only been for a second.

They were alone at the bar. The customers had all moved forward to watch the act. He showed her to a table in a dark corner. A waiter came forward and he waved him away. The boss knows how to pick his crumpet, the waiter thought; that little bird certainly had what it takes. It was making him feel randy just watching her. He caught Gallo's eye flick in his direction and he moved hastily away. Mr Gallo was not the sort of person you wanted to upset.

254

"Do you remember what I said to you this morning," Milla asked, "about some trouble I have and how I might need your help?"

Gallo had forgotten that she was still there on business, however she might have changed from the morning. He felt let down as he remembered. For a moment he had thought that she was there just to see him.

She seemed to sense what he was thinking and turned on a smile that would have melted most men at once. Gallo thought he had better be careful, or she'd get him going as well. He wasn't sure if it wasn't already too late. He said, rather more abruptly than he had intended, "What can I do for you? I can't imagine that a lady like you would want anything illegal." It was meant as a joke but she took it seriously.

"I don't think the law would be much good to me," she said. "The fact is, Mr Gallo, that I'm being blackmailed and the law is the last thing that is going to help me."

Gallo wondered what she had been up to. You didn't get blackmailed for no reason at all. "That can be very nasty," he said. "Blackmail is for scum and you're going to have to be very careful. People who do that would do anything. They're about as low as you can get."

A strange look came over her face as he said it, as though he had hit a nerve. The strain must be taking more out of her than he had guessed from the way she behaved. He felt sorry for her but pleased at the same time that she should have a problem that made her seek out a person like him to sort it out. "You'd better tell me about it," he said, "and I'll see what I can do." She looked relieved as she sat and sipped her drink. He was starting to know her a bit better now. He thought, here it comes, the big story; it was going to be good.

"It's a man, as you may have guessed. Somehow he imagines that I've ruined his life. I mean really ruined, taken all his money and made him get the sack from his job. I used to work in the store where he was a director and he must have had some sort of fixation about me. He's much older than I am, at the menopause age I should think, which is the only explanation that makes sense. Anyway, he gave me a terrible time, and I had to leave in the end." She looked down at the table, suddenly demure and innocent.

Gallo thought it would take a lot more than a dirty old man to make Miss Milla budge if she didn't want to, but he asked, "What is it he's got on you? There has to be something, or you wouldn't be taking it seriously."

There were tears in Milla's eyes as she looked up. Gallo thought it was beautifully done. "I was very young at the time and I'm afraid

255

I allowed myself to be flattered. He was an older man and a director as well. I suppose I thought I was helping my career." She was silent, for a moment, as if it was all too much for her. There was a burst of laughter from the audience. Gallo glanced at his watch. There was time to go yet before the bar became crowded, but all the same, she had better hurry up.

"What does he have, photographs or letters?"

Milla looked up. "It's not as easy as that. He claims it was me who was blackmailing him. He says that he paid me a whole lot of money and I used it to start up my business. Now that he thinks I'm successful and he is disgraced, he wants a part of my company. He's actually demanding to be my partner, otherwise he will go to the papers and then to the police. I can only imagine that he's absolutely desperate, but he's making me frightened of what he might do. I have arranged to meet him here at your club, tomorrow evening at nine o'clock, before it's too crowded. I just didn't know what else I could do."

Not much, Gallo thought. Something smells fishy here; this little Milla is a girl to be watched. He waved to the waiter and ordered two brandies. It would give him something to do, instead of staring at Milla. He couldn't blame the waiter, really, he had been doing the same himself all evening.

"I suppose you want me me to talk to him," he said, "explain that he should behave himself or something might happen?"

She looked at him, and her eyes were shining. "Oh, would you really?" She put her hand on her arm. She had overdone it this time. One day he'd tell her, if he had the chance. He could see that she was relaxing, that she'd got what she came for. Now all she had to worry about was that he'd change his mind.

It gave him a problem, though, about how he would play the rest of the evening. He had two choices really: grab it now while it was going right and she needed him, or do her the favour and see what happened afterwards. There was a very good chance that she would dump him, but that was a risk he thought he would take. There was a lot more to Milla than a roll in the hay.

Milla was surprised by the way Gallo behaved for the rest of the evening. She could have sworn that at one stage she had got him going. She had fully expected him to come on strong. She had heard of Gallo and the way he treated ladies and he was definitely not the type to hang back. She wondered where she had gone wrong. It was really quite worrying; she had dressed for the kill, and it never failed to work. She hoped he wouldn't go back on his promise.

The whole thing with Bramley had been quite unexpected. She

had no idea that he had been given the sack until a girl whom she had worked with in the store came into her shop. She was bubbling with the news that there had been a scandal. Bramley had been caught with a girl from the pet department. Her parents had followed her to a hotel in Victoria. They had burst into the room and found much more than petting and Bramley had lost his job the next day. The way it had happened, it didn't look as though he'd be able to get another. Milla had thought that it served him right.

She had forgotten about it until Bramley had rung her a few days later. He had sounded drunk, but his message had been clear. He was blaming her for all of his problems, for leading him on until he couldn't do without it, and saying that her success was due to his money and he wanted his share in the future. His logic had been frightening. He had continued to ring, saying he had nothing to lose and he'd bring her down with him, until, in the end, she had agreed to see him. If he did call in the police she knew she would be in trouble. She could never explain how she had saved enough money to start up the business.

It was a long time since she had been to bed with a man. She had not fancied anyone since the trouble with Bramley. Gallo drove her home in his car and she desperately wanted him to reach for her, and not just because she was worried that he would go back on his promise, although she supposed that was part of it.

She was disappointed when he made no move towards her, just said, "See you tomorrow", and waved her goodbye. She stood and looked at herself in the mirror. She knew that any other man would have flipped for her. But then, perhaps Gallo wasn't any other man. She was glad that she was seeing him the next evening. Maybe Bramley was doing her a favour after all.

36

Milla liked to get to her office early, long before anyone else. When they did arrive, she was ready for them; the day's work already planned so that she could greet them with a stream of instructions and then leave them to get on with it. It avoided a vast amount of time-wasting discussion and all the posturing and ego-tripping she would have to endure if she gave them a chance to catch their breath.

If they didn't like it, they could leave, and all of them knew it. It was not exactly a happy atmosphere in her office, but she paid them well, and the constant publicity her shop attracted meant that there was always a queue of people eager to replace them.

Even Willie, who was her partner — although he had only a minor share in the company — was not exempt from her authority. She sometimes wondered how far she could push him before he broke, but he seemed almost to enjoy her dominance and spent his days in a frenzy of efficiency, making sure that her orders were carried out. It made him a marvellous manager, but it ruined his chances of ever becoming closer to her in a more personal way. It was one thing to have a man to wipe your feet on during the daytime, but at night it was something else. It was tough for Willie: the better he was for her business, the less were his chances of getting into her bed.

She was in her office at seven-thirty the next morning. She was half expecting another threatening call from Bramley, checking up that he was still going to see her that night, so she was cold and abrupt answering the telephone when it rang a few minutes after she had arrived.

She was astonished to hear her Aunt's voice. It was the first time they had spoken in over three years.

"Milla, is it you?" asked Eva. "Good. I know this is a surprise and believe me, I am only ringing you because there is no one else I can speak to. There is a problem, an urgent problem with your sister. I have tried all that I can do to deal with it and now I am desperate. Is it possible for you to meet me at once? I fear there is little time left."

Milla thought: why of all days did you have to pick today? But there was something in her Aunt's voice, and the mere fact that she was frantic enough to ring her, that made her say, "I don't have very much time to spare. I'm very busy today, but we could meet for a few minutes in half an hour." She suggested a coffee bar on the Brompton Road, almost opposite Harrods. She was damned if she was going to go to that ghastly flat, with her Aunt sitting in her chair in the drawing room, as overbearing and tyrannical as she'd always been. The very thought of it made her feel frightened and miserable, as if she were still fifteen and scared of what new torment Eva could unfold.

It was too early for the coffee bar to be crowded. Her Aunt was sitting at a table at the far end of the room. Milla was startled by the way that she had aged. Her smooth and vibrant face was lined and wrinkled, and even her eyes, always hard and glittering like gemstones, were dull and faded; but she still sat with the same stiff back and domineering set to her head that Milla remembered so well.

She gave a half-smile as Milla approached. "You are looking very smart and sophisticated." Milla searched her eyes, but there was no sign of the usual glint of sarcasm. It was the first time that she could remember Eva paying her a compliment. It gave her a strange feeling as she sat down.

Eva wasted no time. "I know that there is no love lost between you and your sister, but this is a matter of family and therefore we are all involved, whether we like it or not." She stared hard at Milla, waiting for her to argue, but Milla stayed silent, wondering what on earth her stupid sister had done now to cause all this upset.

"I'm afraid I made a mistake," Eva continued, "sending her off to Nice after the trouble in the newspapers. She seems to have met some most unfortunate people there who have persuaded her into a way of life that has been all together too much for her. The fact is, I have not seen her for the last few months and I have heard stories about her friends that are making me very worried indeed. She refuses to talk to me, or answer my calls, and I am afraid that if I go round in person to that ghastly shop where she seems to spend her time, I'll make her run away from me, and perhaps lose her forever."

It had started as a formal, rehearsed sort of speech, but as Eva continued, Milla had seen the sad and helpless look that had crept into her face, and her voice had trembled as she finished. She was unsure and vulnerable as she sat staring at Milla, waiting for her to respond.

Milla had felt almost triumphant as her Aunt had started to talk, but now she was not so sure. She supposed she should have been cock-a-hoop, seeing the years of scheming and coddling that Eva had spent on her sister blowing away into the thin air. It was her moment of revenge and triumph over the endless years of her miserable childhood; the rejection and the jealousy that had driven her on, first to her independence and now to her success. It was a scene that she had imagined countless times, almost since she could remember. She was angry with herself for not feeling elated.

"Is she still with that idiot Cosmo?" she asked. "I heard a rumour that they were hanging about together." She had heard a lot more than that through her connections in the business. There was an awful little man called Levinson and his daughter, Chrissie, who seemed to have become dead set against Cosmo, going round saying that he was a thief and a con man who got credit from everyone, with no intention of ever paying his bills. Cosmo must have done something terrible at some moment in the past for Levinson to be so vindictive. It would have been amusing if Levinson had not been so dangerous, owning a big company that made dresses for the chain stores, and very respected in the trade. It was rumoured that he had reported Cosmo to Customs and Excise, claiming that his books weren't in order. His daughter was telling anyone who would listen that he was going to jail for fraud. Milla wondered what Cosmo could have done to have made such bitter enemies.

Eva said that she thought Cosmo must have some sort of hold over Georgia from the way she refused to be separated from him. Even a few hours away from him would make her nervous, and she would start to make up excuses why she should go back to the Teapot — which was a ridiculous name for a shop.

Milla could see Eva's point. She would be so out of her depth if she visited Georgia in Cosmo's little drug den that it probably would drive Georgia away from her forever. Most likely it was already too late, from what she had heard.

"All right," she said. "I'll go round there later this morning. They won't be in until about lunchtime and I'll ring you with any news as soon as I can."

For the first time in so many years, Eva smiled at her. "Thank you," she said. For a moment it seemed as though she were going to say something else, but she stayed silent and they looked at each other across the table for a long time. Then Milla stood up and they exchanged formal goodbyes. Her head was spinning as she walked down Sloane Street. She had a terrible desire to run back and put her arms around her Aunt. She was silly even to consider it for a moment, but the thought would not go away.

She waited until one o'clock before she walked down the King's Road towards Cosmo's shop. Many of the stores that she passed were being redecorated as eager, would-be leaders of fashion scrambled to buy the tobacconists and family grocers that made up the bulk of the shops at this end of the road. She knew that their owners were making a killing; selling their properties for eight or nine times their value of even six months ago, as boutique-mania swept across London. She had bought her own shop for next to nothing and she was already having offers for over ten times what she had paid. Often she was tempted to take the money and move elsewhere, to a less expensive neighbourhood. It would be one way of getting Bramley out of her hair, grabbing the money and living on an island in the sun for a few years; but she knew that the boredom would soon bring her back.

Milla nearly gagged at the smell of incense, pot and unwashed bodies as she opened the door to the shop.

There was a dirty-looking girl in a long, flowered smock and a headband who came forward half-heartedly to meet her.

Milla gave her a stony look. She would have sacked her in two seconds, if she had been working for her. "Don't you ever open a window around here?" she asked. The girl sniffed in surprise. She obviously wasn't used to customers.

There was a noise from the back, and Cosmo appeared from a doorway. He looked a sight, wearing a long, black kaftan, heavy with gold thread, and sandals with no socks. He looked as if he were very, very stoned. His eyes were red and slightly watering; they stared at her in surprise and then suspicion as he started to focus. His mouth began to work and he cleared his throat a couple of times, but it was going to be a while before his mind would connect with his vocal chords.

· "My name is Milla Frayne," she said, "and I've come to see my sister. I'm told that she works here, or something." She was trying to keep the distaste out of her voice, but she knew that she had not succeeded. It didn't make much difference; Cosmo was beyond noticing such subtleties. He looked around vaguely, as though he expected Georgia to be somewhere in the room, and blinked several times when he failed to see her. Then he went and sat on the platform at the back. The fabric that covered it was stained and someone had tried to burn a pattern in it, using cigarette ends as far as she could see.

"She was here a few moments ago," he said. "I wonder where she's gone." There was the noise of a lavatory flushing and Georgia came into the room. Milla was hard-pressed to recognize her sister. Her hair, once so full and lustrous, was uncombed and lifeless, and her firm, oval face was white and bloated. Her eyes were withdrawn, almost dead, as she stared at Milla.

She said, "Oh, hello," as if she had last seen her at breakfast. And then, "I was just in the bathroom, washing my hands." She looked guilty as she said it and quickly went to sit beside Cosmo on the platform. They both sat staring into space, as if they were seeing a vision.

"Georgia," said Milla. "Aunt Eva's very worried about you, and by the look of you, she is right to be. You must go home and see a doctor. You're killing yourself with whatever you're taking, so for heaven's sake, have some sense."

Georgia turned her face slowly towards her. "You don't know anything," she said, dropping her head and looking at the floor.

The telephone started to ring in the office and the shop girl went to answer it. "It's Customs and Excise asking where you are. They're sitting there, waiting for you to come to a meeting. Hugo's there too, and they're all getting mad."

Cosmo waved his hand in front of his face, as if he were brushing away a fly. He shook his head vaguely when the girl repeated what she had just said. He did not appear to be taking it in.

"That's terribly serious, to be called to a meeting," said Milla. "How long is it since you haven't paid?"

Cosmo shook his head jerkily. "We never had the money," he said.

Milla thought: Christ, he *is* in trouble. They could put him in jail for a thing like that. From all that she'd heard about Cosmo, that was exactly what they were going to do.

Georgia stood up. "Why are you here, worrying us?" she said. "We're trying to get away from all that." She plucked at the sleeve

262

of her kaftan, giving all her attention to a loose thread that she had just noticed.

There was something funny about the way she moved. Milla went over to her and pulled the kaftan tightly against her stomach. "Oh no," she said. "You're not pregnant! They've got pills for that now." But it was pointless being angry. "Who's the father, or don't you know?"

It was Cosmo's turn to stand. "I'm going to look after her, don't you worry." He was swaying as he spoke, but she could tell that he was trying to be a gentleman, for all the good it would do either of them. "We're going away," he continued. "To a place in Wales, as a matter of fact."

"Do you have any money?" Milla was worried, but Cosmo said that they wouldn't need very much when they got there. They were joining a commune and that living was cheap. He would sell his car once they arrived and that would see them all right for a while.

The phone rang again and the girl came back after she had answered it, white-faced. "They've arrested Hugo. Your lawyer just called. He said they'd be coming for you very shortly. I'm going home, it's really too much."

Milla said that they had better be on their way, if they were going to Wales. She went with them to their car. It was parked close by, just around the corner. The rear seat was already loaded with suitcases and bedrolls, so it was obvious that Cosmo was not so far gone that he hadn't anticipated the need for a rapid exit. Georgia kissed her on the cheek. "It's funny it's you who has come to see me off," she said. That was the last Milla saw of them – Georgia sitting stiff-backed and oblivious, staring straight to the front, and Cosmo looking wildly about him, trying to focus his eyes on the traffic. It was a sight she would never forget.

It was lucky that they had been parked round the corner. There was a police car in front of the shop as she walked past. She went back to her office and sat at her desk. There had been no calls, outside the normal run of business. She sat wondering what she should tell Eva. There was no point in upsetting her more than she had to. She thought how once she would have welcomed the chance. She must be getting soft. Then she remembered Bramley and the meeting that night and decided that she wasn't weakening at all. But something had changed. There was no doubt about that.

It was surprising how pleased Druska was to speak to her, when she answered the phone. She said how glad Aunt Eva had been to see her: "Remember she loves you, whatever you think."

When Eva came on she was hesitant and nervous, and Milla

decided to let her off lightly. "I saw Georgia a few minutes ago. She was just off to the country, somewhere in Wales, I believe she said. She was looking a bit peaky and I'm sure the fresh air is just what she needs. From what I could see, the shop was closing down, so she won't be going back there again, I'm quite sure of that."

Eva seemed much happier after she had spoken. She thanked Milla very much and asked her to let her know if she heard from her sister. Milla asked her to do the same. They were both awkward as they said goodbye.

Milla thought she would go round to the club early, to make sure that Gallo had taken her seriously. It would be a nightmare if Bramley turned up and he was not there to deal with him. She wondered what Gallo had in mind and what Bramley's reaction would be. She was suddenly nervous about the whole thing, wondering if Bramley would get a chance to make any accusations against her and, if so, what he would say and whether Gallo would believe him. She remembered what Gallo had said about blackmailers. Suddenly, his opinion of her mattered very much.

37

Thick as shit and twice as nasty would be an accurate description of Danny Morgan and Dosser; enough to scare the daylights out of anyone and Bramley had been no exception.

Gallo sat in his office, waiting for the two of them to come back for their money after they had escorted Bramley out into the street. He thought that life was full of surprises. You start falling for someone for one set of reasons and then you found out that you had got it all wrong, and you had to go back and start again.

At that moment, he was not too sure what he felt. Bramley had been all bombast and bluster to start with. When he realized that he had been tricked out of his showdown with Milla, he had begun whining, and then tried to get man to man, making out that he was a bit of a lad who liked his crackling and that it had seemed Milla had liked a bit as well, leading him on until suddenly she had turned nasty and taken him for all his money.

Gallo thought that Mr Bramley was a very unpleasant man and not the type to be in charge of a load of young girls. He was most likely a liar as well, but there had been something behind all the self-pity and bravado which made you wonder if he wasn't telling at least a part of the truth. It was not the sort of story that someone would make up about himself. It had been near enough to the truth

265

to bother Milla, and she was not the type to panic over nothing, that was for sure.

All of which meant that the classy lady he was starting to fancy – just a bit too much for his own comfort – was not at all the sort of person that he had imagined. She could be anything from dream lover to blackmailing little cow. He thought he had better find out before he fell any deeper.

The lads came back and they had a drink while he counted out two bundles of oncers and handed them over for them to double-check. They were not the sort of lads you wanted to short-change. They were both very pleased with their money and Dosser asked whether there was anything else that he needed doing, as things were a bit quiet.

Gallo thanked them both very much and said that he would let them know. It made him nervous to have them around for too long, they took offence very easily.

He poured a drink for himself and stood looking out at the narrow, teeming street, still thinking about Milla and Bramley and what must have been going on between them. He was sorry now that he had let Bramley walk away so easily. He should have allowed the boys to play around a while – nothing too serious, but enough to put the shits up the pompous little git and loosen up his tongue a bit so that he could have asked him a few more questions about his love life and how he had got himself in such a mess with a nice young girl. That would have started him talking, telling all sorts of nasty stories about Miss Milla and her ways with men, and Gallo would have known what he was getting himself into. Then he thought that he wasn't too sure if he wanted to find out that way. It might be better if he did it for himself.

Milla was waiting for him in the empty club. It was still half an hour before they were open. He saw that she had been given a drink, which was against the rules, but he would be out of there in a few days, so there was no point in making a fuss. She looked strained, probably wondering how much he had found out. "That should do it, I think," he said. "Your Mr Bramley doesn't seem to like the idea of having his head smashed in, so he wasn't too happy when he left. If you hear any more from him, just let me know and we'll have to do something else, but somehow I don't think it will happen." ‘

He could tell she was bursting with questions, but he didn't feel like talking about it anymore. She was too smart to be fooled for very long and it was best to leave her wondering what he had found out.

It was not that easy to shut her up and they had a row about it in the end, with Milla walking out on him in a huff. It would be interesting to see if she came back. He thought he would give it a few days, but then he might have to do something about it himself.

Milla was furious with Gallo and the way he had clammed up on her. She had every right to know how it had gone with Bramley; after all, she was the one who was being blackmailed. She thought that Gallo was a pig, which was what you would expect from someone raised in the gutter. She decided she was thinking too much like her Aunt, but his secrecy and the offhand way he had treated her had made her angry and worried at the same time.

She had hoped he would ring her the next morning and it worried her when there was no word from him. She had thought he was taken with her enough to have got over their silly argument, unless he had learned something from Bramley — and believed him — so that he had gone off her for keeps. She was surprised how much that thought hurt.

Her Aunt rang her again and asked if she had heard from Georgia. She must have given too rosy a picture about her sister and her trip to Wales. She thought it was time she started to prepare Eva for the truth, or she would be forever ringing her up and she was getting tired of lying. They arranged to meet at the coffee bar. She thought that she had better not let it become a regular event.

It was another eighteen months before there was news of Georgia, and by that time she was dead. There had been a reverse-charge call one morning. The operator said it was from a telephone box near Welshpool and she had felt a tingle of apprehension as she waited for the connection to be made. There was a strange girl on the line who asked whether she was Georgia's sister. Then she said, "I'm sorry to tell you, but Georgia is dead."

She went on to say that they'd had a meeting and the group had decided to look after the twins and bring them up as free-thinking children of the earth. She said that the others didn't want anyone to know about it, and they would kill her if they ever found out she had rung. She sounded scared, but she gave Milla the address of a farm which she said belonged to the commune, and made her promise again that she wouldn't tell. She said that there were some very nasty men in the commune and that Milla should not come there alone.

Milla rang Eva. She had only seen her that one time since Georgia had left. She had tried to warn her that her sister was in trouble and had said that she thought it might be drugs, but she had done nothing to prepare her for the shock she was about to deliver.

She thought Eva stood up to it remarkably well. She said they must go up there immediately, to bring back the two babies. She would be ready in half an hour — would Milla collect her from her flat?

Milla was worried about what would happen when they arrived. She had heard that some of these communes were no more than excuses for orgies, with the girls being passed round by the men. She couldn't see Cosmo and Georgia being too keen on group sex, but who could tell how low they had sunk? It was no good calling in the police. It would only need one of the men, not even Cosmo, to say he was the father and they would be held up in court for years. She thought of taking Willie with them, but he was no good at violence and that sort of thing. She realized she had been thinking of Gallo the whole time, almost welcoming the disaster as an excuse to get close to him again.

They had met only once since the evening he had dealt with Bramley. It had been at the party that the mail-order company had given. He had been polite and efficient, busily organizing the evening. When she had tried to approach him he had made some excuse and rushed off to the kitchen. She had left as early as she decently could. She had been too upset to stay. She'd tried to ring him the next morning and somebody had said he had gone. He had sold up his share of the business and nobody knew where he was.

It was by chance that she had seen him only a few days before the call from Wales. She had been driving past a building site and he had been standing outside, talking to a workman. She had almost stopped, but she did not know what to say to him. He had made it quite clear at the party that he had no interest in her.

Nevertheless he was the only person she could think of who would know what to do in the sort of mess they were in. She drove as fast as she could through the traffic, to the street in Kensington where she had seen him. There was a Rolls Royce with its wheels on the pavement. It had its hood down, in spite of the cold, and Gallo was sitting in the driver's seat. He was checking through some notes attached to a clipboard.

She pulled up behind him and tooted her horn. He looked round and started to get out of his car as she walked up to him. She said, "I'm in trouble again and you're the only one who can help me. Can you come to Wales with me, at once?"

Gallo had been in some trouble himself during the last few months. The sale of the club had not gone quite as smoothly as he had hoped. There had been an unpleasant falling out between the boys from north London — who had bought his half-share in the enterprise —

and his now ex-partner, Malinski, who had been less than pleased to find himself rubbing shoulders with several hard men from the Angel, Islington, who had no appreciation at all of his own peculiar and rather specialized form of amusement.

The fracas had resulted in several members of both factions requiring urgent treatment down at the Charing Cross Hospital, where they were used to such things. Both parties had become seriously miffed, and had sought to relieve their bile on Gallo, blaming him for ever having got them into the whole messy business in the first place.

Gallo had thought it prudent to take a trip to Dublin, where he had some unbiased and violent friends of his own who would come in handy, should the necessity arise. It had taken him somewhat longer than he had imagined to cool them all off, so he had only recently been able to return to London without the near certainty of a nasty accident happening to him at a moment when it was least expected.

He had been hesitant about contacting Milla. He was still unsure whether he really wanted to have any more to do with her, after her involvement with Bramley. The more he had thought about it, the more certain he had become that there was more than a grain of truth in Bramley's story. He now had no doubt that she was both a dangerous and a tricky lady, but then there were some who had been saying the same thing about himself in the past several weeks, so who was he to talk.

He opened the passenger door and Milla climbed in beside him. She was wearing a short skirt and tight-fitting suede boots that ended just below her knees. Her face was tense and she was preoccupied with her problem, which she described to him rapidly as they drove. He was so totally occupied by her presence that he had to ask her to repeat what she had just been saying; he had missed the point at which her Aunt had been introduced into the conversation. He was disappointed to find out that they were going to have to take the old lady with them. It was not going to be the sort of trip that he had been savouring a few seconds before; but even if she did have a chaperone, it was better than no Milla at all.

He was quite shaken when he saw Eva. She was not quite the old dear he had imagined. He could see she was rich; sable coats didn't grow on trees and nor did the diamonds that flashed from both hands. Even her voice was a surprise: heavily accented, but strong and determined as she questioned Milla about the telephone call that had started the panic.

He listened to the two women as he drove through the heavy

north London traffic towards the new M1 motorway. It would be the first time he had used it. He had been looking forward to letting rip with the big engine in the Rolls Royce, but the sound of their sad, shocked voices as they talked of Georgia made him remember his own last encounter with the beautiful, blonde-haired girl. If only he had known what was going to happen, maybe he would not have been so concerned with his own deflated ego, and tried harder to convince her of the terrible consequences of her addiction. He felt sick with his guilt as the big car thundered towards the north.

Eva sat in the back of the car and watched Milla and the stranger. He was an odd sort of man for Milla to know. She could tell by his voice that he was not born a gentleman, but there was something about him of which she approved. She was surprised at herself. He was not at all the type that was suitable for a Lubinski to have as a consort, but there was a strength and sureness about him that she found comforting. She wondered what might have happened if she had met him twenty years ago. It was a disgraceful thought and her loyalty to Andrzej prevented her from taking it any further, but her mind kept on straying back to it as she dozed — anything to prevent herself from thinking of her beautiful Georgia. If only she had known what she had been doing. She blamed herself for her negligence.

It was mid-afternoon by the time they reached the outskirts of Welshpool, and another half an hour before they found the narrow, rutted track that led to the farm. It was a ramshackle building and appeared to be deserted, except for a wretched-looking dog chained to the front door, which started barking hysterically as they approached. Then the door opened and Eva found herself in a world that was beyond her most horrific nightmares.

Gallo and Milla walked towards the front door. They had agreed that Eva should stay in the car until they had discovered what was going to confront them. The dog must have alarmed those inside, because four wraith-like figures appeared in the doorway. You could tell by their tattered clothes that they were female, but their faces were so lined and weatherbeaten, so covered in grime and sores, that they had all the appearance of zombies.

They moved in a solid phalanx, barring the way. Milla and Gallo stood still as they approached. The women stopped a bare two yards in front of them and started a low keening noise, swaying from side to side in unison as they did so. Milla stepped forward but one of the women screeched and held out a bony hand to stop her. Close up, you could see that they were only young girls.

Two men came out of the house. They were dressed in filthy trousers and torn sweaters. They had long, greasy beards and matted hair. One of them was wearing a jerkin of uncured sheepskin, ragged and torn. Both of them were very big and looked well fed, certainly in comparison to the others. The women parted as they appeared and Milla stepped forward to confront them. "We have come for my sister," she said. She could hear her voice tremble as she spoke.

The man in the jerkin laughed. "Oh, we have, have we?" He was enjoying himself, imitating her tone. The other man brought out a long and vicious knife from behind his back. He walked over to Gallo and started to finger his dark, city overcoat. Gallo was very small beside him. Watching them, Eva could see that Gallo was hopelessly outmatched. The man in the sheepskin took a pair of brass knuckle-dusters from his pocket and said that they were all going to have some fun. Two of the girls ran to the car and started to pull Eva out of the door. They held her against the bonnet, calling for the others to come and see their prize. Eva remained stiff and silent. She thought that it was a stupid way to die. The specialists had promised her at least another year, and now they were going to be wrong. She took some satisfaction from the thought.

The others all started to move towards the car, herding Gallo and Milla in front of them. Eva searched for Gallo's face in the gloom. He caught her eye and she thought she saw him wink. There was a half-smile on his face. He said, in a quiet and reasonable voice, as if talking to a drunken customer in the club: "One moment, please, ladies and gentlemen. I'm afraid this whole thing is going to get out of hand in a moment. Perhaps you would like to calm down and see what we can work out." Eva thought he was a fool and decided that it was the end of them. The man in the sheepskin evidently thought the same. He turned round and spat in Gallo's face, standing back with a jeer that was taken up by the rest of them.

Gallo smiled and wiped the spittle from his face, everyone watching his hand. He leaned forward slightly and the other hand snaked out and attached itself to the nose of his tormentor. There was a terrible scream and the man was on the ground, thrashing and moaning and holding his hands to his face, but he was unable to stop the blood that was spurting through his fingers. Gallo turned, almost lazily, to the man with the knife. Again his hand went out and there was a sharp crack as he gripped the man by the wrist. The knife fell to the ground and the man stood, staring in disbelief at his arm. It was sticking out at a strange angle.

Then Gallo turned back to the first man and hit him with a flurry of blows while he was still on his knees, trying to stand up. The man stopped moaning, and lay motionless on the wet turf. The life had gone out of the women. They stood with drooping heads, their arms limp at their sides. Milla ran to Eva and asked her if she were all right.

Inside, the house was filthy, with piles of rotting rags and mildewed sacking littering the floor, and there was a stench of damp and urine so strong that Eva's eyes were watering within a few seconds. Gallo was moving quickly through the house, slamming open the doors to the bare, unlit rooms, peering into the darkness.

There was nothing on the ground floor and they stood at the bottom of a lopsided, creaking staircase which looked as if it would collapse under Gallo's weight at any minute. He disappeared around the top landing and there was total silence in the house. Outside they could hear the noise of the women. They sounded shrill and desperate and without hope as they milled helplessly around their men. Then Gallo called out, his voice tight and strained. Milla went ahead, holding Eva's hand as they inched up the inner edge of the staircase, pressing themselves against the wall as the rotten wood groaned and gave beneath their feet.

Gallo was standing at the head of the staircase. For the first time in the whole nightmare he was looking shaken. He put out his arms to hold them back. "Brace yourselves," he said. "There's something just ghastly in that room – in fact, I think you'd better both stand here and let me sort it out." But Eva pushed past him before he had finished. Milla followed her into the room, with Gallo close behind them.

The daylight was almost gone and it was hard to make out anything at first, just the shape of a double bed in the corner, with heaps of old rags piled haphazardly on top of it. Eva turned her head, intent on searching the rest of the bare and freezing room, when they heard a high-pitched, plaintive sound, like the mewing of a kitten and, for a moment, one of the bundles stirred.

Dreading what she might find, but already with an inkling of what it was going to be, Eva approached the bed. There were two long bundles, reaching almost the full length of the mattress and two little lumps dumped between them, one of which seemed to quiver as she came close. She reached out and touched one, and then recoiled in shock as she felt the outline of a fleshless shoulder beneath her hand.

Milla reached over beside her, disturbing one of the larger bundles as she did so, and they both sprang back as the sheet fell away to reveal a waxen, white face, framed by long blonde tresses. Even in death, Georgia had a strange and luminous beauty. For a split second, Milla found herself growing jealous as she looked at her sister, and then all other thoughts were swept away in the horror of the situation.

Gallo leaned across and picked up one of the small bundles. He pulled back the filthy cloth and they all stared at the small head and wizened face that hung helplessly from a neck too weak to support it.

There was no point in wasting time on Cosmo; it was obvious that he too was dead. Like Georgia's, his body was thin and emaciated and there were the marks of countless needles along the insides of his arms. There was an odour of decay already spreading throughout the musty room, in spite of the freezing air. They had been dead for quite a while.

They picked their way carefully down the rotten staircase and out into the yard. The women had formed a circle around the two men. They were holding hands and swaying from side to side, making a wordless chant that rose eerily from their blank faces. Whatever good it was intended to do, it was not working. The two men were lying in the centre of the circle. One of them was groaning, while the other, the one with the broken arm, appeared to have passed out.

Eva and Milla sat in the back of the car, each one with a bundle in her arms. Gallo gunned the engine and they shot past the chanting group and out into the lane. No one looked up as they passed. Gallo drove as quickly as he dared through the darkness. Milla said something about the police and Gallo said they were the last people they needed right now: he'd call the rozzers later, when the kids were safe.

Then Milla asked about a hospital. This time it was Eva who said no. "Stop as soon as you can and we'll buy them some milk. Then I'll ring Druska to have the doctor waiting. The important thing is to get them home."

Milla was surprised at her authority and the calm determination with which she spoke. Gallo grunted his approval at the plan and settled down to concentrate on the road ahead. After the milk, the children seemed contented and slept for the rest of the way.

38

Even in death, Georgia couldn't keep out of the newspapers, and this time she made the television news as well. There were a few days during which the nation wondered about what had happened at the farmhouse, and some of the Sundays ran features on Debs and Dropouts and how useless they all were. Some Frenchman, whom no one had ever heard of, called a press conference to tell the world about how Georgia would have starred in his new film, *Les Jeunes Filles de la Nuit* – coming soon, at selected cinemas only – but that she had *disparu*ed at the wrong moment and he was *desolé* at her death. It was terrible what people would do to cash in on misery.

It could have gone on much longer but then an American pop singer was found in bed with seven underage nymphets and two other men, one of them the father of one of the girls. It led to a further week's amusement, with long articles on the breakdown of family life in our swinging society. Georgia and the commune in Wales dropped out of the picture.

It had been a tough few days while it lasted, and Milla had borne the brunt, giving interviews and appearing on the television news, saying how shocked she was – all of which did no harm to her business, and had at least kept Eva out of the public eye and allowed her to look after the children.

By the time it came to the funeral, there was no interest at all from the media and there had been very few people at the graveside – just Eva and Druska and the two little girls, with Lady Pamela and her brother, and the Prince, who had looked nervous the whole time, avoiding everybody's eyes, and leaving as soon as it was decently possible.

Gallo had gone along as well, but he stayed away from the others and seemed to be lost in his own thoughts. It was the first time Gallo had seen the twins washed and clean and in the light of day. He had found his eyes wandering in their direction throughout the service. There was something in the back of his mind that refused to go away, however much he resisted it. Several times he had caught the two little girls staring at him. Their eyes were jet black and already their brows were dark and determined slashes on their baby faces – which was strange, as both Georgia and Cosmo had been fair-haired.

It had come to him with a sudden and absolute certainty. They were his own eyes at which he was staring. They were his twins, his daughters, who were looking back at him so gravely. He needed time to assimilate what had happened.

The service was ending and he walked over to Eva and said something trite and meaningless, kissing her on the cheek for no apparent reason. Then he had stooped and kissed his daughters, and felt their young bodies and the quickness with which they had responded to his touch. It was impossible that they could know he was their father, but he felt their subconscious reaction to his presence and knew that he was not mistaken.

Eva had been thinking about those eyebrows as well. She knew that she was an old woman and cursed with an illness for which there was no cure. It worried her, what would happen to the children when she was gone. There was no time left for her to bring them up and perhaps atone for the mistakes she had made with their mother. When she was gone there would be only Druska left to look after them and, good soul that she was, their education would be beyond her. Then there was Milla, the last of the Lubinskis, but she had kept away from her Aunt and the children since the night they had returned from Wales.

Thinking of Milla had made her look at Gallo, standing opposite them on the other side of the open grave. She would never have given him a second thought if someone had described him to her. He was the sort of person who should be avoided. He was completely unsuitable as a man for the Lubinskis. She watched him as he stared at the children. There was a strange look on his tough and normally expressionless face, a softness and light in those black, hooded eyes that she found most unexpected.

It was then she realized that they were the eyes of the children who were staring at her, and she suddenly knew, with complete conviction, that he was their father. It was shocking, really, Georgia's promiscuity, but Eva felt a great relief growing inside her. At least the girls had some strong blood to help them. It set her thinking about the Lubinski bloodline; maybe it was not so strong after all. On the one side was Milla, who took after Eva herself, if you followed that line of thinking. On the other, Georgia, a true Lubinski who took after her mother — and there was the weakness, Eva decided. It made her feel better about the whole business: let those who were alive look after the living; that would be her task for the future. There was not very much time left for her to complete it. The pain in her stomach came back to remind her.

She went straight to her room when they came back from the funeral. She opened the drawer and took out her will. It was hard to remember how many times she had changed it. First the two girls had shared equally, and then there had been Lilianne, who had been in and out several times, and Milla, who had been cut out forever, and Lady Pamela, who had come and gone over the years. All of it depended on so many stupid things, so important at the time and now so hard to remember. She thought that she had better be serious with this one; there would be little time left to make another.

Milla did not know what to do about Gallo. The death of her sister must have shaken her up. She was no longer finding that running the business was enough to keep her mind from wandering, from thinking about Eva and how she was getting on with the little girls. But she was still determined that she was not going to allow herself to have anything more to do with them. It would all be pointless if she lost her independence. Willie was becoming brave again. Asking her out to dinner and looking soulful and upset when she wouldn't go, as if he had a right to be close to her outside the business. She supposed he did, if you looked at it his way; after all, he had never hidden the fact that he wanted her. The problem was that she didn't want him. If only Gallo would make some sort of move. At least she would know where she stood. She was ashamed of herself and of her weakness, but it was there and there was no point in hiding from it.

Gallo, too, was wondering what came next. He was sure that they were his children, but there was no possibility of his ever proving it and he was not at all sure that it would be the right thing for him to do, anyway. His world was not exactly suitable for young ladies and there was no doubt that Eva had the money and the connections. He had checked her out through friends of his own.

He was surprised when she rang him and asked him to come and see her. He went round that evening. It was the first time he had ever been in a place like her flat. It was no good pretending to himself that he wasn't impressed. Druska was wearing a black dress and white apron and she curtsied as she opened the door. He thought that he could grow to like Druska. From the little he had seen of her she was all heart and devoted to her mistress. She was one of the few left, he supposed – the old retainer, and a good thing too – but it would upset her if she knew what he was thinking, which was something he would hate to do.

Eva was waiting for him in the living room, if you could call it that. It was as big as the average house where he came from, with old, expensive-looking furniture and plush curtains: it was more like a palace than a home. Eva was dressed for the part as well. She was wearing a long silky gown and she was glittering with jewellery. She had a tiara, thick with diamonds, across the top of her sleek, still-black hair and the eyes beneath reflected their hard, bright intensity as she stared into his own. Druska poured champagne for them both and she curtsied again as she closed the heavy oak door behind her.

Alone with Eva in the vast room, Gallo felt the force flowing out of her. He thought that he had better watch himself here; this was a very strong lady he was looking at, and she had not gone to all this trouble to ask him how he was getting along.

She started in on him right away, no messing about, straight for the jugular and no pretence. "Mr Gallo, what I'm going to say might well sound impertinent to you, and it might also lead on to other things that I might not like to have repeated in a few months' time, when I am gone."

Gallo sat up with a start. He was going to say something, but thought better of it. She was not the sort of person who would come up with something like that unless she meant it.

"I'm not going to ask you to keep anything I may tell you secret," she said. "I will leave that to your own judgment, but I will promise that I will tell no one of anything you might tell me. Do you understand?"

Gallo nodded his head slowly. He thought he knew what was coming. She really was a sharp old bird.

Eva's eyes locked with his own. He felt their power as he forced himself to stare back at her. It was an effort to keep his eyes steady as he fought against her dominance. The brilliance of her eyes seemed to obliterate everything else in the room.

Her voice was hard and brittle as she continued. "First, I must know your intentions towards Milla. She is a strange girl and, I'm afraid, not always as good as she should be, for which I take most of the responsibility. Of course, I won't tell your answer to anyone, least of all to her."

Gallo could see no point in telling a lie, "I honestly don't know. There's something about her that I can't work out. Maybe I'm frightened of what I'll find, if I look." He sat back and felt uncomfortable with his answer. He hoped she didn't think he was trying to avoid the issue.

It didn't seem to worry her. She nodded, as if it were what she had been expecting. "My second question is much easier to answer. Did you ever go to bed with Georgia?"

There it was, straight out in the open. He thought she was one hell of a woman. She deserved a straight answer.

"Not only that, but I believe that I am the father of her children, if that's what you're getting at. In fact, from the look of them, I can almost guarantee it."

Eva gave a deep sigh. "I must say, it's nice doing business with you, Mr Gallo."

He smiled and bowed his head towards her. "Likewise, madame, I'm sure."

And then she said, "I have over three million pounds to my name at this moment. What if I said I was going to leave most of it to you?"

"You'd be mad to do that, not meaning to be rude. How do you know that I wouldn't just bugger off with the money? In fact, I'm telling you now that I most probably would. You just leave it to someone else. It would worry me for the rest of my life if I had it. I'm perfectly able to make some for myself."

Eva seemed to ignore his protestations. "What are you going to do about Milla?"

There was no stopping her once she was started, he thought. He was going to tell her to mind her own business, but then he remembered that she was dying. "That's not really up to me, is it?" he said. "There're plenty of fellows who'd be crazy to have her. There's that chap Willie, for a start."

"Don't tell me that you're scared to ask her," she said. "I thought you were too much of a man for that."

Gallo wished she'd shut up for a minute. He was not used to being rushed like this, but the look in her eyes had suddenly altered.

278

The glitter was going and their edges were blurred. He stood up and sat beside her. Her small, jewelled fingers wrapped around his hand. "I know that I'm just a pushy old woman, but somebody has to look after my children. There's Druska and Milla and now there are the twins as well. In all of my life I seem to have failed everybody. Please don't let them be all alone when I die."

He could hear Druska talking on the telephone. She was speaking to Milla, begging her to come quickly. Then Druska came into the room and sat on the other side of her mistress. She put her arm round her shoulders and cradled her head.

Eva was staring, transfixed at the doorway. "Andrzej, I knew you would come." She lifted her arms to greet her lover. They heard the rattle as her last breath left her. Her face was radiant as they laid her back on the sofa. Her eyes were still shining, as Druska closed them for the last time.

Milla arrived a few moments later. She stared in disbelief at the tableau in front of her. Then she knelt with her head on Eva's shoulder and begged for forgiveness. She felt Gallo's arm go around her, and she knew that it was going to be all right.

Shirley Eskapa
The Seduction £2.99

How delicious it was to be seduced . . . and how dangerous

The only remarkable thing about Emily Bradshaw was that she had written a book. Apart from that she was ordinary — married, with a young son and relatively happy.

A single phone call from her American agent asking her to promote her book in the States marked the start of the seduction . . .

The transformation begins. Slowly at first — hair, clothes, make-up — and then faster as Emily finds herself drawn into the world of limousines, photographers and first-class hotels. To her surprise she is excited by the pace, and revels in a new assurance that comes with her burgeoning success.

But success has another side which includes the admiration of a glamorous lover, an obsessive gunman, and a feeling that her husband and son are a long way away.

All Pan books are available at your local bookshop or newsagent, or can be ordered direct from the publisher. Indicate the number of copies required and fill in the form below.

Send to: **CS Department, Pan Books Ltd., P.O. Box 40,**
            Basingstoke, Hants.   RG21 2YT.

or phone: 0256 469551 (Ansaphone), quoting title, author
            and Credit Card number.

Please enclose a remittance* to the value of the cover price plus: 60p for the first book plus 30p per copy for each additional book ordered to a maximum charge of £2.40 to cover postage and packing.

*Payment may be made in sterling by UK personal cheque, postal order, sterling draft or international money order, made payable to Pan Books Ltd.

Alternatively by Barclaycard/Access:

Card No.

Signature:

Applicable only in the UK and Republic of Ireland.

While every effort is made to keep prices low, it is sometimes necessary to increase prices at short notice. Pan Books reserve the right to show on covers and charge new retail prices which may differ from those advertised in the text or elsewhere.

NAME AND ADDRESS IN BLOCK LETTERS PLEASE:

....

Name ————————————————————————

Address ———————————————————————

————————————————————————————

————————————————————————————

————————————————————————————

3/87